FALLING INTO CHAOS

AN ANTHOLOGY BROUGHT TO YOU BY KNOX PUBLISHING

A.K. KOONCE   COURTNEY LYNN ROSE
IRIS SWEETWATER   KELLY A. WALKER
KENDRA MORENO   LULU M. SYLVIAN   LIZ KNOX
NIKKI HUNTER   NIKKI LANDIS

CONTENTS

Hopeless Untold	1
Queen of the Pack	45
Lillie of the Woods	93
Moments	185
Pharaoh-mones	271
Into the Storm	323
Fated By Blood	385
Seven Souls	419
Nocturne	481

This book(s) is a work of fiction. The names, characters, places, and incidents are all products of the authors' imaginations and are not to be construed as real. Any resemblances to persons, organizations, events, or locales are entirely coincidental.

All rights reserved. No part of this book(s) may be used or reproduced in any manner whatsoever without written permission from the author, except in the case of brief quotations used in articles or reviews.

Fated by Blood. Copyright © 2019 by Elizabeth Knox

Queen of the Pack. Copyright © 2019 by Courtney Lynn Rose

Into the Storm. Copyright © 2019 by Lulu M. Sylvian

Lillie of the Woods. Copyright © 2019 by Iris Sweetwater

Moments. Copyright © 2019 by Kelly A. Walker

Hopeless Untold. Copyright © 2019 by A.K. Koonce

Nocturne. Copyright © 2019 by Nikki Landis

Pharoah-mones. Copyright © 2019 by Kendra Moreno

Seven Souls. Copyright © 2019 by Nikki Hunter

Cover design by Clarise Tan, CT Cover Creations

Content Editing by Courtney Lynn Rose, Knox Publishing

Copy/Line Editing by Kim Lubbers, Knox Publishing

Formatting by E.C. Land, Knox Publishing

Proofreading by Jackie Ziegler, Knox Publishing

❦ Created with Vellum

HOPELESS UNTOLD

A.K. KOONCE

Hopeless Untold

Copyright 2019 A.K. Koonce

All Rights Reserved

Cover design by Ravenborn – Book Cover Designs

No portion of this book may be reproduced in any form without express written permission from the author. Any unauthorized use of this material is prohibited.

This is a work of fiction. Names, characters, places, and incidents either are the products of the author's imagination or are used fictitiously. Any resemblance to actual persons, living or dead, businesses, companies, events or locales is entirely coincidental.

❦ Created with Vellum

A NOTE FROM THE AUTHOR

Hopeless Untold is written as a prequel to Book One, Hopeless Magic. This was a fun novelette that I wanted to do just for the fans. This is a sort of bonus book where we get to see what brought these powerful asshole fae men to depend so much on one snarky fucking human woman;)

I hope you enjoy it and if you haven't started The Hopeless Series yet, the complete series, books one through four are all available.

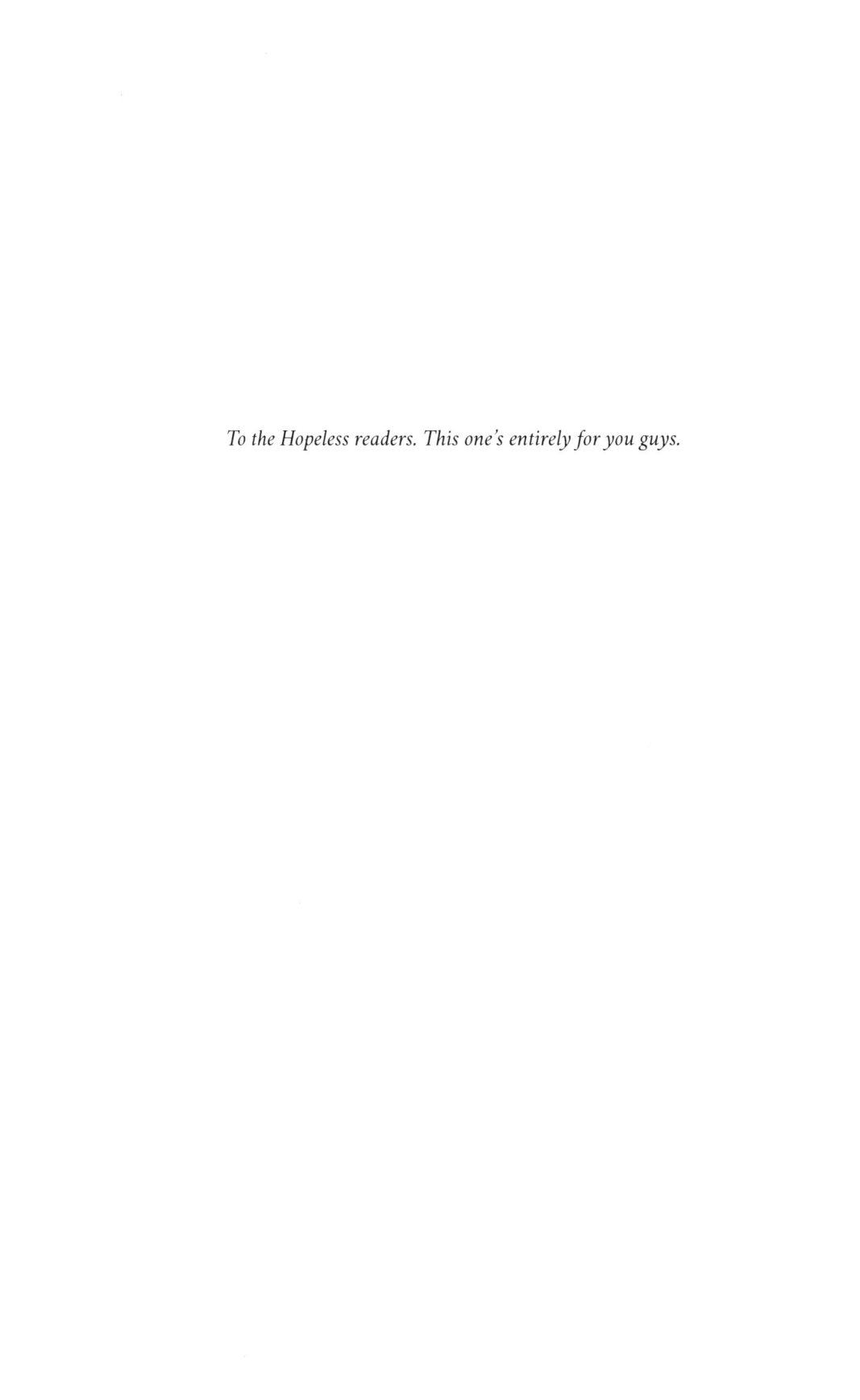

To the Hopeless readers. This one's entirely for you guys.

PROLOGUE

Darrio

The first time I met Zakara Raelix Storm, she ended up lying dead at my feet, bleeding out across ancient stone floors I'd walked mindlessly across a thousand times.

And I couldn't have given a shit less about the beautiful fucking human who risked her life to save mine. It was stupid of her really. A stupid risk for absolutely zero rewards.

Except the possibility of saving a destroyed world.

But that wasn't why she did it.

She did it because we all make irrational, life-ruining mistakes simply because of our emotions, ambitions, and of course, greed.

That's what our chance meeting was.

It wasn't fate that brought three Hopeless fae and one reckless woman together.

It was a perfect mistake.

1

MISERY LOVES COMPANY

Ryder

THE INKY WATER LAPS IN, nearly touching my boots, threatening to tear me away from the fae realm and right into the fiery world of the humans. The glint of the water like glass reflecting the pale moonlight is all I focus on.

Why am I doing this though?

At first, when I started fucking my brother's wife, it was pure, cruel satisfaction. I wanted to ruin something of his. I'm a fae and he's human. I live in a realm of magic and he lives in a realm of burning hell.

Clearly, I'm on the better end of things.

But at the end of the day, none of that makes up for the fact that he killed my father.

And for what? A throne? To be King of a world that's so fucking ruined it's beyond repair?

So, at first, it was easy to fuck Tristan's wife. *Queen Anna.* A woman who hates him almost as much as I hate him.

Nothing brings two people closer together than a common hatred of the same sniveling man.

The allure of ruining his marriage faded with time. And I'm

still here, still sneaking into the human realm . . . because it's my life now. Repetition is easy even if it's miserable.

I hate that I do it, and yet I still do it.

She's meaningless to me, but so is everything else lately.

Shit.

I'm at least ten minutes late now. She asked me to meet her tonight for *something special*. Humans with such a short life expectancy try to make everything *special*.

Special doesn't work like that. It isn't planned and created. Special falls into your life when you're least expecting it.

Nothing's been special in a long fucking time.

"*Fuck*," I whisper to the silent night, pushing my palms harshly through my blonde hair and glaring back down at the calm, drifting dark waves like they're the source for all my problems.

"Leaving again?" The quiet voice sneaks up on me like he always does.

Daxdyn bumps his shoulder into mine, and the two of us hold our gazes on the ripples in the water, letting it reflect our distorted images right back at us.

His lean frame seems so much taller than mine in the depthless waves. The smooth, carelessness of his sharp features sinks my own emotions lower. He's always so relaxed. I can physically feel his calm trying to drift into me.

I've known the man at my side since I was a little boy, but I don't know how to talk to him about this shit. With his empath abilities, it's safe to say he already knows some of it. Already knows the shitty way I feel and the shitty way I keep making myself feel.

I have no one to blame but myself.

"You should break up with her," he states flatly.

Gods above, now he's giving me advice. Daxdyn Riles is giving me advice on my love life now. I've officially hit an all-time low.

"Is that what you do when you're screwing someone who's

not really dating you? *Break up with her* seems like the wrong phrase." I close my eyes at how ridiculous that all sounds when I say it out loud.

He nods; his mess of dark hair skimming along his features.

"Right. Right. Try this . . . maybe you should send her a formal suggestion to stop fucking around behind her husband's back. Though, in front of his face isn't a good alternative either." A smirk highlights his words and when I glare at him out of the corner of my eye, it only makes the asshole smile more.

With his shaggy dark hair and taunting smirk, he looks young. Younger than myself even, but it couldn't be further from the truth. More than a century spans between me and the fae at my side.

But he's right.

I take a single step and my boot sinks into thick mud.

Dax steps right up to my side, meeting my eyes with the most serious look.

"Maybe I want to double date. Human women love fae, you know." His brows lift high above his silver eyes.

He won't say it, but he's going to make sure I do what we both know I need to do.

Break up with Anna.

My stomach twists uneasily at that thought. I can do it. It's what needs to be done. It is.

"Both of you idiots are going to fucking get yourselves killed by human men who find you with your cocks buried in their human women. End whatever it is you're doing with that fucking woman." Darrio's growling words are less than kind and the last thing I hear before his big hand collides with my back, pushing both of us into the pool of inky water.

The moment it touches my skin, sliding right over my flesh, it pulls me into its depths, swirling around me with so much magic, I can't even breathe. It's like being suspended and drowned all at the same time.

But it only lasts an instant.

Smoke burns up my lungs in a painful gasp of air. I fall flat onto the damp grass, taking my time to roll over and look up at the sky that's tinged with a red hue tonight within the thick white smoke that blocks the stars, moon, and heavens above. The fires all along this kingdom can't be seen from my incredibly low point here, like the literal scum of the earth, but I can feel it. The cool night air isn't breezing about. It's all sticky humidity that has me considering crawling right back into my realm before I even meet with Anna tonight.

This fucking world.

The gods must hate the humans more than anything to let it become this chaotic mess of a world. It's a shell of a realm and yet, the humans here refuse to give up. They're either more resilient than I am or more stupid.

Probably both. Seeing as I'm in the relationship that I'm in, I might be the idiot here.

That's only reconfirmed when my gaze lifts higher to find Darrio and Daxdyn both standing in front of me, protecting me from whatever is directly in front of them. Their shoulders block out the faint lights from the castle just yards away. The golden hue of it falls over the scowl on Darrio's face, his back shadowed from the forest behind us. The trees look like inky nothingness from where I lie.

My palms push into the dry earth with tension cording my muscles, preparing me for whatever it is that's making Darrio look so angry.

Angrier than usual anyway.

I barely peer around him when her taunting smile turns my way.

"Ryder, my son. I missed you." The aging woman looks centuries older than I remember when I was just a small boy. Silver streaks through her long hair, chasing out the last few strands of shining black locks.

My stepmother is different. But that conniving look in her eyes is still the same.

"Anna and Tristan send their love, of course." Lines crease her cheeks as the widest smile consumes her features.

Darrio lunges for the small, elderly woman. It's the quickest move but he tenses midway through. His entire enormous body jolts, halting still, and then he drops to his knees. The strongest fae I know falls to the ground right in front of me.

When he lands face first in the dirt, a prickling pain stings my neck. A thudding sound tells me Daxdyn has reached the same fate as his brother.

A slow beating drums in my ears and it takes me several seconds to realize that lazy pulse is my heartbeat. Trembling fingers skim along my throat, my mind growing hazy with every move I make. I pull the thin object from my skin. The shining metal of the tiny needle glints from the Kingdom of Juvar's lights.

It's . . . a dart.

My knees give out all at once and her smile is still beaming at me.

"You're the key, my boy. I always knew you'd be good for something." She smooths her deep blue gown, her chin tipping a little higher. "Now, all we have to do is wait." Her attention shifts, her words barely audible as black spots ink across my vision. "Guards, take them to the tower."

I fall as so many things circle my messy mind.

I came here to finally do the right thing. I fucked up. I fucked up my friends' lives as well as my own. All because of a human woman.

This is the worst night of my entire life.

2

ONE YEAR LATER

Zakara

This is the best night of my entire life.

"And then, and then I tell the bastard, either release my balls or give me back my ferret," the drunk slurs, head thrown back as he laughs and laughs.

And I laugh and laugh, draped around him with him clutching one hand around a mug of beer and another hand slipping precariously low on my back.

The pub is wall to wall, the noise climbing with cheap discussions and empty laughter. It's an easy place to rob literally every single belligerent person you pass. Which is why I'm here. It's been slow though. It's a slow night for a thief. Numbers are down, investments are poor, my motivation is falling. Even thieves have their slow days. Mondays, Mondays suck for everyone. Especially thieves. Mostly because of my lack of motivation.

But full moons, I'm always ready when the full moon is out. People are idiots then. Careless. Careless idiots, my favorite type of clientele.

Tonight's just off. I can't explain why.

Maybe it's just me though.

I refuse to steal from women, especially working women which is what this classy establishment is made up of, and the men here are just so broke, I'm beginning to wonder why they even came out tonight.

I'm about to warn these ladies that the men are in no position to be flirting with an escort. Trust me, I've counted their funds and they can't even afford the smiles some of these women are offering.

To be honest, I was more than happy when this guy grabbed ahold of me and pulled my small body down onto his lap. It was a relief from feeling the soles of my boots stick to the old wooden floorboards.

So, I wrapped my arms around the stranger with disheveled black hair, and eyes so hazy it's impossible to tell if they're blue or green. It doesn't matter. All that matters is I hit the jackpot with this one tonight.

I'm not a whore. *I'm not.* I'm just very good at deceiving people. And drunks, drunks are my kind of people. No one is more trusting, more talkative, and more stupid than a drunk.

Take . . . *shit, what was his name again?* It doesn't matter, take this guy for example.

"That's very clever, but what were you saying before about endless wealth hidden in a tower?" I tilt my head closer to his, his shining gaze blinking several times before lowering to my lips.

His fingers dip lower while he thinks through his thick skull about what the hell he said to me less than two minutes ago. That drifting palm trails down my hip and then he gets even more distracted as he skims down the length of my blade at my side.

My palm snaps out at his so fast, he barely sees it. The sound of my slap can be heard above the chatter, and his eyes widen with surprise from my lashing outburst.

The sword, that's off limits.

I smile sweetly at him, my most seductive smile as if to say I was only kidding.

Even if I wasn't.

"How do you know about this tower?" I ask again, trying so damn hard to pull the answers out of this painfully sidetracked man.

"Oh, the tower. Right." He swallows and tries it again. He focuses so long on simply swallowing that I consider slapping him all over again. "Well, if you can believe it, years ago, I was running so fast in the North Haven Forest that I fell right at the base of the tallest tower I've ever seen. The peaks of it tried to pierce the heavens themselves."

A real storyteller this one. I just hope what he's saying isn't complete fiction.

"And when you got inside, you found treasure?" I'm so close to him his beer-stained breath is wafting over me in retching waves but I swear, if he gets distracted before he gets to the good part again, I'll gut him right here and now.

"The entire room was wall to wall gold, glinting in the sunlight. It beamed so brightly it nearly permanently blinded me in my right eye if you can believe it."

I. Cannot.

"I speculate it was a royal's tower, hidden away for safe-keeping," he tells me, eyes zeroing in on my lips once more.

He leans into me with as much romance as a man with bloodshot eyes and bread crumbs hanging in his beard can manage.

And I pull away.

"So, you're rich," I purr, stroking my index finger down his chest and distracting him all over again with the small touch I'm rewarding him with.

A slow, sad smile pulls at his lips, and that little beam of hope inside me starts to fizzle out.

"No. No, I never even got my hands on it. I reached the window, got a gander inside that glorious tower, and then I lost my grip and fell. The feel of that fall thundered right into my skull." He slams his palm into the side of his head so abruptly that I reach for my sword. "Broke my leg in four places. Couldn't move one inch. I was stranded there for three days." He holds up two fingers, confusing me more and more with every fucking random number he says. "I laid there for so long, I nearly drowned in my own piss."

Charming.

I pause just long enough to push my fingers to my temple and release a slow, calming breath that ensures I won't murder this man for wasting my time. I bet there was no tower. He was probably drunk, came across a slightly large barn, climbed it, and then blacked out at the bottom of it.

Or . . . the little voice in the back of my mind runs away with thought after thought of all the glorious gold this man might have taken a *gander* at.

My eyes open slowly, my greedy mind already making a decision.

"You said it was deep into the North Haven Forest?"

The second he nods, I slide out of his grip, standing in an instant, and setting my gaze on the open door across the room.

"Wait a second, pretty lady." His fingers clutch my wrist and all that pretending I was doing falls away, my body going rigid from his touch. "The night is still young and the drinks are still hard. As is my cock, if you know what I mean."

Gods above, help this man with his inability to form a real pick up line.

My free hand slides over the shining silver of my hilt, and the drunk's drifting eyes finally settle there before he releases my wrist one finger after the other.

Good boy. Smart boy.

I should thank him really.

Today, I'm a common thief. This time tomorrow, I'll be richer than my wildest dreams.

3

THE MISTAKE

Daxdyn

He's doing that thing again. For as smart as Ryder is, I'd think he would have realized by now that his SOS signal isn't helping. But no, here we are again, lying in our own filth while he pulses beams of light between his hands.

It's useless. No one's seen us up here in a year. Why would they notice his broken magic now? Tonight, of all nights?

Let it go, Ryder.

The bright light flares against the grimy brick walls once more just as a hand grips the edge of the window. Hope fires through my heart just as the color fades from the room. With wide eyes, the three of us stare at that hand.

Until Morton stumbles into the room.

"Another light show tonight, ah, boys?"

"Fuck." Ryder's jaw clenches as he takes a step back from the iron bars.

"Your stepmother always enjoys hearing about your pitiful attempts at luring someone here for help." Morton's voice is this slow, gravelly sound like he can hardly remember how the English language is spoken.

"Did you send her my warm wishes?" Darrio asks, taking a step forward just as Ryder takes another back.

Shadows fall across the man's face as he stares hard at my brother.

"Do you mean did I tell her you promised to burn the ugly off her face the next time you see her? No, I must have forgotten." Morton settles into his routine of emptying his bag of the meager food the palace sent to us. This week's entrée appears to be slightly molded bread and a half-eaten ham.

Great.

My shoulders slump as I keep my seat on the damp ground, letting my head tip back against the cold concrete.

This is how the last remaining fae in the human realm is meant to die, huh?

Isn't the most beautiful of deaths. Starvation in the tallest tower in the shitty mortal realm with only Morton for company.

As if sensing his newfound importance in my life, our jailor grabs his cock, scratching and adjusting for several long seconds before palming the food and extending the offering to Darrio.

Fucking kill me now.

The fire fae's lip curls, letting the moonlight strike against the scarred side of his face. His disgust looks more loathing because of that deep etching line along his cheek. It gives him a case of Resting Asshole Face for sure.

"Morton, would it absolutely destroy you to wait to grope your dick until after we've eaten? I'm sure it's small but it isn't going anywhere, I promise." I tip my chin up at him as he glares down on me from his side of our cage.

Tormenting the Queen's guard is the only fun I have in my life. I try to make the best of it.

The man pats his knife against his belt affectionately. "If you were on this side of the bars, you'd be a dead man."

Darrio leans his head against the metal, his voice skimming

low through the room until it reverberates right through me. "If we were on that side of the bars, I'd cut your cock off and hand it to you personally so you'd never have to search for it again."

"You fucking—"

Slender fingers grip the window, nails digging into the brick in an almost painful attempt to haul the person into the safety of our small room. You'd think the small woman pulling herself up was making a total ruckus the way silence drops into the room.

She's not though. Total stealthy quietness makes up her every move.

I watch her with my mouth hanging open. I haven't seen anyone aside from Morton's fucking face and the former Queen Alexia's glaring gaze in years.

So, of course, she's gorgeous but at the moment, I'm honestly not sure if she really is or if Morton is just one ugly fuck by comparison.

Probably both. Isolate someone long enough and the whole fucking world becomes a prettier place.

The blonde dusting herself off lets her fingers push through her long hair, brush over her toned, sexy abdomen and then skim lower against the perfect curve of her thighs.

Yeah, I don't think that's the isolation talking.

She pulls a blade from her belt. Moonlight glints along the edge, giving her an appearance of deadly confidence. The way she holds it, she'd cut through the whole realm just to find whatever it is she's looking for.

The shadows of the room fall across her features and I feel the moment her eyes shift over me, not adjusting to the light enough to really see two feet in front of her. Not seeing Morton lurking in the darkness.

"You should leave. *Now.*" Ryder's voice is an urgent sound but the warning does no good. He might as well have welcomed her to her death for all the good his words did.

Morton's blade glints in the moonlight, a blurring image as he slams it hard into her side. It happens so quickly, I can't even say when I stood. I can't tell you when I walked the space of our tiny cell to try to get closer to her.

Fear washes over her face for only an instant despite how hard she tries to mask it. It takes a lot for someone to hide their emotions, as an empath fae, I know that better than anyone. And this woman, this petite, beautiful mortal would rather scowl in her murderer's face than show him an ounce of fear.

"You should have listened to our little Prince, love." Morton takes a taunting step closer to her, a pleased smile stretched across his fucking face.

I'm not a violent man, not at all. But if I ever get out of this cell, I'll kill him for hurting an innocent woman.

Too bad the blonde beauty beats me to it.

With strength shaking through her arms, she thrusts her blade through the guard's stomach. She shoves hard, so hard I hear when the metal exits his frame and hits the wall behind him.

Morton's grunt is a shallow sound, a breath trying to escape and failing.

Silence lingers while she glares at him, her hand trying to hold in the blood that's slipping through her fingers. All I can do is stare at her with shock. I can't believe she fucking killed him. An inch from death and she fucking railed him like it was her final wish in life.

"Get the key," Ryder urges, his face pressed against the bars while he tries to cling to that hope that we'll leave this miserable prison someday.

She turns. It's a slow movement. So slow, I wonder if she even notices the delay. When she finally looks our way, Ryder pulses his broken magic between his palms. It flickers across our features, it shines into Darrio's silver eyes. Most of the time, I forget that our eyes are the same. We were exactly the same so many years ago.

Now, our eyes are the only similarity. He's fuming aggression while on the outside, I'm his opposite— calm and happy.

It's an appearance. My entire life is an appearance.

But Darrio's isn't. What you see is what you get.

As he reminds us right now. "Come on, we've been here for over a year, love. Get the key." The rumbling sound of his voice is as harsh as it always is. I flinch from the sound of it.

He could have asked in a different way. Our lives are literally on the line right now and he still manages to be an asshole.

Fucking perfect. I might as well just sit back down and eat Morton's dick meal he so lovingly brought us.

"Did you see what happened to the last man that called me *love?*" The way her chin tips up pulls a smile from me. She matches my twin's confidence and it makes me smirk in a weird way to see him fumble for words.

"Please, lo—*woman*, get the key."

Yeah, we're fucked. Someone pass the moldy dick bread.

That's seriously as much charm as my brother has to offer.

My head turns to him, that smile still tilting my lips. His attention shifts to me for only a second, he doesn't have to see my judgmental look to feel it.

To my surprise, she stumbles and starts to walk toward that shining key against the wall. With the breath caught in my lungs, I watch her every staggering step. She could fall at any moment. She could let her life slip away so easily. But she doesn't. The glass encasing the key teeters above her head before falling. Slivers of it shatter over the old bricks, scattering through the room and still, my wide gaze watches her struggle to reach that damn key.

She's so close. *We're* so close.

Shaking fingers grip the little metal object and the breath that shoves from her lungs makes my own ache. I pause and concentrate on hearing her. Really hearing her. The heartbeat that's keeping her going is this feeble, faint rhythm. It sounds like it's going to halt at any moment. Still, she forces herself to walk toward our cell.

With unsteady hands, she pushes the key against the lock. Metal scrapes against metal. The four of us watch that key with so much intensity, I wonder if our hope alone is pushing her to keep going.

It turns— slowly, she turns the lock and the door opens just minimally before Darrio's pushing his way out of the room. Ryder and I follow after him and I've barely taken a step when her knees give out.

The fuming aggression she held just moments ago starts to drift out of her. I feel it fading away like the faint beating of her heart. When she hits the floor, her emotions become this mixture of fear, sadness, and emptiness.

I hate that feeling. It's too familiar. And when it mixes with mine, it's a consuming sense of pain. It's the first real emotion I've felt in a year thanks to that iron cage we were locked in.

It's crushing.

The gritty floor meets my jeans as I kneel at her side. Warm blood seeps into my dirty clothes. Closer, I lean into her— no one deserves to die alone.

"Thank you," I whisper. The sound of my voice flutters her long lashes.

White moonlight strikes across her eyes, making them a deep mossy color. The depths of them hold a lost look. She's beautiful— young and beautiful, and full of anger.

And I feel that connection so deep within me, I know I can't let her die a simple death— not here in a forgotten tower. Not alone.

I want to reassure her. I want to push out the fear that's building within her. Our closeness warms me and my lips skim across her temple gently. She's going to be alright.

My palm settles over the hot blood slipping from her abdomen. I put so much effort into the task of healing her that the magic bursts from my palms in blinding white colors. I don't know why I'm so desperate to save this human. I don't know why her emotions are flooding me so deeply, but it strikes right through my chest. The moment the pain tears through her, it tears through me as well.

Her lashes flutter gently closed. Fuck, she's beautiful.

The pounding of her heart is a strong and steady rhythm. It beats with anger and aggression, and it pulses through me no matter how much I try to blanket it with a wave of calming thoughts.

The gruff sound of Darrio clearing his throat catches my attention. "We need to go. She'll be fine." His harsh words make me tense. I'm still holding her in my arms, letting my body warm hers.

"We can't leave her up here." With the hem of my shirt, I wipe at the thick blood coating her skin.

"We can't keep every stray you come across either. That woman's more than capable of fending for herself." My brother's tone is a gravelly sound of frustration.

What if she's the one? What if she's the Eminence Ryder's mother told us about?

"She saved us. We owe her a little more than just abandoning her in a tower like a fucking forgotten princess." My thumb brushes over the soft curve of her cheek.

Ryder's steps are heavy as he stalks over to the arching window. The moonlight washes out the colors of his face, making his worry look harsher in the pale lighting.

"You just gave her life. What more do you want to give her? A family and a happily ever after? Let's get the fuck out of here." Darrio walks away, ending the discussion without another word.

My palms never release her. If anything, my arms tighten around her even more. Her curves are soft against me. She feels weak but the aggression within her tells another story.

Her head jostles as I cradle her body and lift her from the damp ground. A mess of dark blood stains my clothes but I hardly notice it. She shifts slightly, turning in my arms to get closer to my chest. My heart soars from the small gesture.

The bow of her lip holds my attention as I study her pretty features.

"What are you doing, Dax?" Darrio's posture is stiff as he looks down at the woman I'm cradling in my arms.

"No, he's right." Ryder turns his gaze toward me. "We need her to get us back to Juvar. We can part ways when we get to the kingdom."

Fuck, yeah! I weirdly do want to keep her. My brother's right; I have a thing for wanting to take in the broken and the damaged.

But I also think I made a mistake. Because I've never felt someone's emotions on such a deep level. I'm almost confused if they're even her emotions at all. What if they're mine? Fuck. That's terrifying. But I can't shake how strange it all feels.

Her head settles against my shoulder, making me lean into her a little closer. My heartbeat mimics hers, beating in tempo at just the right time.

When I saved her, when I shared my magic with her, something weird happened. The sensation of it scares the shit out of me. It's terrifying and amazing all at once. I feel her fierce emotions. I feel her pain. I feel . . . my own happiness and excitement.

With her near, I feel *everything*.

4

THE FUCKING HUMAN

Darrio

Perfect. Now his pet is awake.

The three of us walk quietly through the woods, her lifeless body slung like a bride across Daxdyn's arms.

I pretend not to notice when her long lashes flutter. She's his responsibility, not mine. If she whines all night to go to the bathroom, it's on him. She pisses on the floor, it's on him. She fucks us over like all humans do, it's definitely on my fucking brother.

And I'll be sure he realizes that.

She paws at him a bit affectionately in her sleep, and I note how his lips tip up in a slow smile as her fingers tense over his pecs.

Gods above, his cock is all but worshipping this nameless fucking woman already.

All we need to do is find the castle in this hellhole of a world and get back to the Hopeless realm. And now, we have her groping him and making him fucking smile like his puppy just learned a new trick.

"She's awake," he finally whispers.

She's been awake for several moments, but I guess blood just now came back to the main brain for him to remember how to speak again.

Her palm becomes a bit slower down his chest. It's ridiculous to watch the two of them. Completely idiotic.

Until a rasping, sleepy moan parts her lips.

And then all three of us stop in our tracks to look down at the slender blonde wrapped up in my brother's arms. Moonlight crawls through the tangle of limbs above and it spotlights her the moment her eyes fling open.

Her hand jerks away from him fast as if he was feeling her up instead of the other way around.

And then she leaps right from his arms. She lands as stealthy as a cat, her boots barely cracking the leaves and brush below her.

I know exactly what she's about to do next.

Because it's the same thing I'd do.

When the small palm of hers brushes over her loose weapon's belt, she comes up empty. Impassive features give nothing away but the small tensing of her shoulders is more telling than she must realize.

I force myself not to look at her blade on Ryder's hip, the one he took from her because She. Cannot. Be. Trusted. If only Daxdyn knew that as thoroughly as the rest of us.

We're Team Let's Get Back Home. And as always, Daxdyn is Team Let Me Get My Dick Wet.

It's a losing fucking team.

There's a moment where she looks as fragile as her small body appears to be. Her black boots stumble away from Daxdyn, the dry leaves crunching loudly underfoot. She backs away like a little animal. It's a cautious movement.

Until her back collides with Ryder's broad chest. There's amusement in his pale eyes. To be honest, none of us have spoken or seen anyone in so long, it is nice just to watch her.

Damn. That sounds creepy. Isolation does strange things, clearly.

"Looking for this?" Ryder asks, a smirk tilting his lips slowly.

Her big green eyes leave Ryder for less than a second. For one single second, her shifting attention trails from me, to Daxdyn, and then back to Ryder.

It's the quickest glance.

That I never saw coming.

In a flash of movement, she jars her knee up, connecting hard with his balls, hitting him where it hurts and taking the hilt from his hands in one swift move.

Then she runs.

Daxdyn mumbles something behind me, Ryder's commanding tone urging me to capture the one person who saved us. I'm already gone. I rush after her, never taking my eyes off of that damn blonde hair of hers. She's definitely fast, boots barely meeting the ground as her small frame weaves in and out of the thick, dark forest.

And I'm right behind her, cracking branches that collide into my shoulders and not even pausing to flinch from the splinters of wood that sting into my skin.

All I know is, she fucked up. She saved us, but we saved her from *death*.

One of those outweighs the other, and I think she knows that.

It takes one small misstep, the briefest delay of her boot snagging on a limb. She's in my grasp before she can even gasp from surprise. My arms wrap around her thin frame, imprisoning her there against my body. But the relentless woman never stops squirming.

There's something about holding her like this, even if it is a little fucked up that I like the way she feels against me. It's completely fucked up and no matter how hard I grind my jaw against the thought, it's still there prickling through my thoughts with how smooth her skin is, how soft her curves are against my body, how perfectly she keeps rolling her ass into me.

Something cracks and the pain in my grinding back teeth is the only thing that finally snaps me the hell out of my ridiculous thoughts.

"Get off of me." Her small footsteps— *stomps*— down on mine with all the might of her tantrum but it's barely felt. "You'll regret ever laying a hand on me," she warns with an almost convincing rage shaking through her tone.

She must practice that line often. She almost had me there.

"Calm down, human," I growl at her, all but treating her like the pet she is. New puppies are the hardest to train. Daxdyn will learn that soon enough.

When I pivot us, turning toward the distinct careless sound of my brother's footsteps, I'm met with his shit eating smile.

"Darrio, shit, you're scaring the hell out of her. Let her go already," Dax says, his smirk growing with every word he speaks. "You two look cute like that, by the way," he adds in the most obnoxious taunting voice.

"Shut up, Daxdyn." My annoyance is beaten down by my exhaustion and I know he knows it just by his pleased smile. It's his life's mission to get under my skin. He succeeds every day.

"Both of you knock it off. We need her." Ryder studies the woman, her messy hair, her erratic breaths, her heartbeat that I can both hear and feel pounding into my own chest.

She's so determined. Fearless. Stupid.

"What do you want?" Her voice carries a confidence I rarely find in human women. She's a fighter, but that was obvious in the first three seconds we met her.

"You got a lot of fight in you for someone who nearly died an hour ago," Ryder says, mirroring my thoughts exactly.

A pause lingers between them as if she isn't sure she heard him right.

Death does that to a person. Unless they don't remember it like this woman. Perhaps she thinks she's too strong for death.

She's wrong.

Death will always win. No matter how courageous or flat out overly confident a person is, death finds us all. I'm the best warrior in the fae realm— and someday, death will beat me too.

"What do you want?" she asks a bit quieter.

The way her shoulders square and her body stiffens in my arms, causes my mind to dwell on how good she feels against me all over again. Shit. I thought I was past that.

My head tilts subtly towards her, inhaling the scent of pine and . . . vanilla? She smells good. She feels good. Too good. I roll my eyes at myself and my quickness to try to switch to team Wet Dick.

Focus.

"We need you to take us somewhere," Ryder says on a cautious tone, pulling my attention away from the distracting woman in my arms. "We were drugged and captured over a year ago, and we need to get home. We don't even know where we are."

"And why would I help you?" The way she cocks her head at him isn't a good sign. "*Again,*" she adds on a cutting tone.

Yeah. Definitely not a good sign. She's fucking unbelievable.

"Do you really feel you're in the right position to be sounding so condescending?" I growl at her, meeting her deep green eyes from over her shoulder and studying that glint of determination in her gaze up close and personal.

Fuck, even her eyes are beautiful.

Fucking distracting human woman.

A human woman was what got us into this mess to begin with.

It won't happen again.

Simultaneously, she shakes her head and rolls her eyes at

me. Two things at once from the snarky mortal woman. Maybe she is more dangerous than I originally thought.

I glare at her, she glares at me. Then Dax takes it upon himself to smooth things over. I know it's just his natural way because of his powers, but he's so fucking pretentious about it.

"We did save your life. Isn't that reason enough?" Dax asks, charming smile on full display.

Now, I'm rolling my eyes.

"You'll have to do better than that; my life isn't worth very much." Her taunting words hold a hint of sarcastic sass but the words themselves pull at my heartstrings.

They're more honest than she's letting on.

"I like her," Daxdyn says with a slow smirk pulling at his lips.

He likes her because she's so obviously just like him. But I bet he doesn't even realize it.

"You like everyone." I arch an eyebrow at him but it doesn't deter his spreading happiness.

"Her especially." And then the bastard winks like his little mind and his— I can't say little because, we are twins after all— not-so-little dick are all on board with the same thoughts.

As usual. Gods above, can this day be over yet?

"I can pay you," Ryder finally says, stating the first intelligent thing I've heard all night.

"Hmm, a prisoner paying a thief. Sound's reliable." The woman's tone is all biting snark and I can actually see where she's coming from.

"You're a thief?" Ryder cocks his head at her, studying her the way I've been studying her since I made the mistake of wrapping my arms around her delicate body.

"You're too pretty to be a thief." Daxdyn's beaming smile touches his eyes then, flirting so heavily I nearly glare at him again just from his inability to give his poor cock a break every now and then.

"I'm not too pretty to save your ass, though, am I?" She tips her chin up, her fearlessness on full display, and I don't think I've ever been more attracted to such a bad idea in my entire miserable life.

"Have you ever heard the term, *Rich and Hopeless?*" My attention cuts to Ryder and his overly blatant words.

What the fuck is he doing saying something like that about the Hopeless fae to this woman?

"What about it?" she asks with skepticism drenching her words.

She's right to be so disbelieving. The hopeless haven't come to the mortal realm in so long, most of the fae have nearly forgotten about it entirely.

Except for us. Clearly.

"Call me Hopeless, beautiful." A smile so filled with royal charm it lights up Ryder's eyes with more happiness than I've seen from him in . . . years.

"You're lying," she whispers.

If I wasn't a fae myself, I'd have to agree with her. Our race is a fairytale in a world that's crumbling around these poor people. And we want nothing to do with them. They used us. We won't be helping them anytime soon.

But people like this woman, this beautiful, broken woman who's adjusted and overcome her fate, she makes me want to change my mind. She makes me wish I gave a fuck about her.

The tension in my muscles settles, holding her in my arms for just a few seconds like I really might be enough to protect her from this shitty life she's living.

What the fuck is wrong with me?

I grind my jaw and tighten my hold on the . . . prisoner? Is that what she is now?

"You think I'm a liar?" Ryder asks, that smile still marring his face. It's the strangest sight to see him happy. And I know he's about to do the dumbest thing.

He's about to tell her.

If I could scream at him to back down right now, I would.

But I keep my mouth shut and pretend like we're in control of our terrible situation.

Even as he makes it worse, and pushes up the long sleeve of his shirt, revealing one angled line after another. The inky black slashing symbols crawl up his skin and I can feel the air halt in her lungs the moment she sees the Hopeless mark.

Daxdyn follows suit, showing his mark in the moonlight, proving himself just like Ryder did.

And now . . . it's my turn.

Shit.

We have to get home. We have to have her help. They're right. But all of this feels so wrong.

My arms lower from her body, fingertips skimming her sides just because I'm a stupid fuck who wants to know what it'd be like to really feel her held against me in a completely different way.

She shivers from my faint touch but then she's turned, facing me fully, trailing her big gaze across my features and I hate thinking about what she sees.

Too many scars, too many fights, and too many terrible memories line my face. But the way she looks at me seems like she doesn't see any of that. No one's ever overlooked the jagged imperfections in my features before. There's always a pause and a quick averting of eyes. She doesn't do that at all.

It sends a burst of strange warmth searing through me.

Then, I push up my sleeve and show her the only scars on my body that I'm most proud of— The sign of the Hopeless.

Big emerald eyes show her very apparent shock. She glances from my steely eyes to the lashing marks on my forearm. Again and again, she does that back and forth look before finally tearing her attention away and focuses on anything other than myself.

She seems to be thinking all of this through. She's smart. Distrusting but smart.

"Take us to the city," Ryder says with more confidence in his voice now. He's given her proof but the human woman clearly isn't sold yet.

"I can't. The City of the Hopeless is a myth. It does not exist." Her tone is harsher now, not a hint of that playful snark in her words.

"Take us to the Juvar Kingdom then," Ryder pushes, clearly determined to get us home.

He feels guilty. I can tell. And he should if I'm being honest.

The human woman's arms fold over her chest but the way she looks at Ryder is full of curiosity. "It's near Juvar?"

Just like that, he has her where he wants her.

Ryder smirks that princely smile. "You sound very interested for someone who doesn't believe me."

"Let's say I take you to Juvar. What will you give me?"

Ah. They always want something. And that's why the Hopeless would rather forget about this race entirely. Greed fuels humans. Their lifetimes are too short for them to see a bigger picture. For them to realize there's so much more in the world than money.

"Whatever you like. Name your price," Ryder tells her, his words filled with a low sensual promise.

Daxdyn and Ryder both are good at doing that with their words. Their bodies.

Me, not so much. If I tried to distract a woman with my sexuality, I'd end up growling and barking at her like a pissed off mutt. Something tells me I wouldn't be getting laid with that type of alluring personality.

"What's your name?" She nods to him.

He's breaking her down little by little. She's growing more and more intrigued, and the fact that she gives the smallest shit about what his name is proves that she's already in.

"Prince Ryder." He lifts his hand between them.

I look to Daxdyn and he meets my eyes. We both know he's winning. Mostly because he's really selling that Prince card.

"*Prince?*" she asks, her voice rising with the use of that little promising word.

Exactly. He's selling it. She's buying it.

"Before I was a Hopeless fae, I was the son of the King of Juvar. I'm the exiled Prince of Juvar," Ryder explains.

Exiled isn't a word I would have tossed out there to an intrigued buyer but he's too damn honest to keep it from her. The way she pauses though, I can tell she's seconds away from running again.

We need her. We really do. My palm slips over her small wrist, reminding her of who's really in control of this bargain right now.

"You're not really in a place to be *considering* his offer." My fingers squeeze just slightly even if I can't imagine really hurting the pretty human.

"If you do not stop *manhandling* me, you'll regret it."

There she is again with that *you'll regret it* line. She's definitely practiced that phrase a time or two in the mirror.

Her glare stabs into mine, both of us refusing to back down. This woman and I, we're not like fire and gasoline. We're like gasoline and gasoline, and the whole fucking world is already on fire. My head shakes slowly at her and the simple movement just seems to piss her off even more as she closes her eyes and releases a slow breath.

In a flash, her other hand twirls a glinting object. I barely follow her movements in the shadowy night. But I fucking feel it the moment her blade sinks into my thigh.

Everything in me tenses up. A growl of repressed frustration shakes out from clenched teeth and there are several seconds where I can't look at that exasperating fucking woman.

"Fuck, she tried to warn you," Daxdyn whispers with laughter shaking through his words.

He's such an asshole. I cannot believe I share features with someone so patronizing.

My fingers release her one by one. It's the slowest reluctance to let her go but I know it's the right move. Even if it completely kills me to bow down to a five foot nothing stray cat that my brother adopted. The stray is now looking up at me with a cocky smile lighting up her conniving eyes at the fact that she just got the better of me.

Fucking human.

My eyes close slowly and I turn the blade in my hand and return it like I'm not a threat to her, like we're at a strange truce, like I don't think my new ally will try to murder me in my sleep the first chance she fucking gets.

"Thanks," she chirps with so much sarcasm in her tone I want to strangle her. She turns her back on me, writing me off without a second thought. I barely glance at Ryder before she's making demands of him. "I want an exchange."

I glance to my brother but he's watching her like he might eat the beautiful woman alive.

Starting between her thighs, I'm sure.

"Everyone has a Hopeless price," Ryder says, his amusement growing by the second.

He's won. Finally.

"If I take you to the kingdom," she makes a show of wiping my damn blood off on her jeans, the moonlight shining along the metal while she thinks and speaks slowly to the three of us like we're total idiots, "I want a Hopeless exchange. I want something only magic can give me."

Something only magic can give . . .

It's odd to think she doesn't want money. It's even stranger to think I might have misjudged her.

"What do you want?" Ryder studies her slowly, drawing his attention along her slender frame in a way that tells me he's thinking about her the way I was thinking about her— before she fucking stabbed me that is.

"I'll name my price once we come to the ocean that leads to the island of Juvar." She smiles sweetly at them.

I look to Ryder. *Do not agree to that. Do not. Don't.* Gods above, I hope he's not stupid enough to agree to such ridiculously vague terms.

And then he nods.

Fuck.

"What's your name?" Ryder asks.

That's what he has to say for himself. He just made the worst deal in an attempt to get us home. He'll give this dangerous woman whatever she asks for— but suddenly, I'm just as interested as he is.

I'm dying to know the pretty, reckless woman's name.

Besides, it's always nice to know the name of the woman who may or may not kill you. That single thought brings the smallest smile to my lips, and the smirk stays there when she utters the most unusual name that fits her perfectly.

"Zakara Storm."

I can't take my eyes off of her, blonde hair wafting around her porcelain face, her name echoing around my skull like an oath.

Zakara Storm is going to lead us to the Hopeless realm.

Something tells me she's going to be more trouble than she's worth.

The End.

THANK YOU

Thank you so much for reading the prequel to a series that I loved writing. The complete Hopeless Series is now finished and available. Start book one today!
Hopeless Magic, Book One

ALSO BY A.K. KOONCE

The To Tame a Shifter Series
Taming
Claiming
Maiming
Sustaining
Reigning

The Villainous Wonderland Series
Into the Madness
Within the Wonder

The Mortals and Mystics Series
Fate of the Hybrid, Prequel
When Fate Aligns
When Fate Unravels
When Fate Prevails

Resurrection Island Stand Alone
Resurrection Island

The Royal Harem Series
The Hundred Year Curse
The Curse of the Sea
The Legend of the Cursed Princess

The Harem of Misery Series
Pandora's Pain

The Severed Souls Series
Darkness Rising
Darkness Consuming
Darkness Colliding

The Huntress Series
An Assassin's Death
An Assassin's Deception
An Assassin's Destiny

ABOUT A.K. KOONCE

A.K. Koonce is a USA Today bestselling author. She's mom by day, and a fantasy and paranormal romance writer by night. She keeps her fantastical stories in her mind on an endless loop while she tries her best to focus on her actual life and not that of the spectacular, but demanding, fictional characters who always fill her thoughts.

QUEEN OF THE PACK

COURTNEY LYNN ROSE

Queen of the Pack

Written by: Courtney Lynn Rose

Copyright 2019 ©Courtney Lynn Rose

This book is a work of fiction. All characters, places, names, and events are either a product of the author's imagination or are used fictitiously. Any likeness to any events, locations, or persons, alive or otherwise, is entirely coincidental.

All rights reserved, including the right to reproduce this book or portions thereof in any form.

This ebook and the print copy are licensed for your personal enjoyment only and remain the copyrighted property of the author. Please do not redistribute this book for either commercial or non-commercial use. Thank you for respecting the hard work of this author.

Publisher: Knox Publishing, LLC

Editor: Kim Lubbers, Knox Publishing

Formatter: Erin Osborne, Knox Publishing

Proofreader: Jackie Ziegler

Trigger Warning: This book contains adult themes and situations that are intended for readers 18 and older. These themes and situations include, but are not limited to, extreme violence, sexual abuse/assault, vulgar language, and explicit sexual encounters.

❦ Created with Vellum

To my friend and fellow author, Lulu M. Sylvian— if it wasn't for you, I never would have read reverse harem, let alone ever tried to write it.

1

AMARA

THE BOTTOM of my tattered cotton dress sways over my feet, tickling the tops with each push and pull of the light waves hitting the edge of the river bank. The fabric was the purest white when Papa first brought it back from his last trip, but it's been two years, and nothing in this godforsaken town stays pure for long. Not the cotton, and certainly not the townsfolk. It wasn't always like this. Before I was born, the town had no rulers. It was busy with trade between the citizens, and every neighbor looked out for the other.

The year I was born, Papa says was when it all changed. A rich family by the name of Dumitru moved into the biggest home in the town, and slowly, things started changing. They helped the poorer citizens but for a price, and almost overnight, they took hold of everything. Eighteen years later, and Papa and I can hardly get good food without going into debt with them. Not that we aren't in debt already.

When Mama passed from a sweating sickness three years ago, the family's eldest son, Alexandru, offered his aide in making sure she had an honorable burial so that she may rest peacefully in the afterlife. But again, his help came with a price. Neither of us knew what that price was until six months ago.

Alexandru wants my hand in marriage. As he's now the head of his family, he needs a bride, and I'm the one he wants.

For what reason, I can't fathom. Alexandru is handsome enough— rather tall with pale skin, well-defined yet lean muscles, blond hair that is almost white, and the strangest light blue eyes I've ever seen. It's not his looks that put me off, it's the feeling I get when he or his family are out in town. It's like this knot in the pit of my stomach that screams danger through every nerve ending in my body. There's something off about them, all of them. For the life of me, I can't figure it out though.

It's been several days since any of them have come into town, but that's nothing unusual when the weather is nice. Hell's Den is somewhat known for the bleak and dreary constant that hangs over it in the clouds. It's always dark from cloud cover, an almost constant overcast, and rain happens to be the one thing we never lack. After only three mere days of sunlight, today is back to the gray drizzle I'm used to.

That's why there's nothing odd about standing at the river's edge in the rain, skipping rocks across its surface. I'm sure Alexandru will be in the center of town today, and I want to avoid going there at all costs. Papa told me last night that on my birthday, in three short days, he will deliver me to the Dumitru home to marry a man that I hardly know and don't want to marry. In doing so, Alexandru will forgive my family's debt and ensure that Papa and I are taken care of, debt-free, for the rest of our lives.

I love Papa, I do, but I would rather drown in the river than be forced to marry Alexandru Dumitru. I pray that doesn't make me a bad daughter, but no amount of love for Papa will make me love Alexandru, and I don't want to be his wife. Hell, I don't even want to be his friend. I've no desire to have a conversation with him let alone be his wife and bear him children. The thought repulses me.

I have to do something to keep this from happening, I'm just not sure what, and I only have three days to figure it out.

The rain grows cold as it comes down harder, pelting my skin like tiny ice shards. I curse under my breath and turn away from the river, trekking my way back to our hut of a home. Papa owned a big house in the village once. He and Mama lost it to the Dumitru when I was only two. Now, Papa and I reside in a tiny, two-bedroom slum on the very edge of town, closest to the river. I prefer it if I'm being honest.

If I stay close to home, it's less likely I'll run into Alexandru or any of his off-putting family members.

I honestly can't say why they're so strange. There's a rumor around town, and even some travelers have whispered about them when passing through, but I don't believe in the myths and legends of the world. If I haven't seen it with my own eyes, then I'm skeptical that it exists. Hell, it's been forever since I prayed to the Gods. I've never seen them, and they've never answered a single prayer, so why believe in them at all?

As I approach the house, my stomach turns at the two figures standing under the thatch-roof awning Papa built over the front door. He's standing closest to the house, looking more frail and disheveled by the day. His hair is salt-and-pepper, leaning more toward going full white, and he stands with a hunch in his back, his skin loose on his arms and sagging under his eyes. The years have not been kind to Papa, but no matter what, he's always worked his hardest to care for me and love me.

Next to him in a sleek, shimmering black cloak trimmed with fur is none other than Alexandru Dumitru. His blond hair shines with water droplets, and his skin is so pale today that it's luminescent in the grayness of the overcast. Some of the women in town openly fawn over him, and it's not that I can't see why. I'm just intelligent enough to pay attention to my gut feeling about him. I can't avoid him today, after all though, so there's no sense in standing here in the rain longer, especially since I went to the river without a cloak, and my underthings are visible through the worn cotton of my dress.

Walking up to the house, Papa looks up and gives me a sincere smile. "Ah, there's my girl. Where have you been, child? You're soaked to the bone."

Stepping under the awning, I run my fingers through my hair, and it sticks to my neck and shoulders like raven tentacles attached to my head. "I walked down to the river, Papa. Just taking a moment to relax is all."

"Amara, my dear, you're freezing," Alexandru says in his deep tone as he unfastens his cloak and pulls it from his shoulders. "Here. I'm going to have winter cloaks sent down to you by this evening. For both you and your Papa." He places his cloak around my shoulders and pulls it snuggly around me.

I keep from rolling my eyes because I am freezing, and his cloak is warm with a velvet lining. I can't remember if I've ever owned a piece of clothing with velvet on it. The price is so high on finer fabrics that Papa and I can only afford tweed and cotton. It's why I've had this tattered dress for so long.

"Amara, why don't you go inside and dry your dress," Papa says his eyes twinkling with affection.

"Ah, Papa, I will later. Surely it would be rude to leave Alexandru here while my clothing dries." I try for my best playful smile when I glance at the Dumitru man staring at me in confusion.

"Have you no other dress to wear in the meantime," he asks.

My eyes dropped to the ground. "No, my Lord, I do not. Fabric is not easy to come by at this end of town. So, we make do with what we have to avoid furthering our debt."

Alexandru sighs with a strange gleam to his eyes before he reaches out to cup the side of my face. "Amara, my sweet, you and your Papa no longer incur debt with us. I have asked for your hand, and your father has promised it to me. You're going to be my wife, and you and your Papa shall want for nothing. Tell me what you need, what clothing you both want, and I will have the most beautiful garments brought to you."

"Alexandru, I could not abuse your affection in such a way. I am still at a loss for words at the knowledge that you're interested in me at all," I say in an attempt to feign the ruse of someone unworthy of his interest.

"Oh, my dear, you think too highly of me. I am but a simple man, who has fallen for your fierce and beautiful soul. It is my pleasure and high honor to have you as my wife for eternity." Alexandru takes my hand and kisses my knuckles.

The way he says eternity makes goosebumps rise across my skin. Something in his tone has set little warning bells off in my head. I cannot show this in front of him though. Part of what has kept Papa and me alive, and in the Dumitru good graces, is my ability to keep Alexandru in the dark about my true disgust toward him. With only three days to find a way out of this, I cannot disrupt that guise just yet.

He and Papa talk for a few more minutes, and before he goes, he insists I keep the cloak until the one he is commissioning for me arrives later. The angry fear in the pit of my stomach only worsens as I watch him walk the path toward the town center.

Three days is all I have, and it's not nearly enough time

2

ALPHA

STANDING HIDDEN in the trees on the far side of the river, I watch as the raven-haired beauty from the town speaks to my enemy. Alexandru Dumitru has not changed in a thousand years, nor has my rage toward him. When the abomination reaches out and touches the girl, I growl low in my throat. We've quietly watched her for years. There's something about her that has drawn the attention of the entire pack, and any time we lay eyes on her, it is like a current of lightning running through our bodies.

"Why is she with him, Sorin," my Beta, Dacian, snarls from his position beside me.

"I don't know, brother, but whatever he's playing at, we will make sure we get to her first." I take one last glance at her home as Alexandru walks in the opposite direction toward his lavish home on the other end of the town.

When we first encountered the girl, she was no more than six years old. The pack's pull to her happened instantly, and the need to protect her was like a tidal wave over us. It was unlike anything we'd ever experienced, and a few weeks later, I sent my Omega, Adi, to a soothsayer to get answers. What she gave us was enough to keep us here, but not enough for us to understand.

Pack lore since long before I was born says that certain packs are ruled by more than just the Alpha. The female-Alpha is the Queen, for some, and she alone is all the pack needs. While only the Alpha-male breeds with her, the entire pack is at her service. Whether to love her, worship her, or protect her — they are hers. In my thousand years on this Earth, I've never seen such a pack, but that isn't to say they don't exist.

The only true details the soothsayer gave us was that if that is what this girl meant to us, then to complete the bond, we would each have to mark her, my mark being the last. I believe in the soothsayers, but not enough to mark a random girl. So, for years, we've watched instead. Trying to know and understand the girl from afar.

Her beauty is unlike any female I've ever seen. She is not glamorous or seductive. She's subtle, independent, and humble. Her eyes are the most striking violet, and I've spent the last twelve years being haunted by those eyes every time I sleep. I know the others have as well. We share a bond, the pack, and depending on the circumstances, we can feel each other's emotions, sense another's intent, and in the rarest cases, see through each other's eyes. But those are moments of extreme emotion, whether good or bad.

Lately, she's come to the river often, and each time she gets close to the edge, we can feel the fear coursing from her. It's strong and hits us hard, we just haven't been able to find out what it's about. We've been able to put together that her Papa is in some sort of debt to the Dumitru family. Alexandru's courting of our girl is obvious, but she's not as affectionate toward him as we would have thought. We're hoping that is a sign that she isn't truly interested in becoming his undead bride.

Gods know he has had many of them over the centuries. Sadly, immortality with a Dumitru is never really immortality.

That family may turn humans when they please, but they will stake them just as quickly if they grew bored with them or have no other use for them. The war between our families began from this greed. Our pack was once the keeping family of Hell's Den, ages ago. The Dumitru ruled the territory to the north, but wouldn't dare cross into the town.

Our pack was ruled by my father and mother then, and we were a few hundred wolves strong. But then my sister disappeared while hunting the northern ridge one night. We found her on the edge of their territory with a fatal bite to her neck. She died within hours and that's when the war began. Werewolves and vampires are toxic to one another with no cure known for either. We thought that our numbers would give us the upper hand when we stormed their village with two wolves to every vampire in their coven. We only need to bite them to win.

We did not expect them to call on other vampires, and in the end, the five of us were all that remained of the pack.

And here we still stand, just this time, we will not let the Dumitru take what is ours— and the girl is ours.

"Come, Dacian," I say turning away from the river's edge and heading into the forest. "She is in for the night. I shall have Darius swing through tonight, and we will come back at daybreak."

He takes one last look at her home before he turns to follow me. We could shift and make it back to the den faster, but I enjoy the forest. A longer walk will not hurt either of us, and it will keep Dacian out of my thoughts. The ability to tap into each other's thoughts and emotions might be the only thing I tend to dislike about being pack. Sometimes, I would prefer to keep my thoughts and my pain to myself.

"Have you come up with any more theories on what she's planning," he asks as he falls in stride next to me. Dacian is a true Beta— intelligent and strong, with a cunning mind and ruthless when provoked.

As pack law dictates, he is weaker only to myself, and one day my mate, but that is all. In human form, Dacian is over six-foot-three, only two inches shorter than myself. His hair is shaggy and wild, the brown and red equally reflected in the coloring of his fur as a wolf. Yellow eyes that are ever leery stare from him in both forms. He is a force to be reckoned with for anyone outside the bond of the pack.

"I don't know, brother. I think she may be trying to find an escape. Her eighteenth birthday is in three moons, and something tells me that's when Alexandru will come for her."

He stops mid-stride causing me to stop and stare at him as well. His eyes raise to the sky, taking in the almost full moon between the trees. I do not find it a coincidence that the girl's eighteenth birthday also falls on the full moon. "Perhaps we should give her a lifeline?"

I tilt my head and contemplate his words as he brings his eyes to meet my emerald ones. "Hmm. Perhaps you are right." The ideas begin churning in my head as I think of ways we can nudge her to escape the town, and Alexandru before he can turn her. She is too beautiful, too wonderful and pure, to be a vampire. We cannot allow him to succeed.

Plus, she is ours.

As Dacian and I enter the den's opening, the succulent aroma of roasting boar wafts through the air, making my mouth water. Turning the corner into the massive expanse that is the common area, my Delta, Cezar, is pouring a marinade over a whole boar turning on a spit over a roaring fire in the center of the room. A smaller fire next to it holds a rack with several types of vegetables roasting as well.

Cezar is intent on his cooking, his long silver hair pulled back and tied at the base of his head with twine, his red eyes sparkling in the firelight. He must have gone hunting while Dacian and I were watching the girl.

"This is perfect timing, Cezar. Dacian and I have an idea about the girl, and a sit down is required," I say as I pick up a piece of twine from a table as I pass it, pulling my own raven hair back and tying it. Mine is only a little past my ears, which is far shorter than Cezar's, but anything half as long as his irritates me.

He looks up at me from the boar and grins. "Have you two come up with a plan?"

"We will discuss over dinner. We have no details, but whatever we do, it may take all of us to make it work, but if it does, we may be able to bring her to us and see if the soothsayer was indeed telling the truth all those years ago."

Cezar nods with a grin before going back to his cooking. I take a seat at the head of the circle and get lost in my thoughts, thinking of different possibilities to present to the pack about getting the girl.

We've waited twelve years for her to come of age, and I will not lose another woman to the likes of an undead, bloodsucker like Alexandru Dumitru.

And once we have her, we will find a way to eradicate the Dumitru coven and take back our town, once and for all.

3

AMARA

I woke this morning to one of the Dumitru servants banging on the front door. As promised, Alexandru sent us new cloaks and a wagon full of clothing for Papa and I. The wardrobe is exquisite. Much nicer than anything I have ever owned or worn in my entire life. But I don't want any of it. Even wearing the cloak he sent, which is fashioned from silk, velvet, and fur, feels like me showing him affection in return, and that is the last thing I want to do.

I do not want his affection, and I sure as hell do not want to give him mine in return.

As I stand at the fireplace inside our home, making mine and Papa's breakfast, a simple porridge with what is left of our bread, I can't help but cringe at the overwhelming knot in my stomach. I am down to two days to figure out my escape, and still, I am clueless on what to do.

I turn around at the creak of my father's bedroom door opening. A small smile graces my face. Alexandru included new work clothes for Papa, and today he is dressed in new dark brown cotton pants with a loose-fitting cotton shirt in a light tan coloring. He's brushed his graying hair back and for the first time in a long time, he has a little sparkle to his eyes.

"Amara, my child, why are you still wearing that tattered dress? Change into something new," he says as he comes into the room and stands next to me.

I shake my head and sigh. "Papa, I can't accept those clothes."

His brows pull together before he reaches out and takes my hands in his. "Why not? Has something happened? Did Alexandru do something untoward?"

Smiling sadly, I pull Papa over to the rotting wood pieces that make up our table and chairs. "I do not want to marry him, Papa. I know that you think all our problems will be solved if I do, but I can't shake this feeling in my gut about him. It's like a warning."

Papa chuckles and reaches up to lightly touch the side of my face. "Oh, little one, that is just nerves. I would probably feel the same way if someone of his status showed interest in me. Alexandru has fancied you for many years now. Give him a chance."

I shake my head and open my mouth to protest when there is another knock at the door. It is just past daybreak and far too early for more visitors. Papa pats my knee as he gets up to answer. A moment later, a chill sweeps into the room and a shiver runs down my spine. Turning slowly, my eyes widen a little as none other than Alexandru takes a step through our front door. His eyes meet mine and as much as I want to look away, I can't.

"Amara, my love, did you not like the things I sent?" He struts into the room, and drops to one knee in front of me, wrapping my hands in his. It's like holding snow, the chill filtering from his palms into my very soul.

"I did not want to soil them while cooking this morning. They are all far too beautiful to wear for such mundane and messy work," I say quietly as I avert my gaze to the floor.

He lifts a chilled hand and gently touches my chin so that I will look at him. "That is not the only reason. Pray tell, what is wrong?"

I feign for innocence, knowing deep down that angering Alexandru is an unwise thing to do. "I am unworthy of such lavish gifts. Surely, there is someone of a higher standard, someone more deserving of your affections."

Alexandru chuckles and cups the side of my face. It makes me want to cringe away from him, but I know better. "Oh, sweet girl, that could not be further from the truth. So much so I came here this morning to ask you to join me at my home tonight for a proper dinner. I would like you to meet my family, officially, and see the life I want to give you. Would that be alright?"

"She would love to," Papa says taking a step toward us.

My face goes stoic for a moment before I quickly wipe away my irritation and plaster a fake smile on my lips. "Of course, Alexandru. I would be honored."

He stands and takes my hands, pulling me up from my chair. Kissing my knuckles, he smirks at me with eyes full of something that makes my nerves twitch. "I'll come to collect you at sundown. I am looking forward to tonight."

Before I can utter another word, he turns and shakes Papa's hand and leaves the house, shutting the door behind him. When Papa turns to look at me, I can't hide my anger now. "How could you say yes, Papa? Did you not hear a word I said to you just a moment before he knocked? Does what I want matter so little to you?"

"Amara, this is a good match for you. Alexandru can give you a life we will never be able to achieve for ourselves."

Rolling my eyes, I throw my hands up in exasperation. "I do not care about a glamorous life, Papa. I would rather go hungry and spend my days tilling our small garden, than live out the next thirty years as his wife. I want nothing to do with him."

Papa's eyes flare, his face going taut. "I have given you free rein since your mother passed, but finding you a proper husband is my job as your father. I have done that, and the argument is closed."

He turns and grabs his gardening gloves from the small table beside the door and leaves, slamming the door shut behind him.

Tears threaten to spill from my eyes, and I grab my old, ripped, ruined, and tattered red cloak from behind the door and walk out into the coming storm. The sky is much darker today, and the rain is just starting to fall. I put my hood up as I walk quickly toward the river. I need a moment to myself, away from home, Papa, and my impending doom of a marriage. By the time I reach the riverbank, my shoes are soaked through, my toes cold enough that I can hardly feel them. My cloak and dress are the same, clinging to my body, and the rain falls so heavily it's hard to see but a few feet past my own body.

I drop to my knees on the rocks and mud of the bank, the tears spilling over as my whole life hits me. The loss of my mother, who never would have sold me off to the Dumitru like some bargaining chip, Papa's indifference toward my feelings, and all the dreams I had in my younger days of finding a man that would love me the way I remember Papa loving Mama. In the end, that is all any girl really wants in a marriage— someone who loves her even when she cannot love herself.

Alexandru Dumitru does not love me this way. I do not know why he wants me at his side, but I can be sure it is not for love. He knows nothing about me aside from what he learns from watching and hears whispered on the tongues of the townsfolk. Those bits of information are not enough to love someone. And there is no doubt that I do not love him. I will never love him. How can I love someone that I'm being forced to marry when I would rather shrivel up an old maid and die years from now alone in my home surrounded by little to nothing more than my own memories?

Someone behind me clears their throat, and I spin around,

squinting through the rain. My eyes widen and my jaw drops at the man standing but a few feet behind me. His skin is a little tanner than me with muscled calves that lead up to a taut, stomach of abs, a wide chest and shoulder, and a face that could make the gods jealous. There's not a man in town that looks like this one— not even Alexandru. His cheeks are prominent with a short, almost stubble of a beard covering his skin. Black hair flows down to his shoulders in direct contrast with the light blue eyes that stare at me.

"You're soaked," he says in a deep, rippling voice that makes me freeze. It's husky and full of authority. I don't know this man from any other traveler, but the tone and richness to his voice demands obedience and my very core wants to give that.

I nod and continue to stare. After a moment, he comes closer and kneels in front of me. It's only when the heat from his body washes over me do I realize how cold the rain is and shiver.

"You're ice cold," he says on a whisper as the rain picks up and pelts down on us harder. "Can you walk?"

I shake my head, unable to find the energy to even answer this man. He shakes his head and mumbles something I can't decipher. When his arms go around me, one behind my back, the other sliding under my knees, a wave of dizziness washes over me, and sleep unlike anything I've ever felt pulls my eyes closed as I'm lifted from the ground and enveloped in a blanket of warmth.

4

ALPHA

HER BODY IS like ice against mine just from the short time she sat in the rain. I've trekked down the riverbank to the broken bridge. It's the only crossing without having to wade through the water, and with the temperature as low as it is and how poorly the girl is dressed, I don't want to risk her getting ill. Dacian waits on the other side, making sure I am steady on my feet passing from the rotting wood to the river bank.

"Is she alright?" he asks with a touch of panic in his voice.

"She's okay. Let's get her back to the den and warm her up though. My body can only do so much, and she's not dressed for this weather."

It's three-quarters of a mile to the den, but with our speed, even in human form, it doesn't take us long. The moment I step into the common area with the girl in my arms, the pack moves so precisely it's as if we'd planned this. Which was not the case. I only meant to find an opportunity to talk to her. Instead, I find her shivering and in some kind of mental fog, I took her.

Adi, our Omega, steps out and into his room, coming back with several fur blankets, which he lays out on the ground as close to the fire as he can get them. Darius brings several pillows from his area, and Cezar appears with more blankets.

Walking over to the bed they've made, I lay her down gently and step back as Darius pulls a few blankets over her. She hasn't woken up, but we must keep an eye on the time. If she doesn't return home, surely Alexandru or her Papa will come looking. As much as I want to rip that vampire's heart out, we aren't prepared just yet.

"Did you notice anything watching her today," Cezar asks leaning forward to stare at her face.

Having her here in the den feels right, but also very powerful. It's like invisible tethers pulling each of us toward her. The energy is palpable throughout the den.

"Alexandru called on her. It was not long after he made his leave that she fled to the river's edge." I don't take my eyes off her face the entire time I speak. There's no worry etched on her features like we are used to seeing when we watch her from the woods. Her skin is light and smooth, the fire dancing off it so perfectly it's hypnotizing. Her long black lashes make me want to kiss all over her face before exploring the rest of her body. Having her in my arms for that walk was enough to make my thoughts go to places they had not before now.

"We must find out what he wants with her," Adi says sitting back in his seat. "We still have no clue how close she is with the Dumitru family. As much as we want her, this could backfire on us."

He may be the Omega, but he is more level-headed than the rest of us when it comes to things like this.

A soft moan grabs our attention, and our eyes train on the girl as she rolls onto her back, pulling her arms from under the blankets and stretching them above her head. The blankets have pushed down, and my eyes roam of the rise and curve of her breasts, my cock twitching against my pants. If the soothsayer is right, and she is meant to be our Queen, it won't be long before this pack grows in number.

When her eyes flutter open, they meet mine first. A ghost of a smile crosses her lips until she looks around and notices the other men. My heart thumps as her eyes go wide and she scrabbles to her feet, tripping as she tries to move away from us. I stand, holding one hand out toward the pack so they stay seated, and holding the other up in submission to the girl. She is panicked and frightened, I can feel it in the air pulsing around her.

"Calm down, love," I say in a low, steady voice. "We won't hurt you. You have my word."

"Who are you? Where am I?" She backs up a few more steps and trips over an unleveled spot in the floor. I rush over and she topples toward the ground, catching her just before her back hits the floor. She whimpers as she clutches my arms, her eyes welling with tears as she looks up at me.

"My name is Sorin, and this is my pack." Slowly, I stand upright, keeping her in my arms.

She looks over at them with uneasiness plain on her face. "Pack?"

"What is your name, love?" I gently guide her back over to the fire, pulling her into my lap as I sit down in my chair. I take her hands in my one while keeping my other hand around her back.

"Amara," she says, and a grin takes over my face before I can stop it.

"You have a beautiful name, Amara," Dacian says tilting his head toward her. "I am Dacian. And these other men are Cezar, Darius, and Adi." He points to them each in turn.

"Sorin. Dacian, Cezar, Darius, Adi." She lets her eyes roam over each of us as she repeats the names, and then she turns her head to look back at me.

Every fiber of my being wants to lean up and press my lips to hers, but it is too soon. "Amara, we've kept watch over you for a long time now."

Her eyes widen again but never leave mine. "I don't understand. Why?"

I shift my body to set us up some so that the pack can see

her as well as I can. "How much do you know of Alexandru Dumitru and the history of Hell's Den?"

She shrugs her shoulders and shakes her head. "I confess not much. I have lived in Hell's Den my whole life. But the Dumitru family came shortly after I was born. My Papa, he has made an agreement with them which I cannot honor, I just do not know how to get out of it yet."

The pack gets up from their spots and move to sit around Amara and me. Their pull to her is as strong as mine, and they waited longer than I expected before allowing that energy to get them out of their seats. She scoots into me further, looking at them with weary eyes.

"Relax, love. No one here will ever hurt you or do anything you did not ask them to. Tell us, what has your father agreed to."

She sighs and turns her body toward the pack for the first time. "Papa and I have been in debt to Alexandru for many years. To settle that debt, he's agreed to give Alexandru my hand in marriage."

Darius growls low in his throat, and Amara startles a little. He reigns himself in at the realization of her feelings. "My apologies, beautiful. I did not mean to scare you."

She relaxes into my arms again. "No, I'm sorry, Darius. This is just so strange to me."

I reach up and tuck a strand of her silky, raven hair behind her ear. "What is strange to you, love?"

She turns her eyes to mine. "I do not know any of you, and yet, this is the safest I have felt in some time."

"How do you feel when Alexandru is near you," I ask preparing myself to finally learn her views on our sworn enemy.

She stares down at her hands. "He frightens me. There is something about him, about all of them, that feels strange, and not in a good way."

She jumps a little, tearing her eyes away from me when

Dacian reaches over and lays his hand on her thigh. "Do you want to marry him, sweets?"

Tears well in her eyes again, and the protective spirit in me beats against the inside of my chest. "No, Dacian, I do not wish to marry him. I wish to find a way to disappear. I would prefer death than to be Alexandru's wife."

My arms tighten around her. "No, love. Death is what awaits, Alexandru, not you."

She looks to me with questions dancing in her eyes.

"What if we could give you a way out? Ensure that you leave the town and are protected from Alexandru?" Dacian says gently rubbing his thumb back and forth on her leg.

Amara surprises me when she lays her hand over his. "I would be forever in your debt."

"There are some things we need to tell you first," I say sternly causing her to tense in my arms. "Truths that you may not believe, but we must tell you anyway. Then you can decide if you want to accept our offer."

Amara straightens and takes deep breaths before nodding. "Then tell me."

5

AMARA

I HAVE NEVER FELT such a pull to more than one person. Being in the room with Sorin and his pack, as he calls them, it's almost as if I can physically feel the invisible tethers running from them to me . . . or maybe it is just me to them. That I cannot tell.

"Do you believe in the monsters of your myths, Amara," Sorin says in his deep voice. It sends shivers down my spine.

My brows pull together in confusion though. "What kind of myths and legends, Sorin? I believe in the gods. But I haven't believed that little fairies clean my home since I was but six-years-old." I try to chuckle. I have heard so many stories throughout my life, that believing in them all would certainly make me mad.

"What about those stories of beings that feast on human blood or men that turn into wolves?" Dacian says causing me to freeze.

Those stories I used to believe in. But to actually give them credibility . . . it seems almost impossible. "I do not know, Dacian. Are you trying to tell me that vampires and were-wolves are real?"

"They are," Sorin says with no trace of humor anywhere in

his eyes or tone. "We are what is left of an ancient pack of werewolves that once ruled Hell's Den. How do you think the town got its name?"

I think back to the stories I heard about werewolves as a child. Wolves live in packs and their home is called a den. Hell's Den would make sense. "I should be running right now. The thought of being in a cave, hidden from the outside world, surrounded by five very large men claiming they turn into wolves at the full moon."

"Not the full moon, love," Sorin says with a chuckle. "I have not been on this earth for thousands of years to be controlled by the moon. I shift as I so choose. Or when I am too emotional to stop it."

"Wait," I say sitting up a little straighter. "You're serious? You're a werewolf?"

Sorin nods his head. When I look to each of the other men, they nod as well. The most youthful-looking, Adi, smirks at me and winks. His eyes are the oddest color gold with blond, ear-length hair that makes him look almost boyish.

Looking back to Sorin, I shake my head in disbelief. "Okay. So, you're a pack of werewolves. I'm sitting in the middle of werewolves . . ." My heartbeats accelerate and dizziness sweeps over me. The most handsome and delicious men I have ever seen are claiming to be mythical beasts that there has never been any proof that they actually exist. Is it possible that I passed out next to the river, and am now in some dreamland?

"Amara, love, take a deep breath. You are ours, and no harm will ever come to you by us." Sorin reaches up and cups the side of my face, trailing his thumb across my lips.

Such a gesture should not turn me on, but it does. From the tingle in my scalp, down to the pulsing in my sex, his touch moves me in ways no one has ever before.

"What does that mean?" I cannot stop myself from leaning into his touch. His palm is so warm and feels comforting against my skin.

"Many years ago, we spoke to a soothsayer that prophesied you to be our Queen one day. For you to be the alpha female of our pack and help us take back our home."

A thousand questions flow through my mind, like the way the world spins when a child twirls in a field playing. "Which one of you did this soothsayer predict I would be beholden to?"

Sorin smirks and causes goosebumps to flutter across my skin when he pulls me close to him, his mouth next to my ear enough that when he speaks, his lips lightly touch my lobe. "All of us, love. We are a pack, and we are all to be with you. You will be the bind that makes us truly whole."

My sex throbs at his words. All of them? One woman to five men. Surely the gods would frown upon such a lifestyle. "I cannot think of a single reason as to how I would deserve one of you, let alone all of you. I am a peasant, coming from the dirt without a speck of nobility or higher class in my body."

Sorin cups my face again and brings my lips down to his before I have the wits to pull away. His tongue dances with mine and my head can think of and process nothing else. A different hand slides around the back of my neck, soft and tender, with just enough pressure to break me away from Sorin. The lust in my blood makes everything hazy, and I bite my lip as Dacian pulls me to him, his lips taking Sorin's place.

The electricity pulling me to them comes from all around me, sensitizing every inch of my being. As Dacian consumes my mouth, another set of hands trails up my arm, and Dacian releases me. The new hands gently grab me and turn me, so my back is facing Sorin. These hands belong to Cezar, and he runs them across my shoulders to cup both sides of my face as he too leans in to consume my mouth.

Sorin's erection presses into my backside and he lifts his hips, grinding it into me, and I moan into Cezar's mouth. When he releases me, I glance to either side, finding Darius and Adi to my right and left. Darius tangles his fingers in my hair, turning my head so my lips meet his, while Adi runs his fingertips across my collarbone before the men trade positions. When Adi pulls his lips away from mine, Sorin turns me all the way around so that I am straddling his lap, crashing his lips to mine again.

"Did any of that feel wrong to you, love? The energy and want radiating off you tells me you rather enjoyed it."

My cheeks heat as I blush and try to hide my face. He places his hands on either cheek, forcing me to look him in his beautiful blue eyes. "Do not be embarrassed. You are ours, we are yours. We will just have to figure out what works for us all."

"Have you never shared a woman before?" The question rolls off my tongue before I can stop it.

Sorin caresses my face in a loving way that I've never had someone do before. "No, love. Wolves mate for life. Once we have you away from Alexandru, we will mark you as ours, and you will be the only woman for the rest of our time on this earth."

The moment the Dumitru name leaves his lips, my reality comes crashing back on me. "Sorin," I say softly. "What is Alexandru? He is not normal, is he?"

Shaking his head, Sorin sighs. "He is a vampire, Amara. All the Dumitru members are. You must keep clear of him."

"I cannot," I say in defeat. "Papa agreed for me to have dinner with him this evening. If I am not there or I try to refuse, I fear what may happen."

Sorin is the one to growl this time. "When are you to marry him?"

I shudder with a sigh. "Tomorrow night Papa is set to deliver me to their home for our wedding to take place the next morning."

Several of the others growl behind me. Sorin sits up and places his hands on my hips. "If that is not what you want, meet me tomorrow evening, just before dusk at the bridge. We will come for you, and Alexandru will not have you. The choice will be yours."

"I will meet you," I say with more confidence than I feel. With shaking hands, I take his face and lean in to kiss him.

Clearly, I have lost my mind, engaging this way with men I hardly know, but yet, it feels perfect and right— as if this is where I am meant to be. But I must go back to town and have dinner with Alexandru tonight. I cannot tip him off that I will disappear before he can force me to be his bride . . . an undead bride if what Sorin says is true.

Tomorrow night, I will leave Hell's Den behind.

6

ALPHA

TOMORROW NIGHT WILL BE INTERESTING, to say the least. If Amara can make it through the dinner tonight without tipping Alexandru off to her leaving, then we may just get her out of the village without a war. As we stop, hidden within the trees behind her home, she turns to me and looks up so her eyes meet mine. She comes up to my chest, tall for a woman considering I'm six-foot-five. Before she can say anything, I grip the back of her neck and lean down to kiss her.

Her tongue battles with mine as she devours my very soul with her kiss. It's like she's tasted the air for the first time and realizes she needs it to survive. That's the passion she kisses me with. Pulling away from her, I wrap one arm around her waist and lift her. She wraps her arms around my neck and legs around my waist, giggling in a way that's very unlike what we have come to know of her. At this moment, it dawns on me that in all the years we've watched Amara, we have never truly seen her happy.

"Amara, you seem most happy, love," I say as I slowly spin in a circle, making sure to stay under the cover of the overgrown brush.

"Who would have thought that five deeply handsome

strangers would give me a reason to be most happy," she says before leaning down to kiss me again, this time slow and soft. "Now, set me down so that I do not blow our plan by being late for a dinner I'm going to hate."

I fight not to growl at her words. We understand that she must go to this dinner, but it still bothers me greatly. "I will meet you tomorrow at dusk, on the bridge. Bring whatever you need from your home, Amara. Once you leave with us, you cannot come back. Not until we take the town back under our protection. Do you understand?" I let her down from my body but still gently grip the back of her neck.

"Yes, Sorin, I understand. I will be fine. Stop worrying so much," her tone is sweet but irritated underneath.

"You are our woman, my female-alpha, I will always worry when you are not with me," I say.

Her eyes soften as she leans into my touch. "Tomorrow night. Do not be late, Sorin or I will be most displeased." She winks before turning away from me and heading back toward her Papa's house. I stare after her until she enters the dwelling and I can no longer see her.

The entire walk back to the den, I think of all the things we must accomplish before tomorrow night. It being the night before the full moon, we will all be a little more aware, more irritable, more hands-on . . . more everything, if I'm being honest. While we can control the shift, we cannot control the way the full moon heightens the very energy in our being. That is something we will never control because it is the evidence of the very magic running through our veins that makes us what we are.

Being a Lycan is something you are born into, not changed into like when becoming a vampire. We're nature's magic. The protector that Mother Earth gave to the lands as if she knew one day the world would need it. Darker magic from humans created the vampires, who are the very unbalance that plagues this world. Something that feeds off humans and can never die throws off the very line in which all of nature in this realm hangs on.

Our pack is not interested in restoring the balance to all the worlds, but certainly here in Hell's Den. Now that we know Alexandru's intentions with our woman, it is all the more reason to eliminate him. Amara is in danger, whether she realizes it or not, and I will not risk her life. By the time I get back to the den, the pack has cleaned up the blankets Amara napped in, hanging the wet one close to the fire for drying.

"Let's get this place presentable, and later we can work on a back-up plan in case something goes wrong between tonight and tomorrow. Alexandru is collecting her tonight at dusk for a dinner with his family in their home. She is scheduled to go back tomorrow night, an hour after full-dark, to prepare for their wedding. Thank the gods we're taking her at dusk." I grab some more wood and carefully place it in the fire pit.

"What is the plan, Sorin," Dacian asks as he moves around the room picking things up and placing them where they belong. "How do we know her Papa won't try to send her to Alexandru early?"

I sigh and run my fingers through my hair. "We have no guarantee something like that won't happen."

"What the fuck do we do if it does? What if she doesn't leave tonight and doesn't meet us tomorrow?" Cezar stops next to Dacian with wide eyes.

"If she doesn't meet us, brothers," I say sternly. "Then we'll storm that fucking town until we find her, and kill every Dumitru that gets in our way."

They nod and go back to handling things around the den. I must work out a plan for tonight and tomorrow. As their Alpha, it is my job to ensure not only the pack's safety but Amara's as well. Though I certainly can't get too close to Alexandru. It has been many years, but he would still recognize me. During the last battle, it was I who almost took his life. I doubt my face has slipped his mind as of yet.

Once dusk is moving into full night, I lead my men through the woods to the river bank, staying on our side. We stop across from Amara's home, each finding spots where we can see the home. It isn't long before a wagon and escort come from the main road, stopping in front of her home. It's not Alexandru, and whoever it is, he's human, that much is clear. The scent through the air has no hint of vampire on it.

When the door opens and Amara steps into the night, my jaw drops at her beauty. The lust coming off the others is thick in the air as we watch her, in clothing far too expensive, looking as beautiful as ever. She's clean, her raven hair mixing like ink with the night sky. As the moonlight hits her dress, it shimmers a deep purple that accents her eyes when she stops next to the wagon and turns her eyes to the riverbank.

She scans the hills on our side. I know she cannot see us, but she is searching. A howl goes off from Cezar behind me and I snicker as Amara's escort turns toward the river and shudders before leaning toward her and whispering something. She gives the river and woods one last glance with a smirk on her kissable lips before allowing the man to help her into the wagon.

"That was probably unwise, Cezar," I say with amusement in my voice. "Alexandru is sure to have heard it."

He claps me on the shoulder as he moves down the hill to my side. "I wish he would hear it, Alpha. He's grown arrogant in the years thinking we were gone. I truly hope to teach him a lesson on arrogance very soon."

I laugh again. Cezar holds a grudge worse than the rest of us. I have spent too many nights over the last three-hundred-years talking him out of silly revenge notions. Once or twice, I have had to command him as his Alpha because it was the only sure way to make sure he didn't do something careless and stupid. In the last few years, he has calmed down some. But not enough for me to stop keeping a close eye on him when dealing with issues. Amara already holds us bound to her; I can only imagine what lengths Cezar would go to in order to protect her.

Then again . . . I already know how extreme I would take things for the same reason.

I swear, she will be the death of us or what makes us thrive again— we just have to wait and see which.

7

AMARA

The Dumitru home is much larger when standing on the doorstep. It is a castle in comparison to the rest of the town. A large, covered porch made of fine wood with a deep red hue, elaborately carved pillars hold up the awning that shelters visitors from the snow. Even the door is a heavy oak with an ornate silver knocker hanging from the center, silver knobs to match. Everything about this home is pristine and expensive . . . while the majority of the town is dilapidated and rotting.

After knocking, I turn my back on the door and step to the edge of the porch, staring up at the moon while I wait. It looks full, but not quite. Tomorrow will be the full moon, and I can't stop my mind from traveling to Sorin. Every time I found myself thinking of the pack while getting ready, the thoughts always start with him and then move to the other men. I paid enough attention when with them to conclude that Sorin is the Alpha, just by the way the others respond to a mere look from him.

It is silly that I wish he were with me right now. If Alexandru is a vampire, as Sorin claims, then I am about to head into the most dangerous place I have ever been. Even a den of werewolves does not scare me as much as the thought of a vampire. But Sorin is right, I must not give Alexandru any indication that I know something secret about him. I cannot lead on in any way that tomorrow night while he is preparing for me to come here, I will be running away.

"Amara, my lovely lady, you are most stunning." Alexandru's deep velvet voice causes me to twirl around to face the door. As I do my hair is like a fan following the movements, matching the way my dress expands at the bottom. Alexandru's eyes grow darker as he watches me. "That was very sexy. Spin again for me."

I must be as normal as possible. Possibly even more so as to keep him in the dark, so I nod my head toward him with a seductive smirk on my face and spin again. "I fear you are once again too complimentary of me, my lord. I am sure there are far more beautiful ladies that have tried to get your attention."

Alexandru steps out onto the porch, leaving the door open behind him. Stopping just in front of me, he reaches outs and gently holds my waist and then pulls my body against his. "You think too little of yourself, Amara. There is no woman as beautiful as you anywhere that I have been." He leans down and kisses me softly.

I rest my hands on his shoulders and return his kiss, but all the while screaming in my own head and part of me wishing it was Sorin with his lips on mine.

When Alexandru pulls away, I look down to his chest, hiding my face as best I can in an attempt to feign embarrassment.

"Forgive me," he says with a slight hitch in his voice. "Your first time here and I'm being intimate with you before I've so much as invited you in. That was not my intention. I hope you will forgive me."

He cups the side of my face, but I keep my eyes downcast. "There is nothing to forgive, Alexandru. Though, I am beginning to feel the chill."

"Of course, of course, my dear. Come, let's go inside.

Dinner should be set out at any moment now, and I'd like to introduce you to my family."

As Alexandru leads me into the house, a young blonde wearing a maid's frock with a black scarf tied around her neck approaches me, offering to take my cloak. As I try to take it off, Alexandru comes and helps, his fingers skim across my shoulders and down my arms. His lips touch the bare part of my shoulder, something all his dresses minus the work ones have in common. I've never worn such provocative garments that showed so much skin.

"Come, my mother and father are very likely to come looking for us soon if we don't make an appearance." Alexandru takes my hand and walks me through the foyer and down a long hallway. Through the door at the end of the hall, I can see part of a table and chandelier. When we enter, my eyes roam over the vast expanse. The table is actually large mahogany that seats eight. There are two chandeliers adorning the ceiling littered with tiny crystal spheres that spark as the candlelight hits them.

The table has two ornate silver candelabras and a gorgeous red silk table runner down the center. The whole house is a bit dark for my taste and makes Alexandru's complexion a stark white in comparison. Something I notice is similar as my eyes find the rest of his family, standing on the other side of the room near a large fireplace. The knots in my stomach tighten, and Sorin's words ring in my ears.

If Alexandru is a vampire, that means it's likely his entire family is. So, little human me is standing in the presence of not one, but six blood-thirsty undead that may or may not try to kill me before I can get back out of this house. He must feel my tension because he pulls at my hand and stops me from walking, pulling it enough so that I turn to face him. Bringing his other hand up to cup the side of my face, he gently forces my eyes to meet his.

"What's wrong, my dear?"

I cast my eyes down. "What if your family doesn't like me? Papa would be most displeased if I come home and tell him that I wasn't liked by your family."

Alexandru chuckles and rubs his thumb against my cheek. "You will have nothing but amazing things to tell your Papa later tonight. I know my family is going to love you." He leans forward and softly kisses my lips before standing and continuing toward his family. When we get to them, he stops and clears his throat.

The couple closest to us looks to be in their mid-fifties. Both have dark brown hair and blue eyes, perfect porcelain skin, and the most exquisite clothing. Their outfit choices even match in a deep gray.

"Oh, she's beautiful, Alexandru," the woman coos as she steps forward and hugs me. "Simply a vision, son."

"Let's not smother her, mother. Amara this is my mother Mihaela, and my father Andrei."

The man gives me a comforting smile and nods but thankfully, doesn't move to hug me.

"She'll have to get used to affection once she's your wife. We're a close family," his mother says linking her arm through mine and turning me toward the other three, equally beautiful people standing next to us. "Now, this is Alexandru's brother Florin and his wife Elena, and my youngest daughter Katarina."

They all say hello and both the women hug me just as his mother did, mutter how beautiful I am and other such compliments.

After fifteen to twenty minutes of chatter in which I believe they ask me every question a person could ask another about their family and childhood, a bell rings signaling dinner is to be served. Alexandru sits at the head of the table with his father at the opposite end. I am to his right with his youngest sister next to me and his brother's wife next to her. Across from us are his mother and brother as well.

I do my best over the next hour to stay calm and seem like

I'm enjoying the conversation. I laugh when appropriate and don't shy away from any of Alexandru's affections. His family doesn't let on that they are anything other than what they appear to be. It almost makes me question if what Sorin and the others said about them is true. Nothing about them except possibly their skin color is strange.

It's hard to contain my surprise when the food comes out and I watch them dig in just as any normal human would. Clearly, either they aren't vampires or they can eat human food and drink blood. By the time Alexandru stands and offers me his hand for a stroll through their gardens, I am full, exhausted, and doubt everything Sorin spoke. But somewhere in the back of my mind, I know he told me the truth, just Alexandru hides it well.

"Amara," Alexandru says as we walk down the outside stairs and into an elaborate garden that shimmers under the moonlight. "Do you trust me?"

I look at him with confused eyes. "You have yet to give me a reason not to."

"There are some things I must tell you before we marry, and I hope they will not dissuade you from being with me."

I stop and sit on a stone bench at the edge of the path we are on. "I highly doubt you could tell me something that would make me think ill of you, Alexandru."

"Please do not run, Amara, but I must tell you, I am . . . a vampire."

Well, hell. Sorin was right,

8

ALPHA

I sent the pack back to the den two hours ago, but I stayed, sitting down with my back against a tree trunk waiting for Amara to come home. The rumble of a wagon pulls my attention, and looking up, she waits for the wheels to stop and Alexandru to come help her down. I sit forward and watch through the trees, a low growl escaping my throat when he tangles his fingers in her hair and leans in to kiss her. It shocks me when she rests her hands on his shoulders and lets him trail his lips across her jaw and down her neck, stopping as he whispers something in her ear.

My blood boils as she smiles at him, watching as he turns and gets back on the wagon and heads back to town. Amara stands on her doorstep until he has disappeared from sight. I sigh when she rushes into the house. Now that she is home, I should head back to the den. Instead, I sit and stare at her home, illuminated in the moonlight, for just a little longer.

The front door opens again, and Amara emerges. She shouldn't be coming back outside this late at night. It's dangerous, even if she wasn't in the midst of a war between species. She looks up the road toward town for a moment before fully stepping out of the door and slinging some kind of sack over her shoulder. She uses one hand to hold her dress up, clearly still wearing the same clothing she wore to her dinner and running down the path toward the river. As soon as she gets to the tree line, she turns and picks up her pace, running away from the town . . . toward the bridge.

Jumping to my feet, I take off down the river bank. Once the trees open up, I let out a loud whistle. Amara stops and her eyes frantically search the river bank. I emerge from the brush and run straight across the water. Even at its deepest, it only comes up to my shoulders and I make it across quick enough. As I emerge onto the bank closest to her, she drops her sack and stalks toward me.

"What the hell are you doing, love?"

As I reach for her, she smacks my hands away and stands on her toes to grab both sides of my face and pulls me down until my lips slam into hers. Her tongue invades my mouth, and she pushes herself into me so hard, her arms going around my neck as if she's trying to climb inside me. I slide my arms around her waist and lift her, kissing her back with matching intensity.

When she pulls away from me, she looks down into my eyes and all I see in her's is panic and fear. "I cannot wait until tomorrow. Take me now, I won't stay here."

Just as I open my mouth, there's shouting in the distance. I curse under my breath and drop her down to her feet. Reaching down and grabbing her sack with one hand, I toss it over my shoulder and grab her hand with my other. Pulling her, we run, heading toward the bridge. The shouting gets fainter, and I know it's still at her house. Whatever made her leave when she did, I am suddenly thankful for it.

Alexandru came back early for her, and she wasn't there.

Thankfully, he does not know we still exist so close to the town, so there is little chance he will come searching for her where the den is. I move her with haste anyway. It takes us longer to get there with her running beside me, but eventually,

I sigh in relief the moment we are inside the safety of the den. The pack gets up, startled at our sudden arrival. I have to keep the smile off my face when I drop her sack and watch as she walks right into Dacian's arms, muttering with the hint of tears in her tone.

He wraps his arms around her and holds her to his chest, his eyes finding mine.

"Alexandru came early for her. She'd already fled, but she can't go back now," I say to the collective sigh of the pack.

I lean against the wall as the others join Amara and Dacian, giving her gentle kisses and caresses. We have our woman now, so the next step is to mark her and make her ours, and then we take out the Dumitru to take back our home— our town.

This is just the beginning of what is going to be a very long battle, but with our Queen, the pack can accomplish anything.

To be continued . . .

ALSO BY COURTNEY LYNN ROSE

Arctic, an Emerald Isle MC series prequel

The Auction Block, Agents of Interpol series, Book 1

The Gallows at Midnight, Agents of Interpol series, Book 2

Dominated by Desire: a bdsm anthology featuring Courtney's story, In Her Stilettos

Bad to the Bone: a bad boy anthology featuring Courtney's story, Accidental Revenge

Hearts of Steel: a Pittsburgh charity anthology featuring Courtney's story, Jersey Love

COMING SOON

FROM COURTNEY LYNN ROSE

Drunk Me, Southern Dreams: Oregon Coast series, Book 1 coming September 30, 2019

Shamrock, Emerald Isle MC series, Book 1 coming October 28, 2019

CONNECT WITH COURTNEY

Newsletter: http://bit.ly/NewsletterCLR
Facebook Fanpage: www.facebook.com/clynnrose87
Facebook Reader Group: www.facebook.com/groups/courtneysbookconcubines
Twitter: www.twitter.com/clynnrose87
Instagram: www.instagram.com/clynnrose87
Snapchat: www.snapchat.com/clynnrose87
Website: www.courtneylynnrose.weebly.com
BookBub: www.bookbub.com/authors/courtney-lynn-rose
Goodreads: www.goodreads.com/courtneylynnrose
Amazon: www.amazon.com/author/courteylynnrose

LILLIE OF THE WOODS

IRIS SWEETWATER

UNTITLED

Lillie of the Woods
A Reverse Harem Retelling of Beauty & the Beast
By: Iris Sweetwater

1

LILLIE

I rode my horse, Sylver, along the river, looking out for the seventh time that day. The water glistened with the glow only the sun could cause, almost mocking my reasons for being there.

I had done that exact same thing for just over a year, hoping that his boat would be on the horizon. I would have given the horse itself just to see one look of the first part of the bow of his ship rising over the water's edge, but it wasn't there . . . again.

It was never there, no matter how much I hoped and wished it would be. I had asked everyone as far and wide as I had traveled if they had seen him, but always, I came up empty-handed. It had grown exhausting, but I was never going to give up.

Malcom was my Papa, a merchant sailor that would travel all over France to deliver and return cargo, but every time, every single time, he would return on the day that he said he would. On the rare occasion that he was going to be late, he would send a missive from where he was to the Merchant Mariners' office in Paris.

If he was one day late, I would ride Sylver to the Mariners' office and find the missive there telling us when Papa would be home. I had ridden to Paris once a week since he vanished to make sure they hadn't missed something.

It was possible that they had been overlooking it for a year, wasn't it?

The other merchants that knew my father and the situation stopped in every now and then to bring my sisters and I some food, but for the most part, I was the one who provided for my family. I hunted, fished, and bartered for just about anything we had gained in the year following our papa's disappearance.

My blond hair was strung down my back, flipping in the wind as I rode home. I didn't want to go, but the triplets were hungry, or starving, as they would have said. They were far from dying, but I had made my decision— that was going to be my last night home. I just needed to work up the nerve to tell them so.

Rose, Dahlia, and Aster, the triplets, were twenty-one, two years older than me, but they thought they owned the world. They were good for nothing other than going to soirees, chasing after the men they would marry, and keeping up their good looks. They almost always whined, never cleaned the house or went after food, and for the most part, other than the occasional question from Rose, they didn't care to know if I had any more information on Papa or not.

It was funny how they tried hopelessly to find a man to marry or to call mon mari, but there had not been one that stayed around much longer than to get to know them. On the other hand, I had never been one to want to get married. I wanted to take after Papa and be a mariner myself, one of only a few women that would do the job, but I couldn't wait. However, the men flocked toward me like moths to a flame, and I never understood it.

The triplets were always voicing their hate for me, I was the one who killed our mere after all, the day I was born, but once our papa had been gone a day longer than he should, they would beg that I go to town and barter for the things we needed. I would do it for books, but that was the only reason . . . I knew how to take care of myself, what did I care if the little twits starved?

Other than for my books that were . . .

They could eat like princesses if they wanted, but only if I could get something to read out of it. It wasn't my fault my mere died giving birth. Our papa had been sad for years, but he rarely mentioned her any longer. He was proud of his daughters, and she had given them to him.

The first time that papa went away after I was old enough to hold a bow, he taught me how to shoot it. Then, he taught me how to fish, then hunt, and took me to town to barter and use what he had earned on the ship. My sisters said it was because he had never gotten his boy, but I knew it was because if something ever happened to him, he wanted to make sure that someone could take care of herself and the others if she so chose to.

I walked in the door and immediately wished I wasn't there. I hated being home since Papa wasn't, and I had learned to despise my sisters almost as much as they did me. I had no reason to be there other than to feed them.

Rose was looking in the mirror trying on a hat that looked like she had refashioned a ladies' hat out of one of our papa's fishing hats . . . I wanted to scream. Aster was painting her fingernails with the only bottle of polish I ever had. Papa had gotten it for me for my thirteenth birthday. It was the only thing he could afford, and it made the best gift ever. Dahlia was sitting on her cul doing nothing.

"Here, cook this," I said to Dahlia as I plopped the raw, skinned rabbit on her lap.

"*Grose*," Dahlia whined and then she screamed out a small tantrum about it ruining her dress.

"Fine, starve," I said as I took the copy of Les Misérables off the shelf. "It's not like you don't have twenty dresses just the same."

The book had once belonged to Dahlia, but I had my eye on it since I was ten. I had let them grow hungry for a few days while I ate food I had bartered from town. Rose, the more practical one, begged Dahlia to give up her original copy of the book, and so I went hunting for them. The thing was, they were just as capable of taking a few of the things Papa had gotten from his trips into town and barter with them in exchange for food and cleaning supplies, but they didn't.

They wouldn't.

That night, we sat around the table, I was nervous about telling them my plans. I couldn't figure out why it would matter, but I knew they would have something to say about it.

"I am going to look for Papa," I blurted out over dinner.

Aster had given up and fixed the rabbit, and I made a pot of stewed vegetables I had gotten in town. It was a feast, to say the least, but I didn't think I could live like that any longer. I knew I needed to get out, away from them, and away from Azay le Rideau and The Loire River where my father had vanished from.

It was eating me alive.

"What are you talking about, Lillie?" Rose blurted out. "You are not going anywhere."

"You are not my keeper, Rosaria, and before you say a word, either of you Dahlia Marie, or Asterannah," I used their full names for effect, "I am old enough to do what I want."

"Okay, Lillianna," Dahlia said in a cocky tone. "Who is going to feed us?" she demanded, as she stood up and pounded on the table.

"Do you know how awful that sounds?" I asked her.

"Papa taught you to hunt and fish, not us," Aster said.

"It's only because you would not do what he asked," I yelled. "He attempted to teach you many times, but you gave up. You know what," I was screaming, "I am going, and I will be gone by morning. I will make sure you have enough food for a month, but that is all . . . don't expect me back unless Papa comes too."

I stood up and marched out of the house, grabbing my bow and arrows on the way. I had a plan set forth in my head, and I wasn't going to let anyone stand in my way of doing what I felt was right.

As I tied the bags I had already packed earlier in the day to Sylver, I got on him and trotted towards town to see what I could get for my sisters while I would be gone. I took the few things I wanted to give up to trading, and so I found the first marketplace I would stop at for the night.

The markets ran only at night because most everyone worked during the day and because some of the things that went on weren't exactly in concordance with Parisian law. I had never partaken in illegal activities, but I needed to be in the mix to do what I needed to.

I slid off my horse and untied the bag that I would be trading that night. I tied him up and walked towards the tents that were set up on the waterfront in the woods and caught myself looking over the water. I shook my head to bring myself to the present and walked on to the first vendor.

"Martel," I said as I walked up to one of the men I most liked to do business with.

"Lillie." He smiled. "Any word on Malcom?"

I shook my head. I hated that I didn't have any word on that subject. It had been that way for twelve months.

"No," I sighed. "I plan on going to look for him, but I need some supplies for my sisters while I am gone." My eyes darted around the rest of the market as others arrived surveying them. Some looked as if they had done this many times without being caught while others were pulling shawls around them so no one could see their faces and walking slowly, ready for something to jump out at them.

"I think I can help you with that." He smiled as he pulled a basket of tradeable goods out from under his table.

After an hour of going stall to stall, and getting rid of everything I had brought with me in exchange for things both my sisters and I would need, I got back on Sylver and made my way back to the woods where I liked to hunt, my bow on my back and determination in my heart. I was so glad this life I was living would be over soon. I could no longer be their little slave. I needed to be free.

2

ONE YEAR BEFORE

Malcom

I GOT READY ON A SUNDAY. It had always been hard to leave my girls ... Lillie mostly. She was the apple of my eye, she was the most like me, and unlike the triplets, I didn't blame her for her mere's death. I loved my job, though, and for that, I would be gone two weeks out of each month.

I enjoyed when I was able to be home with them, but the waters called to me, especially those of The Loire, and even more than that, the Atlantic Ocean where The Loire spilled out into it. I had the best of both worlds, but I had always worried about the day that something might go wrong.

I saddled my horse up, her name was Lenora. She would go with me on the trip as always. She had once belonged to ma femme, but when she died, I couldn't stop taking Lenora with me.

I had made it a practice to ask my girls what treasure they would like for me to find while I was gone, and so I would ask them right before I left once again.

"Aster, my love, what do you wish I find for you this trip?" I asked her as I lined the four of them up to say goodbye.

"I wish a mirror made from glass from the sea, Father," she whispered with a curtsey and a smile.

"I will do my best, love." I kissed her on the cheek. "And what for you, my Rose?"

"I wish for a hat made of jewels and the finest cloth." She smiled at me and bowed slightly.

"Your wish is my command," I said, and I knew I would find it, I always found what my girls wanted. I kissed her on the cheek as well. "What of you, Dahlia?" I asked her.

"I would like *un mari*," she said, asking me to find her a husband.

"I will do my best, Dahlia, but that is better left to you," I said, and she too allowed me to kiss her on the cheek with my goodbye. "My Lillie, my beautiful Lillie," I said as I put my hand to the side of her face. "What would you like your papa to bring to you?"

It was hard not to favor the girl. The eldest were dressed in fancy dresses, and they wished for things of expensive taste, but not my Lillie. I thought about the gifts of her bequest. A book, an apple, a feather for her arrow, so, I wondered what she would ask of me again.

"Only a rose, my papa," she said to me with a small bow.

Her jeans and puffed mariner's shirt made her contrast against her sisters. She had blond hair while they had brown, and so on, were the differences.

"You wish only a rose, my child?" I smiled down at her from the top of my horse. "Are you quite sure?"

"A rose is what I asked for," she said. "Thus, a rose I would like."

"Could you, at very least, make it hard for me?" I smiled at her.

"I want a black rose with diamond water drops," she said. "Is that hard enough my, papa?"

"Whatever made you think of a black rose with diamonds?" I asked her.

"Simple," she said, in usual Lillie fashion. "I read about it in a book."

Her bow and arrows bobbed up and down on her back as she laughed, and I could see that she already had Sylver tied up in the background. I knew she was going to go hunting as soon as I left. It was a way to work off her worry, and it kept her away from her sisters whom she didn't quite fit in with.

"I will do my very best," I said, and then I kissed her on the cheek. "Goodbye, my girls," I said, and then I gave Lenora the command to go.

As I galloped out of sight, I could hear Lillie give her horse the same command. I could hear her follow me until I made it to the ship. I felt her eyes on me until Lenora and I boarded the ship, and then she was gone. She had done that each time I had gone on a trip, and I couldn't wait until I returned.

But alas, that was not *dans les cartes,* or in the cards as one might say.

THE SHIP HAD BEEN off course for a while, and half the crew was dead. There had been a horrible outbreak of influenza on board, and six months or so after we departed, I took the sickness. I had worked so hard not to get it, thinking that since our navigation system had failed, someone was going to have to keep track of the map.

A mariner named Otis and I were the only ones well enough to run the ship, but neither of us knew how long that was going to last. A two-week trip had lasted six months. We were out of food and the conditions were bad, to say the least.

I hated every moment being on the ship when we were lost at sea . . . I knew that I was dying, but what kept me going was

Lillie, Rose, Dahlia, and Aster. I knew I had to get home to them.

AFTER ANOTHER MONTH, it was down to me and only me, and I steered the ship until it hit land several miles from home . . . I hadn't made it all the way there, but I had navigated via the stars enough to get the ship that close.

After the ship docked, I crawled to Lenora, as sick as could be, mounted her, and let her lead me out of the ship. She was nearly as sick as I was, but I had no other choice than to ride her onto the land.

I knew the area, but only barely. I hoped my thoughts were incorrect about what things I thought existed in those parts, but I felt deep down that I was right. I turned to head back upriver in the direction I knew I would need to go to get home, but then something caught my eye.

It was that moment that changed everything. I should have known better than to turn away from my path to go home, but something crossed my line of vision. Black roses with droplets of diamonds on each petal, and hundreds of them. The bad part was that they were each within the fences of a castle.

An old, dark castle.

I thought for a moment that I had let all my girls down, if only I could get one rose from inside the fence, then I would at very least have the hardest of things to find for Lillie. So, I slid off my horse, tied her to the fence on the outside of the castle, and quietly and sickly crawled in the gates.

The wind began to blow on me which brought on a cough that wouldn't quit. I tried to be quiet because I didn't know if the castle was occupied, but by the looks of it I would have thought not. The roses were the only true signs of life.

I touched one of the roses with one hand while I coughed in

the other. As I pulled it from its stem, it turned to droplets of red fluid that resembled blood, and then it smelled that way too. I gagged at the sight of the red lifeblood on my hands and wondered whose blood it might be unless the plant itself was bleeding, but that was impossible.

In moments the entire thing had melted into a bloody mess on my clothes, hands, and some on the ground, and then it began to storm.

It was almost like it was a fabricated storm, meant only for the castle looming over me. I got cold fast, and with the cold came more coughing. I was dying right there with blood on my hands.

Rose blood.

Before my eyes, a man swooped over me with eyes as red as the sunset. He looked young yet old at the same time. I didn't know where he had come from, he wasn't there one moment, but then was the next, and he swooped in and grabbed me up.

I was thrown into a dungeon of sorts which was cold and wet, but I was given care immediately. Servants of the BEAST that had taken me began to treat my sickness and give me what I needed to try to get better.

Three months later I was still sick but was holding my own. I prayed for my daughters every day, but I also hoped that they would not come looking for me. I knew Lillie would have been the only one to look for me, but I didn't want her to ever find me . . .

Not ever.

I wouldn't wish the torture of living in a cold, damp place, or risk being killed by the Beast on anyone in the world, most of all, my daughters.

And so, I lived in the dungeon of a castle with a *beast* that I had not seen since that first night he had taken me in. I knew I was going to die at some point. I was that sick and could feel it, my body was not getting better as it should have, but I knew if my girls were safe, even if they had to miss me for all their days, wondering what had happened to me, then my death would not be such a bad thing.

3

PRESENT DAY

Lillie

EVER SINCE MY PAPA VANISHED, my head had brought me to every scenario of what could have happened. I tried not to allow it to do that, but sometimes, I couldn't stop it. No matter what I did, it wouldn't stop coming. The good and bad alike would float through my mind, and I hated it, but for some odd reason, I needed it, I needed the thoughts and memories.

I needed to remember what my papa looked like, and that was the way I got to do that.

As I rode Sylver into the woods, full of trees and darkness with the sun gone, I pulled him up in the heat of the night and tied him to the tree I often chose to tie him to. I walked several paces to get away from where he was. The deer and other creatures would smell him and stay away, that was why I needed to get as far away from him as I could. I didn't like being that far from him, but it was a must.

I needed to get enough food for my sisters before I went to look for my papa. They would not be able to fend for themselves, and so I would do my best for them. I had always tried to do my best for them. Rose was the oldest of the triplets, she should have been the one to step up into the motherly role, but that had never happened and was not going to.

She had made that clear.

Although, I wondered what they would do if something happened to me and I didn't make it home. I knew they would be forced to figure it out, but I couldn't imagine one of them making it, let alone all three. All they needed to do was work together, but for my sisters, that was unheard of.

I grew as silent as I could and hoped Sylver would do the same in the background. I wanted to find something big enough, and on occasion, at night only, I had been able to catch a bobcat or small bear. I had gotten lucky enough to get a deer or two, but for the most part, it was mostly rabbits, squirrels, and the like.

After an hour or so of being quiet, I finally heard the footsteps of an oncoming animal, and I climbed into the nearest tree. I knelt in the branches and lifted my bow and arrow. I wanted the best vantage point for the kill. I needed something big in order to feed them for a while, that I knew, but anything at that point would be better than nothing.

I didn't know if they would know how to fix a deer or bear or even freeze parts of it for a later date, but I was doing my part. That was the best I could do ... wasn't it?

It was not my fault if they didn't know how to use what I had provided them, I would have a clear conscious.

Sure, enough a large buck walked out in front of the tree I was in. I pulled back on my bow strings and took a deep breath. I centered myself for the kill and released the string with the exhale of my breath. The arrow flew into the deer's eye and out through the back of his head. I smiled at the sensation it gave me when the creature dropped right where it stood.

I jumped from the tree and went right away to make the deer ready to take home to my sisters, but then I smelled something else in the air, something I had smelt before.

The scent was sweet and had the hint of a wet musk mixed in the sweetness. I thought hard and could remember every time I had smelt that smell, and it had been on several occasions, but I had never found the source of it. It hadn't worried me, but that time it was stronger than any other time.

"Tell me you are not just killing that thing for the sport of it," a man's voice came from behind me.

I spun around and had my bow and arrow pulled faster than I could process hearing the voice. Standing in front of me was a man. He was strong and handsome, and then came the smell that I had been smelling for months. I let down the arrow a little, but not all the way. He had his own bow on his back, but it wasn't drawn at all, it just rested there, ready for the kill. I felt like I had seen him before, but I couldn't place where, surely, I would have remembered.

"How, how long have you been following me?" I asked, hands still where they needed to be on the bow for an easy kill.

"Today?" He paused. "For a while."

"For a while, my ass," I said, picking the bow back up. "You have been around here for months, maybe close to a year . . . haven't you?"

He nodded, which caused me to lower my bow a bit. He was telling the truth so I didn't know if I should be afraid of him or not. My gut told me that he wasn't there to hurt me, but I had always been guarded, and letting him in didn't seem like a good idea.

"I don't mean you any harm, Lillie," he said.

"Wait," I said, as I threw my hand up. "How is it that you know my name and I have no idea who you are?"

"Let's just say I have been around for a while, months even, and I have been looking out for you from afar," he said, the last part a bit lower. "My name is Remington. I am not from these parts."

I looked at him in awe. How was it that he had been "looking out for me" as he worded it and I hadn't known about it? I growled in frustration and wanted to get on with my journey. I knew I didn't need any hold-ups.

"Looking out for me?" I said through gritted teeth. "Does it look like I need to be looked out for?" I asked as I put a foot on my fresh kill.

"Well," he stammered. "I guess not."

"That's what I thought," I said, and then I bent down and grabbed the freshly skinned deer by the back legs and began dragging it behind me.

He chuckled a little as I walked towards my horse to string up the deer. As I lifted the animal over the back of the horse, he stood by and let me do it without offering to help.

If he had been watching me like he said he had been, I was sure he had noticed that I didn't need his help. I had grown accustomed to doing things on my own. Lifting a hundred and fifty-pound deer was a walk in the park for me.

"So, it looks like you are going to finally find your father, Lillie." He smiled.

"Yes, I . . . wait," I paused. "How do you know about my father?"

"Remember I said I had been following you for a while," he said.

"What? Why?" I squealed, as I got up on my horse.

I began to ride off towards my house hoping that the hunter didn't follow me.

"I know where your father is," he shouted behind me, and I came to a halt. "Or at least what direction he went when he made landfall a few miles that way." He pointed down the river.

"How do you know it was my father?" I questioned and waited.

"Because he was mumbling your name, he talked of a girl with beautiful blond hair who liked to read, and then he disappeared into the woods to the North," Remington said. "Then I happened to have already stumbled upon you and put two and two together," he paused. "I can take you as far as those parts if you would like."

"Thank you, Remington," I said as I took off on my horse. "I don't need your help."

I rode as fast as I could towards the house where I dropped off the things I had gotten for my sisters. I walked into the kitchen and placed all I had on the counter, apart from the deer. I had left him in the *sel cabane* to make sure it could be cured in the salt so the girls could cook it.

"Are you really leaving?" Rose's voice came out of the darkness.

I washed my hands in the sink and dried them off with an old fishing towel of our papa's. I didn't want to have to talk to Rose, but I figured I wouldn't get by without saying goodbye to at least one of my sisters. I picked up the ladies hat I had gotten for her at the market and handed it to her. Her eyes lit up great big at its beauty.

I knew that was one of the things that weren't necessary that I got, but I knew it would make her happy. I had gotten a mirror and a book on courting for the others in hopes they would know how much I really did love them.

"Yes Rose, I have to go try to find him, I have heard that he made landfall just east of here but did not head in the correct direction."

"Who told you that?" Rose asked defensively.

"A scout, a hunter of sorts," I told her.

"Of course, it would be a hunter," she laughed, but I felt a little offended.

I then leaned down and kissed her on the cheek.

"Tell the others that I said goodbye, there is a deer in the salt shed to be cured, and if you ration, there should be enough food, and necessities to live for a month."

I turned to walk away, but she stood and walked after me, she brought me up in a hug, the first I could remember coming from her or Dahlia or Aster. I didn't know if I was going to ever see them again, but what I did know was that I was going to figure out what had happened to our father.

The hug broke and I nodded. Rose had a tear running down her cheek, and I wondered if it was more from the fear of the unknown with me gone, or if she truly was going to miss me, but I didn't think that much about it. I needed to stay focused, and if I worried too much about them, I wasn't going to.

I walked out the door with a tear of my own. I didn't let Rose see it, but as soon as the door was shut behind me, I could hear her sobs break out into an uncontrollable cry. I looked behind me and saw the lights come on from other parts of the house and knew that was the perfect time to get away before they had the chance to try to stop me.

I gained a quick stride on Sylver as we began to ride down the river to the east. It was hot and dark, but none of that mattered, with each gallop of my horse, I was closer to figuring out what had happened to my papa.

4

REMINGTON

I HAD WATCHED her from afar for several months. Her blond hair that floated behind her like a cloud, never tied back made my heart race with wanted anticipation. When she thought no one was watching, and I was unbeknown to her, she would dance, and sing, she would hunt and fish and was free. I watched her read in her favorite tree, the big oak on the outside of the woods . . . a different book every day.

She cared for her horse as if they shared a soul, and when she cried, I cried with her. I felt awful for stalking her like that, but there was no other way I could do it. I was forbidden to approach her in the way that I wanted in fear that my heart might boil over . . . it wasn't allowed to do that.

I had made those parts of the woods my home for a while. My people had moved there because we were nomads and moved every year or so . . . or voyaged as they liked to call it. We wondered all over France in search for a better place to live, one that would accept us, but no place had been better than the last . . . we were despised everywhere we went, once people found out about us.

After so long, it slipped out what our people were and what kind of life we lived, and I just about despised all of it. That was until I saw Lillie. She had become the rainbow at the edge of the storm I constantly lived under. Untouchable, but a beauty to look at, so complex with her colors melting together, making her the most interesting person I had ever met . . . well, not met because up until the point, I hadn't talked to her in the woods, I had only watched her.

I belonged to the *Decaleur de Loup* people and they had been around for a long time. Thousands of years in fact. Many people had heard about us, but we were in hiding for the most part so much so that it was very unheard of for us to be seen by non-nomads. One of my people would spill it who and what we were on occasion, and an entire town would go on the hunt for us, but before they could even gather together with their pitchforks and guns, we were gone.

I didn't know what it was about Lillie that drew me to her, but I was drawn. I was supposed to find a mate among my people, but for reasons I could not decipher, I wanted her.

I first saw her when she was hauling fresh corn on her horse, Sylver from the black market in the woods. I had been in the mouth of the woods hunting rabbit.

She was fair and beautiful, and I was attracted to her in many ways, but I knew she was not an option and would never be accepted by my people . . . so, I would spend my time looking out for her in hopes that one day I could be with her, if only for a little while.

I thought that perhaps I was prepared to leave my people to be with her, but I was not going to tell them that. I didn't want to let them down or myself down by betraying who I was, but Lillie was the girl to do that for.

I had known that Lillie's papa had been missing when I came to town and saw her for the first time. Curiosity had gotten the better of me, and I had asked around about her in the markets, and the mariners spoke freely of the girl's situation.

In my search for information, I found out a lot about the

girl. She had three sisters, but none of them matched that of the beauty, intelligence, and ingenuity of their younger sister, Lillie. The mariners all said that, every one of them, which made me fall for her even faster and harder.

She was the kind of woman I had always looked for in a mate, but then again, I had never seen anyone quite like her.

Then, a few months back, I saw a ship approach the banks down the river in no man's land. It came in fast and crashed. A single man came crawling out of the boat and managed to climb up on his horse which looked equally as sick as he did. I watched as he began to head up the river, but then his attention was caught by something deeper into the forbidden forest . . . no man had survived those parts.

The entire time he had mumbled something about a daughter as beautiful as Lillie, as calm as the stillest waters, and the black rose he wanted for her. I could tell by the way he spoke about her that it was my Lillie, and my heart jumped in a way that physically caused me pain.

I felt bad, but I kept that information to myself. I didn't want her to get hurt by wandering into the forbidden forest, but then when she told me that she was going looking for him, I only felt I should let her know I had seen him, so she didn't go off and get herself killed.

I spoke to her in the woods and watched her trot off on her horse back home. I knew I only had a few minutes to set things in order before I followed her to make sure she was safe on her voyage. I was bound and determined to make sure that I was with her.

If only in the shadows.

I was sure by that point that I cared a great deal for her, perhaps even loved her. Her voice as she spoke to me set my body on fire. I wanted to confess to her that I did love her, but she would have thought I had lost my mind for sure.

While she was in her home, I ran the distance between the mouth of the woods where I had seen her make it there, and to the place of my people a few miles away. It only took me a few minutes to get there, and I was less than winded, I felt free.

The head of the *Decaleur de Loup* was my papa, Monsieur La Andre, a man of both stature and authority. His father had been the head before that, and his father before that, it was only natural that I would rule one day after my father was gone. That wasn't going to be for a long time I hoped, and so I knew I had time to do what I was about to request from him.

"Papa, Monsieur," I said as I ran up to him. "I need to be gone for a fortnight, please grant me my voyages."

"What is the purpose of this *mon fils*, my son?" he asked me. "It is not like you to request to be away from our people for so long."

"I must take a voyage to protect Lillie," I admitted.

He had heard me speak of her many times but had no idea how I felt about her. I had told my papa that I felt protective of her, and he told me that our people did that sometimes. He told me it was called *Le Gardien* and not uncommon for our kind.

"And you think such a voyage will take two weeks?" he quizzed.

"I requested a fortnight," I said. "I do not know if it will require such time or longer, I thought I would be safe by my request," I sighed. "She is going to look for her papa! I need to be there for her. I don't know why but I do feel the connection to her. The one of *Le Gardien* and I know I could never have her as a mate, but as long as I can keep her safe that will make me happy enough," I lied.

I had always wanted her to be more but knew that wasn't possible. My body yearned for her to be mine, and I felt guilty for lying to my papa. I had not made the habit of doing that, and I didn't want to start. Somehow, deep down, I thought maybe he knew the truth.

"And this girl, she knows what you are?" My papa asked, ever the noble one.

"Not exactly, but she will," I said. "I promise I will make myself known to her this day."

He nodded and stuck his hand out. I shook it and turned to run away.

"Stop, Remington," he halted me. "I will be sending three of my scouts out to keep an eye on you, at a distance, of course, but this is your first voyage this long away, and I don't want you to be without help, should you need it."

I didn't like thinking he thought I needed to be babysat, but I nodded, nonetheless and took off running back in the direction of the opening in the woods by Lillie's house.

Once I arrived, I sighed. Her horse was still tied out front. I wasn't going to have to track her by her smell. I smiled a little, what a smell she had too. I had memorized it from the moment she first came within one-hundred feet of me.

Then I saw her figure coming from the front door, lights came on in the house, and she quickly made her way onto her horse and strode toward where I was. Once she saw me, she came to a stop, but only once she reached the safety of the tree line.

"What are you doing here?" she scolded me with bitter lips and a tear streaked face.

"I had to warn you of something, Lillie," I said, as I took the chances of taking a step closer.

Her bow stayed on her back, which I was glad for, that meant that she trusted me a bit. I knew, however, that it wouldn't take long for her to access it.

"What's that?" she asked, still sounding a bit annoyed.

"The parts of the woods that I last saw the man I think was your papa in," I paused, trying to decide if I wanted to tell her or not.

"Go ahead," she commanded.

"It's part of the forbidden forest, it's bad in those parts," I warned her. "The bravest men in the world go in and never come back, it is filled with creatures only your nightmares can dream up."

I wasn't trying to stop her as much as I was trying to warn her. Somehow deep down, I knew she couldn't be stopped. I wanted to go with her, but I knew she wasn't going to let me do that willingly, I would have to stick with following her in the shadows.

"First off," she said, as she set herself down in the saddle, "my father told me the stories, second, I don't have nightmares, third," she paused for a second, then took a breath as if trying to assure herself that the next part was true. "I am not afraid, and lastly, you said the bravest men had not come out alive . . . well, I am a woman," she said and sent Sylver into a quick stride as she rode down river in the thick of the wood.

I fell into a stride of my own as I felt my body change to allow me the speed I needed to keep up with her horse. I was going to stay up with her if it killed me.

I watched her from behind as she made her way to the forbidden forest, my heart bled for the fires of a thousand thoughts, but then I could tell that she could sense that she was being followed.

5

LILLIE

I HAD GOTTEN AWAY from the house only to be stopped in the mouth of the woods by the hunter, Remington. I didn't know why it bothered me so much to find out that he had been watching me for so long. I should have been flattered, to say the least, my sisters would have been, but I was annoyed about it... really annoyed.

He seemed to think he knew where my papa was, and that worried me. If he was correct, then I was going to be heading into the darkest parts of France. My papa had told me all the stories, but I hoped that was all it was; stories. The way Remington spoke, I needed to be cautious, and for whatever reason, I hadn't been able to place my finger on it, but I trusted him.

As I rode further towards the outskirts of the forbidden forest, I could have sworn that my mind was playing tricks on me. The trees shifted to something darker, the beautiful leaf green trees of my woods turned hunter green, nearly black in some places in the new one. I had never been that far out to notice that they did that, but it didn't sit well with me at all. Even Sylver seemed to notice that things were different from the way they had been only a few moments before.

An even more eerie feeling set in the further I went into the woods, and scary sounds began to sound around me. I felt like eyes were on me, and I half laughed when I thought about Remington.

I thought about not feeling his eyes on me the whole time he was watching, but somewhere deep down, I wished it were his eyes. But that was not possible, I had left the hunter in the woods, and unless he was on horseback, there was no way it was him.

There hadn't been a horse in sight both times that I had seen, so deep down, I knew there was no way it could be him.

I scolded myself for the way I felt. For some reason thinking about Remington was making my heart race. I couldn't believe that I was thinking about it being him that was looking in on me.

I took a deep breath when I heard the sound again, and the nerve to look behind me increased. With everything in me I wanted to keep my eyes forward, but they would not stay fixed there. I looked behind me as Sylver stayed moving forward.

When I did, I wished I hadn't. There was a blur of sorts that flashed behind me from one tree to the other. It was nearly hard to see. The blur was nearly black in the already darkening woods, so I was surprised I had seen it... or had I?

I thought that perhaps I had imagined it, but no, I looked behind me and there it was again... and again.

I sped up on the horse as I whispered in his ear.

"Come on, Sylver, you got this boy," I said as I commanded him to go faster, and still the blur kept up with us.

I continued to look back, and sure enough, it kept flashing from tree to tree, never failing to keep up. I didn't know what to do, and even more than that, I couldn't quit thinking that perhaps I was seeing things.

Suddenly, I got the idea to stop and see what it was. After all, I wasn't afraid... or was I?

I pulled Sylver to a stop and jumped down off him. I threw

up my bow and arrow and waited for the blur to either stop, make itself known, or pass me, but it did not pass me at all. Instead, it came to a stop not fifty feet in front of me.

There was a massive dog, wolf, if you will, standing there. It was easily as tall as I was on all fours and was as black as the night sky. Its fur was silky and shone under the minimal light being given off by the moon and what few stars were up there, and the even fewer that were allowed to light up the darkness that was the forbidden forest.

I was shocked when the wolf did not advance any further. It just stood there looking at me, and then came the familiar scent that I had smelled every day for several months before.

"Remington?" I asked, but I knew I had to have lost my mind, how was I smelling him so far away from where we had once been?

Maybe I had called to him on the off chance that he was there and would protect me from the wolf that stood as still as could be. But then, before my eyes, the wolf changed into a man, a very familiar one . . . it was Remington.

"Surprise," he said. "I told you I would keep an eye on you."

"That you did," I said as I lowered my bow. "What are you?"

I felt silly for asking, I had never seen a person turn into a creature and back again. Matter of fact, I had never seen a creature that was supposed to be a person.

The stories that my papa had told me about were just that. Stories of vampires, wolf shifters, and other things that were never seen, but heard of often.

People had thought my papa was crazy when he told about a wolf that was a man that he saw once when he was a boy, but I never did. He would read and study about the creatures in the hopes that if he ever came across one of them, he would know how to react, but there I was, standing in front of a wolf shifter, and I had nothing other than my stories to help me.

"I wanted to tell you when I saw you in the woods, but how was I to explain this?" he asked.

I walked a bit closer to him and smiled. He was only wearing boxers, and I wasn't sure how he had managed that, but it didn't leave much to the imagination. I blushed a little as I looked over his body.

"You know I saw it happen in front of me, and I am still not sure that I believe it," I said.

"Believe it," he said as he took a step closer. "But more than anything I wanted to protect you."

"From what?" I asked out of curiosity.

"There are things much scarier than I am out there, things that will feed on you, or kill you," he warned. "You may be brave, but they don't care about bravery . . . even some shifters would have killed you by now, they would have taken your body and have you killed before your head could spin, and one ounce of bravery will not stop them."

I nodded. I couldn't figure out why he felt like he needed to warn me like that.

He stepped closer to me, and I wanted to step away, but I couldn't. There was no way that I could, I was connected to him like a magnet that would not let go.

"What are you doing?" I asked, as closer still he came.

"Just," he paused. "Stay still," he breathed.

I stood as silent as could be, my breath held in as I panicked, but still could not move. Then, his lips brushed against mine, causing heat to pool between my legs.

I felt wrong for what I was feeling, I barely knew the man, why was I allowing him to kiss me?

Also like a magnet being drawn to him, I allowed him to kiss me deep and strong. I felt my body press against his half-naked one which made my heart beat like a drum. Before I could stop myself, I wrapped my arms around him as he put his hands in my hair.

I moaned a little as I could feel the heat inside my stomach ignite more than it ever had.

Then, Remington pushed me back against a tree as his

hands roamed my body. I couldn't tell if it was the heat of the night or the forbidden forest that wanted me to do forbidden things, but it felt right and wrong all at the same time.

Remington growled like a wolf as he made himself even closer to me.

There was something wrong with me. I didn't want to find a man that could take care of me, I was fully prepared to do it alone, and here I was, kissing someone I had only met a few hours before.

Then suddenly, I got my wits about me and pushed him away a little.

"Wait," I said. "I need to go find my father. I'm so sorry, but I am not ready for this right now.

He nodded as he looked me in the eyes. He placed his hand behind my neck and pulled me in a little and kissed me once more.

"I understand," he said, sounding a bit sadder than I hoped.

I wondered how long he had wanted to do that, which made me feel guilty that I was cutting it short. He backed up a bit, and I escaped from between him and the tree. I mounted Sylver and let him take a few strides in the direction we would be going to get away, then I stopped him once more.

"I need to go," I said. "I am so sorry this is bad timing. Will you be following me?" I asked.

He nodded a little right before he turned back into his great black wolf. As I continued on my way, I could feel him right behind me all the way.

6

LILLIE

I TOOK off on a good trot begging the horse to move faster than we had before. We needed to get moving. I didn't want the darkness of the woods to take either of us, yet I feared it might. Sure, I had not been afraid of much, but something about the trees themselves felt like they had stepped right out of a bad dream.

They loomed over us as we made our way. Each of them looked like they had faces looking at us. Their eyes, that really didn't exist, peeked through dark leaves like hair that hung in their faces.

I rode further into the woods with Remington on my mind. I could feel him still back somewhere behind where I was, and it continued to make me feel safe, but then he started falling behind, and then his presence went away altogether. The already dark woods got a few shades darker with what looked like teeth forming in knotholes until the moon and stars were blacked out completely.

Then the air grew cold, colder than a winter's chill. I began to shiver to the point I couldn't control my body. Sylver was doing the same, and I felt bad for him. I didn't know if the shiver was coming from the lack of Remington's presence or if the atmosphere had changed.

Then there they were— the roses from my book. They were rather beautiful, more beautiful than the book made them out to be. Their petals dripped with diamonds that sparkled without any light. It was marvelous. I was enamored by them as they drew me in.

They were all kept in an iron fence and looked like they had been tended to well. Then, off to the right of the beautiful iron gate was a horse, my papa's horse.

I got down off Sylver and ran to Lenora. She was sick looking, but there was a bucket of apples and oats sitting in front of her. I gained a little hope at that fact, wondering if my papa had been the one to feed her, but with how dark things appeared, it was hard to believe that he would have willingly stayed in a place like that.

She was skinny and looked like she had not been taken care of properly. My papa would not have allowed that to happen.

I searched around for a while, then took the chances of entering the gate. I tied Sylver up beside Lenora so that he could share her feed and water. Then I tiptoed through the gate into the fences of the beautiful garden of black roses.

I took a deep breath of their aroma and loved the way they smelled. It made me think of home in the springtime. The thought of home made me think of my papa, and the want to find him deepened even more.

I reached out for one of the roses. I watched one sparkle for a moment before I took it in my hand, then something peculiar happened. Each petal fell off one at a time into a trickle of blood. It was really a sight to behold, but I wasn't afraid. I felt like I was supposed to be, but I couldn't find it in me to be afraid of the blood.

As one droplet fell through my fingers, I watched it hit the ground, then under my hand, I saw a sparkle of gold. It gleamed under the same lightless night sky. I bent down and picked the item up and gasped . . . it was my papa's pocket watch. I held it close to my chest and cherished it dearly.

As I held it to me, a wind picked up that pulled at my chest. I began to cough out of nowhere. It felt angry and unrelenting, both the cough and the wind. Then came a roar of thunder that sounded like it was seeping from the roses themselves. I looked around to see if I could figure out the source of the sound, but I could not.

"Papa?" I screamed into the void.

My scream was not near loud enough to echo over the thunderous noise, but still, I screamed. I screamed until my voice went hoarse. And then came the lightning and more wind. There were bolts of lightning that cracked against the ground just off the property of the castle. It was almost like the storm had been designed just for the castle, just for me.

I tried to take a step with very little voice and blood from the rose on my hands, but it was near impossible. Every step I took towards the gate to make my way out of the storm, the more I was forced towards the castle. I couldn't figure out why when I changed directions with my footing, the wind changed just the same to continue to push me towards the door of the castle . . .

Until I was against it.

I looked around, there was no way I was going to be able to stay there with the storm growing more rapid. I turned to face the large oak door with the wrought iron knockers that resembled bats. They were beautiful and alarming at the same time. I tried to pick the knocker up, but the wind blew against it so it was too heavy to move.

Then I tried the second and the same happened.

Off in the distance, a tornado made its way off the ground and into the sky, reverse of how it was supposed to be. The tiny twister ignored Sylver and Lenora and headed straight for me.

In a moment of panic, I reached out with blood-stained hands and turned the doorknob, and sure enough, the grand door opened. The wind quit blowing enough that I could enter, and I wondered how it was that I could pull the large door, but not pick up the light knocker.

As soon as I entered the large vestibule, the door quietly shut behind me on its own, and as if I had gone deaf, the winds and wild storm outside ceased to exist. I took that opportunity to try to leave, but each time I would reach for the door, the storm would pick up and the wind blew against it, making it impossible to open.

I gave up after my first five tries and turned to face the room that was on the other side of the great greeting hall. I looked around, my bow and arrows still secure on my back.

I took a few steps and found myself in a large sitting room with several Victorian-style wing-backed chairs that looked as good as new, almost like they had not been sat in. The room was dark and not very welcoming despite a fire that I immediately went to in order to warm my bones.

The one chair that faced the hearth was the only one that looked like it had ever been sat in. It was different than all the others. It resembled a throne, but much smaller than one would have expected. I looked to make sure there was no one around, and other than the echoes that filled the halls that surrounded the great room, I didn't see a soul.

I sat in the chair, thankful for the comfort. I let the heat sink into my bones which seemed to have been nearly frozen. I worried about Sylver outside, but I knew that he would be alright as long as he had Lenora by his side, and the storm had appeared to have stayed away from the livestock.

I sat and pondered the storm and what the castle was like as I spun my papa's watch in my hands over and over. I looked at it a few times to see if there was anything different about it, and the only thing I could see was that it had stopped.

Then, I flipped it over and saw that the backside had been marked with tiny scratches perfectly in a row. I counted them and knew exactly what my papa was doing. He was counting the days that he was away. I knew that he would not have counted the two weeks he was due to be gone, and I could only assume he quit marking it the day he lost it.

I sat and did the math. There were exactly eight months and two weeks of markings, which meant that he had been away from home for nine months almost to the day since he lost the watch. I thought for a moment of all the possibilities. That meant that he had been missing for three months since he quit noting each day on the watch.

My heart dropped thinking about how Remington must have known for three months where my father had gone, and that made me angry at him, more than angry, I was pissed. I began to cry in the dark and quiet with only the echoes and pops of the flames.

Until, in the chair, in a castle, I had never seen before, I fell asleep.

7

PRINCE AMBROSE

I GROWLED out my grumbles as one of my servants came to tell me what we had caught in our castle grounds . . . a girl, a woman. There had never been one of them at my home, and I didn't think there ever would be. For the most part, the storms and roses sent men only, most of them bad and in need of the punishment that they would receive, but on the rare occasion, there was the one that was different, like the mariner that had only come into my gates to grant his daughter's behest.

A woman was what I needed, but I didn't know what I needed to do to set things right. Three weeks shy of six hundred years I had been stuck in a lifeless life, and I knew I only had a short amount of time until my time was up. I didn't know what to do, and that made me afraid. A *beast* like me had never been scared of anything, but the oncoming woman made me fear everything.

I had conceded to live out the remainder of my days alone and unhappy until I died of a curse that hated me anyway. But then, I saw her, she was riding from the distance. I saw a wolf behind her, and he continued to trail her until he caught sight of me standing amongst the steeples of my castle. His eyes were on her and so were mine.

The animal backed away a bit but continued to watch her from far away. I knew I needed to keep an eye out for the wolf, there had not been wolves in those parts for hundreds of years and when those were there, the nomads as they liked to be called, they caused problems for me and my castle.

They had even tried to take it over, but that did not happen.

I watched her as she rode up to the gates and pitched her horse beside the other. I knew right away that she belonged to him, the man I had taken in a few months before. They looked a lot alike, though if I had to guess, I would have thought she had a bit of her mother in her too. She did not look like the typical woman. She was not wearing skirts, and she had a bow on her back. By the looks of her, I could tell that she was used to holding her own. I could see the dirt under her nails with the vision granted me by the curse.

She had long blond hair that blew behind her in the wind, and when she picked up the rose and even as it melted to blood in her hands, she did not flinch, she was not afraid of it, nor was she afraid of the castle. I was sure she had already put it together that the horse out front belonged to her papa, but I didn't see a tear in her eye.

He had been entirely too old to be of any use. I couldn't feed on him, and I couldn't put him to work, but for some reason, I didn't want to kill him, which was my usual nicety.

He gained favor in my heartless heart, but he had stolen lifeblood from the roses and therefore from me. I wanted to kill him I was angry enough to do so. I called upon the storm to do the job for me, but then let up a little when I saw her in his eyes.

It was amazing how even when I had not seen her in the flesh, I had seen her in his eyes.

"Prince Ambrose," Blaize called out to me from where he had been standing.

He was my most trusted servant and a good friend if I ever

had one. I would have never told him that just as he hadn't told me that he had been taking a cure for my mind control for years. I knew why he stayed, but I liked the kid, nonetheless.

I guessed he was a man by that time, but compared to six-hundred years, twenty-five was a child.

"Yes, Blaize?" I asked through a grumble as I climbed back through the door of my balcony.

Blaize was the only servant I allowed into my chambers, the only anything I would allow in there. There were many private things that contributed to my life, what little of a life it was, and my impending death.

"So, you saw her?" he asked.

"The woman?" I growled as I walked across the room pacing.

"Yes," he smiled. "She is quite beautiful."

"So, she is," I said, trying not to sound so grumpy, but I was always grumpy. "What of her?"

"Are you going to storm her inside the castle monsieur?" he asked. "After all, she may be the one to break the death curse."

"I have three weeks, even if I was a true and handsome prince, I would not be able to win the heart of true love in three months let alone three weeks," I scoffed.

"Do give it a go," he begged me.

I let a loud roar escape my throat as I threw a bit of a fit and tossed several items off a table beside my desk. Blaize immediately went to work cleaning it up.

"Forget it," I scolded him.

"Sorry." He scurried up off the floor.

"Well, Blaize," I paused for a moment, "if you insist, I will storm her in, but I demand a meeting of mind control to be set up in the grand hall in the east wing NOW!"

He went out of the room immediately as commanded to gather the servants together for me to address them, or compel them, whichever worked better. As soon as he left, I walked to the balcony outside my quarters. There was no way she could see me as dark as the curse kept things around there.

I rubbed my hands together and called on the storm that would bring her inside to me. That tidbit was one of the things that I loved about the abilities I had. The bloodlust and insensitivity were the parts I didn't like all that well . . . oh yeah, and the fact that I had three weeks to live, who could forget that?

I watched as she swirled around with the blood from one of my roses on her hands. She screamed, and for some reason, it took all I had not to stop the storm or at the very least sweep down and save her, but I didn't.

As soon as she had made it inside, I let the storm sit outside quiet and still like a century guarding the doors against her potential exit. I made sure that she nor her papa's horses had not been touched; I knew that was a bad way to get things started.

Once I knew that she would not be going anywhere, I left the upper west wing and headed to the place I had called a meeting of my people. Once I got down there, in true fashion, Blaize had done as I had requested, and he had each, and every servant waiting for me.

"Attention," I said through an authoritative tone as I made sure I had looked into each of their eyes. They each snapped to attention, which I knew they would . . . even Blaize who I knew was the one servant I had that was immune to my tricks. "We have a woman in our castle."

At that, they all gasped and murmured amongst themselves.

"A woman, a woman, there really is a woman," an older man said from the corner in celebration.

I looked at him that one look that I knew would quiet him, and so his mouth sealed shut on my silent command.

"As I was saying, there is a woman in the castle. Blaize has requested that we give it a go with her." I took a moment to think, as I made controlling eye contact with them all. "Please cater to this woman . . . anything she wants . . . apart from leaving, releasing prisoners, or going to the upper west wing, do anything for her. Be quiet for a while as to not make her afraid."

I couldn't believe I was doing what I was doing. Somewhere deep down I knew that I was making the right decision, but I couldn't put my finger on why I felt that way. It wasn't common practice to feel much at all, let alone feel for someone other than myself.

I knew that sounded selfish, but I didn't care, I had gotten the life I deserved, no more, no less.

Each of them left the room at their dismissal apart from Blaize. He looked on in utter concern, and I bounced back and forth between wanting to kill him and hugging him, which I knew was a combination that was not normal.

"Do me a favor, Blaize," I said to the boy.

"Yes Prince, what can I do for you?" he asked.

"Make sure that you personally attend to her needs. I know that you want this to work as much as I do, but we all know who and what I am . . . this is not going to work unless we put all of our time into it."

"I understand," he said.

I turned to walk away knowing that Blaize would do what I had asked, he had his mother and sister's lives to risk if he shouldn't listen to me.

I turned once more and looked at the boy.

"Oh, and Blaize . . . thank you."

He nodded, but I could see the look in his eye that suggested that he was shocked. Hell, I was shocked that I had said it; perhaps the woman was already doing something to me?

I made my way back to my quarters as I watched the object that clicked down my last days, the last hours and moments of my life. I had been trapped in that castle, and what I wouldn't have done to get out, just once, but there wasn't enough time . . .

I had already spent too much time messing up to make things right for me.

8

LILLIE

I woke sometime later to the fire half worn out. The sky was still dark outside, but something told me that it was always like that. I couldn't figure the sun shining through the dark trees any more than the stars and moon had. I felt warmer than I had when I first arrived, but I didn't like that I didn't know how long I had been asleep.

I got to my feet and poked at the fire a little to see if I could raise it anymore. Not much happened, but then I stopped to listen. I turned around to see if I could see anyone. I wondered how it was that I had been able to sleep there for however long I had and not have gained the attention of at least one person. Then again, maybe no one lived there and the roses just grew on their own.

But then who would have started the fire?

Then I heard a crackle and a rush of wind that sounded behind me. I spun around to see the fire was light again, bright and bold. I could feel the heat roaring off it, and I wondered how that had happened.

"Is anyone out there?" I hollered into the large room.

There was not a response which sent my mind reeling. I decided that if no one was going to respond to me then maybe

I would go looking for them. Still, with my bow on my back, I turned to the large hall that crossed the mouth of the great room.

I listened for a while and could hear murmurs from what sounded like people, but I could not see them anywhere. I turned to the left in the hall to see what I could find. I wondered what kinds of rooms were in a place such as that. I passed a kitchen where I heard pots and pans banging, but by the time I made it inside, whoever had been in there was gone, leaving the pots spinning where they had been dropped on the counters.

I walked over to a bowl of what looked like cake batter and took a taste. It was good, and I wanted more, but I was already being rude by being in there.

"Is anyone here?" I asked. "I know I heard someone in here just a moment ago."

I figured I was imagining things, but that would have meant I was losing my mind, and that wasn't something I was going to allow myself to do.

I left the kitchen, wandering further down the hall. There was a dining hall, another sitting room, two powder rooms, living quarters, and then at the very end was the room I guessed I would live in if I was a residence of the castle.

The library.

It was massive with books lining every shelf from floor to ceiling. Some I had read and others I had never heard of. They were in various states of worth. Some had golden spines, and others were simply parchment bound.

I ran my fingers over them as I walked past each one. There were large ladders leading to the tops that slid from side to side for easy access.

I turned to scan the wonderful room to see if there was anyone in there, but there wasn't a single soul. Then, out of the corner of my eye, I saw a large hand-written book sitting in the middle of the room on a lectern. I walked over to it and ran my fingers over it. It was hand-written, but it looked to be at the very least five or six-hundred years old. I couldn't imagine ever seeing a book that old in its original script.

It was flipped open to the first page, and even that struck a chord with me. The title of the hand-written missive was "The Curse of a Beast" by Prince Ambrose.

I wondered if the castle that I was in belonged to the prince, but then I thought about how old the missive was and how old the prince would have to be to still be the owner and dweller of the castle. I laughed a little at myself thinking about how silly the thought was.

I flipped the first page open and sunk into the tale within its pages.

A curse, a hate, written of a monster a man that was a BEAST long before he was made so. He treated his people with the utmost ill regard. They lived much like a pig to the slaughter. The Prince monster would think the servants a slave. They were worthless and therefore their souls did not mean a thing to him alive or dead.

Then one day a lovely woman joined his ranks, and his heart quickly grew for her. A woman that would tame his heart of stone, but alas, that would never be. His lust for blood, for it to be spilled, topped that of even the love she had for him and in reverse the same way.

The woman ended up being a premonition, only an elemental of Mother Earth herself. The elemental was granted one chance at love, and so she had wasted it on him . . . the BEAST. A man made a monster by his own philosophies and even more so by the morals taught to him by his father and the fact that he was the first bastard born to the nation.

He hated his parents, he hated his people, and he hated his birthright.

The woman, the elemental, cursed the man for the hate he gave. With the words remembered to the very day of the last drop of blood spilled.

"Abide your soul in the utmost low, crawl into the ashes of the hole

of your heart to depart," she screamed through hot tears at him as her birthright drug her backward, Mother Nature was taking her home. "You shall be sealed by fate for six-hundred years to date, when the last richly covering of the blackest foliage falls on the six-hundredth year of your torture, you shall die, your servants frozen in time will perish, and your nation will turn to ash . . . let it be."

Before I could continue reading, a sound like footsteps sounded softly behind me. I spun around to set my eyes on a very handsome man, one who looks tired and sad, but handsome, nonetheless.

"Are you the dweller of this castle?" I asked him.

"While I do dwell here, this is not my nation to rule," he said. "This nation belongs to Prince Ambrose. I am but a lowly and humble servant here at the *Le Chateau de L'Obscurité*."

"A junior, I would wager," I smiled at remembering the name from the front of the book. "Or perhaps twenty-second in a long line of Prince Ambrose?"

"No, mademoiselle." He smiled at me. "There is now, as has ever been, and will ever be, only one Prince Ambrose of *Le Chateau de L'Obscurité*."

I nodded, but I didn't know what to think of the lies.

"Tell me, how can it have been possible that one man has lived for what . . . ?" I paused to think for a moment. "Nearly six-hundred years."

"Believe me," he paused, "it is possible," he took a step closer to me, "very possible. Think about your worst nightmares, think about things that go bump in the night, things like leaches and the biggest mosquitos, and you will have found Prince Ambrose in the mix . . . the current Ambrose that is. I knew him from before when he had a softer side, but that was many years ago."

I shivered outwardly.

"Who are you?"

"I am Balaban DeLlacroce, but you may call me Blaize, my lady, and you are?"

"Lillie." I gave a small curtsy, still in a state of wonder. "May I ask you . . . " I paused thinking about how horrible my question sounded, but I needed to know. "How old are you?"

"Well, Lillie," he smiled when he spoke, "I was twenty-three when I stopped aging five-hundred-ninety-nine years eleven months, and one week to the day ago."

I backed up a little out of breath. I didn't know what to think. Either he was a good liar, or he was telling the truth and I was in for way more than I bargained for.

"Are you a . . . " I began, but I certainly could not bring myself to ask that question I knew sounded ridiculous.

He took my hand and guided me to a set of seats on the other side of the library. I sat down and looked at the man, then almost on cue, hundreds of servants began swarming around the castle as if they had come out of hiding. Not one of them came into the library as if they weren't supposed to, or if they had been commanded not to.

They walked around like less than human, but I couldn't put my finger on it at all. I wondered why Blaize looked so different than they did. Their eyes were all glazed over with something hidden behind them.

"Would you like a drink, my dear?" he asked, bringing my attention back to him.

"Thank you," I said at realizing how thirsty I was.

He snapped his fingers, and an older woman in a maid's uniform and a small boy with the biggest smile on his face came in with a cart full of cakes and teas.

"Tea, my dear?" the woman asked me.

"Just leave it, Madame Potter, Bit, thank you for your services," Blaize said.

The little boy named Bit smiled up at me and winked with one of his glazed over eyes. I didn't know what was making them look like that, but for some reason, I wanted to do something about it, I had to. I wanted to find out why all of them looked like they had been brainwashed.

After they were gone, I turned back to Blaize and dared to work up the question I had burning inside me.

"Are you a vampire?" I asked, still feeling silly.

"No, I," he emphasized the word I, "am not a vampire; I am one of the servants from the story you started reading."

"So, you are frozen in time?" I asked.

"Basically," he said.

"Why do you look different than the others, your eyes, that is?" I wondered.

"Let me tell you something about myself," he offered. "I used to be a seer of things to come. When I saw Prince Ambrose going down, I started taking an herb that would ensure, that I did not go down with him the way the other servants did. Yes, I am frozen in time, yes, I am a servant of the prince, but no, I cannot be controlled as they can."

"Why didn't you run?" I asked.

"Because I have a sister and mother here. And it is far more complicated than that. They would not take my word for it, and when they didn't take the herb, then they were able to be controlled . . . I had to stay."

He reached into his coat pocket and pulled out a vial of what looked like chopped up herbs. I didn't ask what he was doing when he sprinkled some into my tea, and I took a sip. I didn't want to risk Prince Ambrose controlling me in any way.

"So, the stories are all true?" I asked.

"Yes," he said with a bit of a frown. "And because of that, you will never be able to leave this place.

9

BLAIZE

I saw her coming.

My heart quickly beat in my chest like I had run a marathon. I knew it was because I was excited that the one and only chance at freeing all of us from the curse was coming up the path to the castle, but then there was something else.

She was beautiful, and I felt jealous that she was meant for Ambrose and not me. I knew it was silly to be thinking about that, but it crossed my mind as I wondered if I would rather die a happy man or live a sad one watching Ambrose with her. That was crazy, I didn't even know who she was.

When she posted her horse next to the old man's I knew right then and there that she was his daughter, she had to be. She had the same nose, and when she was concerned, her eyes crinkled just the same.

I ran as fast as I could to the west wing of the castle, the quarters of Prince Ambrose, and I was happy to see that he was already seeing what I had seen. I could sense the worry in his eyes as I reminded him of the oncoming end of the curse and the potential she would have in breaking said curse.

Then I saw her come into the library. Somehow, I knew that she was going to be drawn to it. She looked like the intellectual kind, had books strapped to her horse, even. I watched from the shadows until she saw the book that Prince Ambrose had written . . . I didn't know how far I should have let her read, but the moment her eyes read a smidge of realization, I knew it was my time to come in and introduce myself.

The introduction had gone much like I thought it would, but I had one problem. I could not picture her with Ambrose as much as I wanted to picture her with me. Her intellect and beauty were a match for none that I had seen or read about in the thousands of books that were within the shelves.

As we walked out of the library, I saw the curiosity in her eyes. I could tell by her body language and from my years of being a seer that she was ready to fix everything. I had not told her that Prince Ambrose was what he was, but she knew deep down, had even asked me if I was, but it was not my place to tell her those things.

"You are welcome anywhere in the castle or on its grounds as long as it is inside the fence," I said.

"Why do you say that I am not allowed to leave?" she questioned. "What will happen to me if I do?"

I wanted to scold her for being so inquisitive, but it was that part of her that was going to free us all. I knew as well as anyone that once the curse was sealed unto death, that even the servants that had been immortalized, frozen in time, would die. If the curse could be broken, then we would begin to age at a natural progression from where we had stopped all those years before.

"There is a lock on the grounds, once you enter the gates, the storms will not allow you to leave thereafter," I lied.

I didn't want to tell her that it was Prince Ambrose that had created the storms. If she thought there was real danger, then that cut down on the chances of her running away.

"I see," she said. "I understand why you could never leave."

I felt horrible that she thought of me in all that. She didn't even cry.

"Just remember YOU ARE NOT ALLOWED TO GO TO THE WEST WING," I reiterated to her.

"But anywhere else, correct?" she asked.

"Yes," I admitted. "Anywhere your heart desires, you may go, and anything you desire, you may know."

"I desire to know about the horse out front." She smiled. "Not mine, but the other, who does it belong to?"

"It belongs to an older man, a mariner," I said, but I was sure she already knew. "He came this way only three months back and..."

"Where is he?" she asked, cutting me off.

"He was accused of thievery, Mademoiselle," I said. "He was put in the dungeon."

She put her hand to her heart, and her eyes flooded with tears that threatened to come out.

"Is he alright?" she begged the answer.

"He is being taken care of," I admitted. "I have been seeing to him to make sure that your papa is comfortable."

"How did you know?" she hissed.

"You have his eyes, his mouth, and nose," I said. "Malcom is a great man and speaks of his daughter Lillie often."

"Take me to him, NOW!" she demanded, then her eyes grew soft. "Sorry," she smiled. "Would you please bring me to him?"

"I will," I said. "But you need to know now, that he is very sick."

She nodded, and I took her hand. I wanted to offer her some comfort even though she did not know me at all.

I led her down to the dungeon.

"Monsieur Malcom, I have a gift for you," I said as soon as I reached the bottom of the steps, way before he had the chance to see Lillie.

"Blaize, is that you?" he called out into the darkness, and I saw the excited sparkle in his daughter's eyes.

He sounded sick and worn, and I hated having to show him to her like that, but she wanted to see him, I figured that if it weren't for looking for him, she would have never ended up in the gates of the castle, and our chances of breaking the curse would have gone done the drain.

"Yes, it is me."

"What have you brought me?" he asked, and then coughed a wet cough.

I saw the change in her eyes. Worry replaced the excitement that had been there.

"Papa," she yelled and ran in the direction of his cell.

"My Lillie?" He yelled out with a weak voice as his face showed up in the bars.

I watched Lillie run up to him, and they hugged the best they could. Lillie and Malcom cried together, and he coughed even more.

He held a cloth up to his mouth, and splatters of blood sprayed on it. Her eyes lit with knowing which made my guts churn. I had taken care of the man for months knowing what was happening.

"Papa," she said. "Are you okay, are they taking good care of you?"

"Oh, my Lillie," he reached through the bars and stuck his feeble hand out and wiped a tear away, "I am dying. My body is giving up."

"Oh, Papa," she sobbed. "What is this place doing to you?"

"This place has helped me," he assured her. "I have been taken care of by this man." He pointed to me.

Lillie ran up to me and wrapped her arms around me, sending my heart into my stomach. I ran my hand down the back of her head. I continued to wonder what I had done to deserve what was happening.

Was I falling for the woman that was meant to save our lives? The woman who was sent for Prince Ambrose who hadn't treated a person good for nigh on six hundred years? What was I to do?

"Thank you, thank you, thank you," she said through tears.

"It was nothing, my dear," I said. "But you cannot be down here for long, so wrap your visit up."

She looked up and nodded, still with tears in her eyes. She understood that I had rules to follow too.

I watched as she and her father visited a bit more, and then I took her back topside. I wanted to tell her I was sorry, but I couldn't get the words out. I wanted to tell her not to worry, but I couldn't say those words either. Instead, we walked the distance to her room in silence.

We stopped in front of the door I knew would be her room. It had been ready for the woman that would break the curse for as long as the curse had been a thing. It was outdated, to say the least, but it was clean, warm, and welcoming.

"This is you," I said with a grin as I opened the door for her.

Her eyes gleamed with the black and silver decorated room that lay ready for her. She ran her fingers over the silken tapestry that hung from the four-poster bed. I took a deep breath as I saw her smile a little.

"Do you like it?" I asked her.

"It is lovely. Thank you. If it's okay, I would like to sleep a bit."

I nodded as I took her hand up and kissed the back of it. I left the room wondering why I felt the way I did. I scolded myself for the heat in my lower stomach when I looked into her eyes.

I felt bad that she had seen her papa that way but was happy that she got to see him before he died because he was going to. I knew that he was going to when I first laid eyes on him when Prince Ambrose threw him in there. I didn't think I had a chance of convincing him to let Lillie's papa out, but I was going to make sure he did what he could to make her happy.

She deserved to be happy.

10

LILLIE

I looked at Blaize, and he had been a wonderful guide, but I was exhausted and growing more tired by the second. I was perhaps more tired than I had ever remembered being.

I backed up towards the bed trying not to be rude to Blaize, but I really was growing exhausted and wasn't managing my emotions all that well.

He turned to leave, but in the last moments, before he walked out the door, he turned back around. He looked at me for a moment, and I felt like he was struggling about telling me something or saying something that he didn't want to say.

"What is it?" I asked, him hoping I could prompt the words that were daring themselves to come out of his mouth.

"There is one more thing," he finally said as he reached out, "I need your bow and arrow. I cannot leave it here with you . . . I'm sorry."

I looked at him like he had gone mad, but I really did understand where he was coming from.

"Will they be destroyed?" I asked as I held them to my chest.

They had once belonged to my father and meant a great deal to me, but I didn't want to lose them even if it meant they sat somewhere in the castle and collected dirt.

"I will make sure you get them back after a while," he said as he took them from me gently. "I promise."

I knew that he was telling the truth, I could see it in his eyes. I couldn't figure out where the trust I had in him had come from, but it was there, deep down, inside me. I let him take my weapon without a fight, and I watched him as he walked out the door with it in his hand.

I felt lost without my bow, but I understood why it had to be done that way, I really did. I would have been a threat with it, and he knew it.

As soon as Blaize shut the door behind him, I began to panic. It was a real panic, not just one of those moments of weakness we all went through from time to time. My eyes went blurry with tears, my breath hitched, and my heart raced wildly, more than I could ever remember.

I let out a full-on cry and grasped my chest in defeat as each beat hurt like I was being shot. I couldn't believe everything that had happened over the course of a day . . . that was it, a simple day had brought my whole life to an end . . . and that was how I saw it.

My life was over.

I looked around the room to see if there was something I could use if I had to defend myself, but my eyes were blurring even more, and I wasn't sure that I could see to find something even if I had to.

I grew more and more tired as I cried, and finally, there were no more sobs.

I wanted to run, but if what Blaize said about the storm was true, that kept me from trying to jump out the window. I walked to the window to see what it looked like just in case I wanted to try. I was shocked, we were at the back of the castle and it was up on stilts, which felt like one hundred feet in the air.

Even if the storm didn't scare me, I wouldn't make the drop.

I laid down on the bed and took a breath. I couldn't believe

I had let myself get into a situation I couldn't get out of. I had always been on top of things and never one to be off my guard. And I had lost Remington somewhere out there as well. Even if I was mad at him, his presence would have been a comfort.

I laid in bed as a single tear, the last tear, slipped down my cheek and the exhaustion of sleep took me over.

I WOKE to Madame Potter in my room, laying breakfast out on the table in front of my bed. I gave her a smile as I realized that she was clearing another tray that still had food on it.

"Ahh, Mademoiselle Lillie, it's nice to be seeing you awake, love; I thought you were never going to be joining the livin'," Madame Potter said.

I sat up in the bed a bit to get a bit more comfortable. Madame Potter picked up the tray and moved it to my lap and I cut into the eggs with hollandaise sauce and took the first bite. It tasted like heaven in my mouth, and I realized that was the first bite of food I had since the night that I left home.

"Did you have a nice sleep, Mademoiselle?".

"I . . . I think so," I answered. "I feel like I slept for days."

"Well, you did, Mademoiselle." She smiled as she sat a cup of tea on the tray and began to stir in sugar, milk, and another helping of the herbs Blaize had put in the last cup I had. "Three days to be exact."

"Three days!" I gulped.

"Yes, Mademoiselle," she began.

"Please," I said after taking a gulp of tea. "Call me Lillie."

"Yes, Lillie," she said. "You took some of Blaize's herbs, correct, just like before?" I nodded. "He told me to tell you it was normal to sleep a lot afterward."

She smiled at me, but her eyes were still glossed over. I figured they had all been told not to take the herb, but I thought I would push a little.

"Have you ever thought about trying Blaize's herbs yourself, or giving some to Bit?" I asked her.

Her eyes went dark, and she looked sad for a moment before returning to her cheerful self. "No," is all she said, a little more abrupt than before.

"Are you alright, Madame Potter?" I asked. "I didn't mean to offend you."

"I know, Lillie. You best be getting dressed for the morning." She pointed to an outfit waiting for me over the back of a chair in the corner of the room.

"Thank you."

"I will be back to be fixing your hair, Lillie," she offered.

"That is quite alright."

She nodded then made her way out of my room.

As soon as she was gone, I finished my breakfast and put the tray on the table. I slid the forget me not blue dress over my head, slipping on the accompanying white cape. It was not something that I would have chosen for myself, but it would have to do. I couldn't deny that it was lovely-— made from fine materials. It reminded me of something my sisters might be drawn to.

I left my hair down, looking at myself in the gilded mirror. I actually looked pretty, something I had very seldom tried to be. A knock came to the door, and, reluctantly, I went to it. I didn't think that Mademoiselle Potter would have knocked; I thought perhaps it was Blaize.

"Who is there?" I asked from my side of the door.

I heard heavy breathing and a bit of a growl from the other side. I knew in my heart that it wasn't Blaize.

"It is Prince Ambrose," he said. "Open the door."

"I do not answer to commands," I said to him and heard him growl yet again.

"You will open this door, or I will break it down," he said.

"That doesn't help your case." I laughed as I walked over to my bed and sat down.

I wanted to see the show.

"Will you . . . pl, will you ple," he growled again. "Will you please let me in?"

I walked up to the door again and listened. He was breathing heavy on the other side. I didn't know if I wanted to see what he looked like. Blaize had prepared me to expect the things that went bump in the night and I couldn't imagine what that would look like.

"I will open the door under one condition," I said.

"I don't do conditions," he said through a tone that would suggest anger.

I cracked the door open and looked out. The man standing at my door was far from what I expected; he was gorgeous. His fair skin shown in the dark which was a pleasant contrast against his black hair with swooping bangs. His amber eyes were piercing, and the smell that came off him reminded me much of the roses from out in front of the castle.

My heart fell into my stomach. I tried to pull my act together so that I could make my request without sounding like a blithering schoolgirl.

"Free my papa so that he can live out the rest of his days with me?"

"Lillie," he paused as he pushed the door the rest of the way open. He looked at me for a moment before he began speaking again. "This is about your papa," he frowned. "He is not doing well and will not survive the day."

"Take me to him," I said as I made my way past the Prince and headed toward where I knew the dungeons were.

I could feel the Prince right on my heals. I didn't have to ask him where my papa was, I had purposed it in my heart to know how to get to him if I needed to, and so I had.

Even after only being there once.

Once we got there, Blaize was standing with my papa, him lying in a bed, barely breathing.

"Oh, Papa!" I took the bars in my hand.

"It's . . . okay, my Lillie," he got out through shallow breaths. "You are here now, and that is all that matters."

"I am happy I found you, Papa," I said, and then I looked up to Prince Ambrose who I hadn't figured out yet. "Open the bars so I can go to him."

He looked at me as if he were going to protest, but then he nodded and had Blaize open the door for me. I ran to my papa and wrapped my arms around him.

I began to cry.

"Don't," my papa said softly as he reached up and touched the side of my face with a withered hand. "My Lillie," he wheezed out.

And then his hand fell to his side and he took a breath that reminded me of the last breath of a deer when I had dropped it.

He was gone.

"Oh, Lillie," Blaize said. "I am so sorry."

"Go prepare things for a small event for the child," Prince Ambrose said.

Blaize went immediately to do as he was told, and I had to think about how he didn't *have* to do that, perhaps there was more to their relationship than what was first presented. And maybe it meant even though this prince was meant to be a monster, there was something there under his ill manners and striking appearance that might be worth knowing. I just didn't know if I wanted to try or not knowing that my papa lay dead in my arms, and he had at least contributed slightly to the event.

"Thank you," I said to the Prince, standing up and letting me papa lay on the dismal ground. I was determined to remain strong, but then I realized I couldn't. My papa had been the only man that had ever loved me and the only man I ever loved. The prince was the only one there as I half collapsed, wrapping my arms around him.

I began to cry as his muscles tensed. After a moment, he began to relax a little and even lifted his arms and put them around me. He growled a little as he relaxed even more, and I knew how untouchable he had been. I had been told about how bad he was, but I had yet to see all the nightmare comparisons.

My tears dried a bit, and I pulled away and turned to look at my papa's body. It was so hard to see him that way, but I knew it was important. I *hated* knowing that he had gone through the lot of it on his own, but then I thought that perhaps it was better for him to have gone the way he did, in the cold of the castle rather than out at sea where I would have always wondered what had happened to him. I wouldn't have been able to live with myself if that would have happened.

And for that, I was oddly thankful. I was happy that my papa had died in a dungeon next to me rather than in an uncharted bit of water in the middle of nowhere.

11

PRINCE AMBROSE

I PACED BACK AND FORTH, wondering what to do with the situation I had been put in. When the girl, Lillie showed up, I only had three weeks to reverse the curse, but then after she slept for three and a half days, I only had two and a half. I was growing impatient and didn't know what to do to get the ball rolling on what was supposed to be a romance that would save a nation.

"If only I wouldn't have gotten involved with that wench all those years ago," I said out loud to no one in particular.

Then Blaize came to my quarters and let me know that the man Malcom was not going to make it past the hour. I knew he was ill, but I hadn't seen him since the day I had taken him into the dungeons. Sure, Blaize had kept me updated, but I had no clue it was that bad.

I debated on if I should have sent Blaize or Mademoiselle Potter to get the girl to tell her of her father. I had never met her face to face even though I had watched her sleep three nights in a row.

I had grown to be fond of her features, but I had no idea how I was going to make someone like Lillie fall in love with me. There was a reason her father had favored her so. She was beautiful, strong, and pure. All the things a monster like me never deserved to lay his hands on.

I walked back and forth, trying to decide when I finally conceded to going myself. I made my way to her door and was shocked when I knocked on the door and she was so abrupt. That part of her pissed me off to the point I wanted, no needed to ravage something. I had even threatened to break her door down.

I could have too, but then she challenged me, which made the anger and other feelings swirl together in my stone stomach to make something new that didn't make sense to me – not anymore.

Then after her father died, she held me . . . as in wrapped her arms around me and cried. I felt tense and out of practice, six-hundred years out of practice to be exact.

I was confused about how I was feeling and wished my heart worked the way it should so it could guide me. Truth be told, my heart didn't work before the curse, I couldn't figure out how I expected it to work after I was cursed to be the monster I was.

I led her topside as I felt confused the whole way. Once we got up the steps just outside the common dining, east of the library, I turned away to head to my quarters.

"Wait," she said as she put her hand to my shoulder.

I turned around and looked at her.

"Yes," I grumbled.

"Do you have to leave me?" she said. "I mean, Blaize is off preparing for my papa's wake, and," she fell silent for a moment, "I just don't want to be alone."

I nodded at the understanding of what she was meaning, and I felt my stomach twinge with something familiar, something I hadn't really felt since I was a kid. It felt something like adventure and excitement, but I couldn't figure out why I had spent so long not feeling, it being impossible in fact, and there I was feeling excited and close to happy.

"Could I take you on a tour of my castle?" I asked, feeling ridiculous.

"I would like that," she sniffled.

I took off walking in front of her and immediately saw her small smile turn to a frown. Finally, after trying several times to tell my body to slow down, I fell into stride with her. It was odd going at a human's pace again, but it felt good to enjoy everything a bit slower.

"I hear you have already visited the library," I said.

"Yes," the smile returned to her face.

"And, what did you think of it?" I questioned.

"It was the most beautiful thing I have ever seen," she said. "It was like falling into a dream."

I nodded.

"Well, if you like that," I said. "You are going to like this."

I opened the door to the gardens. Black roses lined the walk, making it impossible to pass their thorns, but beyond that were the impossible, except I knew they were possible.

I had seen them before, but I could tell by the look in her eye, she had not.

"What is this place?" she asked.

"This is Le Jardin des Ames," I answered her as an all-black fairy danced overhead.

"The garden of souls," she translated. "May I ask if my father's soul is in here?"

"No," I said, and I was sad I had to tell her that. "These are the souls of the roses, the black ones. Once they are picked, they die a death as painful as torture itself, and their souls are released out here."

"That is why there was so much blood?" I asked.

Just then, a fairy landed on her hand, and I knew by the way she looked at the tiny creature, Lillie had realized that the fairy she was holding was the soul of the rose she had picked upon coming into the castle.

"Yes," I sighed, as I reached my hand out and let one of the pixies stand on my finger. "The blood is to remind us why we are all here, that it is my fault that there is so much darkness."

She looked at me saddened by my words and I knew it was time to go on. At the end of the path was another door, one that stood free on its own. There was no facing or walls around it, only a door.

I took her hand and walked us through that door. We ended up coming through the front door of the castle— like magic. Her eyes grew at the wonderment of it, and she turned and opened the door.

That time it opened for her the storm was not there to push the door shut. I knew what she wanted to see, and so she ran to them. She stood on the inside of the fence as they were on the outside.

"Sylver, Lenora," she said as she rubbed their noses. "When I am ready, I will have you let you free. "Lenora," she began to cry. "Papa died today."

The horse looked sad as if she understood, and I wondered if she did. I attempted to walk closer to them, but then they began to jump and neigh in panic. I backed up but then was shocked when Lillie took my hand and pulled me forward. She used my hand and reached out and slowly placed my hand to Sylver's nose.

"He is good," she said, and my heart that had not moved in hundreds of years beat.

Only one beat, but it was there, and it hammered against my chest like a gong calling in the troops.

I looked up through the woods when a new feeling fell upon me, and I could tell that Lillie was looking the same way I was. I could feel his eyes on us, particularly on her, and I wanted to scream at him, tell him he wasn't welcome and that she was being taken care of, but I didn't want Lillie to know I knew the wolf was there.

I had watched him follow her in and knew he was a shifter. A real wolf would have killed her or the horse by the time she made it to the forbidden forest. I didn't like him already, and I knew that it was a man because his smell was musky and strong.

After a few more moments of petting the horses who then accepted me, we turned around and went back inside.

As I shut the door behind us, I knew if she liked the library, then she would like the place I would take her to next.

"Can I take you one more place?" I asked.

"Yes, of course," she blushed a little, which oddly sent heat into my cold chest.

I led her to the very start of the west wing. I didn't want her seeing where I lived or the thing that would explain my existence, but I needed to show her something.

My personal library.

When we walked in, she gasped. The room was nearly a quarter of the size of the other, but the books in there were older and kept differently than the ones in the main library.

"This is my study," I said to her. "I know how much you love books, I just wanted to show you that I do as well."

She spun around looking at the missives at the very top. I had some originals that at the time I had gotten them people thought were lost for all time. The very firsts of some books that were famous before I became a monster.

"Where are we in regard to the castle?" she asked.

"We are in the first part of the west wing, Lillie," I said, as I picked up my favorite book.

"I thought I wasn't allowed in the west wing," she teased.

"You're not!" I growled, overcome by anger.

"I understand," she spoke softly. "I will only go as far as you guide me."

I knew that she was telling the truth. The look behind her eyes told me that. I walked up to her and brushed a strand of hair away from her face as I looked into her eyes.

Her sweet smell filled the room at the exposure of her jugular vein.

I leaned in as she looked deep into my soul and put my nose to her neck. She didn't do anything but stand as still as could be.

"What are you?" she asked, bringing me out of my thoughts.

"You must know by now," I said.

"I think I am losing my mind with the things I am thinking about you, Prince Ambrose."

"Just Ambrose," I said with a commanding growl.

"Ambrose," she said. "I think I have gone crazy."

"Why is that?" I asked as I took another step closer to her.

I could feel the hunger inside me grow, and I wanted to make sure she knew what she was dealing with when dealing with me.

"Because I think," she paused, "I think, I know what you are, Ambrose, and I feel crazy for thinking it."

"Tell me," I demanded.

"Ambrose," she stopped for a moment. I could tell that she was trying to collect her thoughts. "Are you a . . . vampire?"

As soon as she said it my body quaked with desire. Again, my heartbeat, shortly, but twice that time. I could not contain myself. I pushed her against the wall of books and took her head in my hands.

She did not act like she was afraid whatsoever. She looked me in the eyes as my mouth lowered to meet her neck. She whined only a little as my fangs sank into her flesh, and I moaned when I tasted the sweetest blood I could have ever imagined.

As I drank of her, I worried that I was ruining everything, that was until she put her hands in my hair and thrust her head back a little. She began to match the sounds I was making, and my fangs left her neck.

I replaced my fangs with my lips and tongue and began to kiss and lick her wound until it was healed. Then, I let the kiss travel up her neck as my hands found their way up her body.

I realized what I was doing and again didn't want to ruin things, so I pulled away from her as fast as I could.

"I'm sorry," she said, and I laughed because I didn't know why she was telling me she was sorry.

"Don't do that," I scolded her. "You are not the one to blame here. I have been through a lot, and it had been many years since I have shared my home with a woman, and I . . . "

She closed the gap between us and put her finger to my lips.

"Shh," she said and then she removed her hand. "It may have been your fault that your castle is like this and that you are a vampire, but surely, there has to be a way to fix it all?"

"There is not enough time," I said.

"There is always enough time," she countered, which made me smile.

Heat rose in me again, warming me for the first time as my heart knocked against my chest at least a full minute.

In the excitement of things, I pulled Lillie close and put my mouth to hers. Feeding on her had not made her run away, and I wanted to take my chances. I could feel her body tense up against mine, and I pulled back. She looked into my eyes and then walked out of the room and back down the hall to where I had gotten her from earlier in the day.

I wasn't sure what had gone wrong, but it only fueled the anger inside me, and I ran into my quarters. With one swoop, I broke several decorations and a few pictures on the wall.

I ripped a photo of my mother and father in half and burned the pieces in the flame of a candle. While they were still on fire, I took them to the balcony and let them loose into the wind.

I was always going to be alone . . . until the day I died, which wasn't going to be that long. I turned to see another drop of blood from the timekeeper of my curse, and I broke some more.

12

LILLIE

I felt like I had no purpose or sense of direction. I couldn't even decipher what was going on in my head or heart. It was the oddest thing to not know what you were thinking. I had been thrown off guard, and I didn't know how to process it.

I ran through the halls, out of the west wing, through the living room, past the dining hall, and towards my living quarters. That was the only place I could think that I wanted to go. I had no desire to be anywhere where a servant could watch me freak out.

I wasn't even sure who I was.

I ran to my room and threw myself on my bed. I could not believe what I had just confirmed. At first, I had wondered if Blaize was a vampire, but it had felt so silly to think such a thing. I had not gained the never to ask, let alone think about Ambrose being one. Yes, my papa had taught me about them, told me the stories, but just because you heard a story does not mean you believe every word of it. I didn't think vampires were really a thing, just as much as I didn't expect Remington to be a wolf shifter.

Then I thought about Remington, I knew that he had been

in the woods watching us as we were with the horses. I could feel that both of them knew the other was there, and it felt like a silent battle between the two of them and no words were spoken.

And then, as if that wasn't enough to process, Ambrose had taken me to a place that was private to him, and amazing to me. I wanted to scream, he had both bit me and kissed me all in the matter of a few minutes.

My head reeled around and round as I couldn't figure out why the bite had not phased me. Towards the middle of it even, I had begun to enjoy myself, like it even, but then he kissed me, and I freaked out. I was so confused about all of it.

I began to cry.

I had cried more since I had entered the gates of the castle than I had in all my life. I hated that part. For the most part, I had always been strong and never the one to cry, but my father had died that day, and that was enough to make any person cry.

I laid there and sobbed as I remembered when he and I were home. When he was not on the boat, all the things that we did together. My sisters had been too worried about missing a woman in their life to guide them, they didn't see how amazing our papa was.

He would take me fishing when I was just a little girl. I would sit on his shoulders to cast my pole because I had to have mine out further than him. I thought the big catches were further out.

He got one every time and for years, I went home empty handed.

Until I learned that somewhere between the deep and the shallow was the place to be. My papa taught me that, he taught me how to hunt too, how to wait quietly until the kill was close, and then you would gain the upper hand. It worked every time after I learned the basic steps, and then in a moment, a blink of an eye really, he was gone.

I continued to cry, trying to get out some of the frustrations that I could not shake. I had cried so much that I didn't think it was possible to cry anymore, but then again, I had felt that way before.

I guessed I would need to get used to crying. Disappointment and heartache were going to be my constant companion in the game of life.

I heard someone come in as I laid face down on my bed. I figured it was Madame Potter to check on me, but then I felt a plop on the bed beside me.

"Why are you crying, Mademoiselle?" a little boy's voice sounded next to me.

"Oh, hello Bit," I said as I sat up beside him. "I am crying because I am sad," I answered.

"Why are you sad?" he asked.

"I just miss my papa is all," I said.

The little boy, no older than eight, looked down for a moment. It was as if he was trying to remember something that he couldn't.

"I think I had a papa once," he said. "But I don't remember."

"You know what," I said, "you have a wonderful mother though."

"I do have, don't I?" He beamed.

"You do," I said. "Now, go along and see to it that you don't get in trouble for slacking on your chores."

He stood up and smiled at me. I liked the boy very much. He made me think of my sisters. I wished I had a way to contact them to let them know about our father, and that I would never be home to them again.

I would never be home.

When I left, it was under the understanding that if I didn't come home with papa, I wasn't going home at all. But, I thought that I would at least travel all over France, learn to become a mariner, live on the waters, but none of that was going to happen from where I was.

"I will see you later, Lillie," he said. "Is it alright if I call you Lillie?"

I nodded. "Only if I can call you Bit." I smiled at him the best one I could muster.

"Yes, Mademoiselle," he said with the biggest smile I had ever seen a kid have. "I will call you Lillie, and you will call me Bit."

Then he ran to me and gave me a big hug. I could tell that his eyes were a little less glassed over than they once had been, and I wondered what had happened to change all that. I wanted to figure out what was making things that way, but deep down I thought I knew.

I hugged him back, and then he turned and ran out of the room with his ears as red with as embarrassment as the blush of a new bride.

I sat back in the bed and hugged my knees to my chest. I didn't know what I was going to do, but I figured that if I was going to survive there, I was going to make the best of it. I swallowed my pride and dried my face at the wash basin in my room.

After I had myself pulled together, I walked out and called out to the servants. They listened to me and all came running.

"We are going to do something about this place," I yelled through the hall. "It is too depressing in here for anyone to live, and we have small children here. Open the drapes, let in what light will come in from the forest outside," I commanded, and it was done. "Set the formal dining room for a feast. Find what fabric you can, and have it placed in my room with needles and lots of thread. Oh, and make this place smell better, dust the furniture, and wash the linens including curtains, and last, but not least, get some music playing around here . . . liven some things up a little," then I turned and whispered the rest. "Because I am going to die here whether it is now or sixty years from now."

They all did as I commanded and within an hour, things

were already looking better. Food was being fixed which helped mask the smell of death. Soft music was playing from somewhere in the distance. Someone was playing the piano. The children that were in the castle ran past me throwing a ball back and forth which put a smile on my face.

"My, the castle is coming together nicely," Madame Potter said from beside me.

"Thank you." I nodded. "Bit paid me a visit today which made me think."

She looked behind her to Bit who was right behind her skirts. He looked on a little sheepishly, and both Madame Potter and I laughed.

"Bit," she playfully scolded him.

"It's okay, Madame Potter," I said. "He made me think about a few things. I may not know exactly how to fix you all right now, I know you are being compelled," I whispered that part, "but as long as you have been compelled to listen to me, I might as well use that to the benefit of bettering the castle and the way families are run around here."

She smiled at me and nodded.

"It has certainly been a long time since the kids have run and played opposed to working their fingers to the bone," she said.

"I know that these children, as you say are actually six-hundred years old, but that doesn't mean they don't need to have a little fun every now and again."

"This is true," she laughed.

"Tell me," I said when she stopped giggling so much. "Do you know where Blaize has gone off to?"

"I know that he was meant to go arrange things for your papa," she said, and then frowned. "I am sorry about that, you know."

"Yes," I smiled the best I could. "Thank you. I don't like that it happened, but I count it as a blessing that I got to see him before he died."

She nodded, and then looked around the room for a moment. "My guess is he would be in the west wing right now, talking with Prince Ambrose," she gestured towards that direction.

"He kissed me," I said.

"He did?" She gasped. "Oh, Lillie, I have never been one for kissing and telling, but if you need to talk to anyone, you know I am here for you."

I hugged and thanked the woman before she went on to do the rest of her work for the day. I took that as a moment to return to my room. I wanted to see what they had thrown together in the way of fabric.

If I was going to be staying for the rest of my life, I needed a wardrobe that reflected who I was as much as possible.

I got to my quarters and saw rows and rows of fabrics and tapestries that could be used for many things. I ran my fingers over their rich tones and wondered where all those pieces had been and why they had not been used in that amount of time. As I ran my fingers through each bolt, I came across a specific one that reminded me so much of something my papa would have worn for a special occasion.

There hadn't been many of those in our lives, but on the rare occasion, someone would get married or a baby would be born, and he would wear a tweed suit that matched his eyes, and I loved seeing him like that. It was not his normal, but that was okay, I liked his normal as well.

I went to work on a pattern for a suit that I would make for him to wear wherever he would be laid to rest. Without measuring it to him, I didn't know exactly what size to make it, and so I tried it on against myself.

Papa was a few inches shorter than I was, and a good five sizes bigger, but that was to be expected for a woman to be smaller. And as I sewed, I began to cry again, it was one of the last things I could do for my papa.

I worked and worked until I had the basic form made, tears

spilling over as I went. I was bound and determined to do the best I could do for him, because he had made me who I was, and he was my favorite person in the entire world.

And he was gone. He was truly gone, never to return, and I cried some more.

13

BLAIZE

AFTER I HAD TAKEN care of where we would bury Malcom, I decided that I would go check on Lillie. I had picked a place that was going to be nice for him. The way things had worked in the past was that prisoners had been dropped into the same hole, but I didn't want to do that with Lillie's papa.

"Ambrose, you are going to have to meet me halfway with this one," I said, as I stood with him at the gravesite that I had picked out. "She is going to want to see her father buried in a place that she can come back and visit."

"Don't you think I know that Blaize?" he said in a gruff tone. "I think I screwed things up."

"What did you do?" I asked, my eyebrow raising teasingly.

"I took her to my study," he said. "But things got out of hand and I . . ."

"You screamed at her, kissed her, told her your secrets, you . . ." I paused for a moment. "Oh, for the love of the heavens, please tell me that you did not feed on her . . . tell me you did not feed on her!" I begged him to tell me, but somehow, I knew what the answer was.

"She seemed alright with the feeding part," he said, and then paused. "It was the kiss that threw her off."

"You fed on her and kissed her all on the same day that her papa had died, what made you think that was a good idea?"

He growled and looked at me. "I don't know," he said. "I am a vampire, after all."

I growled too, but it was a *me* kind of growl, not a vampire growl.

"I will fix it," I said, and then I walked away from Prince Ambrose before I slapped him for his stupidity.

I finally made it back to the house, and I was in shock once I stepped in. The castle was buzzing with things that people were doing, they were cooking and cleaning, doing the things they did before Ambrose messed up.

"Hey, Monsieur, excuse me," I said to a servant I knew, by the name of Jacques. "What is going on here?"

"Le Mademoiselle," he grinned. "She has gone out of se hiding to, how you say it? Make things better for her and our people."

"Is this true?" I asked Madame Potter as she buzzed past me.

"Tis true." She smiled as she ruffled her hair playfully.

I had never seen her so playful and it brought a smile to my face.

"This is good," I said to both Jacques and Madame Potter.

"Yes," she said. "And we felt his heartbeat today," Madame Potter said in a sing-song voice as she buzzed past me.

I lifted an eyebrow at the woman.

"You felt it too?" I asked.

"Three times," she said with the same melodic tone.

"If you don't mind, I am going to be getting back to my chores," Jacques said, and I nodded.

He took off in the direction of the library with a duster in his hands.

"So, you really felt it too?" I asked the woman who was still running around as if she were fifty years younger.

"I did," she said. "Did you not feel it?"

"Oh, I did," I smiled, "but I didn't know if it was due to the fact I have the herb in my system, or if it was felt castle wide?"

"Castle wide, my dear." My mother came up behind me and kissed me on the cheek.

She was gone just as quick as she came with a pile of washed and pressed drapes in her hands.

"My, my, I see what I have missed since I was out picking." I was going to say a grave for her father, but I didn't want to ruin the mood or risk her being around and hearing me. "Where is Lillie?"

That question brought on a small frown from Madame Potter, and I wondered why the sudden change. Then in a moment, she returned back to her original mood and smiled from ear to ear.

"She is in her quarters at the moment," she answered.

"Has she been crying?" I asked through a great amount of concern.

"She has been since she left the Prince," she said, and then she went to the dusting of a white china tea collection with purple flowers.

"Thank you," I said, and then I kissed the woman on the cheek and went towards Lillie's room.

The whole way there I noticed the children playing, the rooms being cleaned, and food being fixed that smelled like Heaven. I didn't know how she had done all of it, but I was sure glad she had. When I reached Lillie's quarters, I reached my fist up to knock on the door, but then I heard her soft cry. Madame Potter was right, she had been crying, and by how soft her voice sounded, it had been for quite a while.

I didn't bother to knock, I softly opened the door and went in. She was sitting on the ground over the form of an already put together suit of sorts. Of course, it was in its first stages, but I knew right away who it belonged to. She had her back to me, and I sank to the ground beside her.

She startled, but only slightly.

"I'm sorry, Lillie," I said, as I put my hand to her face to dry a tear. "I heard you crying and came straight in."

"It's okay," she said.

"This is lovely," I said. "Is this for Malcom?"

"Yes, my papa will look nice in this." She picked up the fabric and held it up to the light.

A small smile graced her face, and I was made happy by it, but it was quickly replaced by another tirade of tears. I reached up and wrapped my arms around her to comfort her. I didn't really know what to say.

With us servants being immortalized in time, it was hard to kill one of us. I think there had only been two or three deaths in the six-hundred years since we had all been frozen. It had, in each case, been brutal and unyielding, but for the most part, we did not die. I could not remember the last person I knew to do so.

A servant who had tried to kill himself had managed to do so, but I didn't want to relive those tales.

Finally, Lillie pulled away a bit and smiled.

"Would you do me a favor?" she asked me.

"Anything," I told her.

"Would you try the suit on for me?" she asked with a tear that streamed down her face. "You are taller than my papa was, but around the same waist size."

I nodded as I slipped off my jacket and put on the one, she had been working on. It fit like a glove and she smiled. She turned around to allow me to slip out of my pants, and into the ones she had been working on. They were a little short, but for the most part, they felt great.

"You have done a lovely job," I smiled. "Maybe one day you can make me a suit too."

"I would love that," she said. "It would give me a purpose in the middle of this madness." She looked sad, but I knew deep down her words held meaning.

I got dressed and walked over to Lillie, putting my hand

under her chin. She looked up at me with red eyes, and I wiped a tear away with my thumb. Then, I felt my heart race yet again.

I knew I didn't need to be feeling the things I was. She was meant for Ambrose I kept telling myself. And then she stepped in closer, which did not help me at all. My body tightened, and I grew hard by her very touch. This was not something I was used to feeling, not in these hundreds of years I had been a frozen servant.

"Thank you," she spoke softly as she reached up and touched the side of my face.

"You're welcome," I said, but only barely.

Our lips met in the middle, the impact of both her and my desire for the kiss. I didn't want to overthink things, so I let it happen.

After all, what harm was there in a kiss?

But then it deepened to the point I could feel her body even closer, and instinctively, I had taken her by the small of the back and pulled her in even closer as our kiss deepened.

A sigh escaped her as my tongue danced with hers. I had wanted that moment from the first time I set eyes on her, and while it felt wrong to be doing what we were, it felt so good, and right as if the sky opened up and allowed the sun to shine on the castle.

The kiss continued to the point we found ourselves tangled up on her bed. Her legs over mine, and my arms wrapped around her. I could feel the heat between us, and the passion that threatened to explode between us too.

She took my hand and pulled it up to sit on her breast, and I moaned in excitement. It was a pleasure I had not had truly in hundreds of years. I cupped her breasts and squeezed a little which brought on sounds of pleasure from her too.

Then she lifted her head a little and my lips trailed down her chin, her neck, and to the apex of her breasts. I continued to worship the skin under her collar bone when I felt her unzip my pants. My erection sprang free from where it had been held and rested against her thigh.

I tried to remember Ambrose and the fact that he meant the world to me, but it wasn't at the forefront of my mind now. The thought stayed somewhere to the back where it was covered up with thoughts of Lillie. And then there was the question as to if I was taking advantage of her sorrow, and that was a man I could not be.

And so, I pulled away a little.

"What's wrong?" she asked breathlessly.

"I don't want to do this," I said, and then I paused to think of the rest of my words. "If either of us feels it is out of pity or if you think it is because I feel sorry for you . . . it could never be like that."

"I don't think that," she said, and then she pulled her dress over her head and exposed her bare breasts.

She was only in a set of lacy panties.

I looked on in shock for a moment, then I took in her body, and what a body it was. Beautiful and perfect in every way a body could be. Then, she leaned down and began to stroke my cock with her hands, and I hardened even more.

Then Lillie slipped her mouth over the head of it, and then slowly, she slid her lips further down until she held the size of me in her mouth. I felt the sensation and it was great, wonderful in fact. She bobbed her head up and down until I could feel the tension build inside me.

I put my fingers in her hair and pulled a little, but not enough to hurt her or make her think I was forcing her to stay.

I thickened even more as she came up off me and put her lips to mine, then she laid down, and put my cock between her breasts. With one hand she pushed her breast together, and with the other, she stroked me, making the best sensation replace the heat that was there. Then, she brought her mouth to mine, and I erupted over her breasts, spilling my orgasm all over her nipples.

"Oh, Lillie," I said softly as I erupted with euphoric pleasure, and she smiled.

Then, I spun her around and kissed her deeply. I didn't know where all the passion had come from, but it was there.

I took her panties off as quickly as I could, and as I put my mouth to her wet and dripping folds, she sucked in a breath of air, and I had her right where I wanted her.

14

LILLIE

I COULD NOT BELIEVE what had happened between Blaize and I. I had grown to like him very much, and I was sharing such an intimate moment with him. I had never had such a moment, and my mind went in a million different directions all at once.

I really didn't know how to feel.

Then I felt him between my thighs, and the sensation was endless. My breath hitched as I held my body still. I felt like I was out of control and gathered all together. My body wanted to take him in, my heart was the only thing standing in my way.

Blaize's tongue slid inside me. It was amazing to feel such a thing.

I had attempted the sensation by my own hand, but it had never felt so good. He moved up and down as he circled my nub with his tongue, and then I felt him place a finger inside too.

And then a second which added a whole new feeling to the mix.

My back arched as I felt oncoming ecstasy, and my breasts stuck pert into the air. I grasped the blanket on either side of me into both of my fists and held my breath. He thrust his fingers in a bit more which both hurt and felt good, and then his tongue slipped around my nub once more.

"Oh, Blaize," I said, but then I couldn't say any more.

My body betrayed me as spasms started between my legs and arched its way over my abdomen and settled in my chest. I screamed out as the feeling of pleasure washed over me again and again.

After my body finished its convulsion and the feeling ebbed, Blaize raised up and planted kisses up my entire body.

My mind swirled and I felt guilty and good all at once. I scolded myself for feeling so bad, I was human after all and a woman.

I needed a moment to gather my thoughts. Thoughts about Remington, thoughts of the prince, and thoughts of Blaize. They had each kissed me over the course of less than a week, and my heart raced faster.

I pulled back a little and smiled at Blaize who had the happiest look on his face.

"Can we stop here?" I asked. "I have some things to think about and have been wanting to save myself, at least the most whole part of myself, for the man I would be with for all of my life. I don't know that it won't be you, but I want to think about things for a while."

He nodded, smiled, and kissed me on the end of the nose.

"I will leave you to your thoughts, Mademoiselle Lillie," he said, as he stood to his feet and gathered himself together.

"Wait," I said to stop him for one last moment.

"Yes?" he said with an expectant eyebrow raise.

"Can you do me a favor?"

"Anything," he offered, and my heart fluttered.

"Can you send a message off to my sisters?" I asked. "Tell them that our father has died and that I will not be returning home again. I mean, I wasn't planning on it anyway, but they need to know so that they can move on."

"How would I get the missive to them?" he asked.

"Send it with the horses," I smiled. "They will be able to get home, they have done it hundreds of times, but they will not be able to get back here. Please, do this for me, and do not add any clues of my whereabouts, not that my sisters would come looking for me, but in the matter they would send someone, then I don't want them to find this place, or me for that matter."

Blaize nodded and smiled again, "I will," he said, and then he left me naked on my bed, panting and in need for more, much more.

I got up and cleaned myself then got dressed again. I needed to take a walk and clear my head, although I didn't know if it could be cleared. I needed to sort things out before I went too far with anyone, further than I could ever take back that was.

I walked out of my room and headed for the front hall where two frosted windows stood on either side of the door. They were much cleaner than the last time I saw them which made me smile. I could get used to speaking things into fruition.

I looked out the window and saw Blaize sending Sylver and Lenora away with a note strapped to Sylver. My heart seized for a moment. Sylver was my friend. I felt like I had just lost an important part of my family.

I made my way to the garden. I knew if I was going to think, doing it with the fairies was most likely the best way. Their unknowing company would help me greatly. The air outside was dense and it was dark, night even, but it felt less stuffy than the castle.

I was thinking so much of the three men who had fought for my attention over the past week, and so my mind wandered.

Remington was a hunter, a perfect fit for the life I would have chosen for myself, but I was stuck inside the gates of the castle, and he was a wolf shifter. That made things a bit more complicated, and at that, I could smell him in the air. If I wouldn't have known better, I would have thought he was on the inside of the gate, he smelled that strong. I could feel him watching me.

Remington was the protective type that could keep me safe, but I didn't ever think I was the type of girl that needed protecting. My papa had made sure that I was not such a girl. That was my favorite part about myself, but I had to admit, it felt nice to feel him there with me when I went into the forbidden forest, and even since I had been at the castle.

He was watching over me. I didn't know what Ambrose or even Blaize would think about it, but deep down, I knew that Ambrose had felt him there the day I took him to pet Sylver.

A twinge of pain went through my chest at the thought of my horse and friend once again. I was going to miss him, Lenora even, but it was best that way. They didn't have any kind of life strapped to a pole and would have died like that.

The confusion grew inside me the more I thought about things, and I couldn't stand it any longer. I had taken just about enough of my thoughts swirling around.

Just then, a tiny fairy landed on my shoulder.

"Hi, little fairy," I said. "Can you help make my mind up?"

She nodded her head and flew off, much faster than I could walk, and in seconds, I had lost her.

Then, there was Prince Ambrose. He was strong and handsome, but he was a vampire. That part of him didn't scare me as much as I thought it would. He had even fed on me, and I wasn't fearful.

But then, there was the curse. By the sounds of things, it could be broken, but I didn't know how that was possible

Ambrose too was watching me, somewhere not that far off. I could feel him just like I could feel the wolf, and I had to laugh. I had become the untouchable girl who attracted fairy-tale beasts; three, to be exact. I felt bad for thinking that.

The same little fairy came back to me and grabbed the collar of my shirt and lightly tugged it towards her. She was much stronger than I thought she was. I followed her, but again she out flew my walking speed, and while I kept in her direction, I easily lost her.

I felt like she was trying to tell me something.

As I walked, I thought of Blaize. I had just done so many things with him, felt so much. My heart even had love for the man, but I couldn't place in what way. He was handsome, and kind, which was different than Remington or Ambrose. They each had attributes that if I put them all together, they would make the perfect man, but that was not possible.

I too felt Blaize's eyes on me, and I looked to see where they were coming from. Then, I saw him looking at me from one of the windows up above. I smiled up at him, and all at once, I felt three pair of eyes on me, sending my body into an emotional spiral.

I needed someone to decide for me.

And then there was the fairy again, but this time, she was sitting beside a fallen black rose. I could tell she was trying to tell me something, and then I remembered what I had asked her.

"I asked you to help me make my mind up, didn't I?" I asked her.

She nodded her head and tried to heft the rose upward to me, but it was too heavy. I leaned over and picked the diamond-crusted rose, and before my eyes, it turned to a puddle of blood in my hand.

From it, flew another fairy, she held her tiny stomach at first, but as she flew, she got stronger and faster, and then she wasn't in pain at all.

I was left with her blood on my hands.

The little fairy who I asked for help flew up and landed on my hand. She dipped her tiny feet in the blood and walked all over my arms, sending tiny bloody footprints all over, and then I thought about it.

"Ambrose?" I asked, and the fairy nodded.

My breath hitched, I didn't feel Remington at all, nor did I smell him. I looked up to see that Blaize was no longer in the window, that left only the vampire who was somewhere behind me, I could feel it.

I spun around, and I was wrong; it wasn't Ambrose who was behind me - it was Remington, and he stood on four legs as a wolf. I couldn't place why I was shocked, but the one thing I did think about was . . .

He was in the fence, meaning the three men that I was toiling over were all under one storm-protected roof, and my heart pounded again and again.

To be continued . . .

Read the full-length book, Lillie of the Woods, releasing Winter 2019!

Until then, keep up to date with me!
https://dl.bookfunnel.com/h1qixbnlxg

OTHER BOOKS BY IRIS SWEETWATER

Brothers of Fang
(A PNR series)

The Clans
(Mafia Romance)

Quarter Kings MC
(Bad boy romance series)

MOMENTS

KELLY A. WALKER

For Twyla

"*No one gets out alive, every day is do or die.
The one thing you leave behind . . .
Is how did you love, how did you love?*"
-Shinedown

PROLOGUE

ONE MOMENT. We all have it. That one moment that changes everything. It could be something small or something big. Something bad, something good. Something wrong or something right.

It's just something.

This was my moment. The one that would irrevocably change everything, and not just for me.

It wasn't small.

It wasn't good.

It wasn't right.

But it was mine, and it was absolutely perfect.

1

Twyla

My life has never been easy. Not that it's been bad enough for therapy, it just wasn't anything spectacular.

I grew up in a single-parent home with a momma who worked two jobs to keep a roof over mine and my little sister's heads and food in our bellies. Due to mommas long working hours, raising my younger sister fell onto my shoulders. I resented Bethany when she was first born. Before her it had been all about me. Momma's joy and Daddy's princess. Looking back now I've changed my tune and will tell anyone that the day Bethany was born would be my first defining moment. I was no longer mad at the newest addition. I became a big sister and pseudo mom, after our dad walked out. That role would eventually shape me into the person I am today. It would make me better, more patient and understanding. What it wouldn't do is prepare me for the moment that would completely change my life at the tender age of twenty-two.

"Do you really have to go all the way across the ocean to learn photography, Ty?" Bethy asks me for the eightieth time.

Rolling my eyes, I continue packing my bags. My flight to

London leaves early tomorrow morning, like five in the morning early, and I haven't even finished my laundry. "Bethy, we've been over this already. It's an amazing opportunity for me to be able to spend the next three months overseas studying under Marco Turner," I tell her. Again. "Look," I turn to face her, "the three months will fly by. Before you know it, I'll be back home, you'll be starting your senior year of high school and the two of us will be shopping for the perfect homecoming outfit because you know you're going to be named Senior Queen." Grabbing my little sister, I pull her close and squeeze her until she starts play coughing. I push her back so I can look her in the eyes. "It's only three months, Bethy. You'll be fine."

Bethy sighs and the watery smile she gives me breaks my heart a little more. I know me being so far from home won't be easy for her. Bethy loves momma but let's be real here, I raised her. I fed her, clothed her, bathed her. Heck, I sat up with her a solid week when she had the flu and pneumonia all at the same time. Our bond is more than just sisters. She's mine and I would do anything for her but refusing the chance of a lifetime to study my craft under a world-renown artist? She's just going to have to buck up because I refuse to say no to Marco Turner.

"I get it, Ty. I really do. I'll just miss you. It's not like when you're at college and it's only an hour from me. I can call you anytime, but I can't do that while your off jet-setting all over Europe."

I laugh at the thought of me jet-setting anywhere. "Bethy," I breathe out. "I'm flying economy to London and taking either a bus or train everywhere else. I'm going super cheap." I roll my eyes before speaking again. "I already told you I bought an international calling card so I can call and check in on you. Don't make it sound like I'm leaving and never coming back."

"What if you find *him*?"

"Who the hell is *him*?" I ask her.

"You know who *him* is. *Him*," she throws her arms out. "The one."

I fling one of the small pillows off my bed at her head. "You need to put down those romance books of yours. I'm no princess and there definitely is no white knight prince waiting for me at Stonehenge." I zip up my suitcase and turn my back on Bethy to head out of my room and down the hall toward the laundry room. Leave it to me to wait until the last minute to wash clothes so I can pack. I should have been in bed an hour ago.

"You never know, Ty. Maybe you're leaning up again one of the pillars at Stonehenge and it starts to shift. Before you can move to escape being crushed by a thousand-pound pillar from a million years ago a guy pulls you out of the way and BAM! Fireworks exploding everywhere. You'll fall in love and never come home again."

"Are you finished?"

"Maybe," my little sister sheepishly replies.

"First, I won't be leaning on any pillar. Second, if Stonehenge did start to shift I doubt I would just stand there and watch it fall on me. Thirdly, I'm pretty sure it's not a million years old and lastly, who said I would settle for some English man that thinks eating blood sausage and beans for breakfast is acceptable?"

Bethy finally laughs and I know she'll be okay while I'm gone. It will be hard for both of us. Even though I'm only an hour from her while at college, I still come home every weekend and sometimes in the middle of the week. We haven't gone longer than ten days without seeing each other. As I said, she's more than just my baby sister. Bethy is mine and I worry about her sitting at home all summer pouting and not enjoying her last summer before she had to start preparing for college herself.

"Promise me something," I say to her. "Promise me you'll go out this summer. Have fun with your friends. Go to parties, kiss some guys and just have fun. I'll call you every few days."

"Only if you swear to bring me something awesome back from every country you visit."

"I wouldn't dare return to Memphis without having to buy an extra suitcase just to haul all the loot I'm buying you from over there."

"Love you, Ty."

I hold my sister tight. "Love you too, Bethy."

2

Twyla

"You have got to be kidding me," I grit my teeth, trying to hold in my anger at myself and at the jerk who ripped my purse off my arm the second I walked out of the hostel I'm staying at. "What the heck am I supposed to do now?"

"I'm sorry, Miss. Were you speaking to me?"

I look up when I realize the question spoken in the distinctive British accent was said to me. My first thought is whoa, this guy is tall. He isn't built with the typical manly muscles that some have to overcompensate for other things, but he is built solid. I can tell because this dark auburn-haired man with the amused stone colored eyes is wearing a worn-out wife beater tee that has seen better days. His jeans are no better with holes in both knees and the hems fraying at his ankles. I'm momentarily distracted by the ease in which he holds himself so when I look up at his face again, I am not prepared for what I see. His cheeks look like they've been chiseled out of stone and goes against his entire persona. He has a thick beard that matches the dark auburn color of his hair, but it isn't bushy, it's just right. The slight hump in the middle of his nose, I assume is from being broken at one time, is what transforms his face from something made of wax to human-like. I shake my head in an attempt to stop myself from staring at the stranger anymore. "I..," I clear my throat and start all over again. "I wasn't speaking to anyone. Just myself," I stumble out.

The handsome stranger looks at me closely and I find myself wondering what he sees. "If you talk that harsh to yourself, I'd hate to hear what you sound like when you're mad at another person," his shoulders bounce with silent laughter. He holds out his hand I notice a tattoo of a four-leaf clover on the inside of his arm. I can only see the top of script writing underneath it because a worn brown leather band is tied around his wrist. "My name is Miles Davis and you seem to be having some issues. Is there anything I can help you with?"

I fold my smaller hand into his large, calloused one. "Twyla Hays and thank you but no. Not unless you can catch the jerk that ripped my purse off my shoulder and took off like the hounds of hell were chasing him," I huff out.

"Ah, I see. You must be careful, Twyla Hays. Not all English are as nice and honest as me."

I can't help the laugh that explodes from my chest at his statement. Anyone could see that Miles Davis is no nice or honest man. The mirth in his eyes is telling enough that he likes anything that isn't nice. "Thank you for the advice, Mr. Davis."

"Miles," he corrects me. "Call me Miles."

"Alright. Thank you, Miles." I take a deep breath and look up to the blue sky before dropping my chin and exhaling. "Well, Miles, if you don't mind directing me to the US Consulate I would greatly appreciate it. I need to see about getting temporary identification before they kick me out of your country for being here illegally."

"I can do better," he bends his arm and offers me his elbow. "I'll walk you there." He must be able to see the indecision on my face. "It isn't far, but my mamma would beat me if she knew

I came across a damsel in distress and didn't do anything to help. Please, allow me to help you, Twyla."

I shake my head before taking his arm. "Thank you again, Miles. I would appreciate you helping me."

The smile he graces me with is so wide I'm momentarily blinded by his straight white teeth. Good lord, where did this man come from? Miles lays his other hand on my arm. "So, Twyla," he says as we begin to walk down the busy London street, "what are you doing in England?"

"I'm actually here to study photography with Marco Turner for the next three months."

Miles stops abruptly and stares at me. "Did you say you're studying with Marco Turner?"

"Yes," I answer him slowly. "Is there a problem with that?"

"Oh, Twyla," Miles chuckles and begins walking again. "There is definitely no problem. Just the opposite actually. You see, I am also working with Marco for the next three months."

"Oh my," I think to myself. Me and this yummy man for the next three months. Bethy would definitely approve.

3

Twyla

"I'm pretty sure when Marco sent you on an errand it wasn't to pick up a beautiful woman." My head snaps up at the southern voice speaking directly behind me.

Miles and I decided to stop and have a celebration coffee after taking care of my business at the Consulate this morning. Well, I had coffee, he had tea. The small table we're sitting at is outside with three metal chairs surrounding it. Two of which are being occupied by myself and Miles. I don't have to turn around to see who the new stranger is because in the next second, the one empty chair next to me is being pulled out and a cowboy is sitting down in it.

A southern cowboy. In London of all places.

The cowboy catches me looking at him, tips his hat and winks. You know what I'm talking about. We've all seen the movies where the sexy cowboy jumps up into his saddle and prepares to ride off into the sunset, leaving his simple wife behind to look over the farm and homestead. Right before he leaves, he tips his hat then winks at her. Yeah, that's exactly what he did. He tipped his cowboy hat and winked at me. I can feel the heat from my red cheeks. Why do I have to be one of those girls that blush so easily?

"Ma'am," the cowboy says to me.

Ma'am. Really? Not even his tight black t-shirt covering up what I'm betting is a delicious body, his tight blue jeans, or his dashing blue eyes could make me be okay with someone calling me ma'am.

"Conner, man. Seriously, she isn't eighty years old."

"I told you, Miles, it's called manners and it wouldn't hurt if you would learn one or fifty," the cowboy, I mean Conner, smarts back.

"Twyla, this cowboy," Miles rolls his eyes, "is Conner. Conner, this is Twyla. She's one of the interns that will be working with Marco for the next three months."

Conner whips his head back toward me. "Really? It's nice to meet you, Twyla," he holds out his hand and when I place my hand in his, instead of shaking it he flips mine over and places a soft wet kiss on the top. "It is a pleasure, Twyla."

I have to clear my throat before I can speak. "Thank you, Conner."

"So," Conner claps his hands together, "we get to spend the next three months together touring Europe and taking so many pictures your clicking finger will be numb. Are you excited?" He's practically bouncing in his seat when he asks me.

"I am excited. A little nervous as well," I answer him honestly. "This is such a huge opportunity for me. I don't want to do anything to jeopardize it." Hoping they both get the hint at what I'm saying.

"We're the same way, especially Devon. He's all about business. No fun for him," Miles informs me in the middle of taking sips of his tea. "You'll meet him tomorrow when we get together with Marco at his apartment. He always has a big dinner the night before so everyone can meet and mingle."

"Mingle is one word to describe it," Conner coughs into his

fist. "So, Twyla, what part of the good old US of A are you from?"

"I'm from the great city of Memphis, Tennessee. What part of the US are you from?" I ask Conner.

"Texas. Born and bred in a small town just outside of Dallas."

"Ah, so you're a real Texas cowboy?"

Conner tilts his hat once again. "You better believe I'm a real Texas cowboy."

"He even has the bowlegs to prove it," Miles laughs.

"Shut up, jackass. My legs are not bowed and even if they were it would be because of honest ranching work."

Miles straightens up from laughing, looks Conner in the eyes, and begins to laugh some more. "I'm sorry, Conner," Miles breathes out. "It's just the image of you riding around on a horse roping a bunch of cows. I keep seeing that movie City Slickers where the guys are new to riding and when they finally get off those beasts you call a horse, they're all so bowlegged you could drive a car through their legs."

"Yeah, I'm familiar with the movie," Conner deadpans, "It isn't like that in real life you dumbass."

"Well, yes, I suppose it isn't," Miles says. He takes a deep breath and wipes his eyes. "So, Twyla, tell us a little about yourself. What do you do when you aren't taking pictures? Are you in school? We want to know it all."

"So, this is where the two of you have been hiding while I've been running all over London finishing up everything before we leave in two days."

I look up into a pair of intense dark chocolate eyes and the look on this man's face has me slinking down into my chair like a kid being called out in school. This can't be good.

4

Twyla

OUR COFFEE STOP was cut short when the infamous Devon showed up and both Miles and Connor had to leave to finish getting things ready for Marco before we take off in a few days. I didn't get the greatest first impression of Devon, but tonight I'll be officially meeting him and the other two students that were chosen alongside me to intern this summer.

My stomach is a ball of knots when I knock on the door of the apartment Marco specified in the invitation.

The first thing I notice is how tall he is. The second is the way his suit fits him just right. It's stretched across his wide shoulders and the jacket tapers down to accent his slim waist. His dress pants fit snug against his thighs, and I'll bet if he turned around and bent over, I could bounce a quarter off his tight butt. I force my gaze to move from his body back to his face. Of course, he knows I've been staring at him, the smirk on his chiseled face tells me all I need to know. Devon. His brown hair is thick and wavy and just begs for you to run your hands through it. His eyes are blue like the ocean I flew over to get here. The sound of a throat clearing breaks me from internally stripping this man's clothes off.

"Can I help you?"

Oh. My. Sweet. Baby. Jesus. He has a Scottish accent. I'm done.

I didn't have a chance to speak with him at the cafe and I wasn't really paying attention to him if I'm being honest. The southern cowboy still had all my attention at that time. I hold out my hand, initiating a handshake with the Scottish masterpiece in front of me. "My name is Twyla, we met briefly at the cafe. I'm here for the dinner," I surprise myself with the ability to speak without falling all over myself. "I'm one of Marco's summer interns."

"Ahh," he nods his head and grabs my hand. "I'm Devon Taylor and I work for Marco."

"Right. Miles told me you worked with them."

The infamous Devon I heard about from Miles, tilts his head and studies me. "You seem to know Miles pretty well already?" he asks me with suspicion in his voice.

"Twyla!" Conner chooses this moment to interrupt us. "I see you found the apartment," he leans past Devon, pulling me into the apartment and places a soft kiss on my cheek. "Let me walk you around and introduce you to the other interns and Marco. Miles is around here somewhere and was asking for you a little while ago."

I throw Devon a finger wave with the hand not currently being grasped by Conner. "So, what exactly is his problem?"

"That's just Devon," Conner mutters. "Look, Twyla," Conner stops walking and turns to face me. "Just do me a favor, whatever he says or does, ignore it, okay. He's going through some things and has a tendency to be stupid and not think before acting or speaking."

I look at Conner and before I can ask why I'd possibly care, Miles jumps in between us and lays a loud kiss right on my lips.

"There you are! I was worried you might have a hard time finding us."

"It was quite easy actually," I tell him. "Your directions were spot on."

"You have the cutest little accent," Miles says while swaying a little.

"Miles? Are you by any chance drunk?" I laugh at the look on his face when I ask. I don't think he was expecting me to call him out or maybe he was hoping I wouldn't realize he'd been drinking.

"I'm not drunk," he tries to assure me. "I only had a little bit before everyone got here. I need to calm my nerves just a bit. I mean, it's not every day you think you meet your soul . . ."

"Miles," Conner barks out at him. "That's enough. I'm sure Twyla doesn't want to hear all the mess you're getting ready to spew." Conner looks back at me, a sad smile on his face. "I'm, sorry about that. He doesn't drink often at all, but he's been under a bit of stress and well, you know how it is sometimes."

I shrug my shoulders because really, I don't. My grandfather was an alcoholic and after watching him waste away from all the years of drinking I swore I would never touch it. "So, where are all the other interns?" Conner gets my need to change the subject and winks at me.

"I saw one of them in the kitchen talking to Marco. We'll start in there."

We say goodbye to Miles, and I follow Conner toward the left side of the apartment. On our way to the kitchen, I take in the decor of Marco's home. Unless something has changed, Marco is a confirmed bachelor and looking at his apartment I can tell. There's a huge leather couch with two matching recliners in the small living room. On one wall is the typical bachelor large television and the other is floor to ceiling windows. We walk past a small dining area with a pub style table and six stools and a plant that probably should have been tossed three months ago. Conner opens the swinging door that leads into the spacious black and white kitchen. The floors are checkered like in an old diner, the walls and cabinets are white making the black granite countertops look even bolder.

"Marco," Conner calls out and I watch Marco turn around from talking to a woman who looks to be my age. Marco is quite a few years older than me. His black hair is beginning to turn gray at the sides, but his deep blue eyes still look full of mischievous. Something tells me that even though Marco may be older, he probably acts a lot younger than most of us do.

"Twyla, I am so happy to finally meet you in person," he lifts my hand, kissing the top of it.

"Marco," Conner growls out. "Go find your own woman."

I turn my head sharply to see Conner narrowing his eyes. "Conner?" I whisper. "What are you doing?"

Conner runs his hand through his hair roughly. "I'm sorry, Twyla." He winces and looks apologetic. "Marco is a big flirt and I don't want him trying to mess with you. We'll be together for the next three months and it doesn't go very smoothly with the interns if they hate the mentor of the group."

Marco throws his head back and lets out a barking laugh. "Sure, Conner," he chokes out. "If that's what you want to tell yourself. Twyla," he turns his gaze back to me, "it was a pleasure meeting you, but I need to be a good host and get the food out before these monsters start tearing up the place. We'll speak later, yes?" His British accent becomes more prominent the louder he gets.

"That sounds wonderful," I tell him.

Conner takes my hand again and leads me back out of the kitchen and into the living room. "Would you like to sit until it's time to eat?"

"Sure," I say and proceed to sit at the end of the massive couch. "So, how long have you been working with Marco?"

"I've actually been with him for ten years. He knew my parents and when they died in an accident, I had no other living family, so Marco came and got me. The rest is history."

"I'm so sorry," I place my hand on Conner's thigh. "I'm sorry to hear about your parents, but at least you had Marco."

"Yeah. Miles was already living with him at the time and Devon came to us about a year later." He must see the confusion on my face because he continues with his story. "Marco was friends with all three of our parents. They all went to college together. Miles' father went into the military over here and died in a training accident. His mom tried so hard, but she just couldn't deal with it. When he was ten, she took her own life and he came to live with Marco. Devon . . .,"

"Can tell his own damn sob story," the words being spoken in my ear are rich with that Scottish accent. "I don't need you telling my history, Conner. If I wanted her to know it, I would tell her."

"I'm sorry, Devon," I turn to tell him. I didn't realize just how close he was to me and when I turn, my lips brush against his. I jump up from the couch and I can feel the heat from embarrassment on my face. "Oh my gosh," I cover my face with my hands. "I didn't realize you were sitting on the edge of the couch."

Devon blinks slowly then rises. Before he walks away, he looks at me shrewdly. "If you want to know about me, all you have to do is ask. There's no need to use my brother to further yourself."

My mouth drops open and I turn to face Conner. "What the heck is he talking about?"

"I'm sorry, Twyla, but he's right. It's his story to tell and I shouldn't have said anything. It looks like Marco is done setting out dinner. Why don't we go eat, then see about introducing you to Kelby, Renee, and Matt?"

I let out a long exhale and nod my head. I don't know what Devon was talking about but how dare he insinuate that I'm only talking to Conner so I can learn about him! What a conceited jerk. Like there's anything spectacular about the great Devon. Please.

"Did you say something?" Conner asks me.

Crap. I hope I didn't say any of that out loud. "Nope," I say, adding an extra pop to the p. I was just looking around.

"Okay," he shakes his head, knowing good and well that I'm lying through my teeth. "Let's get you fed before you start trying to figure out ways to rip Dev's balls off. I told you to ignore him."

"Yeah," I say to myself. "You certainly did."

5

Twyla

I HAVEN'T SEEN Miles or Conner since dinner two nights ago at Marco's. Today is the day we are all meeting up and heading to our first destination. This week we will be staying here in London, just going a little further away from the city property and seeing more of the countryside. I can't wait to learn from Marco, but if I'm being honest with myself, I'm more interested to see exactly what it is that Miles, Conner and even Devon does for Marco. Are they photographers as well? For some reason, I can't picture Devon or Conner getting dirty while rolling around in an attempt to capture a picture.

"Hey Ty," Miles calls out to me. "Is it alright if I call you that?"

"Only my friends can call me Ty," I say with a monotone voice. I can't help but laugh at the look of disappointment on his face. "I'm kidding, Miles. Of course, you can call me that."

"Oh, Ty, I can already tell we're going to have an exciting summer together," he winks at me before walking off to talk to Matt, another intern. I met him the other night and wasn't impressed. He's from New York City and his preppy clothes and perfect blonde hair screams "stranger danger" to me. I don't know why, but there's just something about him that rubs me the wrong way.

"So, I see you've moved on from my brother to another intern. You switch partners awfully fast," the Scottish voice that has invaded my dreams the last two nights breathes into my ear.

I whip my head around and come face to face with Devon. Rolling my eyes, I give him my best FU look. "I wasn't looking at him like that. What do you want?"

"He," he nods his chin toward Matt, "is not right for you."

"Not right for me?" I repeat back to him. "First of all, who is or isn't right for me is none of your business. Second, why do you care, Devon? Last time you spoke to me, it was to be a jerk."

"Look," he balls his fist up and crosses his arms over his chest. The light blue polo shirt he has on fits tight across his shoulders and chest and I can't help but notice it. "I'm just telling you to stay away from Matt. I'm not sure why Marco chose him for the internship, but something about him bothers me."

I decide to be nice and smile at Devon. "Yeah, I was just thinking the same thing. Something about him makes me think danger. I can't put my finger on it, but I don't have good feelings about him."

Devon seems to accept my answer because he nods his head then walks off to talk to Kelby. She, Renee and I are all staying at the same hostel. I only talked to her for a second the other night at dinner, but it was enough for me to make up my mind about her. She's what I would consider a typical California girl. Her hair is long, blonde and wouldn't dare insult her by not lying just perfect. Her blue eyes are accented by long fake eyelashes and her tan cannot be from anything other than a bottle. Kelby told me she lives in Los Angeles and her dad is some record executive. I saw her camera this morning when we first got here and other than being about a ten thousand dollar one, I know my cameras and their prices, it looked brand new. I'm pretty sure I saw her taking a tag off the bag it comes in. I watch Devon walk over to her and place his hand on the small of her back. Of course, he would be interested in someone like her. I'm sure they make the perfect couple.

I mentally roll my eyes at myself. Why do I even care who Devon likes or spends time with? He is not my business. Besides, he's a jerk and I'm pretty sure he doesn't like me, and I know I don't like him. Uggg. If I don't like him then why is the sight of Kelby looking at him and laughing at something he just said driving me crazy and making me want to walk over and punch her in the throat?

"Are you okay, Twyla?" Conner sneaks up on me, scaring me half to death.

"Geez, Conner. Wear a cowbell or something so you don't give me a heart attack," I say clutching my chest. "I'm fine. Why do you ask?"

"Oh, it's nothing really. I just noticed you were wearing quite the murderous glare and staring straight at my brother and Kelby," he says with a knowing smirk on his face.

I decide to play this entire conversation off and act like it never happened. "So," I was so trying to change the subject. "Are you excited about our first day?"

Conner chuckles but decides to amuse me and lets me off the hook. "I am actually. The first day is always my favorite. It's when I get to know the most about the interns. How you handle your equipment, the different ways you'll move your body to get that one perfect shot."

Holy hotness. I grab my shirt at the collar and pull it away from my body that is suddenly sweaty. "How long have you been helping Marco with his interns," I clear my throat.

"This is my third year helping him. I had to go to school and intern myself before he'd even consider letting me help. He may love us like we're his own kids, but he takes his photography very seriously. We had to prove ourselves just like anyone else does."

"So, all three of you are photographers?"

"No, not really. I mean, we all do it, but Miles is the only one who does it professionally. I enjoy taking pictures, but I'm more into the developing and technical side of the business. Devon is the business mind behind it all. He makes sure we sell enough prints to allow us to keep going."

"Ahh, I see." I had no idea the three of them lived with Marco much less worked with him. Miles, I can see now that I'm thinking about it. His rugged looks and I-don't-give-a-care attitude is definitely one of an artist. "Will you be taking pictures with us today or just watching to see if we know how to turn our cameras on?"

Conner chuckles and I see the tips of his ears turn red. "Busted," he laughs out. "Today we just watch the three of you. We need to know where your weaknesses are so we can work more on those. We each have one intern to watch closely but all three of us will be watching over everyone."

"Let me guess, you got me?" I ask him.

"Actually, Princess," the haughty Scottish accent comes from behind me. "I'll be with you for the next three months."

My head falls forward, my chin hitting my chest. "Oh, that's just great," I murmur. Lifting my head back up I turn and come face to face once again with Devon. "So, I guess this means we'll be getting to know one another pretty well this summer," I say trying to break the tension between us.

"No, princess. It doesn't mean that" he bites out at me. "You just pay attention to taking pictures. That is the reason you're here isn't it? And try not to get in my way or piss me off."

"Damn," I say to Devon's retreating back.

"I told you to ignore him, Twyla. I'm sorry you have to deal with his moody ass. He just has a lot going on that he has to deal with and he's refusing to. It's beginning to take its toll on him."

"It's alright. I'll do what I came here to do and ignore him," I say this more for my benefit than I do for Conner's.

6

Twyla

"Not like that," Devon hisses at me. "You need to see what you want to capture before you just start hitting the shutter button. Taking a hundred shots does not guarantee you the perfect picture." He begins to shake his head at me. "Did they not teach you basic photography in whatever simpleton school you go to back in the US?"

"Hey!" I stand up from my crouching position and get in his face. "First of all, I don't go to a simpleton school. Second, I wasn't hitting the shutter button a hundred times. I only took three shots, you big jackass."

"Princess,"

I throw my hand up in his face, giving him the sign to stop speaking. "Don't call me that. I am nobody's princess."

"Twyla," he calls out after I start walking away from him, "Hey! Can you slow down for a second?"

"What, Devon? What exactly is your problem with me?" I'm not normally so in your face, but his attitude towards me has been bothering me since I first met him at Marco's dinner party.

"I don't have a problem with you."

"Bull hockey," I call him out. "You've had an issue with me since the first moment we met. It's like you looked at me and that was it. You had me pegged and judged before I even opened my mouth to speak."

Later I would look back on the words that came out of Devon's mouth as another pivotal moment in my life. One, that when I thought of them later down the road, I would realize exactly what he was saying. These words would come to define the two of us in every way.

"It's not you, Princess. It's me," he blows out a breath. "I know that sounds cliché but it's true. You are the last thing in the world that could ever be wrong. In fact, you may just be the one thing that actually is right."

I watch Devon walk away from me and movement catches my attention. Miles is standing off to the side of Matt watching the fleeting form of Devon walking back toward the van we rode out here in. His gaze shifts to me and he raises an eyebrow in question. I shrug my shoulders back, letting him know I have no idea what's going on. Something he said nags me. Why would I be the one right thing for him? What does he mean?

7

Devon

"What the hell is your problem, man?" Miles is on me the second we get back to the flat after spending all day with our interns.

"I don't have a problem," I tell him. "Just because I don't sit around all goo-goo over these wannabe photographers doesn't mean I have a problem."

"Wannabe's?" Conner snorts out. "Is that what we're calling them now?"

"You know what I mean," I spit out. "We all know the real reason he keeps bringing in these interns is for us to meet them. How many more times do we have to go through this?"

"None," Conner speaks up. "This is it. She's the one." My brother, not by blood but by circumstances, looks me straight in the eye. "You know she is, Dev. If you say she isn't you're lying to yourself and to us. I know you can feel it just as well as we can."

"Con," I begin to speak but he cuts me off.

"No. Don't say it, Dev. Why are you fighting this so hard? Your mom loved you, but her heart couldn't take going on without your dad. It sucks, but don't you see? Twyla has the three of us to lean on. If anything were to happen to one, there's still two to help see her through. You need to let go of the anger and those walls you've erected around your heart. She is the one, Dev and the sooner you come to terms with it, the faster we can live our lives."

"He's right," my other brother says. "Don't do this. Not to yourself and not to us," Miles pleads with me. "We can't do this without you, Dev. It's all of us or none of us." With those words he stands up and leaves the room, quietly closing the door to his bedroom behind him and shutting us out.

"You know he feels it stronger than we do. He's been waiting for her to come along twice as long as we have."

"I know," I sigh and rub the back of my neck. "I guess we better get ready. Midnight will be here before you know it."

"We don't have to do this much longer, Dev. If you would just admit it."

I cut Conner off. I don't need to hear it anymore. I already know what he's going to say. Of course, I can feel what they're feeling. I know Twyla is the one. She's ours. Our life, our future, our salvation from this curse. That isn't what's bothering me. "What if she rejects us, Con?" I finally voice my biggest concern. The thought of having everything we've ever dreamed of in the palm of our hands only to see it slip away, I don't know if I can do that. The doubt begins to creep in and it's too much for me to handle. "I'm going out," I tell my brother.

"Wait," his voice causes me to pause before I walk out the front door. "What about tonight? It's only an hour until midnight."

I let out a dry laugh. "It doesn't matter, Con. It finds us wherever we are. I'll make sure to be alone and hidden before the clock strikes. I've done this long enough to know how to not get caught."

"Just be careful, brother."

Nodding my head, I slip out the door and into the dark of the night.

8

Twyla

"That's better," Devon tells me as we start looking through the pictures I've taken over this week as we develop them in Marco's darkroom. The process of developing actual film has become a lost art. The digital age almost wiped out the need for such rooms. The smell of chemicals, the slow tedious process of dropping the negatives into the color developer and watching your art come to life, there is nothing like it. I could spend hours working in here, developing and manipulating my photographs by hand. Who needs a computer or some fancy equipment when you can do it the way Timothy O'Sullivan did?

"The focus is much better on this one," he holds up the one I took of a patch of wildflowers about two hours north of London. They were on the side of the road blowing in the breeze and when I saw them I had to capture the beauty of them. I yelled at the driver to stop the van and after he quit cursing me out for scaring him, he did stop, and I got my picture. "You did well considering the wind blowing that day. I don't think even Marco could have gotten a steady shot out there."

"Thanks," I beam up at him. "I think it's my favorite one so far."

"You just need to take a calming breath before you take this kind of shot. Take the time to really focus on the subject. Don't rush and never try to push it. If you do, they'll never come out good."

"Okay. I'll do that. Thank you, Devon."

"Dev," he says in a serious voice.

"I'm sorry?"

"My friends call me Dev."

"Okay then, Dev. I guess you can call me princess," I roll my eyes. I won't lie and say I enjoy being called princess, but there's something about hearing it out of Devon's mouth in his Scottish accent that has me accepting the fact that he will probably forever call me princess.

"We have tomorrow off, any idea what you're going to do with a full day to yourself?"

"Well," I draw out. "I need to do laundry and I thought I would visit Westminster Abbey."

"Why do want to visit an old cathedral?" Devon asks genuinely surprised.

I shrug my shoulders. "It's silly, really."

"I doubt that. Tell me, princess. What is it about old churches that make you want to visit them?"

"It's the gargoyles," I rush out. "I've been obsessed with them since I was a kid. My grandpa used to tell me stories about all the gargoyles he saw when he was over here during the war. He romanticized them so much that I couldn't get enough of them. Honestly," I lean in closer to Dev, so close I can smell the winter fresh gum he's chewing on. "One of the reasons I accepted Marco's offer of the internship was because of where it was and that all the places we're going to be visiting is full of gargoyle history and stories."

Devon doesn't say anything for a second. He just looks at me and blinks a few times very slowly. "Gargoyles?"

"Yes," I draw out. I swear if the man makes fun of my love for the stone statues I will kick him in his privates.

"You like gargoyles?" He blinks a few more times then throws his head back and laughs. He laughs so long and hard he has to bend over and I can hear him trying to catch his breath. Once he's gotten himself under control, he wipes his eyes and raises one eyebrow in my direction. "Of all the things for you to say, you being obsessed with gargoyles is the last thing I ever expected."

"Why is it so crazy to want to study them? They're fascinating and so is the history surrounding them."

"It's just," he shakes his head. "I don't know, it's just ironic I guess. Did you know that Con, Miles and I all study the stone statues, as you called them, as well?"

"Really?" I begin to bounce on my feet in excitement. "You're into the gargoyles and their history, too?"

"You could say we have a healthy fascination with them as well."

"Would you like to go with me tomorrow?" Mentally slapping myself, I add on to that question. "You can ask Miles and Conner to go with us. I mean, I completely understand if you don't want to. You've spent all week with me, and I imagine you must be tired of seeing my face," I flush in embarrassment.

"I would like that. I bet Con and Miles would enjoy going, too. It's been a long time since the three of us played tourist."

"So, it's a date," I say then slap a hand over my mouth. "I don't mean like a date-date. Just a get together for the day, date." I groan out loud. "You know what I mean."

"I know what you mean. Shall we pick you up from the hostel at ten?" Devon asks and unless I'm reading him wrong, he seems a little excited. "Let us take you to breakfast first and then we'll show you the gargoyles of the Abbey and then the ones that aren't so popular."

"I would really love that," I whisper. "Thank you, Dev."

"It's my pleasure, princess."

The next morning, I wait not so patiently on the steps of the hostel I'm staying at. Renee bounds down them, almost kicking me in her hurry. "Crap. Sorry, Twyla. I didn't see you there."

"I'm literally sitting in the middle of the steps, Renee," I tell her. "Where are you off to in such a hurry?"

"Oh," she lets out a high and annoying giggle while flipping her long brown hair over her slender shoulder. "Matt and I are going to get breakfast and play tourist today. He's taking me to the London Eye," she whispers behind her hand like her date is classified information.

"That's great," I lie to her. Spending any time with Matt is not great. There's just something about him that makes me shiver. The thought of creepy Matt is pushed aside when I see my three dates, I'm only calling them that in my head, walking down the street and in my direction. I jump up from where I'm perched on the steps and call out a goodbye to Renee over my shoulder. "Hey," I say to Conner, Miles, and Dev when I reach them.

"Twyla."

"Ty."

"Princess."

I roll my eyes at the last one. Dev knows the nickname princess gets on my nerves. I'm pretty sure that's why he keeps calling me that. "Well, are we ready? I'm starving."

"We can't keep princess waiting," Dev smirks at me. "The cafe is just up the street, a few more blocks."

"Sounds good to me," I throw my arm out, gesturing at Dev to lead the way.

It only takes us about ten minutes to reach the cafe they've chosen for breakfast. I can smell the aroma of freshly brewed coffee and the divine scent of pastries from outside. I can already tell I'm going to love it here.

Conner opens the door for me. "After you, ma'am."

"Thank you, kind sir," I bow as I cross the threshold and come face to face with the most beautiful thing I have ever seen. "Holy display case," I mumble under my breath. This thing is massive and filled with rows of pastries, bread, petit fours, muffins, and french bread. I discreetly wipe under my mouth to make sure I'm not drooling. The chuckle behind me tells me I was not successful in hiding what I was doing. "Don't judge," I tell them. "You're lucky I'm not laying across the display case already."

I take off toward the counter and I hear Miles behind me. "Maybe we should stick close to her while we're here. I don't want her getting sick attempting to eat everything they have in the cases."

"Too late!" I call out. I'm so ordering one of everything so I can stuff myself later." I wasn't kidding when I told them that. I plan on ordering enough for breakfast, a snack for later, lunch, another snack and dinner. If I'm good I can have something left over for breakfast again tomorrow. Then again, I'll do good to have any left over for an afternoon snack. Maybe I should get a few extra pastries just in case.

Thirty minutes later and I may be regretting my decision.

"Well, do you still feel like walking, princess?" Dev the butt-hole mocks me.

I sit back in my chair and pat my bakery belly. I ate so much I look four months pregnant. "I do, Devy," I laugh under my breath at the look on his face. I'm going to go out on a limb here and say he doesn't like to be called Devy. Good to know. "I'll be ready to go in a few minutes. I need to let my coffee settle."

"Uh-ha," Miles says softly. "I'm sure it was that tiny cup of coffee that got you."

"I'm sorry, Miles. Did you say something?"

"No love, I most definitely did not."

"That's what I thought," I tell him cheekily. "Alright, I'm ready to get going." I stand and stretch, my poor body. It's miserable but happy at the same time. "Onward and upward my tour guides."

"Princess," Dev growls at me. "If it were anybody else."

He lets the sentence die and I can't help but feel something from his words. "Chin up, buttercup," Conner says as he passes by me. "Let's get this show on the road."

For the next four hours, the guys showed me so many gargoyles I had to put in a new memory card just to hold all the pictures I've taken. We visited the Abbey first and then the real fun began. They showed me old churches and buildings off the beaten path in places not overrun with tourists. These were gargoyles I hadn't heard of before and I read and study them a lot. It was fun, exciting, and confusing. One minute Miles would be walking beside me, and he grabbed my hand, placing it in the crook of his arm. Next, it would be Conner walking with me, and he would grab my hand and intertwine our fingers together. Then there was Devon. He would touch me in little ways when he guided me through London. A hand at the small of my back, an arm draped across my shoulders, just small touches from each of them that made me pause and think. What are these guys up to? I'll admit I find all three of them insanely attractive and I seem to mesh well with all of them.

The day was perfect, and nothing went wrong in any way. There was no jealousy, no animosity or pettiness. When one was walking with me, the other two would hang back or walk ahead of us, leading us to whatever new building they wanted me to see next. It was amazing and again, so confusing. Do they have feelings for me? Am I reading them wrong? Maybe they just want to be friends and they all happen to be touchy-feely friends. I don't know and I decided on the walk back to my hostel not to dwell on it. I'm just going to do what I came here to do and not worry about anything else. I do like them but right now is not the time to think about any kind of relationship. Besides, there's three of them and only one of me. Last time I checked the ratio was all wrong there. Oh well, it's best not to think about this anymore. I only have a little more than two months left before I have to head back home. Which is across the big pond and a long way away from them.

Why does the thought of leaving them make my heart ache?
.

9

Twyla

I KNOCK on the apartment door and wait for one of the guys to answer. I was surprised when Miles found me this afternoon on my way back to the hostel and invited me over for dinner. The last few weeks have been unbelievable. Tomorrow we're leaving for Ireland and I can't wait to mark visiting the beautiful country off my bucket list. Aside from the amazing pictures I've been able to capture, I've had a nagging feeling that something is wrong with Devon. He's been pulling away from me lately and I don't know why. I'm hoping tonight to get an answer. Maybe I did something to offend him without realizing it.

The door to the guy's apartment swings open and I come face to face with my favorite cowboy, Conner. "Um, hey Ty."

"Conner." Something is up with the cowboy. For someone who supposedly agreed to invite me over for dinner, he seems very upset to see me here. "I'm sorry. Miles asked me over and told me it was cool with you and Devon. I can go if there's a problem," I ask hesitantly. I really don't want to go. I want to see them, spend time with them and figure out what the heck is going on to make Devon and now Conner seem leery to be with me.

"No!" Conner practically shouts at me. "I mean," he says much softer, "of course it's fine with us. I've been out grabbing supplies for the trip tomorrow and I guess I just forgot and lost track of time." Conner steps back to allow me inside the door, but before I can walk through, he grabs my hand. "Look, Ty," he runs the back of his neck and I see a tick in his jaw. "Please, just . . ."

"Spit it out, Conner. If I need to go, I promise it's alright. Just say whatever you need to." My hands are getting clammy and something in my gut tells me whatever words that are about to come from Conner's mouth will somehow change everything.

"Devon has a date tonight," he rushes out.

"Wow, okay. I wasn't expecting that, but I mean," I stumble over my words, not sure what I'm supposed to say. My relationship with Devon isn't romantic. Do I wish it was? Yes. Do I feel guilty about wanting that because I also have feelings for his best friends Miles and Conner? Oh yeah. It's ironic, isn't it? Here I am feeling guilty for wanting three guys and one of them is trying to protect my feelings when another one of them has a girl over. I do not deserve this man in front of me. "It's fine, Conner. It isn't like he and I are dating." I laugh but it sounds off and I pray Conner doesn't hear it as well.

"Alright, Ty," he gestures for me to enter the apartment. Sure enough, Devon is sitting on their brown leather couch with a girl tucked extremely close to him.

"Devon," I plaster the biggest, fakest smile I can on my face. "It's good to see you." Walking toward the couch I stretch out my hand and put on an even faker smile for the bimbo practically sitting in his lap. "Hi, my name is Twyla. It's nice to meet you."

"Lauri, with an i," she says in a very snotty British accent. Lauri, with an i, gives me one of those horrible limp handshakes and I try not to grimace. "How do you know Devon?" She purrs out his name while running a hand along his inner thigh.

"Twyla is one of Marco's interns for the summer," he answers her. I take note he left off the fact that he is actually my mentor, but I'm trying not to be petty here.

"Oh, of course. That makes sense why you would be here of all places. Are you picking up some film or something" Lauri, with an i, asks me. Is correct this isn't a question

"Actually," Conner chooses that moment to walk back into the living room, smiling at me as soon as he gets near.

"She's picking up supplies for tomorrow," Devon cuts him off. "If you'll excuse me, Lauri, I need to show her where I put the bag." Devon taps her on the knee, and she scoots over maybe an inch. He stands then tilts his head in the direction of the kitchen and I, like the idiot that I am, follow him.

"What is it, Devon? If you didn't want me here tonight, you should have told Miles. He said all of you were asking me to dinner," I cross my arms over my chest, nearly panting I'm so mad. Not only does he have a date, but he lied to her and said I was here for a phony job. I understand I have no logical reason to be angry about him having another girl over but tell that to my heart. For some reason, the harlot seems to think all three of them are mine.

"It's fine if you're here, Twyla," I wince at him using my name, not princess, and he sees it. Devon runs both hands through his thick hair, tugging on the ends. "It's better this way. I know it may not seem like it, but it will be better for all four of us if you and I keep our distance."

"I don't understand what you're saying, Devon. Just spell it out for me. If you don't want to be my friend, then whatever. I can't force myself on you or anyone else. If you want me to ask one of the other interns to switch so you don't have to mentor me then just say something. I don't need you to help me because you feel like you have to. I'm nobody's damn charity case, Devon." Turning on my heel, I march out the door to the kitchen and head straight to the one that will get me out of here.

"Princess."

I throw my hand up to stop him. "No. Don't ever call me that again," I snap at him. "It was nice to meet you, Lauri, with an i," I tell her before throwing the door open and storming out. I temporarily forget that I'm an adult and slam their stupid door to their stupid apartment behind me. "Stupid, dumb, jackass of a man."

"Twyla?" Miles calls out when I pass him in the hall. "What's going on? I thought you were coming over for dinner tonight.

I take in the arm full of brown paper grocery sacks and for the first time, tonight give a genuine smile. "Hey, Miles. Look, it's not really a good night for me and Devon already has company over so I'm just going to go back to the hostel. I need to finish packing anyway," I lie to him and I know he can see straight through it.

"Did you say Devon has a date upstairs?"

I take it by the angry tone of his voice that he was unaware of this development. "Yeah, he does. Lauri, with an i," I say with a snarl. Miles shakes his head. "It's really okay, Miles. He told me it was better if we stayed away from each other anyway. I was thinking of asking Matt if he would trade and let me work with Marco for a bit."

"Ty," he groans out my name.

I gesture to the bags in his arms. "I'll let you get upstairs. Those bags are looking heavy to me and I'm sure the guys and Lauri are getting hungry by now." I lean past the bags and place a tender kiss on Miles cheek. Closing my eyes, I pull back the tears that want to fall. "I'll see you later," I choke out.

I don't look back. Instead, I keep walking, determined to not let him or any of them see me cry.

This moment would come back to haunt me for the next month.

10

Miles

"Are you serious?" I yell after I throw open the door. The bags are all but forgotten downstairs at the base of the stairs where I dropped them after I watched Twyla run from our building like it was on fire. I know what Devon did tonight upset her. I could see the tears forming in her eyes and heard it in her voice. My brother better have a damn good explanation for the stunt he pulled on her tonight. "What were you thinking, Dev? And you," I point a finger to Lauri, our very gay next-door neighbor. Why would you be over here helping this dumb ass?"

"Don't be rude to Lauri," Devon barks out. "It wasn't her fault. She was only doing what I asked. Lauri," Devon turns to our good friend. We met her four years ago when we moved into this apartment. We've been there for her through countless breakups and I may have even gone on a few tampon runs for her. She's the sweetest person I know, besides Twyla that is, and I know if she agreed to do something like this then Dev told her one hell of a story. "Thank you for helping tonight," he tells her. "I really do appreciate it."

I move over so Dev can lead Lauri out of our door and over

to hers. "Devon, is that girl going to be okay? She seemed pretty upset when she left."

I feel my blood pressure getting higher. There's no telling what all my brother did to put her in the state I found her in downstairs.

"Yeah," he answers Lauri. "Everything is fine. Thank you again for helping me out."

"Anytime. You boys have a good night and I'll see you later.

I close the door behind her retreating back then turn my head toward Dev, shooting daggers at him. "You better start from the beginning and tell me just what the bloody hell you were thinking tonight."

Devon sighs and I know I'm not going to like what he's about to say. "Miles, man, it's not going to work."

"What do you mean? We've already been over this. She's the one, Dev. What more can we say to make you accept this? Is it her? Do you not want Twyla?"

"No!" He shouts, jumping up off the couch. "Of course I want her. She's everything to me."

"I don't understand," Conner joins in the conversation. "If she means that much to you, then why are you doing your best to push her away from you?"

"And from us," I add on.

"I can't risk it. Not only are we asking her to agree to be with all three of us, but we're asking her to be with monsters."

"We. Are. Not. Monsters," I bite out. "How many times must we have this discussion? We can't help what we are, Dev. You know as well as I do, once we find her, and we have," I remind him for the hundredth time, "once we come together, the curse will be over. I thought that was what you wanted."

"I do, but at what expense? What if we do mate with her and after she finds out what we are, she runs? I don't think I could handle that, guys," he plops down on the couch, a look of utter defeat on his face. "I would rather live like this than watch her run away from me. I just can't. Please understand," he begs us.

I have never seen my brother so broken. He's the strong one of us. The one that everybody looks at and sees so put together. Some may think he's arrogant, but he is so far from that. What they see is just a shield hiding him and his vulnerability from the rest of the world. Only when it's just the three of us will he allow that side of him to be seen. I have a feeling that Twyla was getting too close to breaking down his walls and it's scared him.

"Dev," Conner sits down next to him on the couch. "You don't know how she's going to take it. She has feelings for us. I can sense it and so can you if you'd just open up to it. It will stun her, but something tells me that girl would never run away from us like that."

"She did tonight."

"Really?" I ask Dev. "You're using tonight as an excuse now? You had Lauri almost laying on top of you. Of course, she is going to get upset. Then you tell her it's best if you stay away from each other? How was she supposed to take it, Dev? She's our soulmate and you just treated her like she was a pizza delivery girl. Like she meant nothing to you!" By the time I'm done talking my chest is rising and falling so fast I put a hand to my heart to make sure it hasn't jumped out.

"You told her what?" Conner jumps up and begins to pace. "How could you, man? It's one thing if you want to take it slow, but to tell her you need to stay away from each other? You're pretty much telling her to stay away from all of us and I'm not going to risk losing her because you're being a complete douche!" Conner stops pacing, looks at Devon and I watch as grey stone skin begins to ripple down his arms. It's true that until we find our true mates, we'll turn into stone each night at midnight. The other truth is that anger, or any strong emotion, can also bring forth the change. Unlike other shifters, gargoyles don't just shift back and forth. Our makeup isn't like wolves or bears. We aren't animal shifters, we're protectors and were made to protect at night when most of the havoc occurs.

"Conner," I place a hand on his arm, "I need you to calm down, brother. You don't want to turn right now."

Conner takes a deep breath and slowly exhales. "You're right. I'm going to go to my room for a while. I'll see you at midnight," he tells us over his shoulder as he walks back out of the living room.

"Dev, you can't keep on like this. One, it isn't healthy and two, you're destroying us. I won't let you push her away. I'm scared too, but what's worse? Risking everything or never even trying? She may not bat an eye at what we are, but you won't even give her a chance. I can't keep letting you sabotage my and Conner's future. You either need to get on board or we're going to have to separate ourselves from you."

"You would leave me?" he asks in a shocked voice.

"I don't want to, but this is my future we're talking about. I'll do anything for her, and you know as well as I do that we are what's good for her. We're supposed to be her everything just like she's ours. Think about it, man. Just don't wait too long. We only have six weeks left before she leaves us for good and we deserve a fighting chance before that happens."

11

Twyla

I DIDN'T GET any sleep last night. Besides the conversation with Devon running through my mind over and over again, Kelby had company and our rooms are next door to each other. The walls are paper thin, and I could tell by the sounds coming from her room that she was having a great night. Much better than mine. Of course, listening to that and thinking about Devon, Conner and Miles made it even harder to get to sleep. After I decided to stop obsessing about Devon's words, I immediately started thinking of all three of them. Of being with all three of them. How would it be? Would they even entertain such an idea? I dismissed it. Of course, three handsome men wouldn't go for something like that. At least not anything longer than a one-night stand just for the fun of it.

"Ty!" I turn to find Miles running toward me from where he was standing near the van. "Hey," he leans over and kisses the side of my cheek. "I'm glad to see you. I wanted to talk about what happened last night."

"It's okay, Miles. You didn't do anything wrong. Neither did Devon. If that's how he feels then I need to respect his wishes and keep my distance. Really, I understand. I won't push myself on anyone."

"You aren't pushing yourself on me," the Scottish accent that has haunted several of my dreams says from behind my back.

I turn and come face to face with Devon. I mentally roll my eyes and prepare for whatever bull he's about to throw in my direction today. "What can I do for you, Devon?" I ask him coolly. I don't ever want this man, or any man to think I'll stand there and take him telling me to go away one day and acting like nothing happened the next. He made his bed, now he needs to lie in it.

"I wanted to apologize to you, Princess."

"I told you to never call me that again," I remind him.

I feel Miles step up closer to my back and place his hand on my shoulder. I don't know if it's for support or to hold me back in case I decide to take out his best friend. "Devon," Miles breathes into my ear. "Why don't we do this later? We have a long trip ahead of us. You can talk in the van or better yet, once we get to the hotel."

"Actually," Devon smirks at me. "Princess, you sit by me. We need to review a few problem areas you're having before we get there. We don't want to waste the small amount of time we have there working out kinks that we can fix beforehand."

"Well, I was going to talk to Matt about switching. You can work with him and I'll work with Marco from now on."

Devon lets out a low growl and I watch him clench and unclench his fists. "No," he says through his teeth. "You aren't switching with Matt."

"But, Devon, last night . . ."

"I know what I said last night, and I was wrong. Just give me this trip to talk to you. When we get to Ireland, if you don't want me to mentor you anymore then I'll talk to Marco myself. Deal?" He holds out his hand.

I look at him shrewdly. I don't trust this man right now, but I really don't want to stop working with him. I've learned so much and not counting last night, I've enjoyed our time together. "Fine," I concede. "You have until we get to Ireland."

"I accept that." Devon looks over my shoulder. "Miles? Are we okay now? I promise not to piss her off or make her run away again."

Miles lets out a huff and I feel him nodding his head. I try to turn around to see just how close he is to me, but his nose stops my movement. I guess he's very close. "Ty," he runs his nose down mine. "Are you sure you're alright spending the next nine hours sitting next to him? You don't have to if you don't want to. I understand if you say no."

I suck in a breath and try not to let Miles see how his touch is affecting me. "I'll be okay," I say with a voice that sounds too low to belong to me.

"I promise to be good," Devon says from behind me.

I shake myself out of the daze Miles has put me in and step out from between them. "Devon? You ready to get our seats?"

He grabs my hand, locking our fingers, and leads me onto the van and to the last row of seats. "After you," he moves aside so I can get in first.

Once I'm seated, I turn my head to look Devon in the eyes. "Alright, Devon," I give him my no-nonsense look. "Say what you need to say, but I doubt anything will change what happened last night. You made it clear you wanted to stay away from me. Explain what changed and why I should care."

12

Devon

She isn't going to let me off easy and I fall for her a little more because of it. I knew the vocal vomit spewing from my mouth last night was rubbish. The truth is, I wasn't ready to face the idea of not having her in our lives. I know my brothers speak the truth. She is ours and I will do anything to make it happen. I didn't just have an ah-ha moment last night. This came on gradually. It was all I could think of and when you're a statue, stuck in the same position for seven hours each night, you have a lot of time to think and plan. Which is exactly what I did.

"Look, Princess," she puts her hand up to stop me, but I ignore it and keep on talking. "I know I came across as a jerk, but I only want you to be happy and safe." I let out a puff of air and look her in the eyes. I want, no I need her to see the truth. I need her to know that she is all I think about; all I dream of when I'm still as stone each and every night. She has to understand what she means to me, to us. I have to fight for her. It may not be the biggest or bloodiest battle of my two hundred years, but it will be the most important one.

"Devon? Are you okay? I seemed to have lost you there for a moment."

"Lauri is our next-door neighbor and she doesn't like dick."

Twyla leans back on the bench seat, moving a little further back from me. "I'm sorry, but what did you just say?" She looks at me like I have lost my mind and I'm beginning to believe I have.

"Lauri is our neighbor," I say slowly. "She's gay." I mentally slap myself across the face. "I asked her to come by last night. I may have told her you were into me and I needed her help to make you go away," I wince at the hurt look on Twyla's face. "I'm so sorry, Princess. It was stupid but I did it for a good reason."

"A good reason?" she asks me. "Devon, you told me last night you wanted me to stay away from you and yet here you are this morning apologizing. One minute you push me away, the next you're trying to pull me back in. My feelings are not a game of yo-yo for you to play with. You hurt me last night and you aren't making me feel any better today. Honestly, I'm over all of this and I need you to go away. Thank you for trying to explain it to me, but you need to go find another place to sit. I don't think I can be around you anymore."

Damn it. I knew I was going to screw this up. Most of the time I come across as strong, resilient, impenetrable by the meaningless emotions people have, but not around her. She makes me feel like a weakling and it terrifies me. I don't like being vulnerable to others and she has stripped away every defense mechanism I have. "Princess," I start but this time she does stop me.

Twyla places her hand across my mouth and shakes her head. "Please," she begs me.

"I can't do this anymore. Please don't play with my heart, Devon. Its had all it can take right now."

The look on her face, it's gutting me and I damn myself for ever putting it there in the first place. I place my hand on top of the one she still has over my mouth. I slowly slide her hand away and place it on my leg. If she won't listen to the words coming out of my mouth, maybe she'll be able to feel the truth in my actions. I keep my gaze locked onto hers, looking for any sign that she wants me to stop. I carefully lean in and run my nose down the slender column of her throat. Today her long blonde hair is up in a bun, giving me full access to her. I close my eyes and inhale deeply, taking time to appreciate her natural scent. Twyla smells like fresh flowers in the countryside. When I need to get away from everything, I always find myself in the country, surrounding myself with fields of fresh flowers. The aroma is so light and pure. She reminds me of my happy place. I open my eyes and pull back, still waiting for her to tell me to stop. When she doesn't, I lean in again but this time I cover her lips with mine. She doesn't do anything, but when I move my lips, using them to capture her upper one, her breath catches and I take the opportunity to push my tongue inside her mouth.

I keep my eyes open now and watch her. Hers are shut so tight she has creases at the corners. I continue to explore her mouth with my tongue when she finally lets go and begins to kiss me back. Our first kiss goes from something sweet and beautiful to a full-on tongue war with teeth gnashing, moans vibrating from the back of my throat, and my hair being pulled by my princess. It's raw, it's powerful, it's everything I never had the courage to dream for. A throat being cleared breaks the spell over us and I reluctantly pull back, but I steal one last kiss before retreating completely.

"Devon, I don't know what to say," she whispers. Her eyes are so big, and her chest is pounding right now. I bring my arm up and pull her closer to me, leaving it to lay across her shoulders.

"Say you'll forgive me, that you will give me one more chance to prove that I'm not a total jerk."

"Devon," she sighs out. Shaking her head back and forth she

lets out a low moan. "I don't know. I mean, uggg. I don't even know what you're looking for. I go home in six weeks. It's not like I can just drive for a visit. Besides, there's Miles and Conner."

I watch her shut down as soon as my brother's names leave her lips. What does she mean there is Miles and Conner? Does she have feelings for them as well? "Princess, what do you mean when you say there is Miles and Conner? Is there something you need to tell me?" I try to come across as nonchalant but inside I'm praying for her to tell me she feels something for all three of us.

"Dev," she rolls her eyes and laughs to herself. I see her lips moving but no sound comes out. I'm about to ask her to repeat what she just whispered but she speaks up. "I find all three of you attractive and, without meaning to even though I kept telling myself I was an idiot, I have developed feelings for the three of you." She pulls her shoulders up around her ears like she's trying to hide.

"Oh, Princess." Taking her face between my hands, I pull her to me and kiss the hell out of her. I can guarantee that she has never been kissed with as much passion or desire as I'm giving her right now. I pull my mouth back and growl. "Ours," I say forcefully. I want her to understand what I'm telling her. "You are ours, Princess."

"What?" Her brain hasn't caught up with my words yet. "What did you just say?"

"I said, you are ours, Princess," I punctuate each word with a swift kiss on her now swollen lips. "Tell me you'll try with us. The three of us all have feelings for you."

"Whoa," she sticks her hand up in the air, again. This must be a favorite move of hers. "All three of you?"

I nod my head. "Yes, me, Miles, and Conner."

"Devon," she whispers loudly to my face. "I can't be in a relationship with three men. First off, it's not right and second,

I already told you, I'm going home in six weeks. I don't think I could start something knowing that it will just end. And thirdly, one woman with three guys," she shrugs her shoulders. "It's not right."

"You said that twice," I point out. I pull my arm back from around her shoulders and use it to wrap both her small hands up in my much larger ones. "Why is it so wrong, Princess? Who says you have to live by traditional standards? The poly world is growing every day. People understand that love comes in all shapes, sizes, colors, and numbers. Take a chance on us. You said yourself, you have six weeks. Get to know us and at the end, we can reevaluate what's going on between us."

I know it's a gamble, but I need her to at least try. There is no way I or my brothers are letting this woman get on a plane and fly out of our lives. I don't want to scare her off by telling her this, Miles would never forgive me for that, but I need her to at least agree to try being with us.

"I just don't know, Dev," she pulls one of her hands free and rubs her forehead. "I'm getting a headache from the lack of sleep I had last night and all of this today. Can we talk about this a little later?"

I take the time to study her face a little more closely. I can see the dark shading under her eyes. I can't believe I missed the tired look on her face. "Of course, Princess." I lean back into my seat, remove one of my hands and put it back around her shoulders. "Lay your head on my shoulder and get some rest. I'll wake you when we get to the ferry."

"Ferry?"

"We have to take a ferry boat across the Irish Sea to get to Ireland."

"Huh," she yawns so big I can see the back of her throat. "That makes sense."

I sit and hold her as she quietly falls asleep. I look up to see both Miles and Conner watching us, both with knowing smiles on their faces. I lift my chin and look back down at Twyla. I pray to anyone listening that she agrees to give us a chance and when she finds out what the three of us are, she doesn't run from us. If anyone can handle being in a relationship with a few century-old gargoyles, I believe in my heart it's the woman in my arms.

13

Twyla

"Wake up, Princess," someone begins to shake me awake. "We're at the ferry. You don't want to miss the boat ride across the Irish Sea."

Yawning, I lift my head and smile shyly at Devon. His kisses are still fresh on my mind. I lift a hand up to feel my lips, sure that they are still swollen. I turn my head to look out the van's window and gasp in awe at the sight in front of us. The water is so blue and clear I wonder if we'll be able to see all the way to the floor of the sea. It's so beautiful and magical I almost expect to see a mermaid pop up to greet us any moment.

"Once we board the ferry, we can get out if you would like to take a few pictures."

I try not to bounce in my seat, but I just can't help it. "Please!" I wince and lower my voice. "That would be amazing, Dev. If you're sure it's alright?"

"Of course it is. Although, you don't want to get too close to the side of the ferry. I would hate for you to get wet or drop your camera overboard."

"Oh, good point. Let me grab my bag with my smaller

camera in it. It's a lot lighter and should be easier to use on this."

I reach under our bench and pull out the smaller camera case. Opening it, I begin to put on a longer lens and double check that my film is inside. I grab another roll, just in case, and shove it down my pocket. I put the camera's cord around my neck and get ready to exit the van.

"Not yet, Princess. We have to wait on all the cars to load and the ferry to take off before we can get out and move around," he tells me.

I sit back down in my seat, not even realizing I had stood up and attempt to be patient. About ten minutes later we get the all clear and everyone shuffles off the van. Conner and Miles are waiting for Dev and me when we finally exit. "So," Conner smirks at me. "Did you have a fun time on the drive up?"

I laugh at him and continue walking toward the side of the ferry. Once I get there I climb onto the bench and sit on my knees so I can get a better look at the sea underneath us. I pull my camera up to my face and the sound of my finger steadily hitting the shutter button begins. I don't know how long I take pictures of the sea, the sky, out in the distance before I'm being jostled by someone sitting down next to me. I look over expecting one of the guys when I see Matt.

"Twyla," he sneers at me. "Trying to get some more attention today?"

I roll my eyes and look back at the Irish Sea. "What do you want, Matt? I don't have time to deal with you and your level of crazy."

"Crazy?" he snorts out. "You were in the back of the van making out with one guy while two others were practically jerking off watching the two of you. What exactly is going on with you and Marco's stone brothers?"

"Huh?" I turn to face Matt and over his shoulder I see Miles racing toward us. "I have no idea what you're talking about,

Matt. Why don't you scurry on now? I have better things to do than listen to you go on about nonsense."

"It's not nonsense," he bites out. "Ask your little boy toys what it means? I think you of all people should be interested to know who, or what, they really are."

"Ty, is everything okay?" Miles rushes out when he gets to us.

"Yeah, it's fine. Matt was just leaving, weren't you, Matt?"

"Sure," he says as he gets to his feet. "Don't forget what I said, Ty," he draws out my nickname from Miles. "Let's see what you think after you learn the truth."

Miles watches Matt walk away then looks to me with a raised brow. "What was he talking about?"

"I honestly have no idea," I tell him. The truth is I really don't know, but I want to. Now isn't the best time to ask them about Matt's accusations, but tomorrow we have the day off to rest. Marco has a meeting with some famous photographer, and he wants us to wait for him before we go exploring Ireland. I plan on sitting the three of them down and asking them a few things. Like, what did Devon mean when he said I was theirs? What is Matt talking about? What is a stone brother?

"Earth to Ty," Miles waves his hand in my face to get my attention. "You sure you're alright?"

"Yeah, I guess I'm not completely rested. I plan on going straight to bed when we get to Dublin."

"If you say so. Come on," he takes my hand and helps me off the bench. "There's a machine a little further up here. Let me buy you a coke or something."

"That actually sounds so good right now. I could use some caffeine."

"Well then, m'lady," he bows at me. "Let me lead the way."

Laughing, I follow Miles and we find Conner and Dev at the drink machines. "Hey, guys. What are y'all up to?"

"Conner here doesn't have sea legs so I'm here in case he needs to get sick over the side of the ferry."

"Oh, Conner. Do you need anything? Maybe a cold, wet paper towel?"

"Nah, pretty girl," he reaches up and tugs on a wayward strand of my hair. "I'll be fine in a little bit. We don't have many ferries in Texas and we rarely come with Marco when he has to visit Ireland. I'm a land boy through and through."

"Try some Sprite. It should help settle your tummy," I lean over and kiss him on his cheek. "I hope you feel better."

"I already do, pretty girl."

"There's the horn telling us to get back in our vehicles," Dev explains to me.

I grab one of Conner's hands and help him walk back to the van. He wasn't kidding about not having sea legs. It isn't choppy, but you can feel the waves. Every time a bigger one hits, he moans and turns a little greener. I'm beginning to second guess our decision about putting him back in the van. "He'll be fine," Miles whispers in my ear. "Once we get him in the van, he can lay down on one of the bench seats. You'll see."

I nod my head but don't voice my disbelief. Once we're in the van I help Conner sit down and before I can leave, he's grabbing my hand back in his. "Sit with me?"

"How can I say no to that pitiful face of yours?" I joke with him.

I sit on the outside, close to the aisle and Conner by the window. "Do you mind if I lay my head in your lap? I do better lying down."

"Of course." I scoot over as far as I can without falling off the seat and he folds his long body in half, his legs stretched out on the floor and his head in my lap. I can't help but run my fingers through his hair. It's something my momma would always do when we weren't feeling good. "Are you sure you're okay like this?"

"I'm more than okay," he hums at me. "Thank you, pretty girl."

"Not you too," I complain. "What is it with the three of you and nicknames?"

"Sorry, not sorry. You'll just have to get used to it."

"Conner?"

"Yeah, pretty girl?"

"Do you think the four of us, me, you, Dev and Miles could take a walk or something tomorrow? I have a few questions I need to ask and something Dev and I talked about that we need to all discuss."

"Anything you want. Just tell Miles once we get to Dublin. He's the one that keeps up with everything, so we don't mess up and forget where we are."

"What do you mean?" I ask a very sleepy Conner. I'm beginning to wonder if Miles or Devon slipped him one of those nausea pills that makes you drowsy.

"We can't forget where we are at midnight. It would be bad to change out in the open. Scary stuff," he shudders.

I sit back, letting Conner fall asleep without any more questions from me. I'll add this conversation to my list of things to ask the guys about.

14

Twyla

THE HOTEL we are staying at in Dublin is better than any hotel I've ever been to. The rooms are spacious, with maroon carpets, beige walls with heavy tartan curtains and matching bedspreads, a television and a small sitting area with two green wingback chairs. The only problem is I'm sharing a room with both Kelby and Renee.

"Ugh," Renee complains again. Nothing in this room is good enough for her. "The towels are so thin. They're not going to dry us off at all. And look at this bedspread. Have you seen anything so atrocious?"

I drop my suitcase down by one of the beds, kick off my flip flops and sit back. It isn't long before I hear her again, only this time she's talking to me.

"Twyla? Are you listening to me?"

I am in fact trying to ignore her, but my momma would beat me for being rude. "I'm sorry, Renee. What were you saying?"

"I asked," she draws out the word, "if you'd mind sharing a bed with Kelby? I just can't sleep next to anyone."

"It didn't sound that way last night at the hostel," I laughed out. "It sounded like you did, and you enjoyed it very much."

"Really?" Renee looks at me like she could kill me. Flipping her hair over her shoulder, she looks down her nose at me. "I guess you are perfect, Miss 'I got it on in the back of a van while everyone was watching me with absolutely no care in the world.' I mean, really, Twyla. Have a little respect for yourself."

"Screw you, Renee. If you want to sleep alone, there are two chairs and a floor. Pick one." I get off the bed, slip back into my flip flops and head out the door. When we got our room assignments the guys walked up with me and when I went into this room, they entered one two doors down and across the hall. I find their door, knock on it and stand back to wait on one of them to open up.

"Hey, pretty girl," Conner answers wearing nothing but a pair of black basketball shorts. I secretly wipe under my mouth before looking back up at his face. "See something you like, pretty girl?" He says in a lower tone than I've ever heard.

I clear my throat. "Renee is being a bitch. Can I hang out in here for a bit?" I look into Conner's eyes and give him my best sad puppy dog look.

"Of course," he says and steps out of the way, allowing me in. "Miles is laying down watching television and Dev is in the shower."

My feet stop at the thought of Dev in the shower and I want to burst in the bathroom and take a peek.

"Hey, Ty," Miles calls out.

My feet stop when I see him. He is indeed laying on the bed and like Conner, he's not wearing anything above the waist. Miles is wearing a pair of worn out plaid pajama pants and holy moly. Both of their chests are perfect. Conner has less definition than Miles, but both have a small patch of hair that runs from their navel to the promised land and both of them are sporting the coveted 'V'. Conner walks past me and jumps onto the bed not currently being used by Miles so I turn to look at the same green wingback chairs we have in our room.

"Come on, pretty girl," Conner says patting the bed. "You can sit by me. I promise not to bite."

"Unless she wants us to," I hear Miles mutter under his breath as I walk past him.

I climb into the bed and sit up with my back against the headboard. "So," Miles looks over to me. "What brings you to our room? Not that we aren't happy to see you, but you look a little flustered."

I wave my hand like I'm swatting a bug. A Renee sized bug. "It's just Renee. Now she doesn't want to share a bed because she can't sleep with anyone. I simply pointed out that she had no problem last night at the hostel."

"No, you didn't!" Conner laughs so hard our bed shakes. "Girl give a high five. That is the funniest thing I've heard in forever."

I try to give Conner a high five, but I can't stop laughing long enough to make contact, instead I slap him on his chest. When my hand lands on him, I immediately sober up and look into Conner's face. The heated look he gives me takes my breath away. "Conner," I start to speak but the bathroom door being flung open stops me.

"God, I feel so much bloody better now. I swear I could still smell that funky van smell on me."

My mouth must have dropped open because I feel a pair of fingers gently lift my bottom lip. "You might want to wipe the drool off," Conner whispers while chuckling next to me.

"Shut up, Conner," I whisper back.

I look out of the side of my eye to make sure no one is watching, and I do wipe under my mouth. Devon Taylor is completely naked. As in, he has no clothes on. Not a single stitch and oh my sweet baby Jesus is it a glorious sight.

"Ahem."

I snap my head up from looking very slowly at Dev when I hear him.

"Princess," he purrs. Dev lifts both arms and places a fist on both sides of his hips, calling attention to himself. "Is there something I can do for you?"

I almost scream out yes, but then I remember that I am not a hussy. No matter what my hoo-ha says, I am not the kind of girl to mess around with a different guy every day. "No," I croak out. Clearing my throat, I try that again. "No," I say a little stronger. "I was just telling Miles and Conner about Renee being a butt and I needed to get away from her for a little bit. I can go so you can get dressed," my eyes begin to roam up and down his body again.

"It's not necessary," Dev tells me. "Conner told us you had a few questions and why wait until tomorrow when we can discuss one of those right now."

Holy hotness. "Okay. Yeah, sure." My brain just left the building.

Unfortunately, he walks over and begins to dig in his suitcase, coming up with a pair of heather grey cotton shorts. I watch as he slowly steps into them, sans underwear. When he raises up, I see that the shorts do nothing to hide what he has inside of them.

"So," Miles breaks my perving of Dev. "You wanted to talk to us? I'm going to assume it has something to do with Dev growling out that you are ours on the drive here."

I feel the blush covering my face. "Well, yes," I look down at my lap. "I'm confused and I wanted to know what he was talking about." I lift my eyes and see all three guys attention is solely on me. "I mean, we don't have to," I rush to say. "I could have misunderstood him or whatever. In fact, I should probably just get going." I go to stand when a pair of arms wrap around me from behind.

"Stay," Conner says over my shoulder. "We want to discuss this with you."

"Dev told us you thought the idea of being with all three of us was wrong," Miles says. I turn my head in his direction. "Who says it's wrong, Ty? We have feelings for you. Do you have them for us?"

I look to each of them and decide I won't lie to them. "Yes," I say. "I feel awful, but I can't help it. I tried not to; I swear I did."

"Hey," Devon climbs onto the bed and sits beside me. "Never feel bad about how you feel, especially when it comes to us. We understand."

"You do?"

"Yes, Princess, we do."

"So, what do we do then? I can't date all of you and I can't choose, I don't want to lose you as friends so tell me what I can do to fix this."

"Fix what?" Miles asks. "I'm confused." He sits up and twists his body so he's facing me, Devon and Conner. "Do you want us, Ty?"

"Yes."

"We want you, too," Conner says from behind me.

I twist around so I can look at him over my shoulder. "You do?"

"Princess, didn't I already tell you? You are ours," he growls at me again. "Now, I need to hear you say it."

"Say it?" My brain is officially mush right now.

"Say yes, Princess. Tell us yes and stay the night with us."

"Yes," I nod my head. "Hell yes."

"Thank bloody hell," Miles says as he jumps forward and grabs me under my arms, pulling me to his bed. "I never thought you'd agree but gah, I am so happy."

I want to agree but my mouth becomes occupied with Miles' tongue. I thought Devon's kiss would undo me but this one. Don't get me wrong, Dev can kiss like the angels sing, but Miles? There's something extra about his that takes me to an entirely new universe.

Miles pulls away and begins to run his lips down my neck.

A pair of hands reach around me and begin tugging my shirt up. Miles releases me so whoever it is can bring it over my head. Once it's gone, the same hands release the hooks on my bra, and it's flung somewhere across the room.

"Damn," Miles takes his time looking me over. "You are absolutely perfect." He finishes his sentence with a thrust of his hips, and I groan. "Someone better move her fast before I lose control," he bites out.

I whimper when I'm lifted off Miles but before I can protest another pair of lips take his place. This time I find myself sitting sideways on Conner's lap, his mouth nipping at mine. "Open up for me, baby." I do as instructed and sweet Mary and Joseph. He latches onto my tongue and begins to suck on it. I almost shoot off the bed from the sensation.

While Conner is working on my mouth, I feel a pair of teeth softly biting my right breast. Ripping my mouth away I look down and see Dev peering up at me. With a wink, he starts lapping at my nipple and I lean my head back and let out a throaty moan. "Those noises of hers are killing me," Miles groans. "Dev," he says, and I watch him adjust himself in his shorts. "Take her pants off, brother."

Devon obeys his brother and in the next moment my yoga pants and panties are flying through the air. I start to giggle at the sight then I lose my breath when a pair of lips latch on to my downstairs. I want to see who is where, but Conner takes over my mouth once again and all thoughts are lost. I blindly reach out for anything and grab hold of the first head of hair my hands come into contact with.

Devon. I would know the feel of his thick hair anywhere. I hold on to him with one hand and using my other, go deeper until I feel Miles longer locks. I grab hold of his hair and with both hands occupied I clear all the thoughts of why this is wrong from my head and I just feel. I feel their hands, mouths, and even teeth being used on me.

Conner pulls back, breaking our kiss and smiles down at

me. "More?" he asks me, and I nod my head, unable to form any words. "Whatever my pretty girl wants," he winks at me. "Brothers, our girl wants a little more."

"Hell yes," Dev says around my nipple.

"Mmmm." The sound is coming from Miles who is otherwise occupied with my downstairs.

"What do you want, pretty girl?" Conner asks me.

It only takes me a second to decide what I want and need. "You," I say against his lips. "In my mouth."

Conner's mouth falls open and I use the opportunity to shove my tongue into it. He gasps then attempts to take over but I refuse to let him. He finally pulls away and narrows his eyes at me. "My pretty girl is a little minx. Guys," he attempts to get Mile's and Devon's attention, but neither are listening and honestly, I hope they continue to ignore him. "Guys!" Conner hollers. Once he has their attention he continues. "We need to reposition her, so I need you to move for just a second."

"Really? You need us to do this right now?"

"Oh," he looks at me and grins. "I definitely need you to move right now."

I let out a throaty chuckle and lick my lips. Miles and Dev see me and they both let out a moan. "Fine," Dev says as he backs away and stands up from the bed. "Make it fast though, man. I am not nearly done with Princess, yet."

A shiver runs through my body and I quickly hop off Conner's lap and get on all fours in the middle of the bed. "Where do you want me?" I ask Connor.

"Jesus, pretty girl," he stands up and quickly pulls his shorts off, leaving his beautiful body completely bare. I don't even attempt to hide my staring. All three of their bodies are works of art and I plan on taking in my fill. "Stop looking at me like that or this will be over before it begins."

"On your back, let your head hang off the bed," Miles instructs me.

"You want my head upside down?"

"Oh yeah," he tells me with a heated look on his face. Miles rips off his pajama pants while I get into position.

At first, it's strange to be laying there with my head hanging off the bed but then Conner walks over, and I understand why I'm like this now.

Lying on my back, Miles and Devon now have full access to every piece of me and they both use this fact to their advantage. Devon begins to focus again on my breast while Miles goes back to the land down under. The reason for my head dangling off the bed? Conner walks right up to me and my mouth is at the perfect height. He grabs himself in his hand and paints my mouth with the small amount of moisture leaking from the tip. "Open up, pretty girl." I do as I'm told and after Conner slides himself as far as I can take him, I swallow him down even further. "Holy hotplate, pretty girl. Do that again," he groans out.

I continue to torture Conner with all the tricks I've learned by reading books while Devon and Miles play my body like an instrument. I feel Devon's hand trailing down from my breast to my detonation button and with one flick, I am gone. As soon as I come down from my high, Conner finishes in my mouth.

"I need to be in you, Princess," Devon says as he leans over me, kissing me even though I just finished swallowing down his friend's semen. "Can I?"

"Yes, please."

My body is pulled to the middle of the bed and I'm flipped over on my stomach. "On all fours, Princess. Let me see you on your knees," Devon pants out.

I get on my hands and knees and give the guys a little butt wiggle. I yelp when a hand comes down on me hard then shiver when Miles whispers in my ear. "Are you ready for me now, love?"

Instead of talking, I open my mouth wide to allow him to slide his thick cock between my lips. "Hmmmm," I hum around him and hear his breath catch. "Oh, love, you don't want to play with me like that. Dev, you need to control your girl."

"I'm one step ahead of you, Miles," Devon says before thrusting all the way into me.

I groan around Miles. He's thrusting into me from the front while Devon takes me from behind. I have never felt so full, or surprisingly, so cared for in my life. Devon reaches down and once again when he touches me, I light up like the fourth of July. He shouts out my name at the same time. My moans must make Miles go off because I no sooner finish than he's shooting down my throat.

"Bloody hell, baby," Miles huffs out. His chest is sweaty and falling up and down rapidly. "That was amazing." He leans over and kisses me, using his tongue to swipe the inside of my mouth clean. "That is so sexy," Miles murmurs.

Devon pulls out of me and I fall forward, my body completely spent. "You okay, Princess?" Dev asks after he lays down beside me.

"I'm more than okay," I can't help but giggle. "It was amazing."

"I don't think amazing is the right word," Conner pipes up. "Miraculous. Earth shattering. Awe-inspiring."

"Sexy as hell," Miles calls out from the floor.

"Miles," I lean over and look down. "Why are you on the floor?"

"I can't feel my legs, love. You turned them into noodles."

I snort and roll over onto my back. Devon rolls toward me and lays his head on my tummy. "You have a perfect pillow," he tells me.

"Did you just call me fat?" I laugh at him.

"What?" His head pops up and he looks at me confused. "I didn't call you fat."

I push his head back down to my tummy. "I'm just kidding, Dev. Lay back down and rest."

"Hmmm, you should rest," Conner chimes in. "We have time to go a few more rounds."

My body shivers in anticipation.

This night? It is definitely a moment I will treasure always. After all, it's one of the most defining moments I will ever have.

15

Twyla

My alarm goes off earlier than I expected. I must have forgotten to turn it off last night. We have the day off and I planned on sleeping in for a while longer. My body definitely needed the extra rest. I roll on my side and groan a little at my stiff and sore body. Conner wasn't kidding when he said we would go a few more rounds. If I had it in me, I'd wake all three of them up and start all over again. Not long after Devon had his fill it was Miles turn to make me scream. After that the three of us were so tired I didn't get to experience being with Conner. Speaking of my guys, I open my eyes and smile at the sight of Devon facing me still asleep. His mouth is slightly parted and for once he looks so peaceful. Like the world isn't resting on his shoulders.

I roll to my left and look at the other bed expecting to see both Conner and Miles, but one is missing. I move the covers off me and try not to wake up Dev. I ease myself out of the bed and tiptoe to the next one until I can see brown hair sticking out from under the covers. Miles. I walk across the room and see the bathroom door is wide open. Maybe he got up early and left to get us breakfast. Since I'm already up, I go ahead and do my business in the bathroom, brushing my teeth with the travel kit I always have in my purse and finger combing my hair before throwing it back up in a knot on top of my head. After I've finished, I walk back out expecting to see Conner but he's still missing.

"Devon," I shake him. "Devon," I whisper in his ear.

"What," he grumbles out.

"Conner isn't in the room and I'm worried."

"He's fine, Princess. He's probably still out. He'll be home soon."

"Out? Why would he be out?"

"He didn't have sex with you so he's still stone," he tells a second before he falls back to sleep.

"Stone?" I say to myself. This is the second time I've heard that saying. The first was from Matt on the ferry and now Dev. What does that even mean? I turn to face the door when I hear the lock turn over. Sure enough, a rumpled Conner walks in. "Where have you been?"

Conner jumps at the sound of my voice. "You scared the heck out of me, Ty. What are you doing up so early?"

"Answer the question, Conner. Where have you been?"

"Ty, maybe we should wait until the other two wake up and then we can talk."

"No! I shout at him, uncaring if I wake up Miles and Devon. "I am so tired of secrets and all this confusing talk about stone. What does that even mean?"

Conner takes a seat on the end of the bed Miles is currently occupying and runs his hands down his face. "I really think we should wait."

"And I really think you should start talking."

"There are more living things on this earth than just humans, Ty."

"Okay," I say to Conner. "What does this have to do with anything?"

"No," he shakes his head. "I'm not talking about plants, algae, all that scientific stuff. I mean there are other creatures out there. People that aren't entirely human."

"Conner," I watch him stand up and begin to pace the room.

"Ty, I'm a gargoyle."

"Look, Conner, if there's someone else or whatever is . . ."

"I'm being one hundred percent honest with you right now. I, well until last night, all three of us were gargoyles."

"What do you mean until last night all three of you were?" My stomach is beginning to cramp, and I have a bad feeling.

Conner lets out a long sigh. "Gargoyles are cursed monsters. Forced to turn into stone to watch over the cities, searching for our true loves, our other halves every night. Once we find her and bind with her, then the curse will be lifted, and we will no longer turn to stone. We will become like every day, normal men. No more shifting against our will."

I look behind me to the two men still sleeping. The two men I had sex with. I didn't sleep with Conner last night. "Oh my god," I whisper. "Did you plan this? Was I just a means to an end for the three of you?"

"No, baby, no. Absolutely not. We have been searching and dreaming of you for so long. None of us thought we would ever find our one and then you just popped up here to work with Marco and it was an answered prayer. I wasn't thinking about the curse last night and I can guarantee you neither were my brothers." Conner sits back down on the bed and I shift away from him. "Please, don't be scared of me. I would never hurt you."

"I know you would never physically hurt me, but what about emotionally, Conner? You pretty much just told me that being with me one time was enough to keep you from turning back to stone and you expect me to believe that the thought never crossed your mind last night? I'm no idiot so stop treating me like one," I raise my voice at the end and hop back off the bed. I can't sit still but I don't know what to do.

Gargoyles? Is he for real right now? "How am I supposed to know if you're telling the truth right now? I mean, having someone tell you they turn into a stone statue every night is a bit farfetched, wouldn't you agree?"

"What can I do to prove it to you?"

"Show me," I demand. "Right here, right now. I want to see you become a gargoyle. A mythical creature." When it doesn't seem like Conner is going to comply, I get in his face and scream. "Show me, damn it!"

"What is going on?" A sleepy Devon sits up, looking at Conner and me. "Why are you two yelling?"

"I told her," Conner looks at Devon. "She deserved to know, and I couldn't keep it from her anymore."

"Miles," Devon calls out, his eyes never leaving mine. "Miles, get your ass up."

"What? It's still early and we're off today."

"She knows," Devon says, and Miles sits up the next instant.

"Pretty girl," Miles smiles sadly at me. "I'm so sorry we didn't tell you first."

"First?" I bite out. "You mean before we had sex? Before I cured you? Before you used me? Or was it before you ripped my heart out, Miles? Huh? Which first are you talking about?"

"Princess, please just hear us out."

"Shut up, Devon. I don't want to hear anything from any of you right now." Getting up I grab my purse, the only thing I brought to their room last night and make my way to their door. Turning my head, I look over my shoulder. "I need to be alone right now. At least respect me enough to give me that." Throwing the door open I stomp out of their room and back down to mine. When I get there, I tiptoe inside and see both Kelby and Renee still fast asleep. As quietly as I can I grab my one suitcase, my duffle bag, and both camera cases. I put the duffle over my shoulder, the two camera cases over my neck and I silently roll my suitcase back out of the room. Once in the hall I move as fast as I can down the hall and to the elevator. The front desk attendant proved to be very helpful and in less than twenty minutes, I'm in a cab and headed to the airport in Dublin. It only takes me three hours to get on a flight to New York and in twenty hours, I'm back home in Memphis, wrapped up in my momma's arms.

It's just one more moment life has thrown at me that I would like to forget.

16

Twyla

"Well," Bethy comes racing down the hall and into the kitchen as soon as momma and I walk in the door. "What did the doctor say?"

I swear. I don't know who's more excited about this baby, momma or Bethy. "She said everything looked good and he," I smile when I tell her, "is doing great. Everything looks good and in three months, we can meet him."

"Oh, Ty!" Bethy starts jumping up and down. "It's a boy? I knew it. I told you yesterday it was going to be a boy. This means we need to start buying everything blue."

"Calm down, little sis," I laugh at her. Pulling her close to me, I wrap my arms tightly around her shoulders. "Let me digest this news first and I promise, tomorrow we'll go shopping and buy something blue."

Bethy pulls back and I'm graced with her innocent smile. "Sounds good, momma number two." She runs out of the room, cackling the entire time. She knows I hate when she calls me that.

"Sit down, Twyla. I'll make us a glass of tea and we can

make a list of things we need now that we know what you're having."

I'm just about to sit on one of the stools at the kitchen counter when our doorbell rings. "I've got it," Bethy yells as she races back down the hall. "Ty?" She calls me from the front door. Before I can begin to walk toward the door, my little sister returns to the kitchen with the last people I ever thought I would see again trailing behind her.

"What do you want?" I stare at the three of them.

"Twyla," momma scolds me. "Where are your manners?" She walks past me and straight to the three men who ripped my heart out and left me with a very big surprise in return. "Hi," she holds out her hand to them. "I'm Norma, Twyla's momma. Welcome to our home." Momma shakes their hands then turns to glare at me. "Can I get you anything to drink?" She asks over her shoulder as she makes her way back to the fridge. "I have tea, lemonade, and water."

"No thank you, ma'am," Conner answers and the sound of his Texas twang almost brings me to my knees.

"Are you sure?"

"They don't want anything, Momma. In fact, they aren't staying. Isn't that right, boys?" I dare them to disagree with me.

Devon shakes his head. "She's right. We just stopped by to see Princess, I mean Twyla, before we head back to London."

"Oh! You must work with Marco then." Momma's face is a little pale. She finally put two and two together. I didn't hide anything from her when I got back from Ireland. I laid in her arms, crying and telling her everything the second I walked through our front door. To say she was shocked was an understatement. I thought she was going to have me tested for drugs, but she knows me and knows I'm no liar. When we found out three weeks later that I was pregnant, we decided to never bring up their names again. I didn't know their numbers and the one I did have for Marco I threw away in a fit of madness. The only thing I knew to do was look on social media for them but none of them were listed anywhere. I figured it was a sign and I accepted it. "Well then, if you will excuse me. I'm sure the four of you have a lot to discuss." She throws me a look before she leaves, and I nod my head. I would never dream of keeping a child from their father. Now that they are here, I will tell them, and we can work out some type of visitation. Although I don't know how it will work with them living in London and me in Memphis.

I gesture to the living room. "We can go in there to talk."

The three of them fall in line behind me and I hear Devon whispering to the other two. "Is it just me or is she glowing?"

They must not be paying close attention to me. Of course, I've been lucky and haven't gained much weight with my pregnancy. My doctor this morning told me not to get too cocky because now is when I should start packing on the pounds. Right now, I only look like I ate too much. I grab the one recliner we have, and the three guys are forced to share the couch. "What brings you this far across the pond?" I ask them.

"You," Miles says. "We came looking for you."

"It took you six months?"

Miles licks his lips, a sign I remember him having when he was nervous. "We had to finish the last few weeks out with the interns. Marco couldn't mentor all of them. After that, we had to find your information which wasn't easy. Marco is not the most organized person in the world. Once we found you, we had to clear up a few things back home then find a flight path that didn't make us fly overnight."

"Right," I draw out. "Because Conner didn't get a chance to get his dick wet and he still turns to stone."

"It isn't like that at all, pretty girl."

"Spare me. So, six months later here you are. Now, why are you here and what do you want?"

"You," Devon whispers. "The only thing we ever wanted was you, Princess. Don't you get it? It was never about the curse or us turning to stone every night. It was always about you. About us loving you and needing you in our lives. Nothing else matters to us."

"Then why didn't you tell me before?"

"We were scared. I was scared," Devon tells me. "Remember the night I tried to push you away? It was because I was petrified that you would find out what we were, turn your back on us and run away. I didn't want to lose you and I knew we would if we told you the truth."

"Devon, I never would have turned my back on you."

"But you did," Miles points out. "The next morning, that is exactly what you did. You turned your back on us and ran."

"You lied to me! You deliberately kept information from me that I had a right to know about. You used me for your own gain and made me feel like I was something special when all I was," I choke back the tears and blink my eyes. "When all I was to you was a means to an end. Nothing more, nothing less. But you," I wipe the tears running down my cheeks. "You could have been my world."

"Princess," Devon pushes up from the couch and comes to squat down in front of me. "You have no idea what you mean to us. You are our world. Please, I am begging you, let us prove it to you. Give us the opportunity to show you how much we love you. We need to be with you, Princess. Don't push us away again."

Propping my elbows on my knees, I cover my face with both my hands. "Dev, there is so much more going on you don't even know about." I lift my face from my hands and look down at him. "I don't know if I can ever get past the betrayal."

"We never betrayed you, Princess. We should have told you before we let that night go so far, but none of us wanted to let you go. We were not thinking right, and we took it too far. For that, we are sorry. But we're not sorry for loving you, princess. We aren't sorry for wanting to build a life with you. One chance. It's all we're asking from you."

I stand up and walk around Devon to stand in front of the

couch. Facing them, I ask Miles and Conner the same question. "How do you feel about me? About this relationship?"

Miles stands first and walks to me. "There will never be anyone who will love you like we do. The four of us together may not be conventional, but it doesn't matter. What matters is that we love you and want to be with you. One chance, Ty. It's all we're asking for."

I look past Miles to Conner still perched on the couch. "Conner?"

"Do you remember the night you and I sat outside under the stars until I made you go back in?" He pauses until I nodded yes, I do remember. "Do you recall what we were talking about?"

"Moments," I tell him. "Defining moments."

Conner stands and walks over to me. He places his hands on either side of my face and looks me straight in the eyes. "You are my defining moment. Good, bad, past, and future. Every moment I have ever had has led up to you, and every moment I have from now and going forward will be because of you."

EPILOGUE

ONE MOMENT. We all have it. That one moment that changes everything. It could be something small or something big. Something bad, something good. Something wrong or something right.

It's just something.

This was our moment. The one that would irrevocably change everything, and not just for us.

It wasn't small.

It wasn't good.

It wasn't right.

But it was ours, and it was absolutely perfect.

"He's beautiful, pretty girl." My husband leans down and kisses first my cheek and then our son's. "You did amazing and I'm so proud of you," Conner whispers in my ear.

"Ty," Miles, my other husband reaches his hand out and runs the back of his fingers down our son's face. "I have never seen anything so perfect."

I look over Miles shoulder to Devon, my third and last husband. "What do you think, Daddy?" I ask him.

Devon kicks off the wall and waltzes over to us. Bending at the waist, he runs his nose down the column of my neck. I've gotten used to keeping my hair thrown up in a topknot for this reason alone. It's his favorite thing to do. "I think you are incredible, Princess. And our son? I think he's the best moment we will ever make."

The End

Kelly A Walker lives in the South with her husband of way too long, and their teenage son who knows everything. She's been reading as long as she can remember. Judy Blume and The Babysitters Club started it all and had her dream of one day writing. Kelly loves Jesus, her family, and SEC football (#HottyToddy).

When Kelly isn't writing, she's driving her kid from one thing to another, going to the grocery store, or spending all her hubby's money at Macy's, or Michael's, or the Dollar General . . . okay, she just likes to shop.

You can follow Kelly at the following:
Facebook: Kelly A Walker Readers Group
Instagram: kellyawalkerauthor
Twitter: kawalkerauthor
BookBub: Kelly A Walker Author
Pinterest: kellywalkerauthor
Email: KellyWalkerAuthor@gmail.com
www.kellyawalker.com

BOOKS BY KELLY A. WALKER

Memphis

The Adventures of Winnie

Book 1

Book 2

Book 3

The Secret Life of Piper Series

Dear Eastside Boys

Anthologies

Moments

Memphis - Bonus Scene

Stacy Lacy (Co-Written with KN Thompson)

PHARAOH-MONES

KENDRA MORENO

1

LADY LUCK IS A FLIGHTY BITCH, *and this was definitely her work*, I think as I watch the customs agent dig through my sensible underwear. He glances up at my red face— the curse of being a redhead — in amusement as he slowly holds up a pair of beige granny panties. Thank god I had left my toys at home. While I'll be in Egypt for months, I'll be bunking with one of my crew members. There won't be enough privacy for such things.

The customs agent grins when he lifts the only lacy pair I'd managed to bring with me, his lewd expression making me so uncomfortable, my eyes shift to the other agents around me, looking for help. When I see their matching grins, I scowl and wait impatiently for them to finish. This is supposed to be the trip of a lifetime, all my hard work paying off, but so far, I'm already annoyed, and I haven't even left the airport yet.

The agent says something in Arabic to his friend next to him and they both get a good chuckle as he swings the lace around his fingers.

"That's really unprofessional," I snap, snatching the lace.

Their laughter immediately stops, and for a moment, I think he'll throw me in jail. I really don't want to become a criminal my first time here. They would immediately turn me around and send me back to America. I should have just let it go. Just when I think he's going to blow, he grins again.

"You're free to go," he says, his voice heavily accented.

He shoves all my underwear back into the bag, the once beautifully organized clothing now a ball of chaos and shoves it towards me. I zip it back up with a huff and yank it from the table, storming away with their eyes on my backside. Assholes.

I walk out of the airport into the blazing sunshine, instantly squinting my eyes at the brightness. Back home in New York, we get sunshine, of course, but nothing quite this stifling. I'm wearing jeans for the long flight but I'm regretting that now. I should have changed into shorts the moment we landed.

I look around the group of waiting taxis, all of them rushing forward and shouting at me in a mixture of Arabic and English to get me into their car. I already know the dangers of a wartorn country, so instead, I bypass them, smiling kindly, before walking up to a man holding a sign. My name, Delilah Jackson, is scrawled across it in barely legible writing, but he's definitely here for me.

"Dr. Jackson?" he asks, his voice not as accented as the Customs Agent, a kind smile on his face. "I've been instructed to take you directly to your quarters."

"That would be great," I sigh, following him to a beat-up green car parked on the curb. The windows are rolled down and I immediately realize there won't be any AC inside. I shove the stray hairs from my face, wiping the sweat that's already starting to trickle.

"Where are the quarters exactly?" I ask as he loads my bags into the trunk. "The paperwork I had never said the exact address, just that I would be assigned a room with one of the students helping me."

"You'll be staying at the Anubis Hotel, Dr. Jackson. It's the closest location to the dig site."

"Please tell me it's air-conditioned," I beg, climbing into the front seat. He gives me a startled look when I do so— I'm not sitting in the back like he's my servant— but otherwise, remains professional.

"Of course. Dr. Crenshaw made sure you would be comfortable for your time here."

With that, he starts the car— I was right! No AC— and pulls away from the curb, merging into traffic that doesn't seem to have any uniformity. I'm not sure how he even maneuvers through the rushing cars, but he does so with ease.

"How long until we arrive?" I watch the bustling city moving around us, the architecture so beautiful, I'm tempted to pull out my camera and start snapping pictures. There would be plenty of time for that later, though, so I restrain myself. Today is all about settling in, acclimating, getting over my jet lag after flying around the world. I'm not even expected at the dig site for a few days.

"About an hour and a half, Dr. Jackson."

I nod my head, absorbing the views outside like a sponge.

When I'd gotten the call from Dr. Crenshaw telling me I'd been selected for the dig of a lifetime, I nearly fainted. I might have blacked out. Dr. Crenshaw says I didn't speak for a few minutes afterward. He'd jokingly said he'd thought he'd killed me. But no, I'd been in shock. I'd watched on the news as they talked about the discovery of a new pyramid, long since covered by the sands of Egypt. It was massive, a giant mystery surrounding how it had remained hidden for so long, how it had been buried. The alien conspiracy people came out in full force, claiming that only intelligent life forms from other planets could be responsible, but I knew otherwise. There have been studies done to show exactly how the pyramids could have been built without current technology. It's fascinating stuff.

I'd graduated at the top of my class with my Doctorate in archeology, full honors, though that didn't guarantee that I immediately got hired for amazing digs. Nowadays, you have to be selected for a project as large as this one. There are miles and miles of red tape you must circumvent. Whatever is found in Egypt belongs to the government, and they decide who's in charge.

For the Mystery pyramid, that is Dagen Crenshaw, world-renowned archeologist. He has so many discoveries under his belt, I'm not sure how he keeps track of them all. He's a celebrity in the world of archeology, his name everywhere in the textbooks I studied. When the opportunity to work with him on a mysterious Egyptian pyramid came up, I filled out the form and jumped through hoops, figuring they wouldn't choose someone with so little experience under their belt. I'd been working in museums since I graduated, great jobs but not the adventure I'd hoped for. Surely there were other applicants who had traveled the world and discovered things of their own. But I was the one who received a personal call from Dr. Crenshaw.

The trip is completely paid for by the Egyptian government, and my name would be written right next to Dr. Dagen Crenshaw when this discovery was placed in the history books. I wish my mom was here to see this. She'd always believed in me, always thought I would do great things. She never got to stick around to see me do them. Cancer took her a year before I received my doctorate. Her final words to me are even now etched into the metal bracelet on my wrist.

Do great things. Be kind. Make your mark. I love you.

The bracelet is one of my greatest possessions, the words written in her handwriting.

She would have been so proud to see me standing where I am now, about to make my mark after all my years of hard work.

Even as a child I knew I'd wanted to be an archeologist, and I credit a lot of that to my mother. When I was little, she used to take coins and bits of things into the sandbox in the backyard of our home and bury them. I'd sit out there for hours sifting through the sand, digging, searching. She did it every single day, always finding new things to hide, and I always got to keep everything I found. When I'd walked across the stage for my doctoral graduation, I'd told that story and watched as everyone understood. We don't always know what we want to do in life, but sometimes, it's an easy choice. My dreams were born from my mother who saw my explorer soul and encouraged it. I was incredibly lucky to have her in my life.

When we pull up to the Anubis Hotel, I raise my brow. It's nicer than I expected, more luxurious than I had planned for. I brought a single nice dress for any special events I might have to attend. Hopefully, I won't be expected to cater to the elite the entire time I'm working on the dig.

The driver, who I learn is named Mohamed, helps me unload my baggage and then escorts me to the front desk. He doesn't leave my side until I'm checked in and heading up the elevator to my room. He's very sweet and I immediately felt more comfortable with his presence through the entire ordeal. He waves goodbye as the elevator doors close and I make my way to the fourth floor.

My bunkmate had already arrived the front desk clerk had told me, and I was looking forward to meeting her. I'd been given her name in the files, so naturally, I'd looked her up. In addition to Dr. Crenshaw choosing me as his partner for the dig, he'd also chosen six grad students to come and assist. I'd had the same opportunity when I was a grad student, although my dig had been far less exciting. I'd gotten to dig for dinosaur bones in the Texas deserts, which was super cool, except we'd only managed to dig up pieces and nothing exciting for the museums. These students would be part of a historical dig, something guaranteed to be written into the history books. They're all looking to make their mark on the world, just like I am. The only difference is, they won't be credited with anything, but that's the sad part of being an assistant rather than the lead. Of course, I'm not even sure how much credit I'll be given with someone like Dagen Crenshaw running the show.

Jessica Bellamy, my bunkmate, is top of her class, ambitious to a fault, a prodigy in her own right. Her father was a deep-sea explorer and had been one of the pioneers of discovery for the Titanic. She grew up with it in her blood. She's brilliant, from what I could tell, and beautiful. I'm looking forward to meeting her and having someone just as excited as I am about the dig.

When I find my door, I knock twice before I slide the keycard in and push it open.

"Jessica. It's Delilah Jackson. I'm your bunkmate," I call out before pushing the door wider. I don't want to catch her undressed or something. Before I can peer around and look further inside, it's yanked all the way open and I'm pulled into a strong hug.

"I've been so excited to meet you! Welcome to Egypt! I only got here an hour ago," she exclaims before releasing me. "I'm so glad we got paired up."

"It was bound to happen since we're the only two women," I tease. It's true; the rest of the students were men. "It's nice to meet you, too."

She helps me pull my bag into the room, a massive grin on her face. "Can you believe we're here? You're like my goals, girl. You get to have your name on this dig. You get to be one of the first inside! How cool is that?"

I open my mouth, but no words come out. It's been months since I'd gotten the news and I still can't talk about it without stumbling over my words in shock. No, I can't believe I'm here. Finally, I manage to answer. "It's amazing."

"Well, I'm really excited to work with you, Dr. Jackson. Honestly. It's an honor."

"Please, just call me Delilah. There's really no need for formalities between us. Especially since we're going to be living together for months."

Jessica smiles kindly before leaving me to my unpacking. I

don't have much with me, only the essentials, enough clothing to last me between washings, extra boots, and my lone fancy dress. It takes barely ten minutes to get it all put away and to slide the empty suitcase under the bed.

"Have you heard about the militias in the city?" Jessica asks her nose in a newspaper. It's written in Arabic so either she must read the language or she's only looking at the pictures.

"Yes. I got all the travel advisory messages with the flight confirmation. It's the reason we're not supposed to go anywhere alone."

"Yeah, but there's apparently still a war going on between the current government and some warlord guy. No one knows what he looks like or anything, just his last name. Har-em-ha. I wonder if that's something we need to worry about."

"Probably not. We're going to be out in the desert most of the time. The fighting happens in the city, right?"

"Well, yes. Cairo is massive but this pyramid has a lot of attention on it with the government wanting to lay claim on everything. You don't think that a warlord that's pitted against the government won't take the opportunity to intercept priceless artifacts?"

I worried my lip, thinking about her words. "That's true. We need to be vigilant in cataloging artifacts and making sure they're escorted to the museum. It would be terrible if they were stolen."

We spend the rest of the night relaxing in the room and talking about the excursions we'd been on and our lives. Jessica went on and on about her thesis that she's planning to write on the mystery pyramid. It's a good call. Not many will have the same opportunity of discovery as we will. Her professors would no doubt be excited to hear firsthand experience of the historical dig.

By the time we lay our heads down, I'm exhausted, and I dream of rushing through a pyramid avoiding flesh-eating scarabs and running from a mummy brought back to life. In my dream, my very own Brendan Fraser comes to the rescue, and we defeat the bad guys together.

When I wake up the next morning, I'm only a little disappointed that he wasn't in my bed next to me.

/-/-/-/

WE'RE ESCORTED to the dig site bright and early three days later by Mohamed — our designated driver apparently— the sun barely climbing into the sky when we arrive. We had to wait until all our paperwork was processed before we were granted access. Egypt isn't taking any chances with its newest discovery. Years of grave robbing and wars have plagued the history of the country. I can't really blame them for their careful evaluations.

"I should have brought my explorer hat," Jessica mumbles beside me.

"You have an explorer hat?" I chuckle as we step from the car. Today, I'm prepared in my khaki shorts and a button-down shirt, the sleeves rolled up, and my boots. I look like I stepped from the pages of Archeology Weekly, but there's a reason we all wear the same outfits. Everything is meant to protect. When inside the pyramid, we would be expected to wear helmets in case the structure isn't sound.

"You don't? I thought it was a thing we did, go out and buy a safari explorer hat."

"I didn't say I don't have one." I grin at her.

Where Mohamed drops us off, we can't see much. We have to pass through gates and a ten-foot fence to get inside, showing our IDs at three different stations.

"At least they're being careful," I comment, watching the bustling activity around us. No one has been allowed inside the pyramid yet, the time spent digging the structure from the sand. It goes down into the ground for at least one hundred feet, and they still haven't found any sight of the end. There's no telling how large it is until we get inside, and even then, we could spend years exploring it. There might be booby traps and curses galore. It's enough to make me rub my hands together in excitement. This is it! This is the moment I've been waiting for since I was a child.

The first look at the pyramid literally takes my breath away. I almost pass out because of it before Jessica pats me on the back. Usually, when you see a pyramid, it's above the sands, rising high into the sky, but this one is sunken into the desert, and so we have to descend in order to get to it. The stone is weathered but intact, still well preserved. Experts have been trying to determine its age, checking if it predates the Pyramid of the Sun or if it was built after. I'm curious to know the answer to that as well.

We have no name for this pyramid yet, waiting until we enter to see if there's anything we can learn from the hieroglyphics. The studying would be slow but well worth it. Today, we would open the main door of the pyramid, prying loose the heavy stone set in with age and sand, in order to take our first steps inside. And I still haven't met Dagen Crenshaw, even though we're meant to be partners.

"You get to walk inside that beautiful thing later," Jessica whispers. "I'm so jealous it's insane."

"You'll be right behind me," I remind her. "You're part of my crew."

"Still jealous," she says in awe, looking down into the carved-out hole. It's as if someone just kept digging. "I still can't believe a man tripping over a rock is how this was all discovered."

That's the best story of all about the discovery. After a massive sandstorm, a man had been walking in the desert, traveling from one city to the next. He'd been walking beside his camel to stretch his legs when he tripped over a rock. That rock had proven to be the tip of the pyramid, which he'd discovered when he'd started digging to try and throw the rock in anger. Except he never found an edge he could pick up. If he hadn't been walking, it would still be lost to history, this grand pyramid hidden from all eyes.

"Sometimes it's the smallest things that lead to great discoveries."

"Can't argue with that."

The other five students hadn't been as welcoming as Jessica when I'd met them the night before. One had been downright rude when I introduced myself, but I wasn't here to make friends. Not really. They were my charges, and I had to tell him that he needed to work on being professional when we would be working together for such a long time, especially when I would essentially be his boss. He'd immediately apologized, but I hadn't missed the glint in his eyes. No, that one was arrogant and thought he should be in my position even though he hadn't even graduated with his master's yet.

"If you'll excuse me," I say, smiling at Jessica's twinkling eyes. She's just as amazed by all of this as I am. "I'm going to go find Dr. Crenshaw and discuss some things."

Jessica nods her head and I leave her to stare at the amazing discovery we get to make, searching for the tent that's assigned to Dr. Crenshaw and me during the day. The whole dig site is surrounded by tents, each specialist taking up residence to set up their equipment. Dr. Crenshaw's and my tent is by far one of the largest, and when I walk inside, it's to find it filled with all sorts of equipment.

"Dr. Crenshaw?" I call, looking around the stacked boxes. I expect to find an older man, verging on the edge of retirement, but Dr. Crenshaw isn't even in the tent. Another man is, though, and he's sitting at a desk carving an apple with a knife. "Hello. I'm looking for Dr. Crenshaw."

When his eyes meet mine, my skin crawls in warning, but

I'm not certain why. He's attractive but there is this certain aura around him that makes me want to get away. His skin is tanned, speaking of long hours in the sun, and when he speaks, it's definitely with an accent common to Egypt.

"He isn't here. Probably taking a piss somewhere," he says, eating a slice of apple from the tip of his knife. "Maybe I can help you?" His eyes run down the length of my body and I resist the urge to cover up more skin. I'm not revealing that much, but I'm so uncomfortable that I'm tempted to cover completely.

"I'm not sure. I'm Delilah Jackson. I wanted to meet with him before they start working on breaking the opening to the pyramid." I eye the large knife he carefully uses to carve more of the apple. "Who are you?"

"I'm Bek. I'm in charge of keeping Dagen from drinking his way through Egypt."

"I've never heard of you," I comment, meeting his slate grey eyes.

"You wouldn't have, no." He smiles, the expression not quite reaching his eyes. No, his gaze is sharp, learning every detail. This man isn't one I want to spend extended time with. He doesn't elaborate on why I don't know him, so I raise my brow, glancing around the tent one last time before turning to leave.

"When he comes back, could you tell him I'd like to have a word with him. It's hard to be partners if we've never even met."

"I'll tell him." Bek crunches into another piece of apple. "Congratulations on being chosen, Delilah. I look forward to seeing you in action."

"Nice to meet you," I reply, leaving the tent as fast as I can without seeming like I'm running. I don't know who he is, but Bek is dangerous. I'd have to warn Jessica. It was best to be careful here, even behind the protected fences of the dig site.

Dr. Crenshaw never comes to find me, and the first time I see him is when the workers start to work on the door. He comes by enough to say, "good job" with a whiskey bottle in his hand, before he turns and starts to leave.

"Dr. Crenshaw!" I call, moving towards him. "I've been trying to find you."

"I don't want to be found," he grumbles, shuffling through the sand. His years and years of discovery haven't been kind to him, not from his appearance anyways. He walks stiffly as if an old injury keeps his gait unnatural. His skin is wrinkled and weathered, appearing more like leather than skin. His khaki clothing is stained beyond repair, and I'm not certain it's stained with just dirt. He smells as if he hasn't taken a shower in days, and I'm pretty sure I smell urine when I get close.

"I'm your partner, Delilah Jackson."

"I don't give a shit. Do your job and we won't have to talk to each other." He shuffles away from me, leaving me standing there in surprise.

Disappointment washes over me. This man was a legend, someone I've looked up to for years, and he's nothing more than a worn-down old man with a drinking problem. I sigh, rubbing my neck. It doesn't seem like he'll be much help during the actual dig. His name will no doubt be slapped on everything as if he's the one doing the work. While it's disappointing to learn that one of my heroes couldn't care less to work with me, I still get the opportunity to enter the pyramid, and I'm looking forward to it.

It isn't until hours later that the workers dislodge the stone, and it rolls away enough for us to stare into the darkness. Jessica and the rest of my team stand behind me, all our gear is worn on us. We're only going into the first chamber today, only hanging some gear and letting the workers put up temporary lighting and equipment to make sure the pyramid is stable, but first, we get to lay eyes on the beauty inside.

The sun is high in the sky when we all click on our headlamps. A harness is worn around me, the rope attached to a crank behind us. As I walk in, it'll allow me to move, but if the floor collapses, it'll provide the tension to stop me from plummeting to my death. The rest of my team— the five students, an Egyptologist, a cartographer, and a few crew members to help carry the equipment we'll be erecting as we make our way through— follow right behind me. They each wear a harness that's clipped to my rope, keeping us all together and strong.

"Are we ready to make history?" I ask, grinning at them. The student who'd given me attitude rolls his eyes but the rest smile and nod their heads, varying degrees of excitement and anxiety on their faces. I face the darkness, my headlamp barely penetrating the gloom. In front of me, I hold a six-foot pole, a way for me to check for booby traps. Dead pharaohs aren't fans of grave robbers, and since they were buried with their treasure, they made sure to keep their riches from being stolen in their death. It didn't stop those clever enough to circumvent the traps — grave robbing is a lucrative business in Egypt — but it did slow them down at least. For us, it forces us to move carefully, the pole stretched out in front of me to tap the stones on the floor and the walls. The triggers could be as simple as a certain stone being stepped on, or some intricate thing that senses pressure from the walls. Either way, I have no desire to have a death on my hands. My team knows not to touch anything other than what I do.

I take a step inside, tapping the stones gently, the noise echoing in the enclosed space. Most pyramids have a grand gallery we should come out in once deep inside. Immediately, I can tell this one is different, the stone smoother as if it was used often rather than from age. The walls are perfectly preserved, the etching in them clear as day. The seal must have kept the stone mostly intact, which is amazing for us. That means we'll be able to read the markings.

"Anything you can take from the hieroglyphics, Dan?" I ask behind me, the Egyptologist humming in answer.

"Nothing but curses and the usual blessings so far. The important stuff will probably be in the grand gallery."

I don't tell him I don't think there will be a grand gallery. This pyramid doesn't have the same layout. An opening appears on our left barely fifty feet inside the entry, leading in a different direction.

"Doorway to the left," I call back to the cartographer who scribbles it into his chart. Until we have a map of the pyramid, we'll be flying blind and have to use the ropes for everything. Someone clicks on a light and sets it on the floor against the wall. Later, the crew will come through and affix them to the ceiling with their equipment. There won't be any damage, the lights attach to a system designed for specifically these sorts of digs. For now, we have to set them on the floor. We move past the doorway, staying straight. In another fifty feet, there's a doorway to the right. I call back the info again and continue, tapping the stones one by one.

We don't run into the first trap for another ten yards. I tap a stone on the floor, relaxed before the pole is ripped from my hands by the giant spikes that shoot from the walls. I squeak in surprise, hands yanking me backward just in case the trap is one that spreads but it stops after the first trigger. My heart threatens to burst from my chest, my breaths coming in harsh pants as I straighten.

"Mark down the trap," I call back when I get my breathing under control. My heartbeat thumps in my ears, but I don't let it discourage me. "We have to tell the crew that we'll need the saws in here." The stakes will have to be cut away to make it safe to return. It'll also have to be checked to be certain that it was the only trap here. It isn't unheard of for there to be a trap within a trap.

"So that's it? We're done for the day?" Jessica asks, disappointment in her words. "I was hoping we would at least get to see the chamber today."

"It's best to move slow." I stare at the stakes sharpened to dangerous points. My pole is clamped between them, hanging precariously. "With traps like that, there must be things some

King never wanted us to find. We'll work again tomorrow at first light, once the stakes have been removed."

There's an obvious grumble from them all but they know not to question it. It's far too dangerous to just go walking through an unknown structure without care. If there's anything we've learned over the years, it's that deaths happen easily when on a dig site. I don't want that sort of tragedy on my soul. I'd rather be safe than sorry.

"Dagen Crenshaw wouldn't have turned back."

I turn to the student who I'd already had a scuffle with — Tommy, I think his name is — and raise my brow.

"Well then, you can go ask Dr. Crenshaw if he'd like to escort you further inside. I'm not risking your lives, and we have plenty of time. We can't do anything before the stakes are cut anyways and that won't be completed until this evening. Then someone has to make sure the structure is sound before we continue." I meet Tommy's eyes. "Unless you'd like to walk through and fall into the next trap, I suggest you check your attitude. It's too hot in the desert and too stifling down here to argue with you. Now turn around and make your way back in the direction we came."

He turned around with a gruffhuff but not before his clear annoyance crosses his face. If he isn't careful, he'll be the reason someone gets hurt, or worse, gets killed.

Tomorrow. There's always tomorrow.

/-/-/-/

IT TAKES us three days to make it to the first chamber. We run into trap after trap— spikes, trick stones, poison spray long since dried up but still deadly to brush against— and not to mention the bacteria and such our bodies aren't used to. A few of the crew members get sick right away, but nothing serious. Not yet, at least. We don't find the name of the pyramid or who it was built for, until we come out into the large chamber. We expected the grand gallery. We weren't expecting the dozens of sarcophagi spread along the walls, each one more intricate than the last.

"What the hell?" Jessica mumbles, glancing around in confusion. "This should be the main gallery. Why are there remains here?"

"Your guess is as good as mine," I reply, glancing around the room. "Stay behind me. We can't walk around freely until we're certain there are no traps."

It takes hours to clear the room, no traps thankfully springing on us, before we breathe a sigh of relief and walk around without worry. There are thirty-nine sarcophagi in all, and each one is marked with a different symbol.

"I think these were all Oracles," Dan comments, studying the hieroglyphics. Then he moves to the wall, tracing his fingers over the pictures there. I'd tried to learn ancient Egyptian at one point but decided I should leave that up to the experts. I only knew the important symbols and things to avoid. "I found the name of the temple," he adds, clenching his jaw.

"Well, what is it?" Jessica shifts uneasily on her feet after her question.

I feel a chill travel down my spine, telling me to leave, that I shouldn't be here, but that's just my imagination. I've been dreaming of mummies and craziness for weeks. This is just my mind playing tricks on me.

"Temple of the Gods." His words echo in the large room as if adding to the drama.

"No way," I whisper, meeting the eyes of the crew.

"It says it right here," Dan argues, his eyes lighting up. "Delilah," he meets my eyes, "We found the Temple of the Gods."

My breath stutters, and I take a step back in surprise, and I realize the exact moment I made a mistake.

Either I missed a trick stone, or it hadn't been triggered by the pole, but I realize what happened the moment the brick sinks beneath my feet and a click echoes in the room. My eyes meet Jessica's for a moment, panic barely starting to take hold before the stones start falling out from beneath my feet.

I scream and scramble to grab hold of the edge, but more stones fall away, making a larger hole. No one reaches for me as they hurry to get out of the way, the hole spreading, and there's nothing left for me to clutch at. I'm falling for a split second, and then I'm sliding, the stones scraping my back and biting into my skin.

I fall for long minutes, going deeper and deeper into the pyramid. I try not to panic, but it's nearly impossible. I slide through webs and dust and creatures and fight the claustrophobia at being in such a narrow tunnel.

When I think it'll never end, I fall into the open air before slamming into a sand-covered ground, and I give into the panic. My headlamp breaks at the impact and I'm plunged into darkness.

2

My first instinct is to lose my shit, but I'm a professional, so instead, I force myself to take deep breaths until I get my heart rate under control. It's pitch black down here with my headlamp busted, and no light penetrates from where I came down. I fell for far too long to just be a level lower in the pyramid. I must have dropped hundreds of feet, much further than any pyramid I've ever heard being built. Dan's words came back to me. We've found the Temple of the Gods. I'm both in awe and afraid of what that means, every legend I've ever read or heard coming to the forefront of my mind.

The Temple of the Gods had been written about in the history books, but only because it was recorded by the ancient Egyptians. Until this moment, there had been no proof that a giant pyramid existed dedicated to the Gods.

It's spoken of as the final resting place for Gods and Goddesses, where their souls would rest in times of peace or contemplation. The Oracles in the sarcophagi we'd found must be those dedicated to spreading the words of their Gods, choosing to be buried within their temple. But that would also mean that the Gods and Goddesses are resting here, too, if the legends are correct, along with so much treasure that no one could imagine. It's good the government is taking security seriously.

My name would be forever remembered as finding the Temple of the Gods. My heart skipped a beat at that realization, and I wish that my mom was here to tell her all about it. I can imagine just how excited she would have been.

I realize I'm just standing in the dark, so I fish inside my pocket for the flashlight I never go without. I even have extra batteries in another pocket. Honestly, I watch too many movies. I don't have plans to be without some form of light if another is broken. I even have an extra flashlight, and both are rugged wear and difficult to break. Yes, I'm a little overprepared. I have a sizeable knife on my hip, too. Just in case I need to stab a mummy that suddenly comes back to life.

I click the flashlight on, and the bright beam penetrates enough of the darkness that I realize I'm surrounded by gold and jewels. I take a step back against the wall and stare. Piles and piles of gold, covered in dust and grime but still no less impressive, spreads before me in a large chamber. Statues of the gods rise around me, each one wearing the animal face they're associated with.

"Holy shit," I whisper, my voice carrying through the chamber and sounding as if I spoke normally.

My flashlight beam falls on a trough with some sort of material inside. I smile, knowing exactly what it is, glad for it. I bite the flashlight between my teeth and search my pockets for the lighter I keep in there. I'm glad I have flaps on my pockets or else I could have lost everything sliding down here. My fingers close around the cold metal and I flick it open, slowly pressing it against the material in the trough. It sparks and catches immediately, traveling along the trough, spreading rapidly to light up the entire room in all its glory.

It's bigger than I assumed it was. There's a statue here for every god and goddess, each one intricate and inlaid with gold and trinkets. Each statue is surrounded by heaps of gold and jewels, an offering to the god it surrounds. *How much money this room must be worth*, I think, stepping forward, aware I don't have a pole to check for traps anymore. In all the pyramids I've studied, I've never heard of any trap mechanisms in the treasure room but there'd been one above that triggered me to fall into this chamber. Not having it trapped with triggers seems unwise if you're just dumping people down here unless there's no way out and I'm going to die.

I turn my mind towards something else, not willing to think that I'm going to die when I've just started making my mark. No, I'm alive and I'll find a way out. I'll just have to walk carefully in case I trigger anything.

Slowly, I inch my foot forward, tapping on the stones and stepping back, waiting to see if anything is triggered before I repeat the process and move forward. When I spot a golden spear in one of the piles of offerings, I heft it and start using it for the same process. Oddly enough, nothing is triggered, and when I get to the other side of the room and stare up at a raised dais, I wrinkle my brow in confusion. That doesn't make any sense. There should have been at least a few traps there to prevent me from making it this far, and yet there isn't a single one. Wariness fills me, and I wonder if I should stop my curiosity and work on finding a way out first.

Upon the dais, there's more gold scattered around the floor but there's also a stone platform with only one item sitting on it. I gasp, recognizing it from rough sketches that had been found in an ancient Egyptian scroll. I take a step up, slowly moving towards it, my eyes wide. This is impossible, two legends in one mystery pyramid. It shouldn't be possible.

To others, it would appear as nothing more than a chalice, intricate and golden, jewels encrusted on the sides, but still just a chalice. Any archeologist, however, would recognize the symbols and words etched in the gold, the paint a little faded but still discernible. I'd read a translation once from one of the most famous Egyptologist in her field.

Carry forth the blood of the gods during great turmoil in the Mother's land. Rise against those who threaten existence at the hands of the bringer of change.

Everyone knows that saying and yet no one knows what it means. And here I am staring at something that is believed to be lost forever, only a sketch on an old piece of leather.

I know I shouldn't— all my years of training and studies and field work telling me not to— but I reach shaking fingers towards the chalice. I just want to hold it, to prove that it's real to my mind and that I'm not knocked out and dying somewhere. I can't be dreaming this all up. Holding the chalice for a moment will prove that. I just want to touch it. That's all.

The movies I watched taught me better than this but when staring at something so amazing, you don't realize what you'll do. I learned nothing from Evelyn and Rick; they would be so disappointed in me. And yet, I still place four shaking fingers against the gold metal of the chalice.

And as if I had known, chaos happens all at once, for the second time today.

The burning flames in the trough had been burning brightly before but now, they lower, as if something forces them to dim. The wind swirls around me enough that the loose strands of my hair go wild, tickling my face. When I hear the gears of giant mechanisms turning, I know I've made the biggest mistake. Those will no doubt be closing off my only exit, something in this room that would lead me back to the surface had I only not touched. I try my best not to panic, but I lose the battle. I grab the chalice in my shaking fingers and rush from the dais, no longer caring if I spring another trap. If I don't get out of this room, I'm going to die anyway. I need to get out now!

I see a doorway to my left and rush towards it, a large stone slowly closing it off. No! I run, pumping my arms as hard as I can to make it before it closes. There's only a small space left when I get there, just big enough to fit through, but like an idiot, I hesitate, my mind revolting against getting squashed by a giant stone. By the time I clear my mind, the stone closes with a deafening crunch. I look around the room. Besides the slide I came down, there's no other way out, and going up the slide isn't going to work without some sort of gear. The flames don't go out, a good sign that I'm not completely sealed into my new casket. I really don't want to die down here.

I grit my teeth, the chalice still in my hand, and move to take a step back into the room when I hear the voices.

My breath stutters. Oh my god, they found me already! Grinning, I move towards the quiet hum of conversation, but when I round one of the statues, the dais coming back into view, my grin falls. I nearly drop the chalice in surprise, just barely keeping my fingers clenched around it.

What the hell?

In front of me, standing on the dais are three men, but not just any normal looking men. Each one appears Egyptian, that much I can garner, and each one is dressed up in costumes. Their waists are covered by cloth, and they each wear sandals on their feet. They're shirtless, sculpted muscle for days that I stare at greedily. They have fancy jewel encrusted collars sitting on their shoulders, each one wearing enough jewelry to fund a country.

"How did we get here?" one asks, the tallest of the three. "Thoth, you must know." His skin is beautifully tanned, natural rather than by the sun. His eyes are rimmed with kohl, bringing out the pale color of his eyes. He's clean shaven, his hair trimmed short, and he has so many muscles, my eyes might be bugging out of my head.

"Your guess is as good as mine, Anubis," one of the others answers. This one has the darkest skin of the three, the color a beautiful mocha shade. Tattoos stand out black against his skin, beautiful lines of hieroglyphics showing brightly. He's slimmer than the other two but no less muscled. His hair is up in a knot, and his eyes shine green as he shakes his head. "I don't even know where exactly we are, or which temple. Everything looks dull with age." He glances around himself, but his eyes never look to where I stand fifteen feet away, staring at these three men in shock. "Horus?"

The final man is the only one with a beard, giving him a rugged appearance. His hair is windswept like it always stays that way. And his eyes are as blue as the clearest sky. His skin is paler than the others but not by much. "I don't remember anything," he says, his voice is thick as he looks at the stone altar, "but something was here and is missing. Perhaps, that will reveal more answers."

It takes me that long to realize they're not speaking English, and even longer to realize that I still understand them even though I've never been able to learn ancient Egyptian. I gasp, and my fingers release the chalice by instinct. Flee! My brain screams at me. Run! But where can I run to? There's no way out.

I watch helplessly as the chalice hits the sand with a soft tink and all three men turn as one towards me. Varying emotions cross their faces— surprise, anger, annoyance— but it's the anger of the one they'd called Anubis that truly causes my body to shut down.

He takes a step down from the dais and his body shimmers, his face morphing before my eyes, until I'm staring at the actual depiction of the God of the Afterlife. He grows at least a foot taller, his skin flashing black, clawed fingers and toes punching out. His face extends into a snout, great jackal ears flicking up as his pale eyes meet mine. He storms closer.

"Who are you, thief?" he snarls, his mouth lined with sharp teeth that can rip me to shreds.

Darkness dances at the edge of my vision but I try to fight it. I open my mouth to speak but no words come out as I stare in horror at a God come to life. But the darkness wins, and I feel myself falling before my eyes even close.

"Look what you did! You scared her to death!" someone shouts.

"One less thing to worry about," another answers.

I don't feel my body hit the sand, but it must have, right? I'm going to die down here, and all I can think about is that I've been watching too many movies.

Where's Brendan Fraser when you need him?

3

WHEN I OPEN MY EYES, I'm staring at the deepest green I've ever seen, so many colors in them that I'm mesmerized even though my head feels like it got crushed under that stone door. The beautiful eyes are attached to an extremely handsome face, concern etched into every line.

"Can you hear me?" he asks, and I blink.

None of this is real, right? I've died and this is just some screwed up vision of heaven.

"It's alright. We're not going to hurt you," green eyes— Thoth the other called him— assures me.

I sit up way too fast, searching for the other two. When I see human-looking Anubis, I breathe a sigh of relief, but I still cringe away when he looks at me. He and Horus are arguing about something. Just thinking that line makes my brain shrink away. I'm just calling these three by god names. I'm sitting with gods.

"What's your name?" Thoth peers at me as if checking for injuries. He seems the most kind of the three, so I edge just a little closer to him. Thoth is the God of Knowledge and Writing. That sounds much better than the God of the Afterlife and the God of War.

"Delilah," I croak. "I'm an archeologist."

My hand trails along my hip, searching for the knife there. My fingers curl around the handle just in time for Anubis and Horus to turn towards me and walk forward. Ignoring Thoth, I scramble backward and yank the knife free, holding it in front of me like I know what I'm doing.

"Stay back!" My hand shakes so badly, I'm not sure if I'll be able to actually stab him. Can a god die? I certainly can. "Don't come any closer."

Anubis looks at me in amusement. Horus raises his brow, but otherwise, doesn't show any emotion. Thoth shakes his head and moves to stand by the other two. Anubis steps forward, taking charge. We're only five feet apart when he stops.

"Stabbing me will do you no good." He tilts his head, studying me. "Though you're brave to try."

"It'll slow you down enough that I can get away," I reply, gritting my teeth. "I won't let you take my soul."

The amusement dies and he clenches his jaw tight. "I'm not here to take your soul, Delilah."

"The dagger will not kill us. We're immortal," Thoth says from behind him, stepping forward. "And somehow, I think you released us from our slumber."

Too many movies, I chant inside my head. "Bullshit," I growl. "I don't know what kind of shit is going on, but if you don't let me go, I'll fight you to the death. I'm not dying at your hands, Jackal."

Anubis rolls his eyes at me. "It would be a shame to waste such beauty fighting non-existent enemies. We're not going to hurt you despite my initial desire to do so. I thought you meant us harm. And besides, I doubt you know which way to go to get out of here. Wherever here is."

"The Temple of the Gods." It's pointless to keep it from them. "And the only thing I did was fall through a trap door and touch the chalice."

Thoth's eyes light up at the mention of the chalice. "That explains it! We've been awakened by the Herald of Change!" He looks at me appreciatively, as if seeing me for the first time.

"What?" Anubis, Horus, and I say at the same time.

"Don't you two remember the plan Ra put into place? When Egypt is in turmoil, we can be awoken by the Herald of Change to fight for her."

Anubis raises his brows. "That wasn't a jest?"

Thoth literally rubs his forehead in annoyance. "Delilah, what year is it? What century?"

"It's the twenty-first century," I whisper, staring at him in amazement. This can't be real. Everything in me rebels against the idea of gods coming to life because I touched a golden cup.

"Thoth, any more insight into how this happened?" Horus asks, shock written all over his face.

"Ra must have entombed our souls within the chalice." He picks up the cup and stares at it, studying it. "I need my books to know more, but right now, it looks like this woman is our savior."

They all turn to look at me and I take a step backward. This is too much everything— too much information, too much excitement, too much man-flesh in front of my face that I want to lick.

"Look, I'm not really sure what's real or not right now. Maybe I was booby trapped and sprayed with some sort of hallucinogen. Maybe I'm licking the stones right now thinking something else." *Like that, I'm licking their chests.* "Are you telling me that I'm standing here with three Egyptian gods?" I realize that for the first time, their collars have different symbols on them, different scenes. "Anubis," I whisper, staring at him. "Thoth and Horus." They all nod their heads and I grab onto the nearest thing to steady myself, which just so happens to be the thigh of the stone Anubis. My hand is dangerously close to his private parts and my face flames while he smirks at me. "This is impossible. Oh shit! I must have died when I fell through the trap. I'm dead right now and dreaming about sexy Egyptian gods."

Three teasing smiles spread. "You think we're sexy?" Anubis asks.

"You're focusing on the wrong word there, Nubbie. I'm dead. And now I can understand ancient Egyptian and I'm having a very vivid dream."

Anubis shakes his head, that smile still on his face. "No, you're very much alive. I'm the God of the Afterlife, remember? I'd know if you were dead."

I grab my head, the darkness dancing at the edges of my vision again. "I think I'm going to pass out again."

"Take deep breaths," Thoth instructs, and I do as he says, trying to calm my racing heart. "We realize this is a major thing you're taking in, but we really have to find out exactly why we're here. We shouldn't have been so easily awoken, not unless Egypt is in turmoil and not by anyone other than the Herald of Change." His eyes take me in. "I don't mean offense, but you don't exactly look equipped for that role."

I grimace. "Technically, Egypt is probably considered in turmoil by your standards. It's been victim to a civil war and the government is trying to fight off the militia. I agree with you about the Herald thing. I'm not going to lie, I'm grossly underqualified for that job."

"Could there be a mistake?" Horus asks. "Some sort of accident that released us." He turns sharp eyes to me. "Are you alone? Perhaps, it's someone else."

I try not to let those words get to me. After all, I'd just said the same thing, that I was underqualified, but it didn't mean I wanted them to look around for the non-existent savior. I don't hide my cringe well.

"He didn't mean it rudely," Thoth hurries to explain.

"Yes, I did," Horus argues. "The woman admitted it herself. She can't help us, and now we're stuck in a century far from ours because our country is at war."

Anubis doesn't interrupt their argument with his own opinion, his eyes trained on me, studying my appearance and the shaking in my limbs. "Are you alright?" he whispers.

"Yes," I answer quickly but then think better of it. "No. I don't know. I'm a little overwhelmed if I'm being honest."

"Need me to distract you?" he asks, a sexy grin spreading. He moves a little closer and I flinch, remembering the way he'd looked coming after me. He frowns and stops, sadness in his eyes that makes me feel bad for flinching.

"I'm sorry," I whisper. "It was a reflex."

"I understand, Delilah." He shrugs his shoulders. "It's natural to be afraid of the unknown."

"That's the thing." I meet his eyes. "I do know you. I just didn't know you actually existed."

"You've studied us?"

"I'm an archeologist. It's kind of my job to study you. This temple was supposed to be my big discovery. There aren't that many of this scale left."

Anubis smiles and takes another step closer until there's only a foot between us. This time, I don't flinch, expecting it. My brain still tells me to flee but something tells me that I don't need to, not from them. It's probably a stupid decision.

"What would they say if you brought us out there? Would they talk about your great discoveries then?" he whispers, an intimacy in the air between us. Thoth and Horus still argue behind him, completely unaware of anything else.

"They would."

His cups my chin with his fingers, tilting my head up so our eyes meet. "Is that what you want?"

I shake my head, certain. "No. I don't think the world should know that you're gods. Humankind doesn't react well to things we don't understand, and while I'm sure you're strong and capable of protecting yourself, I won't hand you over on a silver platter for dissection."

I'm hyper aware of Anubis' fingers on me, of the breath

between us, and of the heat coming from his body. This deep inside the pyramid, it's chilly, and I find myself leaning towards him.

"Is it really necessary to seduce the first woman you find?" Horus asks with a groan.

Anubis clenches his jaw and looks at Horus over his shoulder. "Don't be upset because you didn't act first, Old Bird," Horus growls at him but he returns his eyes to mine. "Besides, why should I resist? I've been asleep for thousands of years, and Delilah here is far too tempting."

I step back and clear my throat. "Let's focus on getting you three out safely before we discuss other things." Anubis' eyes light up at my words, a wicked grin on his too handsome face. I'm pretty sure my ovaries sit up at attention and dance around. Traitors. Now really isn't the time, but I can't help but stare at their man chests one last time before I put on my professional face. "I can help you get out of the temple at least. Best to wait until dark so no one sees you. The dig site is heavily guarded, so we'll have to slip by guards anyways. If I go out alone at first, I can distract them so you can get through." I point towards the doorway blocked by a stone. "First, you three can figure out how to move that."

"Unacceptable," Horus says, shaking his head. "Dusk is too far away. We go now."

"He's right." Thoth rubs his hand on his neck, massaging it as if he has a two-thousand-year-old creak. "We can remain unseen if we wish. We'll follow you out."

"That still doesn't solve the problem of the doorway being blocked."

Anubis grins. "I can handle that."

I watch in surprise as Anubis walks up to the door and starts punching the stone. I'm even more shocked when cracks spread along with it. How strong does he have to be for that to happen?

Thoth rolls his eyes. "There's a mechanism somewhere,

Anubis. There's no reason to be using brute strength when we could be using wits."

"My way is more fun," he growls in answer, hitting the stone again and again until chunks start falling away.

"I don't know if this plan is solid," I interrupt. "Honestly, you say I'm some sort of Herald, but I'm just an archeologist from New York."

"What's New York?" Thoth asks, curiosity written across his face.

"It's a city and a state in America. Um, it's on a different land mass than we're currently on."

"That must have taken a long time to cross with a ship."

I raise my brows, realizing how woefully underprepared they are to see the world. "Um, we don't take ships to cross the ocean unless it's for, like, leisure. I've never been on a cruise so I can't tell you much about that. I flew on an airplane. I think you guys might be a little surprised by the world when we go outside."

"Humans can fly?" Horus asks in wonder. "When did they learn how to do that? Do they grow wings now?" He walks around me to check if I'm hiding a huge set of feathered wings. I don't know if he really expects to find them or not. If Anubis can shift, I'm assuming Horus and Thoth can, too. Thank god, I hadn't awoken Khepri. I couldn't even imagine a god with a beetle head.

"There's so much that's different between our centuries," I tell them, wringing my hands. "I can't even begin to tell you."

Anubis pulls the last of the rubble left from the door free and turns, a self-satisfied smile on his face. "Well, then, you can show us all the differences. You let us out into this strange new world. We're your responsibility now."

I gulp, wringing my hands harder until my bones pop. They all stare at me expectantly, as if I'm some sort of all-knowing person.

How do I tell them that I can't even keep a houseplant alive? Or that I killed the goldfish I bought when I was lonely?

How do I tell them that I keep imagining them making me their queen and running away together?

I scrub my hand down my face. I'm losing my mind. I really hope this isn't a dream. I can't imagine waking up to such disappointment after all this.

4

"Do you have any idea how long it will take us to get out of the pyramid?" I ask, because the moment we stepped through the doorway, we were met with just hallways and more doorways. What kind of crazy maze is this thing built to be?

Horus surprisingly is the one who leads us. I assumed it would have been Anubis since he seems like the one in charge. It makes a weird sort of sense. Anubis is the God of the Afterlife and Mummification. He has no powers that should be for navigation. Horus, on the other hand, has to navigate the skies, so they put him in charge of directing them. Thoth runs his fingers across the markings on the walls as we move, reading them to check for something we might have missed. I notice he taps an image of a crane each time we pass it.

"I remember Ra talking about this temple, about how it was meant to be confusing." Thoth smiles back at me as he talks. "No one is supposed to find the treasure room, and no one is supposed to escape should they be dropped down there. They're meant to die as offerings to the Gods they disturbed."

"Nice. I'm glad I didn't end up being an offering." My voice is far too nonchalant for talking about my death, but I choose not to dwell on it for too long.

"There are other ways you could offer yourself," Anubis adds, winking.

Horus scoffs and stops, spinning on his heel. "If she was offering herself to someone, it's not for you to dictate which one of us she chooses." His eyes are hard when he looks at Anubis but when he glances at me, there's a hidden fire there I didn't notice before. Perhaps the God of the Afterlife isn't the only one interested. I try not to let that thought get to me, to focus on getting out, but I can't help an image flitting through my mind: laying on a bed, surrounded by three Egyptian gods.

I glance at Thoth, the only one who hasn't made any comments, to find him watching me.

"Horus is correct. You are the Herald. That doesn't mean you owe us anything. You've already given us freedom and that is enough," he says, running his finger over another crane image. "Free will is important."

I wrinkle my brow, confused by all the gentle prodding. They aren't suggesting that I can sleep with them, are they? We've literally just met, and they're thousands of years old gods. "I'm a little confused . . ."

Anubis grins. "He's saying we're all interested in you, but it's all your choice. The Scholar never quite says what he means."

Thoth glares at him but doesn't argue.

"I'm literally the first woman you've seen since you woke up. Isn't that kind of like offering dirty water to a man dying of thirst? He doesn't care what it is so long as he gets it?"

Horus snorts, trying to hold in his laughter.

"I suppose you're right," Anubis says, shrugging his shoulders. "But we have a connection to you because you're the Herald. Don't be surprised if we still want you even after seeing what this world has to offer."

"Um," I mumble. I'm a little at a loss for what to say. I'm not the best flirter. I spend my time on books and sand. Honestly, this is so far out of my comfort zone, I don't know if they're teasing me or being serious. They don't seem like they expect anything but really, I don't know if that's some sort of mind trick, either. "Do you have powers?" I glance at Anubis. "Besides shifting into a scary jackal creature."

Thoth laughs and nods his head. "We all shift into our namesakes. But we also have other powers. I'm the God of writing, magic, and wisdom."

"I know that part. But what does that mean for your powers?"

"I can do transfiguration, cast spells, read a book far too fast, and remember everything."

"So you have a photographic memory?"

"Yes." He nods. "Horus can fly."

"You make it sound as if that's all I can do," Horus grumbles, moving forward again. "I'm the God of the sky, war, and hunting. I'm an excellent fighter."

Thoth points to a doorway on the right and we all trail behind Horus as he makes the turn. They placed me in-between Thoth and Anubis, the passageways too narrow to walk side by side.

"And what do you do?" I look over my shoulder at Anubis, studying his face. He's incredibly handsome. It's hard to imagine him shifting into his jackal head again. I wouldn't believe it if I hadn't watched it with my own eyes.

He shrugs, his go-to move, I'm realizing. "I'm the God of the Afterlife and Mummification."

"What does that mean for your powers?"

Thoth and Horus grow quiet, waiting for the answer themselves as if they're not quite sure what he's gonna say.

"It means, little herald," he says, stepping closer behind me and cupping my hip gently, "that I kill people."

Why does that turn me on so much? He literally just says he kills people and I'm practically panting from his touch.

"How?" I didn't become an archeologist because I didn't ask questions. I'm an explorer. That's what I do.

He leans in, his breath fluttering against the loose strands of my hair, tickling my neck. "I suck out their souls," he whispers, and there's absolute seduction in his voice. My legs turn to jelly and I find myself leaning back against his chest a little. "I rip them right from their chests." My eyes slide closed.

"That's enough, Anubis," Thoth interrupts. I peer at him through hooded eyes and see the stern set of his face. "Let's focus on getting out of this place first before you try to seduce her."

Anubis doesn't let me go right away, and I don't move, leaning back against his warm skin happily. Horus turns and levels his own gaze on Anubis, his brow raised in challenge. Anubis growls softly before pressing a kiss against the junction where my shoulder and neck meet, sending tingles all through my body. I watch the arousal spark to life in Thoth's eyes first; he's too slow to hide it. Horus doesn't try to hide his at all, his gaze dropping to take in my body briefly before he spins and continues. Anubis releases me but his hand stays on my hip, guiding me forward, keeping me from stumbling.

I'm so out of my depth here. When a God sets out to seduce you, he means business, and apparently, these three have set their sights on me. I can't decide if that's something I should celebrate or something I should cower from.

"You said you're an archeologist," Thoth says, breaking the silence. "This temple is meant to be your discovery?"

"It is. I'm technically sharing the honor with an archeology legend. However, I'm doing all the work. He doesn't seem too keen on actually working anymore."

"Is this your first discovery?"

"Lay off the questioning, Thoth," Anubis growls, but I shake my head.

"I don't mind answering questions. This is my passion. No, it's not my first discovery but it's my first big one. I don't think there will be too many more at this level left." I smile at Thoth when he turns to look at me. His lips curl up when he meets my eyes.

"When we're free of this place and have time, I'll tell you what it was like to actually be alive in our era."

My heart beats hard inside my chest, and his green eyes sparkle. "You got me. I'll sit and listen to you talk for hours." I chuckle, brushing my hair back, suddenly self-conscious of what I must look like. It's a little late to worry about it now but something tells me they don't mind. I'm a far cry from the gorgeous women they were probably used to, but none of them have even lingered too long on the dirt covering my body, or the tangles in my hair. Of course, I'm still the only woman they've seen since they woke up. That could always change, I think sadly. "So, the crane is the symbol that leads you from the pyramid?" I ask, changing the subject. I don't really want to think too much harder about how things could change when we get out of here.

"You know the trick?" Thoth grins at me, touching another crane image.

"Some people discovered it years ago. It's all about figuring out which symbol it is. I would also like to know how come there are no traps through here."

"There are." He presses his hand against another crane. "I'm just disabling them as I go. That's why I'm touching the images."

My eyes widened in surprise. I never knew there was a way to disable them, but it makes sense. Why wouldn't they make it possible to move freely around inside the pyramid?

Horus leads us through another doorway and the air feels a little less thick as if we might be making headway. My ears choose that moment to pop, almost as if in answer to my thoughts. The steady slight slope of the floor wears on my calves but I continue on. I really don't know how far I fell before landing in the Gods' temple.

I didn't take any of the treasure from the room. The only thing I'd grabbed when we left was the chalice only because we need to figure out more about this awakening thing. Thoth said that it was meant as a protection for Egypt, and yet the chalice had been hidden away and became nothing more than a legend. It was time we learned about how this all happened in the first place.

"Do you hear that?" Horus asks, pausing in front of us.

I tilt my head, listening. At first, I don't hear a thing besides our breathing and the soft scuttle of other creatures. Then the sound of voices reaches my ears, barely piercing the silence but enough that I can make out the gentle vibrations.

"We're close to the top!" I move to go past Thoth and Horus, but Anubis stops me with a hand on my forearm.

"Wait."

"They're probably looking for me," I remind him, wrinkling my brow. "Why should I wait?"

"Anubis is right," Thoth interrupts. "Something doesn't feel right. The air feels heavy with premonition."

"Premonition?" My confusion only increases. "Like visions? What does that mean?"

Horus turns and meets my eyes. "It means something bad is going to happen, but we don't know what."

"Fantastic," I mumble, glaring at the direction the voices are coming from. "So what do you advise oh, God of War?"

Horus doesn't even react to the obvious jab in my words. His face is serious and stern when he speaks. "We proceed with caution. Perhaps, it would be best for us to go invisible."

"I don't like that," Anubis counters. "It takes too much time for the glamour to be removed before we can act if something goes south and Delilah needs our protection."

"That's a valid point." Thoth turns to me. "What do you think we should do, Herald?"

I raise my brows at the formal title. "I don't think any of my crew will hurt me, and no one will believe your gods. They'd be confused as to where you came from but believing you came back to life because I picked up a chalice is a little farfetched.

Best bet is to walk out with me, and we can tell them some story." I wave my hands around in an attempt to think of something. "Maybe we can say you three are here for some sort of production for the government, but you fell into some sort of trap door outside and ended up in the same place as me." It sounds like a stupid idea as I say it aloud and I cringe. "I don't know, honestly. Maybe we can play it by ear?"

All three gods stare at me and I can't figure out if it's in disappointment that those words just came out of their great Herald's mouth, or if it's amusement. Honestly, they're hard to read when they aren't sending me appreciative glances.

"Play it by ear," Horus repeats, looking at Anubis. "I don't think I'm the person to lead us in this sort of mission."

"I'll do it." Anubis steps forward. "This seems much more my style."

We all shift our order. I have to press myself against the wall for the large men to get by. Anubis takes the opportunity to rub far too closely, his chest pressing against my breasts as he sends me a saucy wink. Horus is a little more gentlemanly, but his chest and shoulders are so broad, that he ends up brushing up against me anyways. He meets my eyes but doesn't tease like Anubis. No, he strikes me as someone who is completely straight forward. I'll know when he sets his sights on me.

Anubis takes up the front, Thoth still second in line, then me, and Horus takes up the rear. We start moving towards the voices, the echo getting slightly louder the higher we climb. We walk for I don't know how long before I'm able to make out who some of the voices are.

"We have to go searching for her," Jessica tells someone. We still aren't close enough to see them, but we're close. They sound as if they're just around the corner. "She's been missing for hours now. It'll be dark soon and we won't be able to keep looking. She could be bleeding out somewhere."

"We don't have the capability to go searching in an

unknown and unmapped pyramid right now." That is definitely Dagen's voice. I'm surprised he sounds sober, and that he's even here. "Dr. Jackson knows how to take care of herself. She knows all the tools of her trade. She'll find her way out."

"And if she doesn't?" Jessica argues. Their voices are so close now, I expect to see them at any moment with a turn. "If she dies down there somewhere?"

"Then her death will be written in the history books when they talk about the discovery of the Temple of the Gods."

Of course, Dagen Crenshaw is interested in the pyramid now that he knows what it is. He'll be hoping to seize all the pay associated with such a high-profile historical event.

"How dare you!" Jessica shouts and then there's an obvious scuffle as if Jessica is trying to attack him.

That's the moment we turn a corner and come into the scene in front of us. The first thing I see is that Jessica is, indeed, trying to attack Dagen, who looks a little less for wear. Sure, he might be sober now, but he certainly didn't take any time to change into a shirt without food stains. Two men hold Jessica in the air between them as she struggles. I don't recognize either one. My other crew stands off to the side, watching everything warily. Dan has his nose in his journal, trying to decipher the code to move through the passageway, the one Thoth already solved. There are other men surrounding Dagen, including Bek. They're all focused on Jessica as she spouts all manner of curses at the men holding her. None of them notice my entrance or the three men with me.

I'm tempted to announce that it's the crane to Dan, but something tells me that I don't want these men with Dagen to know how to navigate the temple. Maybe it's just Thoth's words getting to me, the premonition mentioned, but I definitely feel something that holds my words back.

"It's okay," I say instead. "I found my way out."

Every pair of eyes turns to me first, and then the three men who flank my sides and back.

Jessica visibly relaxes. "Oh, thank god. I thought you'd died."

No one else says a word, not at first. Dagen stares at the gods around me in confusion. Bek's eyes light up and I don't think that's a good thing. And then Dan's eyes find the chalice in my hand.

"Is that—" he stops, frowning, and then shakes his head. "No, it can't be."

"You found the chamber?" Dagen asks, surprise written on his face. I don't know how he knows about the chamber to begin with. "How?"

"Well, I sort of fell into it," I shrug.

"And who are they?" He takes in Anubis, Horus, and Thoth, recognizing their imposing presence. None of them say a word.

"Um," I start, not really knowing what to say. "I found them?"

Jessica eyes the naked chests. "You just found three hot naked men? Girl, give me some of your luck. Share the love."

I almost laugh, but it dies in my throat when Bek steps forward, an intensity in his eyes that makes me nervous. That feeling of danger grows stronger and I tense. The gods sense the same thing, each one shifting around me. Something is wrong. Thoth was right.

"You released them from the chalice." He clenches his jaw hard enough to grind his teeth. "How did you accomplish that?"

Anubis cocks his head, his fingers brushing against my own. The touch makes me feel better, even with all the tension. "A better question would be how you know about us, mortal?"

"Mortal?" Jessica repeats, looking closer at Anubis. Whatever she sees makes her take a step back, closer to the rest of my crew. The men who had been holding her had already released her, their attention on the new threat in the room.

Bek reaches slowly inside his vest and pulls out a gun. I tense, along with every one of my crew. This just took a dangerous turn. Anubis, Horus, and Thoth stare at the gun with raised brows, recognizing it's a weapon but probably not quite knowing how.

"We're immortal," Horus says, giving away all his cards. Isn't he supposed to be a God of War? You don't show your whole hand at the beginning. But maybe he just doesn't understand the actual threat here. They're immortal, yes, but my crew is not. I'm not. There are too many people here who can die.

Dagen shakes his head but doesn't interrupt Bek's speech, and I realize he was never in charge.

"Why?" I ask. "You're supposed to be a legend. And you sold us out? For what?"

Dagen has the decency to look ashamed but he straightens his spine. "Being a legend doesn't pay the bills, Dr. Jackson. And besides, Bek Hare-em-ha pays much better than the government."

I hear Jessica's gasp the same time my own slips passed my lips. Bek isn't just some criminal. He's THE criminal. He's the general of the militia fighting the Egyptian government. The danger in the room cranks up a notch.

Bek trains his weapon on Anubis and I resist the urge to step in front of him. It would be a stupid decision really. Anubis can't die apparently. What would be the point in taking a bullet for him?

"I told you. We can't die. We're gods, you spineless human." Horus growls under his breath, his shoulder tense and ready for a fight.

Bek only smiles at their words, as if what Horus had said was funny. "You're right," he speaks, his voice echoing against the stone. "But she isn't." Every man in the room that isn't with my crew pulls a weapon from their bodies and levels it on our party, but Bek, he points his gun right at my chest. I freeze. "And if she's the Herald of Change, then your life forces are tied to hers."

Great. Now we're all going to die. Someone, Quick! Get the Book of the Dead!

Too bad this isn't a movie.

5

"I don't want to shoot her," Bek continues. "This can all be solved if you swear your allegiance to my army and help us bring Egypt back to its former glory."

Jessica snorts and I give her a look to stay silent, to keep the attention off them, but she's never been one to stop her words. "You'll take it back to the stone age is what you'll do. The people of Egypt deserve freedom, not a dictator."

Bek looks over at her, a smile on his face. "Ah, such sweet advice from a woman who has never lived anything but a life of privilege. What right do you have to speak on my people's behalf?"

"I speak on behalf of people who need help." She meets his eyes head on. "I speak for those too afraid or unable to speak for themselves."

"I see." Until this moment, Bek's gun had still been trained on my chest. The feeling in the air sizzles with electricity and Thoth tenses, a twitch of his fingers I barely notice. "Then you're a threat to my goals, Ms. Jessica. And I don't take threats well." Jessica raises her chin as Bek slowly turns the gun and points it at her.

"No!" I shout at the same time that Anubis leaps forward and tackles Bek. The gun goes off and all hell breaks loose.

"What the fuck!?" Dan shouts, grabbing Jessica and shoving the others down.

Anubis shifts while tumbling with Bek, that scary Jackal face making me cringe even as I crouch down to avoid a rogue bullet. I watch Horus shift next, his head transforming into the face of an eagle with a massive beak. Wings grow from his back and he jumps into the fray. I notice his clawed feet next when they slice clean through one of Bek's men who tries to shoot him. Thoth looks at me nervously before he shifts, but when he does, his face transforms into a great ibis, his beak wicked sharp as he attacks. He doesn't use brute strength like Anubis, or skilled moves like Horus. Thoth has his own powers, and I watch in open-mouthed wonder as golden magic glows from his hands that steals through some of the men's bodies. They fall to the ground, dead.

Bek manages to throw Anubis long enough to scramble away. Before Anubis can follow, his men take up the assault, firing their weapons directly at the God of the Afterlife. He grunts as a few sink into his flesh but he doesn't pause as he wraps his claws around two of their throats. I watch, both in awe and fear, as a pale blue haze pulls from their bodies, releasing into the air and disappearing. Both men fall to the floor with a solid thunk. Anubis trains his eyes on the others. He manages to look back at me once, meeting my eyes, a question here that I can't answer yet. I don't know if it bothers me. It doesn't feel like it does, not at the moment.

Jessica screams and I realize my crew is still cowering in the corner, their heads covered in an attempt to stay out of the line of fire. Bek is nowhere to be seen but his men don't leave, continuing the fight even after he's long since run. He won't be gone for long. A man like him doesn't give in so easily, especially when he wants to use the Gods as the weapons they obviously are.

There are only a handful of men left but it's enough to cause damage. I watch as a man, his face twisted into a hateful expression, turns his gun towards my crew, and I act without thinking. I rise from my position and I sprint, pumping my arms as hard I can. The room isn't large by any means, but it's large enough that it takes me a moment to get there. The gun goes off the second I step in front of my crew and it feels like something shoves me hard in the shoulder. Confused, I look down and watch the bright red blood well and begin to spread outward from my shirt.

Anubis roars and I watch in shock as he rips the man to shreds but it doesn't even compute in my mind.

"Guys," I whisper, my voice barely echoing against the stone walls. "I think I've been shot."

My legs collapse beneath me. Someone screams. I don't think it was me. I wait for the impact of hitting the ground, but it never comes. I can't feel anything. Shouldn't I be in pain? Maybe I'm in shock?

The palest eyes I've ever seen look deeply into my own, his face no longer a Jackal but all man. "Hold on for me, little Herald. We're going to get you some help."

"Are you here to take my soul?" I whisper, my voice is hardly more than a croak.

"I refuse to accept your soul, Delilah. You're going to live. I forbid you from dying."

My eyes flutter closed at his words but even at the edge of darkness, I can't help but hear his words repeating over and over in my mind.

I forbid you from dying.

Bossy god. Death waits for no one.

6

THE FIRST TIME I open my eyes, I'm so disoriented, I'm not sure what I'm seeing. Didn't I pass out inside the pyramid? I should be surrounded by stone and sand. Instead, I'm looking up at some sort of ceiling. It takes me long minutes to realize that I'm in my hotel room. It takes me even longer to notice the three gods standing against the wall.

I groan and try to sit up, my shoulder twinging and causing me to grimace in pain. Right, I'd been shot in the shoulder. I glance down at the bandage wrapped around me, touching my finger gently to the sensitive wound. I hiss at the sharp pain.

"Don't touch it," Thoth instructs. "You need to heal."

Finally, I look up at them, taking them in. They no longer stand half naked, a shame really. They're dressed in modern clothing, but they don't look any less attractive. Thoth wears a button-down shirt and khakis. Both Anubis and Horus wear a t-shirt and jeans; they look comfortable.

Together, they move towards the bed I'm sitting on until they're close enough to sit on the edges.

"Is Jessica and the crew okay?" I ask, my voice rough. Thoth hands me a glass of water and I take it gratefully.

"Everyone is unharmed. Jessica hasn't left your side during

your recovery. She's only gone now because she had to find food. Her stomach was growling so loud Anubis thought we were under attack." Thoth grins, teasing as he looks at Anubis.

"And Bek?" Three frowns are my answer. "He got away?"

"He did," Horus confirms. "We don't know how he escaped but once you were harmed, we turned our attention to getting you and the other innocents out of the temple."

"Thank you for taking care of them," I breathe, brushing my hand through my hair.

"You care for them. That means they fall under our protection," Anubis shrugs. "It's really no big deal."

"It means a great deal to me," I reassure him, flashing them a small smile. My shoulder begins to throb, and I lay back against the pillows.

"We weren't entirely honest with you," Thoth starts, and I turn my gaze to him. His green eyes shimmer with what I think is nervousness as he shifts where he sits.

"About what?"

"Before we slept, Ra put a plan into place, a protection in case Egypt ever needed it."

"That's what you said before," I nod, watching him closely.

"We were to be awakened by the Herald of Change," Horus adds. "And our lives were to be tied to theirs to ensure we could complete our mission."

"The Herald of Change is our life force." Anubis meets my eyes. "But there was always a strong chance the Herald would be expected to be tied to our existence in another way."

"What way is that?" I ask, engrossed in their story.

"Ra mentioned an opportunity, that our powers could grow stronger if we were to join with the Herald." Thoth sighs. "We don't just feel a connection to you. We're almost drawn to you as if you're our very breath." He closes his eyes. "Because you are. If you die, we return to our sleep whether the mission is complete or not."

I frown. I don't like the sound of that, that they might not have a choice in the matter. "And what is your mission?"

"To return Egypt to her former glory and bring its people prosperity and new beginnings," Anubis says the words as if they're a mantra. Maybe they are. Maybe they've known their duty since their creation, but I'm just an archeologist. I can't be some sort of savior for Egypt.

"Are you certain I'm this Herald of Change?" I ask, biting my lip. I'm not really the lead-an-army sort of person.

"We know you are, or else we wouldn't have awoken when you touched the chalice." Horus holds up the golden cup before gently setting it on the bedside table. I'm glad someone remembered to grab it before all the chaos started.

"We are in your debt, Delilah," Thoth speaks, "and we offer our protection and our lives to you."

I shake my head. When it jostles my shoulder, I grimace, but I don't stop. "Nope, that's not right. I can't be responsible for three men. I can't. I can barely keep track of myself."

"Do you, or do you not, know much about our culture?" Thoth meets my eyes, urging me to understand. "Don't you want to help us?"

"I do," I whisper, pushing my hair back from my face.

"Then you are prepared. You have been chosen, and it is our duty to protect you and complete our mission."

What the hell did I stumble into when I accepted this job? I was only looking to make my mark by discovery. I never anticipated becoming some sort of Harbinger for three Egyptian Gods trying to save their country. I certainly never expected to be shot and have a warlord out for my blood. I can't deny my curiosity, and my mom would be so disappointed if I turned away from people in need, even if they were all powerful gods.

"Okay," I nod my head. "I can help. But Bek is going to be watching. He wants you three to fight his war for him, and he'll do anything to ensure that cooperation. How are we going to do this?"

"First, we have a problem," Horus growls, clenching his jaw hard.

"What is it?" It can't be good. Their faces are all solemn as they watch me.

Anubis sighs. "Ra said there would be four gods awoken when the time came. Myself, Horus, Thoth—", *please don't say Khepri. Please don't say Khepri,* "— and Sobek." I breathe a sigh of relief.

"We're missing Sobek," Thoth repeats, "and it didn't dawn on me before that something was wrong."

"So what does that all mean?" I ask, staring at each of them. They're sitting close enough that each is touching me gently, careful not to jostle my shoulder. "What do we do?"

"We don't know, but without him, we're all vulnerable."

I don't know exactly when my life turned into my favorite movie, or when I somehow managed to tie three, possibly four, Egyptian gods to my life, but I can't really complain. I was hoping for an adventure, after all. When I stare at Anubis, Horus, and Thoth, I can't help but wonder, what would Evelyn and Rick do?

I grin, and even with the pain in my shoulder, I sit up enough so that I can raise my chin. "Well," I say, "what are we waiting for then?" I scrape my hair away from my face and steel my spine. "Let's go save Egypt."

THE END FOR NOW . . .

INTO THE STORM

LULU M. SYLVIAN

SPECIAL THANKS

With special thanks to Peter Blood, Geoffrey Thorpe, Brian Hawke, Jamie Waring, Will Turner, Jack Sparrow, Fredrick, DP Roberts, Vallo, and most definitely, Rafael Sabatini.

1

The entire Raptor rattled and shook with ferocity. This was not good. It didn't help that alarms blared through my head like a hot spike thru warm butter. Yeah, I got it, this whole thing was not good, with capital letters. I didn't need the fucking alarms.

I scanned the readouts, half of them were dead. What I wouldn't give right now for some old-fashioned analog dials. Analog and space used to work really well together. Why not now?

The joystick between my knees fought me hard, and I pulled with everything I had to port. It barely seemed to help. I continued to pitch to starboard. I fought against the gravitational forces that kept me plastered back into my seat. It was tempting to hit the release on my harness, so I could really put my upper body strength to use, but with the shaking, I would get knocked against the canopy and then knocked into the next life.

The bird leveled enough that I could hold on one-handed. I reached above me, flipped the cover off a dozen switches and began pounding at buttons. "Shut. The. Fuck. Up. Already!"

Blissful lack of alarms. But not silence. The entire bird

creaked and rattled, and the wind made an unholy rush of sound. But I could think.

I slammed my fist against the system reboot, located above and behind my head, in a very hard to reach place, on purpose. It effectively cut power to my control panel and then turned it all back on three seconds later. Two seconds. One.

Everything that had been on came back on with a flicker of red warning lights. The half of my controls that were out before stayed out.

I had no idea where I was, or where I was headed. All I knew I was coming down fast, and it was dark. Dark was good, dark meant no population center for me to become the latest news tragedy of the Jupiter Mission. But dark also meant I had no idea how close I was to the ground.

Fucking ground. I shouldn't have been in the atmosphere. I should have been dozing in a gentle orbit, waiting for my ride to catch me and ferry me in the relative comfort of my own cockpit, without the use of my near depleted fuel reserves, to Juno Station. It always cracked me up, Jupiter with its moons named after the god's nonconsensual lovers, and the station that served as our gathering port before launch, named after his wife. In our case, Juno was enabling us to get to her husband. Back in the time of the Roman gods, I'm pretty sure Juno wasn't involved in getting Jupiter some side action. Maybe she was an enabler by not interceding on his victims' behalves. Maybe she never learned how to say, "Jupiter, no."

Well, I had said "Jupiter, fuck yes," and that's where I wanted to be headed, instead I was headed nose down into a hostile atmosphere— hostile to my Raptor, because it was trying to tear it into small pieces right out from underneath me — with my instruments out, and no freaking clue how soon I needed to pull the eject lever.

Too soon and there wouldn't be enough air to fill my shoot. I'd end up spinning out of control, I'd blackout, and then I'd go splat at terminal velocity. Too late, and I wouldn't have time to gain enough air to slow anything down and I would go splat at terminal velocity. Really too late, I wouldn't clear the canopy, and yep, splat. Terminal velocity sucked.

The shaking doubled down in effort, and I was back to double fisting the joystick. Right now, all I could manage was to keep her steady and pointed toward the dark. Terminal velocity was in my future. At this point, I needed to make sure it was limited to only me.

Damn it. This wasn't how any of this was supposed to go. The launch was stupid easy. I literally only needed to fly the bird out of the atmosphere. No more failed rocket-based launches. Blessed technological advances. Once up there, I needed to park myself at a set point in a geosynchronous orbit and wait for the ferry to make its rounds and scoop me up. Once the ferry had all of us Raptors loaded up, it would leave orbit and carry us to the far side of the moon to Juno Station.

There was no pulling back on the joystick, no matter how much I fought it. I tempted fate and let go, back to one hand. I searched the side of my seat for the emergency "this bitch has got to ditch" eject lever. A simple handle, that's all I needed to do was give a yank, and I would be launched up and out like a chocolatier's glass elevator.

Where was the fucking handle? My hand flailed about. I could picture it in my mind, it was bright yellow, and located just under my right thigh. Fuck, wrong right thigh. I fought to switch hands. No, there wasn't a handle under that thigh either.

"Arrg!" Where was the fucking handle? Damn it. This was a new bird; they moved the handle right between my thighs.

G-forces were doing their job and keeping me back in my chair. There was no reaching down in front of me to yank anything. My hand flailed around between my legs, and then back up to the joystick. I took a deep breath and tried again. My fingertips brushed the top of the handle, but I could not lift myself another freaking inch against the forces pushing against me. The shaking was considerably worse. My teeth were going to start falling out any second.

I needed out of this bird. I needed out— right fucking now! I no longer cared if there was or wasn't enough air to fill my shoot, I didn't want to meet terminal velocity in this tin can. A firefly caught my attention. No, no, no, no, no. There were no fireflies in my atmosphere-controlled ship. That was a spark, and it had friends. Lots of them, and they flew around my head in a happy little fiery deathtrap dance. This took *Not Good* to a whole new level.

The pop sounded very far away.

... and then blackness ...

I AWOKE WITH A START. My eyes opened and I sat up, trying to suck in as much air as possible. The room felt confining. I kicked out from under the blankets. The dog sleeping by my feet lifted his head and whined, while lightly thumping the mattress with his tail.

Did I have a dog?

I didn't recognize where I was. This was not a standard-issue bunk.

The sound of something breaking and roar of laughter rolled in from the open windows. Maybe I was on leave? I lifted my hand to my head. I didn't have a headache. Maybe I really had overdone it, and managed to sleep through the hangover?

My feet hit cool hardwood, and I stood up. A breeze billowed the curtains inward. I brushed them aside and discovered the openings were more like doors than windows. I still had to step up and over to get through them and out onto the small balcony, but only two or three inches.

The crashing of waves and moonlight dancing on water

held my gaze as I stepped outside. The beach was just beyond the courtyard. It was comfortably cooler outside.

"Ah-ha," a deep voice bellowed up from the courtyard below. "The fair mademoiselle has awoken. Speak fair maiden so that we may be gifted with your sweet graces."

The speaker used a fake British accent. He was tall with long blond hair. He wore clothes for some Ren Fair, or Shakespeare revival. I would put my money on Shakespeare. After all, that was some pretty flowery vocabulary flowing from the . . . okay, the man was hot and even hotter in that getup, so yeah, those words flowed from lips that made a girl think naughty thoughts. He was tall, broad-shouldered, defined pecs, and I caught a glimpse of some serious ab definition from the open front of his dark shirt. His pants had that weird square flap at the front of period-appropriate costuming and they weren't form-fitting, so who knows if there was a shapely ass under there, but his hips were slim, and his thighs long. Oh, and those over the knee leather boots about did me in.

"Where the fuck am I?" My voice sounded like a frog, and my mouth tasted like someone killed a goat with cotton balls and hid the evidence behind my teeth.

The laughter from his friend pulled my attention from the tall blond standing below to seek him hiding in the shadows.

"Our fair maiden sounds like she may have spent a little too much time with some of our friends. Who should we thank for teaching such a pretty mouth such foul language?" At least this guy's Spanish accent sounded authentic.

I swallowed when he stood up and crossed the little courtyard to stand next to his friend. Equally as tall, easily as handsome, and dressed for a show in dark red velvet and lace. He bowed low, and the swords at his waist clanked together. He had darker skin, his dark hair was pulled back into a braid, and a thin beard hugged along the lines of his sculpted jaw. And, yes, another set of naughty, naughty, thought-provoking lips.

"Guys, I don't have time for this." I wanted to know what was going on.

The dog from the bed pressed against my hip. He was huge, looked like a wolfhound, but I wasn't up on my dog breeds. My hand instinctively rested behind his ears and scratched.

"We have plenty of time. I have it on good authority that Cavenaugh's fleet is two days from here. We are safe as houses," Blondie said.

"I would rather be safe and under sail. She is better, no? We have done our good deed and pulled the beautiful siren from the watery depths. She has her land legs, we should go."

"I can hear you. You know? What do you mean pulled me from the watery depths?" I asked.

"You were out there, in the middle of the ocean, floating on something I've never seen before. We pulled you in. To be honest, in case there was a reward for your rescue. Who are you, dear lady? And is your father rich?"

"My father?" I shook my head. He just mentioned wreckage. My bird! That hadn't been some nightmare. I had gone down. I blinked hard to suppress the anger motivated tears. Too many years in training, too many years making sure I was going to space, all for nothing.

"I'm Captain Jane Way."

They made an audible taken aback sound, not quite a gasp, but still, I told them something they were not expecting. That was no surprise. I got that a lot.

Everyone at the flight academy had been familiar with the fictitious captain of the same name. While her first name was Katheryn, my full name matched her last. While she had a penchant for coffee, my go-to drink was tequila. Hell, most of us had come from families with fans of the franchise, and I grew up going to school with many Kirks, McCoys, and even a Tiberius or three.

"Captain of what fair maiden?" the Spaniard asked. I think I wanted to see him with a ball gag sooner than later. I mean, why put such a pretty face to waste? I just didn't want to hear him call me *fair maiden* again.

"All pilots rank Captain. So that would be my official ranking. Captain of my Raptor." I leaned over the railing and gave the men my hardest military training stare I could. They bristled under my scrutiny. Good.

The balcony was not a full story above the courtyard. The floor where I stood was maybe only five feet off the ground. I lifted my nightgown up around my thighs with one hand, and bracing the other on the railing, I vaulted up and over. The dog barked.

It took effort, more than it should have. I would never admit that to anyone, my body was not exactly up for what I had just asked it to do. It should have been. I was a Raptor pilot chosen to travel through space to establish colonies on Jupiter's moons. I should be in better shape than these half-drunk Shakespearean wanna-bes. I held the classic superhero half kneel; fist braced on the ground landing a bit longer than I expected. I needed to regain some stability.

Of course, when I lifted my head, I glared at the men. I was going for maximum intimidation effect. I stood slowly. I may have been shorter than the two of them, but that wasn't going to stop me.

In a slow even voice, that no longer sounded like a frog lived in my throat I said, "Now, let's try this again. Where am I?"

The pretty blond one bowed and took a step back, after an appropriate moment of silence. "Mademoiselle Way."

"Captain," I corrected.

"Fair Captain," the Spaniard pronounced it cap-ee-taan.

"Lads, you're missing the point. She's Captain Way." The third man had next to no accent at all. He emerged from under the canopy the Spaniard had been hiding under earlier. "She's used to being in charge."

I hadn't realized there was a third man. I gave this new one a slight nod, maintaining my dominance in the group, not letting anyone know that my knees were growing weak, and it wasn't because I was surrounded by hot men.

"Are there more of you?" I asked as I slipped into the regulation at-ease stance. The shift of weight on my legs helped me to maintain an upright posture.

"Just the three of us Captain." The new one approached and stood a little too close. I could smell the wine on his warm breath.

I had to lift my chin to look him in the eye. I was tempted to thread my fingers through his wavy hair and pull his mouth down to mine. It would definitely give me an excuse to have him hold me upright. A thought worth considering since he had one of those sinfully delightful mouths too. But right now, I wanted answers, and I wanted to assert my dominance over these costumed players.

"You didn't bring in the wreckage I was found on, did you?" I tried hard to ignore this man who was within my personal space. I wasn't about to back down. Besides, I more than kind of liked it. The heat that radiated off his body was packed with sexual energy and not pissed at the female energy— there was a difference, I could always tell. This man would be able to dominate me, but I got the feeling he wouldn't unless I gave him permission. I liked that. I liked that a lot.

"What kind of ship were you on? I've never seen material like that in all my years at sea."

I turned my head to face the blond. That was a bad idea. My vision faded into splotchy gray blobs. I could sort of hear the men. But they were far away.

. . . and then blackness . . . again.

This time when I woke up, it wasn't with a start. This time I groggily rolled over, cracked an eyelid, didn't see a red digital time readout, rolled over and tried to go back to sleep. The pillow I crashed into was the softest I had ever felt, and with the windows open, and the fresh breeze, I was too comfortable. Sleep was where it was at, and that's where I wanted to stay.

Besides, I had been having a lovely dream about a curly-haired pirate, with barely a hint of an accent, a strong jaw, stronger arms, and knee-weakening kisses. He had just taken his shirt off, and I had wantonly pulled my nighty over my thighs, so I knew we were headed for more than some necking. I really wanted to see what happened next. I drifted back into my dream lover's arms.

"Jane." His voice was so soft, like a caress.

"Yes." He had my consent, all of it.

His knuckles ran down the side of my face, and I felt the touch deep in my core. I hiked the skirt of my nightgown up higher. Take the hint man, take the hint!

"Jane."

"Mayhaps our fair Captain should not have jumped down to join us." That wasn't my lover's voice. He didn't say cap-ee-taan, the way this voice did.

"Andreas, get her some water. I don't think she quite realizes what she's been through." The bad British accent said.

Oh right, I had been talking to some Elizabethan re-enactors. I had to pull rank on their drunk asses, and . . .

And it hadn't worked. They barely flinched, and they hadn't told me what I wanted to know.

I sat up and looked around. I was back in bed. That monstrous dog was back on the bed with me, and next to me sat the man who had been making love to me in my dream.

Yeah, okay, that could definitely be something worth pursuing. Hell, all of them were that hot. Bad accents and all. The blond stood at the end of the bed; a tall armoire was holding his languid form upright.

We all turned our attention to the door when the fancy-dressed Spaniard came in followed by a maid carrying a pitcher of water, and glasses on a tray.

I could tell she was a maid because she had a freaking apron on over her clothes, and one of those little folded up hats. It made me think of a vintage nurse's hat, the kind that looks like origami. She wasn't a nurse, and her clothes, how to describe them . . . She was also dressed in the same time period, mid- to late-sixteen hundreds I guessed, full-length skirt, billowy fabrics.

I groaned— it was too dark in here. "Why doesn't someone turn on a light?" I asked.

"I can bring in more lamps," the maid said.

Lover-boy nodded. I should probably learn his name, especially if I was going to continue to have semi-erotic dreams with him in the starring role.

I shifted my attention to him. His brow furrowed as he stared back.

"You want to tell me what's going on?" I guess I felt a connection to him, after all, he was the first one to recognize my authority, and he was the one sitting here. I can only assume he's the one who picked my ass up when I passed out.

"You swooned," bad accent said.

I swiveled to face him. "And you are?"

He pushed off the tall dresser he lounged against and bent into a deep bow with a sweeping flourish of his arm. "Mademoiselle Captain, I am Lord William Montague, Duke of North Ives."

"Lesser Duke," the Spaniard cut in.

"This foul beast is Andreas de Tas-Sliema du Malta, trust nothing he says," the Duke introduced the man I thought of being Spanish. Shows what I know about accents.

"Señior de Tas-Sliema, you English dog."

"If you're going to be like that—"

"Monty!"

I looked back at the man sitting by me on the bed. He lifted his brows in a way that said no matter how grand a title either of these two presented, he was the one who kept them in line.

"Everyone in this room is capable of captaining their own

ship. I have a very strong feeling yours is at the bottom of the ocean, along with Monty's. Proper introductions should never take place in a bedchamber. Allow me to not so properly present Captain William Montague, younger son of a British Duke. You can call him Monty, we all do. Señior Andreas de Tas-Sliema du Malta." With each introduction, he held his hand out to the other men. When it was his turn, he rested his hand across his chest. "And I am Captain Eric Mann, ma'am."

The way he said his name had me giving him the side-eye. That hadn't seemed particularly Elizabethan, he had slipped out of character.

The maid came back in carrying several light hurricane lamps. The power must be out.

"And as you told us earlier you are Captain Way of the Raptor."

"Not The Raptor, a Raptor. I pilot a Raptor-class fighter." I looked at the puzzled expression on the faces surrounding me. The terror that crossed the maid's face made me change my mind, "Yes, Captain of the Raptor, a fighting ship."

I scanned the room, there were no electric lamps, no television, no electronic items at all.

This was less than not good. At least I was no longer in a bird on fire crashing into the planet after somehow being knocked out of orbit.

"Where am I?"

"You are in my home, near Bodden Town," Mann said.

"Where? That sounds like east coast, the Union States, or—" it was entirely too balmy out to be along the north-eastern coast of North America, "— an island somewhere."

Andreas laughed, "Yes fair Captain, an island somewhere."

"Caymans to be precise." I swear Monty was about to add a 'ha-ha' to the end of his sentence. He had the speech pattern about him.

Cayman Islands? That was a hard nope. Those had been underwater with a majority of the smaller Caribbean islands for too long now. "I need to see the wreckage you pulled me from, take me there." I tried to push out of bed. Mann eased me back against the mattress with two firm hands on my upper arms.

He followed me down, his face entirely too close, too familiar. His tone was low, and his breath brushed my cheek. "You are going to stay in bed. You have been unconscious for the better part of a week. Your body isn't as strong as you are clearly used to. You need recovery time. Day after tomorrow we will show you the wreckage."

"I need out of this bed," I whined, but I didn't fight him. He was right, I could feel the lack of strength in my bones.

"Tomorrow. Nero can escort you on a stroll up the beach if you wish."

"Who?"

The dog barked. It was a deeply impressive sound.

"Oh, you must be Nero." His tail thumped the mattress.

"Rest. Mary will bring you some broth. We will take you to what remains of your Raptor later."

I sighed and let all the energy leave my body. Mann let go of my arms and I sank limply into the bed.

2

It wasn't the next day, but the day after that before I was allowed to do anything. Yes, I am a strong modern, fighter pilot. No one exactly allows or doesn't allow me to do anything outside of the command structure. However, my body had very strong opinions about what I was going to be capable of handling.

My first attempt to leave bed was to find a bathroom. Apparently, Mann's choice in beach houses did not include one of those or any modern indoor plumbing. I had to use a chamber pot and hide it in a cabinet when I was done. It was disgusting.

I felt sorry for Mary when she came and took it away. At least she didn't chuck it out the window. After that little adventure, I took a pitifully long nap. The dog Nero became my constant companion. Which was actually a good thing. He was tall, and by my side when I needed to grab on for stability.

"There are no clothes in here," I said to the dog as I searched through the armoire. There were what could only be called shifts. Long cotton, or maybe linen, shapeless tent dresses with a drawstring at the neck. The dresser coughed up even fewer options. I did find a pair of open crotch pantaloons.

No undies, no pants, not even a pair of sweats.

I stormed into the hallway outside my door. Okay, so I didn't exactly storm, but in my head, I was storming. In reality, I was haphazardly tilting out the bedroom door, with not as much balance as I should have had.

"Mary!" I called out. I had no idea where or how to find the woman otherwise.

Mary was scared of me. I don't know why. She was a few years younger than me and very sweet. But also, very timid. I didn't know how not to scare her.

She rushed up the stairs. "Yes, mistress Jane?" she asked rather breathless once in front of me.

"I need clothes. I want to go for a run on the beach. Is there any way I can order some shorts or anything to be delivered?"

"Shorts?" She looked so confused.

"I need to go shopping, but without clothes, I can't." I scanned her up and down. I was taller, but we looked to be about the same size. "Do you have anything I can borrow?"

Her eyes went wide, and she stepped back.

"I'm sorry. I just." I threw my hands up in frustration. "Never mind. I'll find something."

And that would be how Mann found me in his chambers completely naked.

I sat on his bed and examined my scraped knee. Apparently, that was the only visible injury I sustained after falling out of orbit. A scratched knee. Okay, and some medical-grade weakness issues, but no other bruises that I could see. There were no mirrors in this place anyway, so I had to assume since there was no soreness or tenderness that my back and my rump were fine.

Mann's armoire was full of blouses that tied in the front and actual pants, with button flies. In his drawers, I found a lot of knee socks that felt hand knit or were actually made of silk and had seams up the back. No sweats, no jeans, no cargo pants, no shorts. Hell, no underwear.

I sat with a huff and decided to see what real silk stockings felt like. The voluminous nightgown they had put me in kept getting in my way, so I removed it. I had planned on putting on some of these other things that I had tossed onto his bed in my search for anything to wear. I slid my toes into a pair of his stocking and slid my hands up my calf.

I looked up when I heard a gurgled half-strangled sound from the doorway. Mann stood there red-faced and his eyes opened wide. I don't think I realized he had such green eyes. The red really made the color stand out.

He recovered quickly and shut the door behind him with a throat-clearing cough. "Jane, what are you doing?" His eyes finally left me and looked at the mess I made of his things.

"There is nothing in this house for me to wear. You don't have any sweats." The silk slipped over my skin with gliding ease as if there was no friction involved. "These stockings are exquisite. I don't think I've ever known a man to wear something other than just socks. Is this a rich person thing?" I actually don't think I had ever heard of silk stockings for men at all.

"You don't have any that go all the way up?" I lifted my leg and indicated how far up on my thigh I would love these to go.

"Jane." His tone was stern.

"Captain," I corrected.

In a flash, Mann was in front of me, and I was lifted into his arms. A breath caught in my throat. I was naked and crushed to him. One breast was flat against the smooth fabric of his blouse. The other against the rough hairs of his chest. How was I naked? Not good. Or maybe very good. It certainly felt pretty damned nice.

"You are in my bed wearing nothing but silk stockings. Jane seems more appropriate, don't you think?"

Apparently thinking was not something I was capable of. And to prove my own stupidity to myself, I kissed the man. I threaded my fingers into the mess of curly hair, and I moaned into his mouth.

It took him a moment or three to catch up, but when he did, his hands grabbed my ass and pulled me against him, and his tongue plundered my mouth. I felt his hard body all along mine, his erection poked at my belly, and I ground against him, eliciting a groan.

I yanked at his shirt. Okay, these tie open front blouse style shirts, not only looked super hot, they were so much easier to get open than buttons. Buttons were stupid, and I never wanted to deal with another one again. My skin pressed against his chest. He ran a hand up my back. I redoubled my effort to crawl inside of him via my lips. My heart pounded in my ears. I sucked in air as hard as I sucked in him.

Sounds got muffled, all that existed was Mann's mouth on mine. He lowered me back. No, I was falling.

Fuck.

. . . blackness again.

"Janey." Mann patted my face.

I blinked up at him. Well, that put a real damper on the moment.

The passing out thing was getting old fast. My brain needed to be able to keep me upright and functional, and not passing out every time things moved too fast. Damn it, I trained in high gravity combat situations and didn't pass out until a threshold of close to 8.5 Gs before G-LOC hit me, so why the hell was I passing out now every time things got a little exciting?

Right, I survived a crash, and I hadn't had a chance to examine my wreckage to see if I could figure out what had gone wrong.

I let out a heavy breath and then yawned. I pulled his hands away from my face and pushed away from him. Why the hell was I naked?

"Here." He held my nightgown out so I could slip my arms in. He made sure the fabric fell all the way down past my knees as if he were no longer interested in pursuing our earlier activities. Earlier? Seconds ago, and one little fade to black moment and ardor was replaced with concern.

Probably the smarter choice, if I were honest. I didn't want to be. Then again, I didn't want to pass out in the middle of banging someone built like him either. I might miss something fun.

"Let's get you back into bed."

My intention was to crawl into his, it was the nearest bed. I didn't even register a second of surprise when he scooped me into his arms and out of his chamber.

"Good lord, Mann, shouldn't you be carrying the fair maiden into your chambers and not the opposite direction?"

Maybe Monty's accent wasn't as fake as I had originally thought. Was it possibly an authentic seventeen-century aristocrat accent belonging to a man who hung out with all kinds of reprobates, thus bastardizing his natural speech patterns? Could that be what happened when he was put out to sea as an eleven-year-old cabin boy? His parents and surroundings no longer influenced everything about him, including his flowery speech. That's the story I decided to tell myself.

"Shut up, Monty," Mann snapped.

I cut the weak side-eye that I attempted to glare at Monty to Mann. Whatever game they were playing, Mann didn't fit in. He didn't fit in the way I didn't.

Or I was delusional? After all, I had this new fun hobby of passing out, so maybe this really was some re-enactors village vacation that I had subscribed to. Because me being stuck in the seventeenth century just was not a possibility I wanted to entertain.

And yet, the thought was there.

I should have been all kinds of swoony over being carried by Mann into my room. Instead, my brain was trying to spin back up, and pick out all the details I may have missed that would prove I wasn't on some no longer existent island in the middle of the Caribbean.

Monty followed us in, as Mann deposited me back on my mattress.

"So, Captain," Monty really had a hard time wrapping his pretty mouth around my title. Maybe I should truss him up with a ball gag too. Hmm. "Why do I find you being conveyed from one room to another by our dear Mann here?" I really wanted him to put that "ha-ha" in there.

"Captain Way is in need of clothes. She ransacked my room looking for something suitable. I found her admiring some of my finest silk stockings."

Monty scoffed. "I doubt she would find a frock to meet her needs in your room."

I sighed. "Frocks? When I asked Mary if she had anything I could borrow, I think she peed her pants in fright. Look I just need some sweats, and then I can go hit some shops. I'm sure there are some tourist places where I can pick up a few shirts and shorts, and maybe some shoes." I looked from one confused face to another. "Those stockings were pretty sweet."

"Sweats? Just go stand out in the sun if you want to sweat. You make very little sense Captain Way. Are you even sure of the words you are saying?"

I didn't bother to answer Monty's condescending ass. "Look," I turned my attention back to Mann. "I need clothes that I can move in. And that's not going to happen in some authentic period dress as Mary wears. If I have to stay in setting, then get me some men's things. Pants, shirts. But I would like some underwear of some kind. Also, shoes. Something sturdy."

"I will speak to the housekeeper; she will be able to find something that should suit you until we can figure something out. My tailor is in Port-au-Prince. I don't fancy a trip to Hispaniola at the moment to get you clothing."

What I ended up with were a pair of drawers, not my first choice in panty wear, but better than commando, and what, for all intents and purposes, was a linen and ribbon bralette. I was thrilled to not have to fight a corset or anything with lacings. The housekeeper, mistress Liza, came up with a pair of breeches for me. They had that weird square front flap, but otherwise were perfectly comfortable, and I could move in them. And a top, more like a tunic than one of Mann's or Monty's frilly tie-front shirts.

They had no luck with the shoes, so I was left barefoot for the time being.

Andreas felt the need to point out my near urchin-like appearance when I made my way downstairs for the first time and met the men in the dining room. Nero accompanied me and steadied me on my trek.

"Well, then you can pay for the tailor when I finally see one if you are going to be so picky about my wardrobe," I snarled.

"My Captain, I will do just that. For you deserve to wear the finest money can buy." The little wink and lick of his lower lip chased all thought of being pissed at the man out of my brain. His flirt game was much better than Monty's. Had it been his chambers I had stumbled into during my search for clothing, somehow I don't think my passing out would have been any more than a little hiccup in our afternoon activities.

Maybe I should go try on his silk stockings next time?

3

I SAT BACK on a fallen tree. The beach was perfect, well, it would have been perfect if I was here on vacation, and not going insane. It was time to come to grips with the possibility I was dead. If that was the case, then this was one weird afterlife that I had not expected.

No fluffy cloud cities, no fiery pits with demons either.

The men had insisted that I rest for a bit. Inwardly I agreed, I had zero stamina. Mann and Nero took this opportunity to disappear, and Monty and Andreas were strutting their stuff.

I kicked my leg back and forth in a lazy swing, contemplated why I was stressing over why I was here when it occurred to me I should be taking advantage of this situation. Enjoying what I had while I had it. Screw that, I was on a tropical beach. I had two sexy men showing off with flashing blades, and shirts open to their navels. Oh and those thigh-high leather boots.

I stopped looking inside my head for clues and started to really watch Monty and Andreas. Their swords glinted in the sun, their normally billowing shirts plastered to their skin like some wet T-shirt contest, showing off all their muscles.

Monty laughed as he lunged forward. He should have

easily been able to catch a hit on Andreas's arm, but instead, he overreached and went down on a knee. This should have been an opening for Andreas, but instead of attacking he did some fancy flip of his sword while switching hands. He missed the grip, snatching his hand back from the blade before it cut him. His sword landed with a thunk into the sand. He followed it down, and landed on his knees, breathing heavily.

I couldn't decide if their work out was for a performance, for fun, or was this their version of hitting the gym. Clearly, their arm and back muscles responded to this as a workout.

Andreas pulled his shirt off, pealing it away from his skin, his dark sweaty skin shining in the sun.

"We go again?" he asked Monty as he stood up.

Monty took the offered hand to haul himself up from the ground. The two men walked around a bit, shaking their limbs before facing off against each other.

Parry, parry, dodge, miss. That could have been an easy hit.

"Are you missing on purpose, or do you really suck that much?" I asked.

"What is this suck?" Andreas asked.

"It must mean something good." Monty quipped.

I had to remember I was an educated woman with a vocabulary, even though I talked like a fighter pilot when the C-O wasn't around.

"It means . . ." I paused as I was about to say they were crap, again, I reminded myself: vocabulary.

"See she's speechless. The good Captain Jane Way finds our swordplay to be magnificent, why else would she be at a loss for words?"

I couldn't help it, I giggled. He was cute and charming, and that smile made things flutter in my body. I cut my gaze from Monty to the broody sweaty Andreas. I'm pretty sure I blushed. That giddy feeling got hot and raw looking at him.

I let out a hard sigh. "I paused because I wanted to find a

word that would convey just how horrific you are, while not destroying your fragile male egos."

Neither said a word, just raised eyebrows at me. I gestured at Monty.

"You are tall, and you have reach, yet you overextend yourself at every turn. And you," I turned to Andreas, "keep trying maneuvers as flashy as your clothing. Keep to the basics. Look I'm sure you were both mucking about, getting in a good workout, but if you seriously fight with swords, shouldn't you attempt to do your best at every practice? Unless you were actively practicing your worst?"

Andreas scoffed. "And you can do better?"

I shrugged. I could do a whole lot better. I was an Olympic qualifying fencer. One of those little overachiever type things they looked for when selecting pilots for the Jupiter Mission. I had excelled my ass off at as many things as I could conceive of. My skill set included County Fair winning knitting and crocheting. I peaked early with those. I had a handful of martial art skills, sword training— not just the fencing— archery, horsemanship. I knew how to dig a well and engineer a simple solar-powered pump— won the fifth-grade science fair with that little gem. Whether I had been aware of it or not, I had spent my entire life preparing myself to be an ideal candidate.

And damn it, I was beyond bitter that I was here in the fresh air with these hot, half-dressed men, and not surrounded by recirculated air and other pilots in jumpsuits. I shook my head. My priorities must be off, hadn't I just told myself to enjoy the here and now? Once I got to see my wreckage I could start worrying about all that other stuff.

I jumped down from my perch and walked up to Monty with my hand out. "May I?"

With a dramatic bow— did he do any other kind?— he handed me his weapon, hilt first.

I hefted it in my grasp. I twirled it a bit and got a sense of its weight. I glared at the piece. How long had he been working with this?

I examined the blade. It was solid enough and had decent flexibility. "This blade is crap, no wonder you're overextending. The balance is all wrong. Where did you get it?"

"He probably took it off a dead body when he first started privateering."

Mann was a welcome addition to this little party, especially since he joined us with his shirt off, and loose breeches held up by a rope around his waist. He had been swimming, the fabric was still wet, thin, and dear Lord did not hide his considerable package. The fabric plastered to him like cling film, I could make out the ridge of his tip. I swear the beast in his pants moved of its own accord.

I swallowed and forced my eyes to his face. His grin told me I was busted.

"Well, just because someone else had it first doesn't mean it's not—"

"Yes, you said crap already. It's a perfectly fine blade." Monty defended his weapon.

I scanned up and down his body with my eyes. If he thought this blade was decent, I wondered what else he thought was good that wasn't. I stabbed the blade into the sand and held my hand out to Andreas. I wiggled my fingers indicating he needed to hand over one of his weapons.

He placed the pummel in my hand. I expected a lighter blade the way he wielded it. No wonder his moves were awkward.

"Is this one new to you?" I asked.

"Si."

I nodded, that explained a few things. I turned to Monty. "Is this your normal weapon?"

He answered me with an eye-roll, "Yes."

If he was still alive with a piece of crap sword, then he

probably was an excellent swordsman. But how did he not know this sword was off balance?

"How about you? Is your weapon any good?" I looked at Mann.

"My weapon is exceptional, madame." He cocked an eyebrow at me, and I swear my underthings tried to come off my body.

"I mean your sword."

"I did too. Unfortunately, that is not the weapon I have with me at the moment. Unless you care for an audience, I'd rather show you my swordplay in a more private setting."

Monty let out a loud guffaw.

Game on.

"And you?" I turned to Andreas, who seemed to have issues breathing through his laughter.

"My sword is not up for public scrutiny either."

I nodded and blinked my eyes at him. "But with a little encouragement," I toyed with my collar and exposed my neck and collar bones. "I'm sure it would rise to the occasion?" I could tease and deliver innuendo just as well as the next guy. I probably had better follow through too.

I held my hand out to him and Monty made strangled noises behind me. "Your good weapon sir."

The blade he put in my hand was a thing of beauty. The blade was long and curved and flared ever so beautifully at the end before coming to a point. The balance was exquisite, and as I moved my wrist, the blade flowed through the air like a dance.

"Now this is a beautiful weapon." I lifted the blade close to my eyes so I could inspect it, and ran my hand along the flat of the curve. "Turkish scimitar?"

"You know weapons?" Andreas gave me a little tilt of his head to acknowledge that I did indeed know what I was talking about. "My Captain."

He held out his arm, indicating I should give the sword a trial.

I returned his nod, and he picked up his heavier blade. With a small bow to indicate we were ready, the dual began.

I had to pull back in order not to snick his skin. After all, this was for fun, not for real. After a few parries and counter parries, I stepped back and held up my hand indicating I needed to stop. My breathing labored, I was not used to being weak like this.

"I was unconscious for how many days?" I asked. I know they had only mentioned a few, but I felt like it had been weeks. Maybe the air quality was zapping my strength.

Mann reached my side, and with an arm around my shoulders, he took the scimitar from me and handed it back to Andreas.

"Captain, we do not doubt your abilities, but I believe you are not up to your normal level of health."

Before I really knew what he was doing, I was cradled in his arms and being carried back to the downed tree in the shade. While I enjoyed my time in his arms, I did not enjoy the reasons why I was here.

As soon as he placed me down, Monty was by my side with a flask. I would have preferred water, lots of it. I took a swig. It had the distinct lighter fluid qualities of rum and burned.

"Where did you learn to fight like that?" he asked.

"She is a captain with good reasons," Andreas said in my defense.

Mann handed me a leather bag. I looked up at him. Neon question marks had to have magically appeared over my head. I had no idea what that was or why he was giving it to me. My eyes narrowed and I cocked my head to the side in the universal "huh?" motion.

"Water."

I shook my head. I didn't understand, that was not water.

He pulled it back and twisted a cap off, that I hadn't seen.

He demonstrated how it was water. Instantly I felt dumb as a box of feathers. It was a water skin. He handed it back, and I washed the lingering rum burn from my throat.

"She's clearly had training," Mann said.

"She's also clearly right here," I chimed in. "I've had lots of training. They don't let anyone captain a Raptor. Now, is there a swordsmith on this island? I'm going to need a blade, and that dreadful piece Monty has been playing with needs to be corrected."

"The nearest swordsmith that would work with you is on Tortuga."

"Where? How far is that?" I thought they meant the other side of the island.

Monty laughed. "For a captain, you don't know your geography very well. North of Hispaniola, that's a day and a night at sea. Are you sure you're a captain?"

I leveled the blankest stare at him as I could muster. I turned my attention to Andreas and Mann. "Can I see my wreckage now?"

MANN HAULED AWAY a matte of loosely woven together rushes. I was expecting my wreckage to be stored in a cave, or something a little more dramatic. Then again, the population of this island was so sparse, that hiding something under some leaves was very much doable.

I helped to pull the makeshift covering away from my bird.

There was more than I expected. Tangled with paracord, and my silk shute was a substantial section of wingspan. How had this not filled with water and pulled me down into the deep?

I lifted the contoured edge and saw that it was only the top skin, not the actual intact wing. Except for the jagged edges where the piece had sheered away from the body of my ship, it looked perfect.

My stripes and number were all in place. Nothing had burned off on reentry.

Three stripes. My port wing. Lucky number seventy-nine, and the Jupiter shield. Seventy-nine wasn't really my lucky number, it's the number on the bird they gave me.

"This everything?" I asked.

"You expected more?" Monty asked.

I don't know what I expected. But I wasn't going to get any answers as to what happened from a section of aluminum-titanium alloy.

I sat down on the sand. Nero nosed into my face. I pushed his big head away from me and scratched his ears. He lay down with a heavy sigh and rested his paws and head in my lap.

"I don't know what I expected. More than just part of the skin. I guess I should be glad there was that much to survive. Everything should have sunk. It wasn't made for sailing it was made for space."

Mann let out a loud cough as if he tried to cover up what I said.

"Did you just say space dear woman?" Monty asked.

I looked at Mann, his brows were drawn together, his gaze intense.

I blinked up at Monty. "It wasn't made for sailing across large spaces. I must have gotten knocked off course."

Mann noticeably relaxed. Something was definitely going on with that man, and I wanted to find out.

I stood up, displacing the dog. I leaned over and grabbed the loosely woven matte, and began hauling it back over what was left of my Raptor. I wasn't a forensic investigator. I couldn't look at a piece of fatigued metal and tell why it had failed. I don't know what I thought I would find by seeing this. A message engraved across the wing: *this is what happened, this is why you aren't in twenty-second-century space.*

Andreas took the tarp from me and finished covering the wreck. I rested a hand on his bare chest. Our eyes met, and I'm more than certain he read what was in my eyes. I was going to need some serious distraction tonight. My brain and reality were not meshing very well, I didn't want to be alone.

On the long walk back to Mann's, I let Monty carry me piggy-back style. I hinted that I wanted to see what else he could do from the back.

By the time we returned, invitations had been issued. We ate dinner in near silence, not discussing what I had needed to see, or why I had needed to see it. I excused myself and retreated to my room, hoping my subtility earlier wasn't too subtle.

I HAD MONTY TRUSSED UP, and a makeshift gag in his mouth. He didn't really seem to mind. Turned out, for all the complaining he did in the daylight hours, he liked a strong-willed woman. I know he thought he would call me out on some of my more direct flirting by showing up in my room, but little did he know I was serious.

So there I was riding him like a cowgirl, not caring about how loud that bed squeaked when the door to my bedroom inched open. I'm glad I looked up when I did, or I would have missed the most magnificent expression on Andreas's face. Surprise, awe, appreciation when his eyes saw my breasts bouncing around, and finally unadulterated lust followed by completion lightening shock when his eyes met mine.

I smiled. Goodie, more for my party. I could use an extra pair of hands since I made Monty unable to use his. I smiled up at the man as he stood, incapable of moving in the doorway.

"Come on in, and close the door."

He quickly stepped in and shut the door behind him. He

leaned against it. I couldn't tell if he was afraid of me, or of what he had walked in on.

I stopped bouncing on Monty's cock and sat, still impaled. "You are going to join us aren't you? Or are you just going to watch?" I arched up, grinding my ass against Monty and lifted my breasts, pointing my nipples at Andreas. The invitation couldn't have been any more obvious.

Monty made a moan and thrashed a bit. I ignored him. He agreed to be my plaything, and I wanted to play with more things.

"Monty?" Andreas directed an unasked inquiry to the man underneath me.

He moaned and thrashed his trussed up legs, trying to thrust— I had effectively removed his leverage— trying to keep fucking me. I loved the power he gave me at that moment.

Andreas tilted his head to the side and returned his gaze to me.

I groped and rolled my nipples at him. "Are you really going to make me do this part myself?"

His mouth on my breasts was all the answer I needed. I sunk my fingers into his thick hair and thought about how I had considered a ball gag for him when I first met him. Right now, this seemed like a better use of his mouth. One arm wrapped around my back and held me to him, and the other tickled down my abs to find my sweet spot. He knew what he was doing. I began to grind against Monty again, and he did his best to thrust up into me.

"Oh yeah, this is so much better," I moaned into the night.

When my door opened again, I was on my hands and knees, Monty was in my mouth, and Andreas drove into me with brutal force from the rear.

Monty's cock popped out of my mouth when I saw Mann standing there, dark rage crossing over his features.

"I must have been mistaken." He stepped back and started closing the door.

"Where do you think you're going?" I asked, making sure there was a challenge in my tone.

"You are occupied, madame. I thought . . . no, never mind what I thought."

Monty groaned, and I cut a glance up to his face, his eyes were wide. I guess he thought he was in trouble. Had he thought I was Mann's territory? I was going to have to clear up any misconceptions on who was whose territory. If anything, I was claiming them for me, not the other way around. This was my delusional fantasy, I was the one in some kind of near-death coma, so damn it, I was the one going to have the sexy superpower.

Andreas had stopped delivering thrusts to my lady garden, and I could feel him diminishing. Mann needed to step in and step up before he ruined my groove.

"Eric," I spoke softly. "I need you to join us."

"I prefer to play solo."

"The first violinist always gets the solos, they also lead the rest of the strings. I have a vacant chair that needs you."

Not exactly sure of what I was going for, but the metaphor worked. He closed the door and pulled off his loose shirt. Damn, he was fine. My sex throbbed against Andreas but wanting Mann and the promise of that huge cock I saw hints of earlier.

"I see you found a way to get Monty to shut up."

After every position known to man, and animal, and a few I'm sure we made up on the spot, Monty snored lightly through his gag. Andreas rested his head against Monty's chest, curled up and also snoring lightly. They made a cute couple.

Mann rolled out of bed and stretched tall. His limbs were long and strong, and even though he had rocked my world, and had his own come shower release more than once, I was fairly certain, he was not ready to slow down.

"What are you doing?" I asked languidly as his arms slipped under my knees and around my shoulders.

He lifted as if I weren't made of solid muscle.

"I'm ready for my solo, Captain. Shall we?" He kicked open my door, allowing Nero to slip in and climb into bed with the other men.

Mann carried me down the hall and into his bedroom, sliding me between cool sheets. His body slid in next to mine, and before I could find a witty retort about how he had better be able to perform on his own without a supporting band, he had my thigh in a firm grip and was positioning himself between my knees.

His cock, which was as gloriously thick as it had hinted, prodded at my sex, teasing my clit. My nerves were all afire so every soft rub, every pulsing press against my flesh had me whining and moaning. I rocked my hips trying to get him seated to where he could properly pound into me, but he avoided my sheath with expert dodges and blocks. He used the weapon between his thighs most expertly.

Andreas fucked the way he fought, with a continuous onslaught of pounding until the foe relented or in my case until my sex cried with orgasm after orgasm. I hadn't given Monty a chance to demonstrate his skills. He made one little comment about not trusting if a woman could be in command, and, well, challenge accepted. And by the way we made him come like a broken hydrant, I'm pretty sure he'll never make a snide comment again about the skills of a woman, or about letting another man make a delivery in the rear.

Now that had been fun, Monty sandwiched between me and Andreas, and Mann at my back. All of us connect, all of us thrusting as one giant throbbing need. The orgasms that happened had to have ripped a hole in the fabric of reality. I think I orgasmed first, which triggered Monty. Monty came, and continued to come, even as I slid off of him, his seed sprayed all over my chest, and I shared it, rubbing back all over him. Andreas continued to hammer into him. As long as Andreas pounded, Monty came. Finally, Andreas collapsed against Monty's back, clearly, all wrung out. While I admired all of that sexy workmanship in front of me, Mann bit the back of my neck and made guttural noises as he filled me up from behind.

I didn't pity the maid who would be washing my sheets in the morning.

I pulled with the leg I had hooked around Mann, trying to get him back down, wanting him to ram home and stop teasing me. He smiled and shook his head. He was up and out of my grasp. Before I could protest too much, he had me flipped. My hips were pulled up and back, a hand braced against my back and pushed my chest down against the bed.

"Yes, please," I mumbled into the sheets.

I did not expect the smack to my ass. I gasped. Mann smacked me again, his fingers stinging against my sensitized behind.

I guess Mann decided he was in charge now. Fine, I had no problems being a switch. But I didn't give up all control that easily.

"Harder," I demanded.

Smack. He delivered.

"Harder."

That time, he replaced his hand with his considerable member. It didn't hurt, but the fact that he was smacking my ass with that flesh rod made me wet all over again.

He rammed that beast into me and I cried out with joy. My muscles spasmed instantaneously, already so over-sensitized from the near abusing levels of pounding I had demanded from the men all night. Each one of Mann's thrusts elicited a moan, a cry, a whine, some sound from my throat. I don't know how he had more in him, the mess we left behind in my room, included a considerable pool of his own DNA evidence.

The hand on the back of my neck grabbed harder, his thrusts slowed. He sounded pained, I looked back over my shoulder. The contortions of his face concerned me.

"You okay there?"

"I'm." Thrust. "Coming." Thrust. "Hard." Thrust. And then he screamed the likes I hadn't heard before. It wasn't an ear-piercing, rend the night in half sound, but it was more than a roar.

He pushed hard against me with his hips and listed against my back, I could feel his cock throbbing and pulsing as he unleashed his torrential outpouring into me. There was so much come being jettisoned into my system, I wouldn't be surprised if every egg residing in my ovaries didn't quicken with fertilization. Good thing I had been given a ten-year implant. I wouldn't be able to accidentally get pregnant while serving the Jupiter Mission, so as long as I was in the same body here, all of that baby-making froth was going to do no harm.

4

When I woke up I knew where I was, and I didn't care. Well, maybe a little bit, because if I wasn't here, I wouldn't have felt so completely satiated and happy. The weather was perfect, the breeze gentle, the sky blue, and I had three men who rocked my world.

I stepped out onto the balcony from Mann's room, wrapped in the sheet from his bed. The courtyard bustled with activity. Monty spoke with determination to a small group of men. Who untied him? It looked like Mann had just given some kids a few coins before they eagerly ran off. He looked up, noticing I leaned on the railing watching them. His smile made my toes curl.

I wondered if I could convince them to return to bed and have a repeat of last night.

"Get dressed, and gather anything you might want to take with you."

Not the words I wanted to hear. I was hoping for something more like, 'Oh goodie you're still naked, go lie down and spread your knees, I'll be right up.' No such luck.

"What's going on?" It certainly looked like something was going on.

The group with Monty left, and he joined Mann, tossing an arm over the other man's shoulder. He looked as languid and loose boned as I felt. I guess last night had been just what he needed too. His gaze made me think he was trying to see through the sheet I was wrapped in.

"My dear Captain Jane, we are taking a little voyage, and we leave immediately." His tongue rolled around his mouth, giving his speech pattern a lazy almost slur.

"Is there time for anything before we leave?" I teased the edge of the sheet. Monty's hooded gaze said he was up for it. Mann's steady no-nonsense look said, 'No.'

I huffed out a sigh and turned back inside. Mann was no fun at all. I kicked the sheet out of my way and headed to my room to find my clothes. I didn't have anything to gather. I only had the one set of clothes, so I was going to be a very light packer.

The ribbons on my bralette tied in the back. I struggled until a pair of warm strong hands took the laces from mine and finished the job for me.

"Better?" Monty asked.

"Much."

I turned into him and his mouth was on mine. His hands stroked my back before finding purchase on my ass and in my hair. Next time, I'd leave him unbound. I wanted to see what he could do, fortunately, he did not make me wait. My drawers fell to the floor, and suddenly I was pressed against the bed. Monty kneeling above me.

We kissed as if our tongues wrestled for domination. His hand left my ass and found my delicate folds. He wasted no time. His fingers slid around and primed me for action. He did not need a treasure map to find my pleasure pearl. Monty went straight to my clit better than if it had sent up a homing beacon.

A quick fumble with his breeches and his weapon of choice was free.

I wrapped my legs around him. "Do me now," I moaned.

"Always giving orders, aren't you?" He complied anyway.

My nerves were still on fire from the night before. The second he slid in, I was going off like a firecracker. Boom, boom, boom, to his bang, bang, bang.

I was just about to hit my peak and cry my orgasm into Monty's mouth when Mann came into my room. "What's taking you so long?"

Long? This wasn't long. This was a fucking quickie. Or a quick fucky. I could only imagine what he saw— Monty's naked ass pumping away, my legs thrown up in the air. Zero finesse, and one hundred percent grind.

He huffed and turned to leave. "Well, hurry it up. Andreas is getting the provisions to the dock. I'm waiting on confirmation regarding the last sighting of Cavenaugh."

"Who's Cavenaugh?" I asked. Monty didn't skip a beat and kept thrusting away.

"We are not having a conversation while Monty fucks you."

"Why not? I can multi— oh my, hold on, ah." Damn, Monty hit a nerve, a good nerve.

"That's why." Mann changed his mind and leaned against the door jam, arms crossed waiting for us to finish up.

"Hold on I can do— ah, I can do— coming, oh shit, coming!" I yelled as I crashed and muscles clenched.

Monty had me mindless and throbbing and . . . I guess I couldn't multi-task. At that point, I gave up and rode him until it was his turn to spurt his release like a fountain. I felt it throb and pulse from him in a pattern that had to have matched the way his own body clenched and spasmed as he came. Monty collapsed onto the bed next to me, his spent manhood, hanging forlornly and used to the side.

"Mann, what are you doing here?" he asked. Monty stood and tucked himself back in and refastened his pants.

"He's here to tell us to hurry up. Did you miss that?"

"I was rather focused." He gave me a withering stare as if I hadn't noticed. Oh, I had noticed. I still twitched from noticing.

"Now that you're finished, you need to get dressed, and I need you," Mann turned his attention to Monty, "to make sure which direction Cavenaugh was sighted coming from. Hopefully, he's coming in from the south. We'll have the island between us as we leave."

"Where are we going?" I asked. I found a cloth to clean up with before I pulled my drawers back on.

"The other side of Hispaniola, dear. We're headed to Tortuga."

WITH NERO BY MY SIDE, I followed Mann on the short trek to the north side of the island, where the ship Resurrection was moored.

The walk wasn't long, and the ground nicely even, so I didn't miss shoes terribly, but I would eventually like a pair. I wasn't the type of person who took my shoes off every chance that I could, and the bottoms of my feet were letting me know about it. So far nothing horrible. But I kept hitting my toes.

"Why are we leaving in such a hurry?" I dared to ask.

"Not really a hurry. We were planning on ducking out eventually. I believe we got a bit distracted with you, dear Captain, so our preparations were not as well pulled together as they needed to be.

I thought the water outside of Mann's home was the most beautiful shade of blue I had ever seen. It was completely drab in comparison to the crystal cerulean of the bay in front of me. It was picture perfect. Out from shore was another picture-perfect example, this time of a pirate ship. I don't know boats, I know space birds, more specifically Raptors with their VOJ propulsion engines, and the ICA 2312 dual rocket booster being built on Hera Station. I had no idea if what I saw was a warship or a schooner, but it looked lean, mean, and fast. And since I was pretty sure we were actively on the run, fast was good.

Two longboats were pulled up onto the beach, and men were loading barrels and crates. Once full they shoved the boats out into the water and they rowed out to the ship.

"Why not bring the ship in closer?"

"Can't. Resurrection draws low, but this close in the depth is inconsistent, can't risk getting caught up."

"Oh." I nodded as if what he said made perfect sense, and sat with the dog, waiting our turn to get ferried out.

Once on the boat, I found it safer to stay out of the way in the large cabin where I was told to go. Not that I was meekly taking orders, the men, and there were quite a few of them with the crew, were moving about like a swarm of ants and I felt it best to stay out of the way.

The gentle rocking of the vessel lulled me to sleep. We were well underway, and it was nearing sunset when I finally woke up and ventured onto deck.

I found Andreas. "Why are we headed to Tortuga? Isn't that where pirates hang out?"

He cocked a single brow at me. "Hang out? Why no. Tortuga is safe for privateers, no hangings."

I snuffled a weak laugh. Hanging was not what I meant. It was a minor miracle we understood each other as it was. English was a different language five hundred years ago. Good thing I understood Shakespearean, even if it did sound flowery.

"That's what I meant. Pirates are on Tortuga, isn't that what you want to avoid?" I tried to ask a better question. "I mean isn't that why we left to avoid Cavenaugh? I was under the impression he was the pirate type."

"My darling Jane, he is. But then again, so are we." He seemed so completely nonplused by the whole concept.

I swallowed hard. My throat went dry. "Is there any wine around here?" I stood up and crossed the deck, heading back toward the cabin.

"Captain, does this surprise you?"

I turned to look back at him. Did this surprise me? In my delusions, it shouldn't. My fantasies were built upon the kinder, gentler pirates of adventure vids and romance audios, and not the reality of nasty sea dogs who never bathed and believed women were less than possessions.

Pirates, of course, they were pirates. I still needed some wine.

"If Cavenaugh is a pirate, and we are pirates—" I was in it with them now, might as well count myself all in, "— why are we running to Tortuga?"

Andreas let out a hearty laugh. "Cavenaugh has a personal vendetta against our Monty. This was the easiest way to make sure we delivered Monty safely to Tortuga while keeping an eye on Cavenaugh's whereabouts."

"So, we're playing keep-away in the Caribbean?"

"Just so Captain Jane, just so."

I pushed into the cabin. Mann and Monty discussed something over a map. Directions I guess. How many times did they make the journey from the Caymans to Tortuga? Shouldn't it be a familiar route?

I shook my head and checked my navigation by modern technology privilege at the door. There weren't road signs and landmarks at sea, and they didn't have a satellite GPS system to tell them where they were. This was old school, sextants, and navigating by stars.

"How long before we get there?" I asked as means of letting them know I intruded.

Monty gave me a lop-sided grin. "Barring any unforeseen events, we should arrive the day after tomorrow. Our departure from the island was a bit later than ideal."

"Unforeseen? You mean like getting caught?"

"We won't get caught. Resurrection is faster than Cavenaugh's Dutchman."

"Uh, I thought The Dutchman was a sailor's myth?"

Mann chuckled," The Flying Dutchman is. A Merchant Dutchman is a type of ship. The type Cavenaugh sails. This will be a rather uneventful voyage."

"Oh." I think I felt stupider, not smarter, even if I was learning new information. "So what do we do for the next twenty-four uneventful hours?" I toyed with my collar. I know what I wanted to do.

I BALANCED PRECARIOUSLY on a piece of my bird. I gripped the paracord with what little strength I had left. It was hard to hear over the crash of the water around me, but I swear I heard the repetitive thumping of helo blades. A light flashed out and moved around. A spot. I waved my free arm back and forth. I tried to cry out that I was here, but my voice didn't want to work.

"Hang in there, we've got you. We've got you."

... *blackness* ...

Mann gripped my wrist, as Monty tugged on my shirt.

"We've got you!" He yelled above the crash of waves and thunder.

My first instinct was to wriggle out of their grasp. Mann's grip really hurt. I reached up to begin prying his fingers before I realized they were keeping me from falling overboard.

Instead of pulling his hand off me, I latched onto his wrist instead.

What was going on? I was soaking wet, and spitting salt water. I kicked and tried to find purchase for my feet.

Monty's grip changed to the back of my breeches and together they hauled me up. I scraped over broken railings before collapsing across both men. We all swallowed down air in heaving gulps.

I was the first to recover. Sitting up I adjusted my focus to the broken railing. What the hell had happened?

The ship pitched and rocked, as waves crashed over the sides. I looked at the two collapsed men. "Where's Andreas?" I yelled.

Monty lifted a languid arm and pointed. I followed his finger and saw a dark figure manhandling the helm, keeping up headed into the waves.

With a deafening silence, the downpour stopped. Waves still tossed us about, and I wasn't sure if my sea legs would hold me on deck. I eyed the hole in the railing again and wanted to avoid pitching through that. I had a sneaking suspicion that's what had happened, or somehow I was the one that made that hole.

"What was that all about?" Mann panted harshly at me.

I looked at him like he was the one who should have those answers and I should be asking that question. Shaking my head, I scooted to sit next to him.

"That's what I want to know. Did I blackout?" I pointed at the railing. "Did I do that?"

"What do you mean you don't know?" Monty stood over us, adjusting his clothing. He was soaked to the bone. We all were.

"I mean the last thing I remember is Andreas shouting that we were close to where you picked me up, and the squall was off starboard. He was going to swing wide to miss the worst of it, but unfortunately, it was in our way."

The discussion had been intense, but all three men had been in agreement. We tried to work our way to the north of the storm, wait it out as much as possible, and hope we didn't have to divert too far from our course since it lay directly between us and Hispaniola. If the weather got worse, we were going to have to loop north of Tortuga and approach the port from the east. Monty hadn't been a fan of that plan. Something about Cavenaugh and wanting to avoid him at all costs.

After that, well, I would have sworn I had been hanging on to my Raptor's wing while the ocean rose and fell around me. Waves crashed over me. And above me, a light, and a voice, and the distinct thud-thud-thud of helo blades blending with the roar of the storm that surrounded us.

"And after that what do you remember?" Mann held an arm up to Monty, who hauled him to his feet.

Now both men were glowering down at me.

I shook my head and shrugged. "Nothing. And suddenly the two of you were barely holding on, and keeping me from going in the water. I don't know what happened." I could feel my eyebrows knitting together. I didn't know what was happening to me and it scared me. I didn't want to move, afraid of the pull of that gap in the railing, afraid that if I tried to walk, my legs would decide to run, and I would be jumping through that hole and back into the ocean. I felt the pull.

Monty threw his hands in the air before stomping off to direct some of their crew in getting the boat back into condition.

Mann squatted down next to me, elbow resting on his knees. "You became very agitated as we drew closer to the squall. Once it was upon us you kept yelling about needing to go back. You went through the railing, or maybe it broke when you went over it, but Jane, you disappeared. We thought we lost you. I can't explain it any more than I think you can. You were not there when we looked, and then you were. Monty got a hold of you first, and then I grabbed you. This is where we found you, right on the edge of that squall line." He looked over his shoulder, back at the storm. "Those clouds aren't moving."

I decided that moving below deck was probably the safest place for me at the moment. Nero agreed, and he seemed to be happy with my company, once I closed the door to the main cabin and lay down on the bunk. He crawled in next to me, and mostly on top of me. He nosed his head under my arm with a whimper. We comforted each other as the waves around the ship calmed, and we returned to a soothing rocking motion that lulled me to sleep. I dreamed about that squall, convinced there was something hidden behind those clouds.

5

I MUCH PREFERRED Mann's home on Cayman to the squalor of Tortuga. For the sake of preserving my mental faculties, I had two choices, accept that I had traveled back in time, or these re-enactors really took their roles seriously. This place was too smelly, too nasty, and too flea-ridden to be anything but authentic.

I was stuck in a loop of trying to convince myself that this was real. At Mann's idealistic island home, there was the possibility that he just liked to live rustically. Here, no more doubt, I was in the past.

I was grateful for many benefits of being from the future, mostly I had all my shots. But I really wished I had shoes. Maybe even one of those broad-brimmed hats the men wore. I looked like some tag-along street urchin compared to how the men in front of me were dressed. Andreas wore his dark red velvet and lace. Not surprisingly his hat matched. Monty looked straight out of a swashbuckling vid all in black, with belts strapped across his doublet. Mann wasn't quite as coordinating in his fashion choices, blue doublet, brown leather pantaloons, brown hat. And all three had on those over the knee, tall boots. If I hadn't been told they were pirates, it would have been my first guess.

"Is there a clothier here? Can I get clothes that actually fit? How about some shoes?" I wanted to look as amazing as they did. They had all the cool cred, and I was a rag-a-muffin mess. I trudged after the men, they made their way from the port into town, and were all so very serious, and not very chatty.

Monty dropped back to keep pace with me. "If things go well then we can find you a tailor, and a bootmaker. I would like to have my sword refined, now that you have pointed out how out of balance it is. But this is not a leisure trip."

Monty didn't have that delightful twinkle in his eye, and there was no hint of flirting in his demeanor.

I shrugged. What else was there for me to do? It's not like I could go wait in a hotel room for them, and I certainly wasn't willing to find a cafe to wait around in.

In the center of town, we reached our destination. There was no mistaking the building for being the pirate's courthouse. All flags hung from poles that extended from a second story. I recognized the English flag and assumed the fleur-de-lis meant that was the French flag. The rest I could guess as being Spanish, Dutch, and damn if there really wasn't a skull and crossbones.

The men's boots made loud clumping noises as they mounted the stairs. Nero and I padded up behind them. Mann led the way and he pushed open the double doors. I could only imagine the reception he received on the other side. He did cut an impressive figure.

But then again, I was completely wrong. There was no one to greet us. I stepped inside, not knowing what to expect. Maybe a gathering of a pirate council? A throne room for a pirate king? We crossed through a vestibule and into what was clearly a courtroom: benches, chairs, raised daises with railings.

With a loud expulsion of air, Andres collapsed into a chair. Monty did the same.

I perched on a table. Mann paced.

"You guys want to tell me what's going on here? Why were we in such a hurry to get here when there is no one here? What's up with the game of chase with Cavenaugh?"

Meaningful glances passed between the men.

"It's a long story." Mann sighed.

I kicked my heels and cast my gaze around the empty room. "Unless you expect someone to come in any second now, I'm guessing you have time. Hell, you had time on the Resurrection. All I know is Cavenaugh is after Monty for some reason."

Monty leveled a disappointed gaze at me, and then at Andreas. "You shouldn't have told her."

"She is smart, she figures things out on her own." Andreas gestured at me.

A gangly teen crashed into the courtroom just then. "Cavenaugh's Dutchman has been sighted. He will make port by the end of the day."

Mann approached the lad. Words were exchanged, and from the look of it, so were a few coins.

"We have a few hours before the parle begins." Mann turned to me, arms wide. He was about to explain everything, but I think I had figured it out.

"We had to get here before Cavenaugh for some reason, didn't we?"

Mann nodded.

"Power play?"

"This isn't theater." Monty scoffed.

"She means political positioning Monty. And yes, this is a power play. By being here first we are in compliance while Cavenaugh is—"

"Is seen as being a slacker, and thus making his claim against Monty seem less than what it is?" I cut him off.

"Exactly."

I laughed at their deviousness. "No wonder you lured him out to the Caymans. Then you got on your fast boat and sped away to get here before him." I ruffled Nero's ears in triumph. I figured out their strategy.

"Does that mean we have to wait here the entire time? Cavenaugh hasn't made port yet. I'm hungry," I may have let a whine sneak into my voice.

Monty shook his head. "We have to be here when parle is called, which will be as soon as Cavenaugh lands. Can't risk leaving."

I may be a tough fighter pilot, but this was pirate-capital in the seventeenth century. Without a sidearm of any kind, or an escort, this place was very much not safe for women. I didn't want to end up being volunteered to serve in a brothel.

I jumped off my perch and approached Mann. I stepped in close enough for our breath to mingle. I slid his weapon from its sheath on his hip. I held out my hand. "Give me some money, I'll go get us some food."

"It's dangerous out there," he practically purred. Neither of us had backed away.

"And now I have a sword, so I am dangerous too." I stepped back. "Come on, Nero," I called the dog, and we left to find a tavern.

By the time we returned with a roasted chicken, a few apples, and a loaf of bread, I got the feeling Cavenaugh was close. The men were agitated.

We ate, and tensions did not seem to be any less. Waiting was never good for anyone's nerves.

I sucked on a leg bone, trying to find any hint of meat that I may have missed. "So what exactly did Monty do that was so horrendous?"

The door to the courtroom crashed open, and an honest to God sea dog pirate walked in. He made my collection of pretty boys look like posers. "Montague stole my property."

Cavenaugh made an entrance that was meant for intimidation. We may have been there first, but he wanted any witnesses to know he was there with righteous indignity. An attitude that to have been born of his piracy. He was more broad than tall, and his beard took over the majority of his face. He was intimidation on legs.

Mann stepped in front of Monty. "He is his own man. He left of his own accord."

I scrambled to my feet, grabbed Mann's discarded sword, and held it behind me. I felt safer on my own out on the street when I went to find food. Other pirates entered the space behind Cavenaugh's impressive entrance.

"Slavery has been abolished in this region." Monty stepped out from behind Mann.

Cavenaugh growled.

Andreas stood up. "I am not chattel."

I covered my mouth, stifling a gasp. Andreas had been a slave and Monty freed him.

"You are mine. I demand the return of my property!" Cavenaugh bellowed.

"Or what?"

"I demand satisfaction!" He pulled his sword out and leveled it at Monty's chest.

Andreas stepped in front of Monty. "Then fight me, you bastard!"

"I will not fight property." Cavenaugh backhanded Andreas across the face, knocking him out of the way.

If he had that kind of strength in a slap of his hand, he had considerable power behind his sword. Monty wasn't that skilled a swordsman.

I rushed to Andreas's side. Cupping a hand to his face, I said, "Give me the Turkish saber."

He removed the sword and handed it to me pummel first. I hefted the blade in my grip. And stood in front of Monty.

"Then that means your argument is with me." I held my

hand out indicating Andreas, Monty, and Mann. "These men belong to me, therefore, your fight is with me."

I held still, I didn't swish the blade back and forth in an aggression display as Cavenaugh did.

"Jane, no!" Monty surged forward.

"I love you. I can do this." I mouthed to him.

Mann held Monty back and whispered something to him. He gave me a sharp nod. I turned my attention back to the pirate.

"To be clear, I win, these men are no longer a concern of yours and you will cease to pursue them further."

Cavenaugh laughed. He thought he would win, it was written all over his face. "And when I win, you will be dead, and I will reclaim my property, and Montague as payment for any infraction against me."

I mocked him and laughed right back. "That's not going to happen, you aren't going to win."

I gave him a slight nod of my head, and he took that as an ascent to my readiness to dual.

He attacked like a bull. He fought with power, but not with agility, flexibility, grace, or fluidity. I let him advance, and I backed up, climbing as I went. Balanced on the backs of chairs, I held my hand up for a brief pause.

"What?" the pirate snarled.

"To the death?" I asked. I did want to be sure of my goal. I already had my motive.

"To disarmament or yield." Someone yelled out.

Cavenaugh grunted. I took that as his agreement.

One of the aspects of the Turkish blade that I liked, was how much it felt like a Japanese sword in my hands. That meant I could modify my parries, and thrusts and use this weapon in a completely unexpected way.

I lured Cavenaugh about the room, letting him think he had the advantage. When it came to pure brutal attack strength he did. But I had moves he never would have encountered. I was very disappointed in his lack of witty banter and told him so. His response was to growl more and barrel forward like a bull. Fatigue crept up on me. I needed to end this before I was no longer capable of fighting.

Using a two-handed grip, I spun the sword. At the same time, I delivered a roundhouse kick to the side of Cavenaugh's knee. There was a loud crack, and he went down. My sword slid behind his grip, and with a flick, I disarmed him. I was still in motion, and my action continued with a hard blow of my hilt to the back of his head. He went the rest of the way down with a loud thud.

I stopped and composed myself instantly. I cast my gaze over the gathered counsel.

"I believe he yields. Has this been settled to your satisfaction gentlemen?" I asked.

There was some muttering before one of them announced that this issue had been resolved in the favor of Andreas de Tas-Sliema du Malta as a free man. Barron Cavenaugh had no claim to him or to William Montague.

Monty gave them a wildly flourished bow, as he usually did. I managed a nod. Mann was by my side, and I latched on to his arm "Get me out of here before I collapse."

They managed to get me back to the ship before I blacked out... *again.*

I WOKE to a loud crash and the sound of screams.

Monty banged into the cabin. "We are under attack. That mad man is firing on us!"

He left as suddenly as he arrived.

I stumbled out onto the deck. A cannonball whistled over my head and careened through our rigging, and exploding in the ocean on the other side. The only way we were going to survive the attack was to outrun the other ship. The Resurrection was capable of doing just that, but we needed to catch a breeze in order for that to happen, as it was, we were in cannon range.

Cavenaugh clearly did not agree with the counsel's findings. He wanted Andreas returned, and he wanted Monty's neck in a noose for stealing his property. Well, that wasn't going to happen, not while I was around. I had already fought for the men once, I would do it again.

I stared at the squall line to our south, in the same place it had been two days ago. We were making our way north of the pocket storm, but something told me our best bet for safety was inside those clouds. I ran across the deck and up the stairs. I wrenched the wheel from Andreas's hands, spinning us toward the bad weather.

"Abandon ship," I yelled. No need for the crew to get lost with us.

"What do you think you are doing?" he yelled at me, fighting to redirect us.

"Do you trust me? We have to go in there." I pointed at the roiling clouds, lightning flashed in their depths. The same squall line that had lured me to attempt jumping overboard called to me again. This time I knew why the storm that they had rescued me from was still here. It wasn't a storm

"What do you think you are doing?" Mann joined us by the helm.

"It's not a storm, it's a vortex. And I'm fairly certain my Raptor is the cause of it. If we sail into it, I go back home." Mann didn't look at me like I was insane, he understood. He had to be from the future too, had to be.

"Do it!" He shouted at the crew to get in the longboats. He helped to lower the men and the boats so they could get away before adding his strength to holding us on course, straight into the storm.

"I came from a storm, and I shall return to the storm!" he shouted into the wind.

One of the masts came down, bringing the sails with it. Waves washed over us. I was beginning to question my own resolve when I saw the vortex. It wasn't natural. Lightning spun, and colored lights flashed in the spinning clouds.

"Head toward that!" I pointed.

I didn't blackout, and I witnessed the Resurrection disintegrating around us. For once in my life, I wish I had blacked out, then I wouldn't have seen the storm rip Monty from the deck, or Andreas give up, and look at me with a face smeared with tears.

Mann gripped my hand. "I love you. I'll see you on the other side." He gave me a smile, and then he was hit across the back with downed rigging, knocking him out.

"I'm sorry," I said to no one. I had been so very wrong.

... *blackness* ...

THE WEEKS BLENDED TOGETHER. Once I was able to maintain consciousness, I was shuffled off to a rehab facility. My days were repeats of the same thing over and over again. I had physical therapy in the morning. I was ridiculously weak and confined to a wheelchair. After PT, I was wheeled to lunch. And after that, I was parked in front of the large vidscreen for hours on end. Before dinner, I had another round of PT, typically at that time, I rode a stationary bike, trying to get my pitifully weak legs to gain strength.

I think I was doing better before the meds started. The nurses gave me a little pink and white pill right after lunch. At first, I didn't get the pill. But I guess my delusions became aggressive, and I needed some help getting a firm grasp on reality.

Apparently, there were three of us knocked out of orbit by a meteor shower. There was nothing I could have done. Two of us survived. At first, they thought there was only one survivor because they couldn't find me. I was out there for just over a week before I was picked up, floating out there on some wreckage, dehydrated, and incoherent.

The days they were late with my pill were the days that I knew Mann, Monty, and Andreas had been real. So had that damned dog, Nero. Those were the days I typically ended up crying myself to sleep because I knew I was forgetting something, someone I loved.

The vid news kept playing updates on the miraculous recovery of some space jokey. He crashed in the early days of the Jupiter Mission. Knocked out of orbit by satellite debris. Had a similar engine to what was in the Raptors these days. He was found floating on some half-sunken boat. It was a big deal because he had gone missing almost thirty years ago, and he had aged less than ten.

Every time I saw him on the vid I would spend the rest of my day crying. No one knew why, and I couldn't explain it when they asked. I knew at some point, I just didn't know now.

Today was no different. I barely held my own body upright, slumped in the chair, parked in front of the vid. Captain Manerowski, a modern-day super survivor, was on again. I felt that tickle in my brain, I would cry later. Today the news cameras followed him as he met with school children. Apparently, he was Space Force's golden child, and he was happy to do the work. Behind him his companions; two tall men, one all in black, the other in dark red. They were always slightly out of focus, but always there. I started crying earlier than usual.

"Jane." The nurse's soft voice broke into the white noise in my head. They stopped addressing me as captain a few weeks ago. "Why are you so upset today?"

I shook my head. I didn't know. I pointed at the vid. Maybe I was just so pleased he had survived. Maybe I was angry that I was not recovering while he seemed so fit and healthy.

"Oh, it's that good looking astronaut again. I heard a rumor that he might be visiting us soon. You'd like that wouldn't you?"

"I think that would be nice. I was a pilot too, you know." Everything felt slower after that pink and white pill.

"Yes, we know. And maybe if you get better you can be one again." She patted the back of my hand and tucked a tissue into my pitiful grasp.

I didn't see the other nurse behind me, but I heard them. "You shouldn't tell her things like that. They'll never let her fly again."

"I was just giving her a reason to want to get stronger."

Another blur of days, and then something was different. I didn't go to morning physical therapy. I was given a shower earlier and dressed in actual clothes, not pajamas.

"Someone wants to meet you." Was all anyone would tell me.

The smells of lunch were missing from the cafeteria when I was rolled in. It was full of people, important-looking people. There was a crowd at one end, and rows of empty seats lined up in front of a podium. A stern-looking woman, I think she was the director of the facility headed toward me. Captain Manerowski was next to her, and just behind him, those other men.

My heart pounded in my chest.

I couldn't remember something very important. I felt tears well up in my eyes from frustration. What was it that I could not remember?

"Captain, this is Jane Way, the pilot you requested to meet." The woman introduced us. I lifted my hand to shake the one he offered. He didn't look at me but took my hand.

The darker man, the one in the stylish red suit swiped a tear from his cheek. The blond had a wide grin on his face as if he were showing off some perfect new veneers on his teeth. His teeth hadn't been so bad before.

Before?

I knew him from before. Why was Andreas crying?

"Eric?" I may have been a bit louder than intended. I pulled on the hand in mine.

Mann stumbled as I caught him off guard.

"I'm so sorry, Captain. She's been suffering from outbursts since they found her."

He regained his composure but didn't let go of my hand.

"That's okay, she's been through a lot." He kneeled down in front of me so his handsome face was level with mine.

"I know you?" I looked up at the two men behind him. "I know all of you, don't I?"

Mann, Manerowski, reached up and brushed hair back from my face. "You know us, Captain."

He stood and began questioning the Director regarding my routine, my medications.

"I'm not at liberty to divulge that information," she said.

"I know him. You can tell him." My voice was never very loud, but I did try to make my words as forceful as I felt.

She cut me a quick glare, and then guided Mann— I was certain he was Mann, but who was Mann?— away from me. Their heads were lowered together in discussion.

The blond knelt down next to me. He picked up my hand and cradled it in his. "How have you been, darling? Are they treating you well?"

Andreas, I decided his name was Andreas, rested a hand on the blonde's shoulder. "She doesn't know us." He still had tears in his eyes.

"But I should. Something is missing and I know something is missing but I don't know what."

Manerowski and the Director returned to our little group.

"Does she suffer from amnesia?" the blond asked.

"It's her medication, Monty. They're making her forget."

"Mon-ty." I let the name roll around on my tongue. It felt so familiar. He should be tied up with a gag in his mouth.

"I know you!" Sound burst out of my mouth. "I love you!"

"I believe it's time for her medication."

The Director left momentarily and returned with a nurse. The nurse had a little paper cup and that pink and white pill. Manerowski reached over and crumbled the paper cup and the pill into his fist.

"I don't think so. She's not having outbursts that need to be controlled by that." He turned his attention to me. "Jane, dear, are you willing to sign yourself out of this facility so that we can take proper care of you?"

"You asked us to trust you once, and here we are. Now, it's our turn to ask you to trust us," Andreas said in his lilting Spanish accent. Not Spanish. Damn what was it?

I swallowed a lump in my throat. "Yes, I'll go with you."

Somehow, I knew they would take care of me.

What seemed like hours and arguments later, I was wheeled out to a very large black hover. The back door was opened and a large dog jumped out and began licking my face. I laughed as I pushed him back. "Nero? I'm happy to see you boy."

"So, you do remember us in that brain of yours?"

"I told you, Monty, it was the medication. She'll start remembering more and more as it gets out of her system."

"What's going on?" I asked. These men were rescuing me, but I couldn't help but think they should be dressed less like celebrities, and more like pirates.

"You brought me back, Captain. You saved Monty and Andreas from Cavenaugh, and you brought me home. About twenty years off, but yeah." He shrugged.

"Was all of that real or a dream?"

"Does it matter? We're all together." Mann lifted me into the back of the vehicle. The dog put his face into mine, and I had to push him back.

"I'll miss your beach house," I said. "I remember that right? You had a beach house?"

"I did, and I won't miss it. Don't underestimate indoor plumbing and electricity."

"But how?"

"I don't think we will ever know. Both our ships' engines were based on the VOJ. My best guess is there is something in the propulsion system that punched a hole in time. For some reason when your Raptor crashed it created a stable vortex. At least partially stable. There is nothing there anymore."

I looked up at Monty and Andreas. "But what about you guys? Were you also from now?"

Monty scoffed. "No one appreciates how good I look for being over five-hundred years old."

"Seriously? It wasn't all a dream?" I sighed, it had happened. It had really happened. And I really was in love with them, all of them.

THE END

ABOUT THE AUTHOR

Lulu M Sylvian

Bio-engineered to be the only redhead in a generation of blonds, she feels that "aliens" may actually be the best answer for a lifetime of being asked, "Where did you get that red hair from?"

Lulu cannot ride a horse, hula hoop, or play roller derby, but she can make pictures. Encouraged to make those pictures out of words Lulu began writing just to see what would happen. What happened was two full-length manuscripts in three months. She embraces the crazy that comes with that one little genetic mutation, and attempts to live up to the reputation of being a redhead.

She writes sexy hot contemporary and paranormal romance.

Where to find Lulu

Facebook: www.facebook.com/lmsylvian

Facebook group: Lululandia https://www.facebook.com/groups/519202371904484/

Twitter: www.twitter.com/lulumsylvian

Instagram: www.instagram.com/lmsylvian

Pinterest: www.pinterest.com/lmsylvian

Goodreads: https://www.goodreads.com/LuluMSylvian
website: http://www.lulumsylvian.com
Newsletter sign up: http://lmsylvian.com/newsletter/

FATED BY BLOOD

LIZ KNOX

1

The Year 2019...

Rhea

I HAVE LIVED in the Underworld for over two hundred and twenty-three years. I state the amount of time I have been here, but I have never ventured outside the Underworld. You see, I was born here. I am unlike any other creature confined within our gates. My name is Rhea, and before anyone assumes that I am Hades' mother— I'm not. I am actually his daughter. Why he named me after my grandmother, I have no clue.

I want to venture past the confines of my home and see the wonders of not only Earth, but the rest of the Underworld, and even Mount Olympus. My father's three-headed dog, Cerberus, guards the gates so that no Shades or Demons try to break in. My father has also enlisted the help of the highest demons to guard us. It's not exactly like the cream of the crop lives here. Our home isn't just for the average lost soul— it also houses the worst beings, but yet is the safest and most secure place for me.

I live in the primary part of the Underworld, where my

father spends most of his time— Tartarus. We don't live alone either, but with my father's second and latest wife Persephone. They have been wed for roughly fifty years, which isn't very long in our world.

The two other regions are Elysium, where mortals go and home of the heroic gods. All-in-all, it's the closest one will ever get to paradise. The last and final portion of the Underworld is the Asphodel Meadows, which hosts most of the souls who have crossed over. It's where individuals who haven't lived in extreme, good or bad, end up.

Sitting on a couch made of igneous rock, which is what almost all of Tartarus is made up of, I watch lava flow in between the rocks. Sometimes, when I overlook the landscape through my bedroom window, the heat radiates over my face.

I move the white silks of my dress over my legs, my knee peeking out as I ponder what I will do today. Thinking about my mother, I slowly convince myself that I should act *now*— find out what she truly meant when she left me ten years ago. There's only one place I can find the answers I so desperately seek. Only three women can tell me what I'm missing, and they are the Fates. Never have I had the courage to find out the reasoning behind my mother's actions, or the understanding of the words she spoke to me the night before she escaped the Underworld.

I hated her for a while— for her actions, for leaving me here with *him* all alone. Only, I wasn't genuinely alone because Persephone has been here. But, she gets to leave for half of the year . . . and I get no freedom from this place. It may be my home, but I want to feel the wind on my face, and see birds flying through the sky on Earth.

Most of all, I want to go to Mount Olympus and discover another part of myself— the part that my father doesn't like to elaborate on. My Uncle, Zeus, shows up on occasion . . . however, it is almost always on bad terms. My father isn't exactly a rule follower.

My uncle only comes down here when he has to yell at my father for disobeying him in some way. I've only overheard a couple of their fights, although, there was one argument that I was the topic of. I still don't know how to feel about it. I wish I had heard everything so I would understand more. Instead, I feel as if I am trying to put together a puzzle— something about my bloodline, what some have said and the other gods' opinions. It still doesn't make sense to me, but I doubt it ever will. My father does love to keep me in the dark, after all.

When I overheard them arguing, I remember going to my mother. I was much younger, and naïve beyond belief. When going to my mother, she made sure I understood that I'm unique, but that is a drastic understatement.

I'm not like any other demigod. No, I'm an entirely different species. You see, my father is Hades, one of the most feared Gods in the realm. He also happens to be the complete embodiment of evil. On the other hand, my mother is Luminita. She is the sole daughter of Dracula.

I am a half demigod, half . . . something else— from the most royal vampire bloodline in existence. There is not another of my kind, seeing as my parents loathe one another. Their marriage was for a political alliance which kept the gods from going to war with my grandfather. In the agreement was for them to have one child— to unify both species. That child is me, but I'm not sure I've done anything to help unify the species, especially since I haven't ever been allowed to leave Tartarus.

My father has always kept me behind the safe gates of our home, but it has not been an entirely quiet life. There is a fair share of dramatics in our safe haven, but Brenex keeps most of the dramatics away from me. On occasion, when my uncle would visit, he would tear me away from being within earshot.

Brenex is one of the many higher demons who guard our home. I'm not friends with anyone else, really. I assume that it must be far too risky to be friends with me, all things considered. It makes me wonder, is it out of fear for me or the fear they hold for my father? Brenex, though, he's quite a bit different. He's filled with attitude and gives zero fucks. He's said that word quite a bit, but I'm still unsure what it means. I believe it's because of the type of demon he is, but he hasn't revealed that to me. In actuality, most do not.

I stand from the couch and approach the window overlooking the courtyard. It's made of cooled over magma with lava flowing throughout, creating patterns and symbols that glow reddish-orange against the darkness of the stones. My father has never told me what they mean, but they have significance to him. I know better than to ask further.

Cerberus is a few hundred feet away, sitting on the outside of the gates. He scans anyone who comes within his reach, always assuming they're a threat. He's massive, as black as the ground I walk on, with a lion-like mane. His tail is pointy at the end like a scorpion. I've seen him use it on a demon before. One who had worked for my father and got the wrong idea of trying to harm me. Cerberus eliminated the threat, using his tail, and I watched as he writhed in pain, disappearing in front of my eyes. My father explained that the soul of the demon is no more— when Cerberus attacks, someone's mere existence vanishes.

Cerberus stretches out and walks in a circle, coming closer to the gates. This is what he always does whenever he's about to lie down and sleep. I wait, thinking that if he does really go to sleep, I will try and sneak out. My heart pounds in my chest, my blood pulsing through my veins. Nervousness floods over me, partially hoping that he won't sleep and I'll be able to get out of my sudden courage, but as he stretches his paws out and curls up his tail, I know I'll be leaving.

I might not have another opportunity like this for years. At least, that's what I tell myself. My longing to discover what my mother meant will haunt me if I don't act . . . so, here I go.

2

Rhea

HOW IN THE world I managed to slip past Cerberus, I don't really know. It makes me think we can't really live in the safest place in Tartarus if my father's three-headed guard dog can't even notice a small woman leaving. I'm on a mission to seek the answers I need from the only beings that can convey them to me— the Fates. As a child, I was always told that the Fates would guide you in their direction. They are never in the same exact place but stay in the Elysium.

I don't honestly know the extent of my powers, but I have been trying to focus on them. Being that I'm not exactly like my father, he can't give me any insight on what I can control. All I do is think about the Fates and what it is they will tell me as I continue on my journey. My hope is that one day I will know every aspect of myself, and be able to control all of my hidden abilities. But first, I need to know what they all are.

I'm careful to keep my head down and stay on my path, even with the Shades that make me leery of following this avenue. I should've asked Brenex to accompany me, but knowing him, he would have talked me out of it. It's not that he wants to keep me from doing what I need to do. But rather, he's so concerned on whatever my punishments will be for defying my father, so he keeps me on the straight line. Only, this time, he wouldn't be able to do that.

I get out of my head and look at my surroundings— like the lava flowing through the rock. Some of it even pools in giant puddles, big enough that I could swim in it. Scanning over the landscape, it all looks the same to me. A cliff is off to my right a ways and chunks of lava flood over the side. The lava divides into multiple cracks and flows through the crevice in the rock. Everything looks the same, and I'm not quite sure how I'm going to make it there. I was always told that the Fates know when you're on your way to them.

"Please guide me to you." I quietly beg.

I close my eyes and focus hard on these three women, needing them to show me the way. I have craved seeing them for years and with every passing day, my need grows even more. Negative thoughts break through my mind, wondering what will happen to me when my father finds out what I've done. I have to snap myself out of it. There's no point in worrying until after I'm caught, and even then, I need to hope he'll understand. It's doubtful, but not impossible.

Opening my eyes, I'm no longer in the same place. Igneous rock and lava are replaced with some sort of cold, white material. It melts as it hits my foot and with each step I take, it gets caught in between my feet and sandals. Not only that, but it is so much colder here. I have only ever been hot. The drastic change has me shivering in place.

Plus, this new place has me not only curious, but afraid. I yearn to discover the world I am part of . . . but I also am terrified of going outside of my element. I think that is only natural, though. The white ice flakes fall from the sky and hit my face, melting on impact. Running my hands against my face, they're spotted with wetness and I wonder what this is called.

"This is so different," I mutter to myself lowly, looking

around. I am on some sort of cliff, up high in the sky. Surveying the area, I wonder if this is a mountain. More than that, I wonder if this is Mount Olympus. Have I somehow teleported here? I know I am not in tune with my powers, or even aware of them . . . but maybe this is one of them. Maybe I am some sort of time-demigod.

"Come here, child." An old, wavering voice speaks out to me, almost causing me to jump. I whip around, searching for a body, but see nothing. Instead, there is a cave a little ways off and I head in that direction. I don't know how to describe it, but it somehow feels right. I'm supposed to trust my instincts, so I do.

When I arrive at the opening, it feels a tad bit warmer. No longer am I shaking in my sandals, or is the wind blowing through my silks. I don't shiver as I was a few moments ago. "Don't be shy, Rhea. We have been waiting for your arrival, my dear." This isn't the same voice that speaks to me. It's different, the pitch a tiny bit higher.

"Are you the Fates?" I call out, wanting an answer before I continue on. It's never hurt anyone to be a little bit cautious.

A snickering laugh greets me. "Of course we are. Now, come. We do not have much time." This must be the third Fate who speaks to me. No matter what I do, I am continuously worried about what will happen when I get back, but I have waited a long time for this.

Placing one foot in front of the other, I venture into the cave. It becomes warmer with each step. The floor isn't rock like I think, but dirt, and as I continue on there is a multitude of changes. You would have no idea that this cave is located in the middle of a cold climate. Flowers, bushes, and trees grow within the walls of the cave, turning it into some type of paradise. I follow the path, turning at the curve of the formation. An opening is revealed to me, the sound of water rushing down from a higher elevation greets me, along with the sweet smell of something I do not know.

"You took long enough," one of the Fates greets me. Looking off to the right, she is sitting on a tree stump, as old and frail as her voice is. I can't help but seek out the other two and spot them almost immediately. One sits by a pool of water, dipping her feet in, and the other is off to the left, surrounded by flowers.

I wonder if they have brought life to a place where it doesn't exist?

"Yes, we have," says the Fate who is dipping her feet in the water. I had no clue they could read minds, but it does not surprise me. Although, how can they bring life to a place like this when they are all fragile and gray.

"It is simple, naïve girl. While we look old and decrepit, we still have immeasurable power. If you would prefer to insult us, you may leave and go back from which you came," the one on the stump tells me in an agitated voice.

"I apologize. I did not mean to insult you in any way. I just . . . have never been away from my home. So many questions are running through my mind. For instance, how long have you been here?" I've heard stories of the Fates ever since I was a little girl, but not knowing if I will ever have another opportunity like this . . . I want as many answers as I can get.

"Oh, child. We have been in the Underworld for a megaannum, at least."

I'm taken aback by the one's answer. "A million years?"

"Yes. The gods saw fit to trap us here with your father," the one near the water states.

"It is the worst form of punishment that they could have given us. Trapping us in this awful place. It is funny that they want to know what we see, but they do not accept what we say," says the one in the garden with a smirk.

I cock a brow. "So, they condemned you here after you told them something they didn't want to hear? Something that . . . they couldn't accept?"

"Yes," the three of them answer at the exact same time.

"We know why it is you have come here. We are prepared to give you the answers you seek as long as you pay the price."

"A price would be a fair barter for the things we will tell you."

"Yes, the fairest trade of all."

The three of them do whatever they can to talk me into giving them what they want. I've never heard of the Fates being wicked creatures, so I don't think that offering them something in return would be a bad thing. Although, what can I offer them? I don't have anything of value to my name. Instead, everything is my father's.

The one sitting in the garden laughs, making me feel like they have an ulterior motive. It causes chills to run over my body. I'd say I'm uncomfortable, but that's not entirely the right word choice. I have a feeling that out of all three, she's the cocky one– the one who makes most of their decisions.

"Come here, child," she calls over to me. Part of me wants to go from which I came. However, I didn't come here to chicken out last minute. I came for answers, and I will get them one way or another.

I walk over to her and stare at something she has on a pedestal. It looks like an evil eye. My father has shown me this once before. The Fates can see our past, present, and future. It is believed that they all share one eye, but from looking at them, they all have their own. This must be the eye that the stories speak of. "You will slice your hand with this blade and allow your blood to flow into the goblet. This is your price, Rhea, Daughter of Hades."

I can't help but wonder why these women would want my blood so desperately . . . but, I do as they ask. Reluctantly, I grab the blade from the pedestal and bring the dagger along my skin. The knife digs into my skin, separating my flesh and red droplets of blood pour down my hand. I'm not sure how I know to clench my fist and squeeze the blood into the challis, but I do.

I glance up to the Fate smirking, peering into the glass. It's almost like she is waiting for me to get to a certain point. She grabs my hand, forcing me to open it and puts some sort of green mixture on my wound. For a moment, I think it's poison.

"No, silly girl. It will help you heal quickly. You see, this is no ordinary blade. It is one that allows cutting through the thick skin of the gods. Skin like yours. You would have healed anyway, but the ointment I made for you will help you heal quicker. By the time you go back to your father, the wound should be gone."

She grabs the goblet from in front of me and takes a lengthy gulp. I didn't hear the other two women come over, but they quickly grab the cup and do the same as their sister. There is much that I still do not know when it comes to this world, but never have I witnessed someone drinking the blood of another. Ironic considering the fact I'm part vampire.

Within a few moments, the first Fate who had drunken from the cup turns unrecognizable. No longer is she old or frail, but now, she is filled with youth. Long, curly red hair spans down her back, meeting porcelain skin. The old rags she wears change into a lovely emerald green color, starting from the top and expanding down the length of her body, transforming into the finest of silks. I turn abruptly, wanting to see if the other two have changed as well. The one who sat by the water has long white hair that goes down in beautiful waves. Her eyes are a light, bright blue and it compliments her alabaster skin. Their rags have turned to vibrant silks as well, bright in the most beautiful shades of a cyan blue and a soft pink. Lastly, the one who was off in the distance is overcome with dark features. Her skin is an olive complexion, and it compliments her jet black hair and rusty orange eyes.

Not only do their features change, but the inside of their abode grows vibrant with even more life. Colors are brighter, small creatures come out of the cracks of the cave and fill their tiny forest. Something hops on four small feet with long fluffy ears. Tiny animals sit on the trees, chirping away.

I'm amazed to see that with their beauty, comes greater life — life that I have never seen before. I kneel down and place my hand out to the small animal with the long ears. It comes hopping over to me and sniffs before darting away to hide under the bush with flowers spread across it. I stand, and finally realize what has happened. My blood gave them their youth back.

"We have been cursed with old age for far too long. Thank you for freeing us from the madness, Rhea. I am Atropus," the red-headed woman tells me.

"We are indebted to you now," the white haired woman tells me. "I am Clotho."

"No, we are not indebted to you. It was a fair trade. Now, we will tell Rhea what it is that she so desperately seeks," the black haired woman says, but fails to reveal her name.

"That is Lachesis, the hard-headed one," Clotho snickers, shooting an irritated look to her sister. These women have revealed to me that they have been here for over a million years, but yet don't even look as old as I do. I still can't fathom how my blood did this to them.

Lachesis grabs me by the arm, twisting her head off to the side as she peers down, looking over me. "You don't have the faintest idea that you are the most powerful being in the realm. What a shame."

I furrow my brows, confused by what she's just told me. "What do you mean?" There's no possible way that *I* am the most powerful anywhere.

She scoffs. "You are unique. Far more important than anyone else, but we know you do not understand the true meaning of this. You won't, at least not for a while. You don't want to believe what I will tell you, Rhea. So, listen up. You will bring about change in this world— a change that is feared by some and desired by others."

I take in a deep breath, my heart pounding in my chest. I'm not naïve, and I know that the Fates know of the past, present, and future. There is no doubt in my mind that Lachesis is telling me the truth. I only wish I could understand what she means.

"The marks of your destiny will soon cover your body. It is the combination of your bloodlines that give you a power greater than anyone has ever known. As Lachesis has told you, you will bring about change in the world. Some will want to destroy you for it, while others will praise you. You have two choices, Rhea— to either transform into something worse than your father or embrace fate." My eyes go wide at what Clotho has said, trying to understand it.

"You will not be like the other demigods or even the gods themselves. You'll be something else entirely, as you should be. This journey will lead you to many mates, who will all be part of your success or demise, depending on your choices. You are not to choose between them, Rhea. Please understand this. You must accept them for the help they will offer you, and love will grow through acceptance," Atropus states.

"What do you mean, mates?" I take a step back, looking at the three of them like they've lost their damn minds. I've never even left the confines of Tartarus and they're acting as if I'm going to be some courageous savior.

Clotho smiles. "You will love many men, and maybe a woman, if you so choose. She is up in the air, but four have been chosen for you. Four men. Two who share some of the same blood as you do, although, they are not the same. One of them is as trapped as you, and another who constantly fights against half of your bloodline."

They are speaking to me in riddles, and I hate that. I hate that they won't just tell me what this means. "Please, don't toy with me. Tell me what you mean!" I shake my head in disbelief. The only reason I came here was to find out what happened with my mother, not to discover whatever this is.

Atropus takes a step forward me. "You already know what we mean. Think about what we have just told you."

Truthfully, I don't know how to think. I don't even know how to breathe right now. My chest feels heavy and my heart pounds relentlessly. Before I even know what's happening, everything goes black.

3

Rhea

I FEEL the soft green stuff between my hands, and my eyes flutter open slowly. I turn my head to the right and see Clotho sitting there with some sort of rag pressed against my face. "What . . . are you doing?"

"Trying to help you, Rhea. We do not have much time and you must be on your way before your father notices you've left. More importantly, he need not know that you came to us. If he were to find out what we told you today . . ." She looks to the ground, not saying a word.

I use my hands to pull my body up, still looking at her. "If he finds out what? Please continue."

Clotho whips her head back towards me, staring me dead in the eyes. "If he finds out, he will kill you. It is why we must send you off before he notices."

I take in a sharp breath, not wanting to believe that my father would do such a thing . . . I am of his bloodline. He couldn't possibly harm me in any way. I'm his *only* child.

"Don't be so naïve. He will kill you at the first chance if you give him the opportunity. You are his biggest threat, after all, and if there is one thing Hades hates . . . it's someone more powerful than he," Lachesis tells me. She's on my opposite side, cranking her head sideways as she did a short time ago. "Do you remember the story your father would tell you as a little girl? The nightmare he would bestow upon you night after night?"

I think hard, only recalling one story that would terrify me.

"The story of a prophet coming to destroy the world as we knew it. A girl born of multiple bloodlines, unlike any other creature we've ever known. Hades has always assumed this girl would destroy the world, but remember that perception is different whenever you speak to anyone. You will be the villain in his story, but the savior in many others. You must get out of the Underworld before he puts the pieces together, Rhea. If you don't, he will damn us all."

Fear rushes over my body. But why am I afraid? Is it the unknown that scares me or is it knowing that what these three say is my reality? The one person I've always craved to be loved by is the person who would kill me. That is mindboggling. This makes me feel even more alone. Separated from everything I thought I knew.

"You are not as alone as you feel. You know one of your mates already, and he will be ready to help you when the time comes. Please understand that you must go to your grandfather's. Most of the answers you seek are there, including your mother . . . but Dracula will help you, girl. Whatever you do, trust your instincts and know what is right. You must follow the path."

Still, I am having a hard time processing all of this. "What do you mean I know one of my mates?" I ask the question, turning my head around to look at all three of the Fates. Just as I understand, I ask what I already know. "He is a demon, isn't he?"

"Yes," Atropus responds. "We cannot tell you anymore or

any less. It will alter the thread of life and everything will be off balance."

"I will have to defy him, won't I?" I'm not speaking about my mate, but ask about my father.

"Yes, and while it will be hard for you, you must do it. We've already told you what will happen if you do not."

All my life, I have never deceived him. Nor have I even thought about it. My mother had her reasons for leaving and while I respected them . . . it didn't mean I understood. I just think of what she said to me— how I was special and that one day, I'd know what she meant. I think I partially know what she meant now. Only, there is so much pressure that comes with it.

I'd be lying if I said I'm not afraid. I'm afraid for many reasons, but mostly because I have an eerie feeling that my entire life is about to change before I even know it. I want to explore the Underworld and far past the gates, but I don't want my inner peace to be lost. From what the Fates tell me . . . I have no choice when it comes to that.

"Is it wrong that I am afraid?" I ask in a mere whisper, partially worried that I will be reprimanded.

"No, it's not. It shows that you understand the severity of the tasks that are bestowed upon you," Clotho states, offering me a half smile. "This will not be easy for you, Rhea. But remember that in your struggles, you will triumph and become the woman that has been promised to us."

If I had to guess, the Fates view me as their savior and not the villain. This just shows me that the lines will be drawn in many ways. I am not familiar when it comes to war, but it seems to me that I will have to be. I doubt that I will be able to get through this without any bloodshed— especially when I've already shed blood for them. "This is just the beginning, isn't it?"

Nods greet me. "Now get up and get going. We don't have any time for this. You must leave, and quickly," Lachesis growls out. Grabbing my forearm, she tugs me into a standing position. I whirl my head around taking in the scenery and then remember... I suddenly appeared here.

"Wait. I don't know how I got here!" I tell her, worry striking through my body.

She huffs, rolling her eyes. Shoot, I didn't think one of the Fates would be packed with so much sass. "You set a destination in your mind and teleported here. It is one of your powers, Rhea. I don't have time to explain this to you. Think of your home, visualize it in your mind and open your eyes."

I do as she says, closing my eyes and visualizing my home. I see Cerberus sleeping in front of the gates and the lava that flows through the rock. Silent screams of the Shades greet me and as I breathe in and out, I know I'm not where I once was. Heat warms my skin and I am home. Now, I must figure out what to do from here and pray I've made it home in enough time.

4

Rhea

JUST LIKE THAT, I open my eyes and see the iron gates that lead up to my home. I'm irritated that I didn't teleport back through the gates. I imagined my room and yet, I'm outside, a little ways past Cerberus. He is still asleep which causes me to sigh in relief. My worries are alleviated since I was able to get here before he woke up. If I didn't, getting back inside would be so much harder.

I'm careful with my steps, moving one foot in front of the other in a calculating way. I'm meticulously placing my feet on certain rocks, making sure there are no broken pieces that could make any sort of cracking sound. Of all Cerberus' senses, his hearing is by far the best.

I look below me onto the rocks, making sure I don't accidently dip a foot in the lava. My father told me once that it doesn't harm us, but he and I are made up of different DNA, so I'm not sure he's accurate. He's naturally assuming that the things that don't affect him, won't hurt me.

Making my way past Cerberus, I'm as quiet as can be, but as soon as I manage to place my hand on the iron gates and push it open, he's alerted. I place my head against the gates, silently cursing myself. An old creaking sound fills the air, and I cringe as I feel a gush of wind from his body blow over me. If that isn't the worst of it, he's growling ever so loudly. There's no doubt that I'm caught red-handed.

Turning my head, I am nose to nose with one of his heads. "Cerberus . . . it's just me." Reluctantly, I bring hand over the side of his face, rubbing him gently. "Please don't eat me."

I keep my hand on the iron and push it forward a teeny bit but have to stop as the sound grows louder with each push. It didn't do this when I left, but I also wasn't pushing it in. I was going out.

"Rhea. What on Earth are you doing?" Brenex's voice comes out of nowhere. He grabs my hand through the gate and before I know it, I'm no longer in the same spot. Now I'm on the inside of the gates. Did he just take me through the gates?

Furrowing my brows, I speak. "What just happened?"

"I saved your ass. Do you want to tell me what the hell you were doing?" He looks enraged, furious beyond belief. But it's not like the usual anger that I'm used to seeing. I think worry fuels his emotional state.

I take a good hard look at him, watching the way he knits his brows together. His expression is filled with nothing but concern. It is now that I remember what the Fates told me about having a demon mate. Could it be Brenex?

I scan my eyes over his body, taking in his pale skin with the light blue tint. Horns come from his head with a white fire that simmers. His eyes glow with the same tint that covers his skin, however, it is much brighter. His hair is the whitest of whites, looking close to that cold material that fell from the sky when I went to see the Fates. He wears metal armor on his shoulders and forearms with matching boots, while his lower region is covered in some sort of black suede leather material.

"I was . . . out." I keep it simple, not wanting him to know my personal business.

He scoffs, throwing his hands up in the air. "Fuck, Rhea. Do you have any idea what could've happened to you out there!"

I widen my eyes, not liking the tone he's taking with me. I understand he might've been worried, but nothing happened. I'm perfectly fine. "I handled myself just fine, thank you very much."

"Don't be a cocky bitch," he snarls, yanking his hand away from my arm. "You don't have a clue about the demons and shades out there who want to bring you harm. There are entire cults dedicated to your demise simply because of your blood. Don't you ever be this arrogant again. Do you understand me?"

His words instantly make me feel guilty for seeking the answers I needed. Little does he know what else I was told. I keep wondering if he is the one they speak of, but I'm not quite sure. There are so many demons here . . . and it really could be anyone. I'd only be lucky if it were actually Brenex.

I gasp at my thoughts, not realizing what I was thinking. In all honesty, I have always admired him from afar. He's never been afraid to get close to me. Everyone else always is.

A sudden flux of heat covers me and there's no mistaking why. "Rhea. Did you leave the grounds?" His voice is deep, full of disapproval and damn right intimidating.

Turning my body towards him, I look up to my father. He's almost double my size, towering over my small frame. His arms are as big as my torso, covered in rock hard muscle, almost as if he was made from the rock that covers Tartarus. His legs are even double my size, massive in every sense of the word.

Besides his size, there are few things that are different about him except for his eyes. He doesn't have any like I do. Instead, they are open slits with some sort of fire burning behind them. His long black beard goes down to the middle of his chest, and he has armor blocking his shoulders, forearms, knees, and mid-section. It's made up of Olympian steel, which is something that only the gods can wear. "Brenex, you are dismissed. Thank you for finding her."

Oh, crap. He knows I wasn't here. The Fates warned me that I needed him to not have a clue. Now I have to be convincing as I get myself out of this. "I'm sorry, Father. Really, I am terribly sorry." I lower my head and look down to the ground, bringing my arms around my torso. I plan to use my innocence against him in the hopes it will stop his suspicions.

"Do not lie to me, girl. You're not sorry. Try that again and do not tarnish your name. Your grandmother would be sick if she knew you were lying to me."

I look up to him, not trying to glare but it just happens. "I am sorry, so please don't tell me that I'm not. I'm sorry that I hurt your feelings and didn't tell you I wanted to explore Tartarus. I'm just . . . trapped here all the time. My entire life I have been behind these walls and I want to explore my home, Father. The Underworld is my home, so why won't you let me go past our gates and see all of the beauty? Why must I stay trapped here? You can come and go as you please, so why can't I?"

"I know my strengths and weaknesses. You do not. That is why you are not allowed to go past these gates." He stops, pointing from the way I just came. "*You* are not to leave the grounds unless I give you explicit instructions." My father is yelling at this point and I can't help but squint at his wrath. "I do not give you consent to leave by yourself. While I am angered beyond words, I understand your need to explore. So, we will have a compromise. You will be allowed to leave once a week with Brenex."

A smile slips across my face and I give my father a hug, "Thank you so much!"

He rips himself away from me, eyes as threatening as his tone. "Do not defy me again, Rhea. You know what I am capable of." Just as quickly as he came, he vanishes before my eyes.

I gather myself, shocked I was able to keep control of not only my composure, but that I breathed the whole way through that. Many probably assume that I have a lovely relationship with my father, but the reality is that we barely speak to one another. I doubt he even loves me. I'm sure he has some sort of feelings when it comes to me, but love wouldn't be the right word. He is the physical embodiment of evil and represents it in every setting.

Glancing around, I see the typical demons on watch, guarding our beloved home. In this moment, I wonder if they're guarding our home or if they're keeping me from leaving. Have they been here for our safety . . . or my imprisonment? The Fates told me to trust my instincts, and now I can't help but trust them. Something deep in my soul, if I even have one, is telling me that something is fishy.

"You look to be deep in thought," Persephone calls out to me, sitting on the steps that lead up to our home. I pick up my silks so they don't drag along the rock and tear, walking towards her.

"I just might be," I confess, laughing as I finish my sentence.

She gives me a half smile. "I've never sensed deception coming from you, but it's thick in the air tonight. What do you have planned?" My step-mother has many gifts, one of her most valuable being that she can sense the intentions of another.

I sit down on a step below her, taking in the beauty that is her. She always looks so young, as if she hasn't been alive in this realm for as long as she has. She has long, flowing blonde hair in wispy curls that span down to the bottom of her back, and the lightest eyes of anyone in all the Underworld. How she was damned to marry my father, I still can't understand. "Nothing, really." I sigh, "I just don't like how confined I am here." I've never had to worry about confessing my true feelings to her. Even though she's my step-mother, she'd never betray my trust. We keep one another company here being the only two women in the compound.

"I bet you don't, darling. You're condemned to suffer down here alone through half the year while I am in the fruits of the Earth. He still does not even allow you to pass through the gates. He is afraid. He will never admit it, but it is evident."

I interlock my hands. "What is he so afraid of? We both know it's not of losing me."

For the first time in the fifty years I've known her, Persephone doesn't speak. She silently stares at me. I imagine she's trying to come up with some sort of response. "I'm not sure, Rhea. Truly, I wish I knew. All I can tell you is that he's afraid."

Her answer makes me wonder if he somehow knows. If I am really to be the thing that the Fates foresaw . . . it would make complete sense. Although, if he had any indication, why would I still be breathing?

"Rhea. Are you coming or not?" Brenex asks me from a bit away.

I turn my head in his direction. "Huh? What do you mean?"

"I'm going out and your father informed me that I'm your babysitter. So, c'mon. I have plans."

I glance over to my step-mother and raise my brows. She chuckles lowly. "You'd better get going before he changes his mind."

I don't hesitate. Instead, I rise and follow Brenex. I've been waiting for this moment for far too long. No way am I going to chicken out now.

5

Rhea

"How exactly are we getting out of here?" I ask, curiously. Brenex starts walking towards the back of the grounds. I'm unsure why, considering there isn't anything back here. Well, that's a lie. We do have a few things— sculptures, art pieces, that sort of stuff.

He turns his head back to face me while he still walks forward. "You want to get out of here, don't you?"

I nod, knowing I don't need to say a thing.

"Good. We're going through the back door."

I push my brows together and grab his arm, tugging on him in the hopes he'll stop. "What do you mean? Since when has there been a back door?"

He cackles. "There's always been a back door. But not any type of door. This is a special door, one that I so happen to have a key to." He pulls at the metal necklace that hangs over his neck until I see Tartarian fire stone being revealed.

My eyes go wide and I almost gasp at the sight of it. Tartarian fire stone is one of the rarest minerals in all of Tartarus. My father told me that we have a mine somewhere on our grounds, but I've never chosen to look for it. It was a few short years ago that my father also forbade anyone from mining. He stated it would immediately justify Cerberus to be making visits to any demons, shades, or other creatures that call Tartarus home.

The fear caused everyone to honor his wishes. What people sometimes don't understand is that there is life after death. It's how we even have souls here. Just as in life, you must make deals with the devil to live a comfortable life. My father's price happens to be no mining for Tartarian fire stone. If it really is the key to this door, then it makes perfect sense why he wouldn't want others digging it up.

Large trees made of rock line our way to wherever it is Brenex is leading us. We don't naturally have any landscaping here unlike other parts of the Underworld, so my father made sure he had something to look at, enlisting the help of some demons who wanted to work their way into his heart— all my life I have been shown the evil of this world and understand that good things do not come for free.

They wanted favors from my father. I only know because he told me that they expected something from him in return. When he learned of this, he laughed in their faces and told them that the only thing he owed them was a painless death. However, my father did not deliver. He sent Cerberus after the ones who dared to speak out against him.

Brenex and I approach a dark archway. It's not like anything else I've ever seen lit by the flames of Tartarus. Instead, it's a pitch black void. Brenex walks forward, disappearing into the dark. Reluctantly, I stick my hand inside and it looks as if I don't have a hand anymore. I can feel my fingers as I move them. All of a sudden, I'm being pulled into the dark and let out a loud scream.

"Damn. Could you scream any louder?" Brenex grumbles under his breath. My eyes search the space we're in— it's some sort of guard house. There's a demon sitting on a chair, holding a scroll. He glares at me and then looks to Brenex.

"What in Hades are you doing with *her*?"

Brenex shrugs his shoulders. "Our boss told me to take her out once a week. This is the first time."

"Is this some sort of joke? I don't want to be killed because you're trying to sneak out the Princess of the Underworld." He stands up, well over seven feet tall. Crossing his arms, I can see his nails digging into his scales. "Do not fuck with me, Brenex."

"He's not sneaking me out. My father has allowed me to leave the grounds once a week." The scaly demon throws his head over his neck and calls out behind him, "Moira. Come here and tell me if this girl is lying."

A woman appears from the shadows in a beautiful full-length crimson red robe. Along the robe are Tartarian fire stones. They line the bottom of her sleeves and go over the V that exposes her bosom. It is gorgeous, but I know it isn't made of silk. Instead, it is something much different, and looks heavy.

The temperature here is always the same, making me wonder how she can wear such a weighted fabric and not be overcome with sweat. Her hair falls past her shoulders in full, dark curls. Her nails are long and Cimmerian as are most creatures that live here. In a way, I think we adapt to our surroundings. I'm sure one day my blonde hair will turn dark, and so will my eyes and skin. I've seen the same happen to many others before me.

"Rhea, it is . . . priceless to meet you in a way. The Princess of the Underworld, here of all places. Never did I think he'd let you out of his sights."

The scaly demon huffs. "Are you going to cut her and taste her blood, or what?"

She must be a blood mage. I've heard of them before. They're in many books inside the library. Since I can't leave, I've found a way of escaping my father's prison by reading on creatures of the realm and other species. "Shut your trap, Voron. Rhea does not lie."

Voron looks displeased. I think he wanted to keep me from tagging along with Brenex, but given that Moira just told him I'm good to go, he sits back down in his chair. "Get lost you two. Oh, but Brenex, don't let anything happen to her. I'm sure you wouldn't be teacher's pet much longer if that was to happen."

Something in the way Voron says it makes me feel as if these two don't have the best relationship. I survey Voron but Brenex grabs ahold of me and pulls me along with him. We walk down a dimly lit hallway for quite a while. It feels like a century, but I know it definitely hasn't been that long. At the end is an old wooden door. Iron mechanics keep it upright, but red Tartarian stones are placed in specific areas. I look over the door carefully and it suddenly hits me.

I've seen these symbols before. It's the same one that's in the front courtyard. I still don't know what it means, but I'm bound to find out.

"*Mnjorn*," Brenex states clearly, and no sooner does he's finished the last letter, the door opens for him. I don't recognize the language, but I do not know many. I speak English, since almost all species speak this tongue. However, there are trillions of languages throughout the world and while I have studied many, I am fluent in very few.

Instead of following him like I have been, I walk forward and go through the door. It looks a lot like outside of my home, but the ground isn't cracked and the lava doesn't flow this far. Honestly, it's a bit cooler here. "Are we still in Tartarus?"

"Of course we are. I've simply taken you to another part of it."

I nod, taking my time as I take in this new view. The ground is made up of the same rocks that cover my home. However, there is some sort of dusty material. I lean down and pick up some of it, letting it flow through my fingertips. "What is this?" I ask Brenex.

"It's sand. In every part of the realm, the landscapes are a bit different."

I nod, rising to look off in the distance. There is a structure made up of magma with a light brown coloring to it. Loud music pounds from the windows and lights go off inside. "I take it that we're going there?" I point over to the building.

"Yes. It's called Shades and Shadows. For your first outing, I figured you'd enjoy a bit of fun. Although, we should go over some ground rules before we go in. First of all, I will not call you by your name. If anyone were to find out your true identity, it would be a massive security risk. So, pick another name."

"Maya." I pick a random name, one that I've seen before in a scroll. "So, what is Shades and Shadows?"

A sneer crosses Brenex's face. "It's a club. Basically, it's a place where people come to relax a bit. To let loose from our every day lives."

I don't know how, but something deep inside me is telling me that this club is more than meets the eye. I sense some sort of energy booming from it. It makes warm chills run up and down my body. Never in my life has this happened before, but I have to recognize that I've never experienced things such as this.

I turn to Brenex and notice something that isn't normally there. He has two small dots in his eyes like everyone else. Normally, they're solid white with that blueish glow. "Are you okay?" I ask him, kind of wondering if he's ill.

"Yeah. I'm just hungry. Sorry."

"Oh, okay! Well, let's go grab a bite then. I'm sure this place has really good food!" I smile, starting to walk off towards the structure. I hear Brenex's boots hit the rocks behind me. He's normally the type who always has something smart to say, so as we walk, I ask him a question. "What aren't you telling me?"

"They serve drinks, but I'm not too sure we're talking about the same type of food."

"You know you're going to have to elaborate for me," I state. I'm not a mind reader like the Fates are. I actually need people to explain things to me.

"Haven't you ever wondered what type of demon I am?" The tone of his voice has a saltiness, almost like he's offended that I've never asked him.

"I mean, yes. I just never wanted to invade your privacy. I figured that if you had a desire to tell me, you simply would."

His boots stop at a standstill and I too halt, turning my body in his direction and walk towards him. "I'm an incubus, Rhea." he whispers it lowly, but I don't understand why. We're both too far away from the club. No one would be able to hear him unless they had some sort of supersonic power.

"You mean a sex demon?" I raise a brow, unable to help myself from looking over his body like I did earlier today. I mean, it kind of makes sense. How can you look this good and not be a sex demon?

"Yes. Do you have any idea why I've brought you here tonight?"

I shake my head from side to side. "No, I don't."

"I haven't fed in quite a while. I'm starving, and if I don't eat, I'll turn into something vile and I really don't want that to slip out. I want you to know me in a way that you haven't known me yet. Plus, this will be a good opportunity for you to see some other creatures that live here with us."

I've heard what Brenex has said about me seeing other creatures and continued to half listen as he told me it was a good idea to expose me to the rest of the Underworld in this way. Slow and easily. It would be painless. But that's not what I'm thinking about right now. Instead, I'm thinking about something so much different.

If he is one of my mates as the Fates have foreseen . . . his plans would be different. "Do you plan on screwing me here?"

I watch him fully take in what I've asked. His breathing slows down, and he looks at me in a different light— one that shows me how much he's thought about it. Brenex brushes his elongated finger nails against my skin, scratching me in the most pleasurable way. "Only if you want me to."

For the love of Hades, what have I gotten myself into?

Dear Readers,

I know you probably want to throw your kindle right now with how I've ended this. Please know— this is *not* the end. You'll find out what happens with Brenex and Rhea in the first chapter of *Betrayed by Blood*, which will be out later this year. I hope you've enjoyed seeing Rhea meet the Fates and start to understand some of her past. I have a trilogy planned surrounding Rhea and her mates.

Thank you for reading,

Liz

AUTHORS NOTE

Dear Readers,

I know you probably want to throw your kindle right now with how I've ended this. Please know— this is *not* the end. You'll find out what happens with Brenex and Rhea in the first chapter of *Betrayed by Blood*, which will be out later this year. I hope you've enjoyed seeing Rhea meet the Fates and start to understand some of her past. I have a trilogy planned surrounding Rhea and her mates.

Thank you for reading,
Liz

SEVEN SOULS

NIKKI HUNTER

Seven Souls

Copyright 2019 Nikki Hunter

All Rights Reserved

The content of this book is protected under Federal Copyright Laws. Any unauthorized use of this material is prohibited. No portion of this book may be reproduced in any form without express written permission from the author.

This is a work of fiction. Names, characters, places, and incidents either are the products of the author's imagination or are used fictitiously. Any resemblance to actual persons, living or dead, businesses, companies, events or locales are entirely a coincidence.

❦ Created with Vellum

1

THE NAME GAME

First dates are always the worst. They're awkward.

I'm awkward.

The restaurant is filled with the mild roar of people talking over their meals. Perfectly ironed white linen cloths cover each table and even though the sun hasn't quite set candles are lit, the lights dim overhead.

Everything about this place makes me slightly nervous. I don't normally eat at five-star establishments. Normally, you'll find me in the drive-thru. But my date, he fits in nicely. I mean look at him there. He has that casual confidence about him. He doesn't need me; he could get any girl.

Timothy.

My newly downloaded dating app showed me the adventure I could have with him and I couldn't *not* swipe right and somehow it turns out he swiped right on me too. Now here we are at the local Italian restaurant that I could never afford, and his brown hair is perfectly placed. It didn't miss me that he is in a designer suit with a Rolex watch, either.

I may not have the money for designer, but I sure am a fan of it. My dress came from the mall. It was twenty-five dollars . . . but it has pockets!

He doesn't care about pockets.

The overly flirty waitress just left us, but she gives him a second glance, I don't blame her. Thankfully, he doesn't acknowledge it, I'm sure he gets it all the time.

I'm also hoping Timothy doesn't notice how nervous I am, even as I shift in my seat. He smiles. *God, his teeth are perfect.* Is there anything about him that isn't wonderful? Oh God, I hope he isn't a serial killer. I've seen too many murder documentaries.

Mental note— put up curtains in the living room. Not today, stalker.

Wait, don't get ahead of yourself, Jade. Give him a chance.

I'm already getting ahead of myself, creating scenarios that haven't even happened yet. That was the problem with my last relationship. I should probably break that habit now. I'm always assuming the worst, some part of me knowing that something dark can lurk within anyone. No matter their class or how attractive you may find them.

The worst monsters that haunt this world don't look like monsters at all. It's the people you love the most that turn into what you fear above all else.

Now, with those thoughts, you'd think I'd lived through something traumatic. I'll top you there. I haven't. I lead a perfectly happy, ordinary life.

"You look absolutely beautiful. That dress is stunning," Timothy says, eyeing me over his glass of wine, also very expensive. His caramel colored gaze flashes over me in an appreciative way. I'm enjoying the attention and I know he knows as my cheeks blaze bright red.

"Oh, thank you. It's nothing." My hands brush over my dress smoothing the careless wrinkles from my dryer down as best I can. "You look quite handsome yourself."

Yes, I'm sure you hear that all the time too.

Timothy nods and cocks his head to the side as he watches me. I smile back at him, my fingers skimming the bottom of my wine glass. I'm playing with it. Not sure if I can keep myself from chugging it down to calm the nerves flowing through me.

"Don't downplay your beauty. Take delight in it, understand what God has blessed you with. I certainly do." He folds his hands in front of him like a professor bent on giving me a lecture. I've seen that face before.

Well then.

"Do you not think those who know and 'take delight' as you say are arrogant, Tim? Can I call you Tim?"

"Timothy." He smirks. "It's a fine line but it's possible to have pride and not be egotistical. You'd be surprised."

"And do you walk that line? *Timothy.*" I say his name slowly, letting each syllable roll off my tongue with emphasis. There is something about assholes that bring out a . . . I don't know, confidence in me. Tim might need to be knocked down a peg or two if either of us is going to make it through this date.

His eyes dart to my lips and they stay there. He opens his mouth as if to speak but closes it tightly again, blinking harshly a few times. Then, he laughs.

It's a wonderful noise, really. Almost enchanting. I mean, it would be coming from someone like him. The corners of my mouth perk up into a small grin. Maybe he won't be so bad. He is handsome enough, perhaps I can ignore the not so likable parts of his personality.

Timothy takes another small sip of his wine. Maybe he is nervous too.

The waitress returns smiling widely, not at me, of course. "Are we all ready?"

"I am. Do you know what you would like, Jade?"

That's the first time he has said my name. I bite my lip to keep from erupting into a goofy grin. My name sounds so good when he says it in that deep buttery voice of his.

Ugh, I'm disgusting. I'm so smitten right now. But that's what a two-year dry spell will do to you.

"Yes, I'll take the grilled chicken salad. French dressing,

please." Gently, I push the leather covered menu closer to the waitress, but it squeaks loudly against the table as I do so. She all but cringes as she picks it up.

I was trying to be smooth. Trying, being the keyword. Thankfully, my date doesn't seem too worried. I mean it's just a small thing. It shouldn't be a big deal that I just made my menu fart on this fancy restaurant's table. Right?

I'm overthinking it. Jade, stop.

"And for you sir?" I watch our server carefully as she leans closer to Timothy and twirls a bit of her blonde hair.

He stares back, blinking hard and not speaking. Does he have a thing for blondes? Is he regretting this date already?

"Excuse me, sir?" she asks again tossing me an uneasy look when he doesn't answer.

Yes ma'am, I'm still here. But don't look at me because I don't know why he isn't responding. Is he having some sort of seizure?

"Timothy?" I ask, reaching across the table to squeeze his hand.

He turns to me. "Christian, please." Then he clears his throat and gives the waitress his attention. "I wanna go ahead and get the thirty-two-ounce ribeye, medium rare with a side of steamed carrots, broccoli, and mashed potatoes."

Christian? Didn't you just ask me to call you Timothy?

"Sounds perfect. I'll get that right out for you." Our server's petite hands grab his menu.

"Sorry," Timothy/Christian stops her. "I'm not done."

"Oh." She stammers. "Go ahead, my apologies."

"No worries. I would also like to try your salmon and if you could bring a sampler plate of your appetizers that would be awesome!"

I'm staring at this man in awe. That's a heck of a lot of food. How is he going to eat it all? Better yet, where is he going to put it? He is so slim and fit I can't imagine his stomach holds that much food. Oh no, maybe he thinks I'm that girl that gets the salad and then picks off his plate?

I mean, I am, but I wouldn't do it on the first date!

"Hungry?" I don't bother to hide the humor that plays across my features.

Timothy/Christian, *I've got to get this name thing sorted out,* beams at me from across the table like a child on Christmas Day. He loses his perfect posture and slouches back onto the black booth seat.

"I mean I'm only here for the food. Have you read the reviews on this place? People rave about the chef here. I plan on eating my weight in these fancy fucks grub. Hopefully, the pizza I had before I got here doesn't get in the way of that." He pats his stomach cheerfully. "Why did you only get a salad? We're loaded, I could get you the whole menu if you asked."

We're?

"Oh, I don't think I could eat that much." The laugh that comes out of me is nervous now. "Plus, I'm trying to diet. Hints the salad." I pause again. "So, Christian? I thought you went by Timothy?"

His face falls and he sits back up returning to his proper, confident silhouette. Timothy/Christian brings a hand up to his forehead, rubbing at the worry that seems to crease his brow now.

"Sorry, Christian is my, uh, middle name. Timothy is fine."

And now we are back to Timothy.

"Plus, I told you, take pride in yourself. You don't need to diet. I mean eating healthy is essential to taking care of your body but you, you do not need to lose weight."

He is back to his charming, polished manner I see. Maybe he is one of those guys who you just have to break down some walls before they really relax. Sigh. I need to relax. I'm eyeing my wine glass pretty heavily now.

"Maybe we should make a toast," I begin. "Mr. Timothy Christian . . ." *What was his last name? Oh, God. What was his last nammmeee?*

My sentence just hangs there in the cold, overly perfumed,

too expensive for me to breathe, restaurant air. Timothy lifts an eyebrow.

"I'm so sorry. I've forgotten your last name. How silly of me?" I fumble with my glass taking a quick gulp of wine. *Ugh, his expensive wine is very dry. I'm not a well enough versed wine drinker for that.* Trying not to pucker my lips at the taste, I set the glass back down.

"It's McGregor and weren't you about to make a toast?" His finger is almost accusing as he points at my wine glass. While his hand seems to be placing blame, his face, with those perfect golden eyes is full of humor.

"Oh, shit. Yeah, I was. Sorry, again." I'm laughing uneasily. This is it, that terrible point in the date where I start to wonder why I agreed to this in the first place. I'm spiraling. Quick, get some alcohol in me! Nevertheless, I continue, "I'm sure you can't remember my last name."

"Waske," he interjects before I can continue.

It's official, I hate myself. My jaw is almost on the floor. Is there any way I can make this worse?

"Jade Waske."

He is smirking now. He knows it. He knows he is so much better than me and my terrible memory and cheap dress. Bet he can't wait to tell his friends about the ridiculously awkward date he had that started with me practically insulting him and then cheersing to the fact I forgot his name.

But I'm pushing through.

Coughing, and internally wishing I had taken those shots before this date like I thought about doing before my friend Amy talked me out of it, I raise my glass. "Okay, then, Mr. McGregor here is to first dates."

Timothy lifts his own glass. "Ms. Waske, Cheers. May the first date be as wonderful as you are lovely."

With a quick nod, I bring the glass up to my lips taking a large gulp. Sour. So sour.

"And just as *fascinating*," he adds all too fast.

His tone catches me off guard mid swallow and half my wine comes out. It feels like more than half, but I know some of it is floating around in my lungs as I gasp for air.

Timothy doesn't look amused as he dabs at the wine on his white shirt. His knuckles even appear to be white. I mean it is an expensive looking suit, I don't want to know how much it costs, so I understand he is probably mad.

"Sorry. So, sorry," I stammer.

Up and down his chest moves with the deep breaths he is taking. Now, I'm just waiting. He is going to yell, perhaps even spit wine at me. I may deserve it.

But he doesn't, even though his red face suggests he feels otherwise, he says, "You need to be more careful next time. Timothy is going to have a fit over this."

"Are we referring to ourselves in third person now?" I'm starting to think I'm on a date with a psycho. How's he gonna pull this off?

"No, Timothy is the biggety bastard who bought this overpriced piece of fabric. Javen is going to have his head for it too." He pauses with a scowl. "Sorry, my name is Dylan."

What. The. Hell.

2

DON'T SWIPE RIGHT, AGAIN

My keys jingle loudly in the lock of my apartment which sends Pickle, my five-year-old black lab, into a fit of barks. I toss the keys onto my counter with the mail I had grabbed and let Pickle nuzzle against my fingertips for a minute. He needs to quiet before my neighbors file another noise complaint as if they have a right to complain when they have obnoxiously loud sex at two in the morning. Yeah, that doesn't bother me at all.

Glancing around my apartment, spotlessly clean I might add, I smack my lips. *Oh, what a night.*

I had thought that maybe I could be coming home with Timothy, Christian, Dylan, whatever his freaking name was and right now I would be letting him pillage me all over my small one-bedroom apartment, hence the fresh sparkling room. It's the only time this space gets cleaned when I'm expecting company.

Too bad I decided it was safest to politely say goodnight to my date. The date was . . . odd. I have yet to decide if I'll go on another with him. Though all the confusing name changes had me on edge, everything else about him seemed normal. Kind of.

Am I making excuses for him because I haven't had luck in

the dating department, and this is the first guy to show me some real interest in a while? Maybe.

Do I still wish that somehow I could be doing the frickle-frackle with him this very second? Hell to the yes.

He acts like a gentleman. He even covered the whole bill when I was prepared to split it.

Thank God for that because I was dipping into my very limited grocery money for this date.

Sighing, I slip out of my dress and wander to grab pajamas. Though, I'm thinking about also grabbing my vibrator on the way. Maybe not, perhaps my hormones can wait a little bit longer.

Who am I kidding? I'm breaking out that baby as soon as my head touches the pillow.

Once in my night clothes, I head for the kitchen still dabbling in my thoughts on this strange date. Out of the cabinet, I grab some instant pasta and pop it into the microwave. A salad was clearly, not enough.

Food, toy, then bed.

Pickle is already snoring in her bed just outside the kitchen, but her ears perk up at the sound of the microwave beeping and her nose lifts as the smell of the overly salted noodles fill the apartment. My phone buzzes.

Had a wonderful time. Hope to see you soon. - Timothy

The text makes me smile. That reminds me to lock my windows and doors. Oh yeah, I'm going to pin blankets over my windows too.

We exchanged numbers but I wasn't expecting any correspondence so soon. Either he really likes me, or I do have a weird stalker situation going on here. Let's hope it's the first option. Careful not to actually open the message I dismiss the notification.

And into my dating app I dive. Maybe I can match with someone a little less creepy and with one or two fewer names.

So here I go. Leaning over the counter, pasta hanging from my mouth as I sloppily slurp it, I'm doing my thing.

Swipe left, too young. Left, weird chin. Right, hmm he looks fun. Left, he is only here for sex and sex only. Left, that's a woman, not for me, but more power to you. Left, ew.

But then, just as I move to swipe right because honestly, I'm moving too fast, there he is. Timothy, but not? It's his face, his approximate age, everything like him but his name is Ebon.

Is this a fake profile? Or is this dude a freak, for real?

Blinking blankly at his image I screenshot the profile and swipe left. Least I can do is let the poor man know someone has stolen his images. Though his bio is eerily similar.

Moving on . . .

Right, oh God, those blue eyes. I don't even care about your bio you're so pretty. Left, too country bumpkin. Left, and that's my cousin. Left, okay he is lying about his age. Right, he looks sweet. Oh hey, a match!

And then . . . it's fucking Timothy/Christian/Dylan/Ebon again! Holy shit. This dude is everywhere. This time the name is Mark. *Screenshot that!*

Amy should know about this. Amy my best friend since forever who always has some sort of opinion on every situation. Picture after picture, I send Amy the screenshots and give her a brief update on the craziness happening on this one dating app.

It only takes a minute before she has responded. The nighttime is Amy's prime time. Her response? "Holy shit."

She isn't wrong. I chew on my nails and wait as I watch the bubbles pop up while she types some more. Her next message? "You should confront that freak."

Okay, she might be wrong now. What if he tries to kill me? Okay, what if I'm overreacting and there is some simple explanation for this? Worse, what if there isn't?

Someone should write a book about my life. I bet it would be hysterical.

Or sad.

THE COFFEE SHOP IS FULL, and I know I'm going to be late to class, but the caffeine is worth it. Plus, I'll be useless if I don't get it. Who takes an eight a.m. class? Me, the idiot standing in this Starbucks line, that's who. At least, I'm not alone. Amy is also an idiot and took the same class as me.

"So, I'm thinking I need to break up with Brian because he is probably on to the fact that I'm dating Chase now too. That and, he can't break up with me, right? I have to be the one who ends it." Amy blabbers on. I swear, she doesn't need caffeine. No, she can go a mile a minute no matter the time of day no matter the amount of sleep she has gotten.

"Well, it does make it look better if you are the dumper, not the dumpee." It's what she wants to hear. Really, she should probably just stop trying to date other people behind their backs. Honesty is the best policy.

Casually, I people watch as I wait. Nothing more thrilling than wondering what that hipster over there does in his meantime, am I right? I nod along with Amy but it's too early for me to really give her my full attention.

"Jade. Jade." She snaps her fingers in front of my face.

"I'm sorry, what?"

She gives me an annoyed look then points over my shoulder and continues anyway. "Isn't that the guy you went on a date with? The one with the billion profiles?"

Eeek. Let's hope not.

The line moves forward and it's practically our turn to order. I just want to get my coffee and get out at this point. In no hurry, I turn to see if it is who Amy thinks it is. Annndddd . . .

It is. Kill me now.

"Oh, hide me. Don't let him see me. I never texted him

back." I scutter to the other side of Amy trying to hide from his view. He hasn't noticed me, thankfully.

"Jade?" His voice rings out.

"Uh, I think he saw you," Amy laughs. "Plus, he is fine as hell. So much cuter in person. You should just ignore all the weird stuff and just ride his cock off into the sunset."

I cover my face with my hands. If I can't see him, he can't see me. Internally, I'm crying and cringing. "Amy," I whine. "Pretend I'm not here."

"Jade, I know you're there." Timothy/Christian/Dylan/Ebon/Mark chuckles. Even his laugh is attractive.

"Oh, my God. Stop it." Amy pulls my hands down away from my face and stretches her hand out to Timothy/Christian/Dylan/Ebon/Mark. "My name is Amy. I'm the best friend."

"The best friend." He nods, then takes her hand and kisses it. Amy is impressed already, I can tell. She is a sucker for men, any man really. Timothy/Christian/Dylan/Ebon/Mark looks so good today too. More casual, athleisure like, in his jersey shorts and shirt cut open at the sides to show off his ab muscles. *If only he wasn't a weirdo.*

"Hi, Timothy?" I ask unsure of what name I'm going to get right now.

"Dylan." He purses his lips.

At least it isn't a new name. I give Amy a weary look.

"Can I talk to you for a minute?" Dylan continues as he fiddles with the headphones that hang around his neck.

"Actually, we were just grabbing a drink and then we have to get to class." I'm trying to shrug this off and get away as quick as possible. But neither "Dylan" or Amy are having it. Amy is shooting me dangerous dagger eyes trying to subtly tell me I'm being rude. I know I am Amy, point that mean mug somewhere else.

The customer in front of us leaves the register to wait for their drink and I step up ready to order and be on my merry way. I sputter out my order and turn expecting Dylan to have left but there he is, still. His pursed lips have turned into a deep frown. Dylan slaps cash down on the counter and without taking his eyes off me speaks to the barista, "This should cover her drink and her lovely friend's here too."

I blink. Then blink again. This guy can't take a hint.

"That isn't necessary." My voice is rough since I'm forcing the words out of me with the most restraint I can muster.

"Jade," Amy growls. "I'm running on a tight budget, let the nice man buy our drinks." She turns to Dylan and smiles. "That is very sweet of you, thank you."

Well, isn't she just lovely? Ugh, I just want out of this situation.

"You know what," I say scooting over to allow the next customer to order. "I don't really have the time right now, but I'll text you." *No, I won't.* "Thank you for the coffee," *And for making this the most uncomfortable situation I've been in, in a long time.* "But we will be on our way now."

Another barista hands me my drink and I raise it up to him in salute and drag Amy with me away and out the door. Dylan stands at the counter, heavy creases on his forehead from his deeply furrowed brows drawing more attention to his beautiful eyes. Goodbye, Timothy/Christian/Dylan/Ebon/Mark. Hope I don't see you anytime soon.

With the door firmly closed behind us, I turn back to Amy. "I hate you; you know."

Amy tilts her head back an easy, and by easy, I mean slightly evil, laughter fills the air around us. She isn't sorry, not one bit. Her hand quickly finds mine and she gives it a squeeze. "We should give him a second chance."

"We?" I raise an eyebrow at her.

"Yeah, you may have some competition now, girl. Drink your free coffee and let's get to class before Mrs. Webster kills us for being late again." Together we leave behind my embarrassing morning and head off to start our day.

3

I'M A BEAUTY GURU

CLASS WAS A BITCH. Not only did I take an eight a.m. class, but I also took a hard one. *Idiot.* Thankfully though, Amy has agreed to meet me for some drinks tonight at the local bar. Maybe we will get to dance. Maybe I'll find a cute boy. Maybe I'll get a little bit frisky. The possibilities are endless.

I smile at myself in the mirror. I look like an alien. I've managed to get my eyes smokey after many many angry tries that ended in the pile of makeup wipes on my bathroom counter but haven't gotten my foundation on yet. Gotta protect myself from fall out.

Yes, that's right. I'm a beauty guru. I admire my final eye product as I place small drops of my liquid foundation all over my face. *Now, I'm a beauty guru with chicken pox or something.* I pucker my lips playfully at my image and grab my beauty blender to begin the transition from pale and blotchy to just pale. *When in doubt dab it out. And oh boy, am I dabbing it out.* My makeup tonight is gonna look so fine I'll be a totally different person.

I'm about five seconds to setting down the blender and grabbing some setting powder when I hear a knock at my door. I thought I was going to meet Amy, why is she here so early?

Oh, God. Brian must have broken up with her before she could break up with him.

Pickle is already at the door barking loudly. My guard dog. I pat his head as I come up to the door and peek through the peephole to see who it is.

Well, it's not Amy, instead, it's my worst nightmare.

It's freaking Timothy/Christian/Dylan/Ebon/Mark. I'm reeling. What do I do? This apartment isn't at all soundproof he has probably already heard me stomp my way across my apartment right up to this very door that I'm not opening. How did he even find me? I swear if Amy gave him my address, I'll kill her.

But what if she didn't give him my address? What if he really is stalking me? My heart is hammering out of my chest. I bet he can hear that too.

Slowly, I open the door forgetting I look like a drug addict with my pale face and dark eyes at the moment. "Hi." It's all I can manage.

"Hi." He smiles. "Look, I really would like to talk to you. Do you have a moment?"

Yes, I do.

"Actually, I've got to finish getting ready and head out the door. I've got to meet someone." I smile back at him gingerly. *Please go away and leave me alone.*

"It will really only take a second." His smile is fading.

"Sorry," I say. *I'm about to be rude.* Quickly, I close the door in hopes that my terrible actions will make him realize I'm not interested. However, the door doesn't close. I push but am stopped by his foot in my doorway. *Okay, this is it, the beginning of a horror movie.*

I push harder, flattening myself against the door as if that is going to help it close. "Get out." I shriek. Pickle is really getting into it now; he bares his teeth in warning. The panic only lasts a second though, because Timothy/Christian/Dylan/Ebon/Mark moves his foot out of the way and the door slams shut.

I'm terrified and kind of shaking even from the small encounter as I lock the handle then twist the deadbolt locked. Heavy breaths bounce off my door and fan back over my face as I lean against it for a second. Nervously, I peer into the peephole. He's gone.

I've got to tell Amy about this. She will have a fit. Honestly, I might call my Dad too because dang that scared me.

Hastily, I twist around to run back to the bathroom to get my phone. Momentum carries me around until I find my face meeting the hard muscle of the very stalker I was trying to escape. *Holy shit.* I bounce off him and stumble back into the door. I'm yelling, I'm screaming. Someone is going to hear me and by God, I'm not going down without a fight.

"Oh, my God! How did you get in here? Get out! Get out!" Petrified words are fumbling over my lips my shouts seemingly having no impact. Pickle is full on snarling now as I grab the closest thing to me, my umbrella.

"Stop screaming, Jade." Timothy/Christian/Dylan/Ebon/Mark holds his hands out.

I smack his hands away from me with the umbrella. "I'll stop screaming when I don't feel like you're about to murder me!" I stutter. "How the hell did you get in here? What do you want?" I can feel tears filling up along my eyelashes, they may spill over soon. I keep the umbrella between us, creating distance. If I can just get to my purse in the kitchen, I can get the taser my father gave to me and call the cops while he is down.

"Jade calm down. I just want to talk. I'm not going to hurt you. I need you." His voice is deep and gravelly. He is somehow still the picture of perfect husband material that I've always craved even through all the crazy behavior. He sounds sorrowful even.

"No, please leave," I whisper. Fear grips me now more than

it ever has. I try to turn to open the door and run out of my apartment, but he is on me. His body pressing me against the door, his hands firmly clasped over mine so I can't.

"I'm sorry. I'm sorry. I'm sorry." He is practically chanting, quietly. "Please hear me out."

"Help!" I scream loudly, praying a neighbor can hear me. "Help, somebody please help me!"

Nobody is going to save you. This is how you die.

Pickle is at his ankle now, his teeth digging into his pant leg and tugging with all his might, but Timothy doesn't seem to notice. I'm trying to force myself to think, not to panic. But it's so hard, I'm so scared.

I push through my nerves bringing my knee up to meet his groin with as much strength as I can summon. He drops my hand leaning toward the door as he doubles over. Instinctively, I push past him, but he reaches out for me. Narrowly, I avoid him and throw myself into the closest room. My bathroom. The lock snaps loudly as I twist it and press myself into the wall.

"Jade," he calls out, his voice straining.

Desperately, I'm searching the bathroom. Opening and closing each drawer as I hunt for anything, *anything*, that can be used to protect me. The best I have is hairspray to spray into his eyes unless he gives me time to whittle my toothbrush into a shank. Could I be stuck here long enough for that? I don't even know how to whittle!

I can't keep still, and my hands are shaking. I grab my toothbrush and my razor from the shower before I slide against the door until I'm sitting on the ground. The sharp edges of the razor slowly peel away shavings of plastic. My vision blurs. A single tear spilling over the rim of my eyelid.

HE NEVER SPOKE another word to me. I sat for hours on my

bathroom floor clinging to the toothbrush I had finally managed to bring to a sharp point on the end. My only weapon. Now, staring off into nothingness, my body is worn from all the chaos, I flinch at the sound of my front door opening and closing.

"What the hell, Jade? You left me sitting at that bar forever and you can't even bother to respond to any of my messages?"

Amy. AMY.

"Amy!" I cry out. Oh, God. What if he is still in my apartment? I never heard him leave. "Amy. Watch out! He is still out there!"

"Who?" she says confused as she stalks over to the bathroom door and tugs on the handle.

"Bitch, let me in." Amy taps her fingers against the door annoyed.

Reluctantly, I unlock the bathroom door, opening it and gazing behind her to see if he's waiting right there. He isn't. But I can't be sure. I push back Amy and ignore her bewildered look as I hold my shank out in front of me. Where is he?

On shaky legs, I jog over to my purse in the kitchen and pull out my taser. With both weapons in hand, I stalk around my apartment opening every door, looking in every closet, under my bed, any hiding place I can think of.

"Jade, what happened to you? Are you okay?" Amy is flustered and confused trailing behind me.

"He was here." I squeak, lowering the weapons when I am finally satisfied he isn't in the apartment anymore. But those nerves still have me looking over my shoulder. Was it my imagination that he just appeared in my apartment? I give my front door a long hard look. No signs of forced entry. Had I imagined the whole thing? No. My umbrella is still laying on the floor where I threw it from my hands when I tried to get out the door myself.

"Who was here?"

"Timothy. Dating app guy. Cute guy from the coffee shop guy." I'm crying now. I can't help it.

"Oh, my God." Amy takes her purse off, dropping it on the floor, and runs her hands over my shoulders and arms looking me up and down. "Did he hurt you? Are you okay?"

"I'm okay. I'm just shook up. I think."

"We should call the cops." Amy is already reaching for her phone in her back pocket.

We should call the cops. Yes, yes, we should.

I nod my head slowly allowing Amy to take the toothbrush and taser out of my hands. She pulls me close to her for a second, squeezing me gently and rubbing my back even though I'm unable to hug her back. "It's going to be okay. We will get him for this."

"Can we call my dad first?" I squeak into her hair.

Amy pulls away with a sad smile. "Yes."

She scrolls through her contacts clicking on my dad's name and holds the phone up to her ear. She looks at me as it rings, her eyes still continually searching me for injuries. "You won't ever have to see him again."

If only that statement was true.

4

I'M STARVING, DAVID

THE POLICE CAME AND WENT. I explained everything to them. Told them about the date, running into him at the coffee shop, and his most recent bout of breaking and entering. I showed them the screenshots of all his different dating profiles and gave them the phone number that was programmed into my phone. The number that I quickly blocked.

They suspect that he does something with sex trafficking. They promised to look for him, but they said he could be hard to track down, given that we might not even have his real name.

I sigh heavily falling onto the couch. Amy puts her arm around my shoulder and lets me lean into her. My dad waves goodbye to the police and closes the door behind him. Locking both the top and bottom lock then giving it a good hard stare as if he could keep it firmly closed just by his own pure will. Perhaps he could.

"Amy, you go on home now." My dad sighs, slipping his hands into his pockets. "I think I'll stay the night with Jade."

Relief floods me as I know that at least for tonight I won't be alone. I'm thankful for my dad and his protective ways over me. With him, I know I'm safe.

Amy kisses my forehead and pulls away, giving me a hard stare. "If you need anything, *anything*, give me a call. I'll have my phone on me at all times."

I work hard for a smile and give her a nod. "Thanks, Amy." My hands are still shaking as I wave goodbye to my friend.

Amy grabs her purse and pauses at the door. "Seriously, I mean *anything*. Call me when—"

She's cut off as my dad unlocks then opens the door and ushers her out. I chuckle and mentally make a note to text her later and apologize. Dad is not her biggest fan.

"I mean, thank God she stopped by to check on you," he drawls, "but that girl is louder and more annoying than a marching band playing show tunes." My dad sighs and locks the door again, then double checks the locks. "I'm just gonna double check the locks on your windows."

I switch on the TV and let whatever easy going sitcom that is playing go without much thought. Plush and cozy fabric meets my skin as I wrap up in the throw that is over the couch. I curl up in it and let it keep me warm.

The show drones on in the background as I stare blankly ahead until my Dad comes and sits down next to me. He pats my head then pushes the stray hairs away from my face. "Your mom is worried sick. Woman keeps blowing up my phone even though I've told her it's taken care of."

My teeth dig into my lower lip. I doubt he told her much of anything and that's why she is still panicking. I better send her a text. The thought of even reaching out for my phone though seems too daunting. *Later, I'll do it later.*

"I love you, Jade." My dad sighs worry showing in the deep creases along his forehead.

"I love you too, Dad." I reach out of the blanket and give his hand a squeeze. It's a parent's job to worry I suppose. My phone dings and my dad picks it up off the coffee table and glances at the notification, showing it to me after he does. Did he think it was going to be Timothy? It isn't. It's Amy.

"Sweet, Jesus," My dad frowns. "That girl has already started in at it." He sets my phone back down.

Amy is just worried. Hell, I'm still worried myself. I'll just start praying that I don't need therapy after this.

Lying on the couch next to my dad it only takes five minutes and he is snoring. His arms crossed over his body and his head tilted back against the large couch cushion to support him. My mind starts wandering as I curl into myself next to him. It all happened so fast. Really, I'm sure the exchange was only a few minutes long, but it felt like an eternity. I guess true fear can do that to you. I really thought he was going to murder me.

Those thoughts continue to bombard my mind until I fall asleep to the laughter of the live studio audience playing on the TV.

IT'S SLASHES OF GREEN, *visions of red, bursts of yellow and blue. It's all I can see. Different colors invade my vision bringing different voices with them as they do. I can't hear the voices though. There are too many, their overlapping.*

They're soothing though. Somehow like a song, a familiar song. The colors flash through my mind and bring images forward again and again. They're all men. None of them with faces that I can recognize.

They're in pain. They need help.

Each man only gets a second to be with me before another color pushes them away. Then one by one they try and reach out to me. I'm not scared. I try to reach for them too. It's like we are on a roller coaster that brings us together and takes us apart. Every time one of them leaves me, something in my soul aches, even though a piece of it is soothed by the new color and image of the man that replaces them.

I don't count the men, but I know there are many of them. I try to call out to them, try to touch them. No, luck.

Then it all stops. Everything is black and I can barely see my hands before me. A small light appears and from it, my attacker appears. I try to stay calm but my heart beats frantically.

"Jade, we won't hurt you. We need you," he says sadly. Slowly, he reaches out to touch me but I flinch away.

I jerk upright, the blanket falling off of me as I sit up on the couch. My Dad is no longer next to me and my eyes quickly scan my apartment. I hear him before I see him. The familiar whistle of an old tune I never quite learned the words to comes to me from my kitchen. I can smell what he is up to as well.

Pancakes. He is the world's best pancake maker. Every important event as far back as I can remember includes us eating pancakes for breakfast.

That's all it takes to make me forget about the confusing dream that woke me so fast. I smile and notice my nerves and fear from last night aren't holding onto me this morning. It just feels like a regular day that I'm lucky enough to have my dad visiting.

Dad peeks out of the kitchen, expertly flipping a pancake in the air and catching it back in the skillet. He smiles brightly. "Good morning, darling."

"Morning, Dad." I'm so happy he is here. Even more happy he is making pancakes because I'm starving. My stomach growls loudly, right on cue.

We both look up at the sound of a soft knock on the door. Dad sets the spatula in his hand down and stares hard at the door as I walk over and look through the peephole.

A happy and familiar face looks back at me. I open the door, smiling at Amy as she walks past me. Wind from how quickly she moves past me tosses small strands of my hair away from my face.

"Good morning, Waske family!" She holds her hands up in welcome before dropping her purse onto the couch.

"Oh, good. Amy's here." My dad doesn't bother to hide his frown.

"David, you know you can't live without me." She winks at him and turns back to me. "How did you sleep, pumpkin?" She's trying to be extra happy; I can tell.

"I'm fine, Amy," I say rather plainly. "I slept okay."

An image of my dream runs through my mind for a second. *We won't hurt you. We need you.* I can feel those words as if they had been whispered and engraved into my soul. But it was just a dream. Just. A. Dream.

"Good." Amy squeezes me with a hug and jogs over to my small dining room table. "I'm starving, David."

"Amy, please," My dad looks pleadingly at me. "Call me Mr. Waske."

Amy rolls her eyes and pats the seat next to her. "I don't know why he doesn't just let me call him, Dad. I mean I'm practically his daughter too."

"You know, I just don't get it either." The chair next to her is cold and sends a chill up my spine as I plant myself in it. My stomach is raging now.

My dad comes out of the kitchen holding two plates and sets them down in front of us. Two pancakes each, both with smiley faces cooked into them with chocolate chips, and two pieces of bacon.

"Perhaps, it's because I've only known Amy for something under a year. I've known Jade her whole life. So, Amy," He gives her a disapproving look. "I'll let you call me "dad" the day that I watch you crawl out of my wife's lady bits."

I wish I gave myself time to chuckle but instead I'm almost choking as I shovel in bites and laugh at my dad's comment. I've met Amy's parents and her dad lets me call him whatever I want. She is actually a lot like her dad. Loud, loyal, and always down for a party.

In unison we look up, my door swinging open quietly. My dad stops in his tracks, his hands automatically balancing on his hips like a middle-aged woman who wants to speak to the manager. "Marla! I thought I told you everything was handled."

He stares with humor in his eyes at my mother as she quickly rushes to my side.

"Oh, my baby! I couldn't sleep last night I was up with worry."

Help us all, my mom is so dramatic.

"It's okay, mom. I'm fine. Everything is fine." I try to peel her hands off me since she quickly wraps me up in a hug. My face is suffocating in her boobs. The harder I try to pull away the harder she hugs me, so I give up.

"Jade, I will personally hire a detective to find the guy who did this to you." Finally, she lets me go and gives Amy a quick peck on the cheek. "Hi, Amy dear."

"Hi, Mrs. Waske." Amy smirks as my dad looks down his nose at her.

"Marla, how on earth are we going to afford a detective." Dad gives Mom a quick hug, kissing the top of her head as he does.

She waves her hand in dismissal. "Don't worry." Mom looks over at me theatrical concern reflecting in her brown eyes. "Baby, we will do everything in our power to make sure everything is taken care of. Don't you fret."

I mean, I am. Fretting that is. But not enough to need a detective, I know they don't have that kind of money. "Mom, it's okay. I'm an adult and I can take care of myself."

"Of course you can, honey." She gives me a sad smile.

I fight back the urge to roll my eyes and instead shove an entire piece of bacon into my mouth. *Yay, the whole family is here.*

Not.

5

WOW, YOU'RE HOT

MY MOM WASN'T LYING, unfortunately. Amy sits up from where she is lying on my couch as I go to answer the door. This must be the investigator she scheduled to show up and talk to me. Before they left to head back home my dad tried, bless his heart, to talk her out of it. However, mom has not been known to be good about compromising or really letting anything she wants slide.

"Can I help you . . ." I trail off.

A young man, probably only a year or so older than me stands outside my apartment. Sandy blonde curls give him an even more youthful look, not to mention the piercing blue eyes. He smiles polity as if he doesn't realize the effect his good looks have on people.

He must think his whole life is sunshine and rainbows where people just hand him things for no apparent reason. But there is a reason, this guy is gorgeous. I wonder if he has an Instagram I can stalk.

"Miss Waske?" he asks.

"Yes." I blink at him. I can't feel my limbs, I'm so nervous to interact with such a fine creature.

"My name is Nick Johnson. I was hired by your mother to

investigate a break in. May I come in so I can ask you a few questions?"

Nick holds out his hand to shake mine. I feel like jello but I gingerly take his hand in mine before I push open the door enough for him to enter.

"Come on in."

Amy jumps up from her seat. "Wow, you're hot." She exclaims, in her not so shy manner.

I cringe. With a warning glance at Amy, I give Nick my attention again. "This is Amy, my best friend. Amy this is Nick, he is the *private investigator my mom hired.*"

Amy strolls up to Nick. Her walk full of that predator sway she has when she sees something she wants. In his defense, Nick seems to be taking it well. He doesn't shy away from the attention, nor does he seem to care to acknowledge it.

"How old are you, Nick *private investigator?*" Amy shakes his hand.

"I'm twenty-six."

"You're twenty-six. Oh," Amy turns to me. "*He's twenty-six.*"

"Yes, I can hear," I say.

Amy, why do you have to be so embarrassing all the time? I can feel the heat rising to my cheeks as both their gazes shift toward me. I'm still in the middle of a really bad date aftermath situation, I don't think getting into anything with Nick would be a good idea either. Plus, he is a professional. I'm sure he doesn't date clients.

I clear my throat, my hands clasping and unclasping in front of me. "Would you like to sit down at the table? I can answer anything you want me to."

None of us talk as we take the small awkward walk through the living room to my kitchen table. It's small, really only seats four people. Nick and I sit across from each other, but Amy doesn't bother to join us. Instead, she hovers behind me like a protective parent. Or like a horny hawk waiting to swoop down on its prey. One or the other.

The pitter patter of familiar feet greets us as Pickle bounds out of my bedroom where he was sleeping and charges for Nick. Pickle wags his tail wildly, jumping into Nick's lap before he can push his chair in.

Poor Nick doesn't know what hit him.

Nick jumps but doesn't make it out of his seat with Pickle weighing him down. Slobber glistens against his cheeks from the endless kisses my old pup is giving out.

"Pickle! No, get down." I order, standing up and pulling Pickle out of his lap.

Nick laughs wiping the spit from off his face. "It's okay. Pickle is it?" He gives me an amused look before reaching his hand out to pet my dog. Pickle is more than willing for any and all attention he is able to get.

"I love dogs." Nick continues, petting Pickle affectionately.

"Jade loves dogs too," Amy interjects earning one of my well-known angry stares.

I choose to ignore her statement and instead refocus the conversation. "You had questions for me?"

Nick pulls out his phone with a nod. "Yes. Do you care if I record this? It just makes it easier for me to have all the information we talk about for me to go back and reference throughout the investigation."

"That's not a problem," I answer.

"Okay, let's begin." He gives me an easy smile. "Your mother said someone broke into your house. Is that correct?"

"Yes."

"Were you home or out when the crime was committed?" Nick looks so serious as he asks this question. I shouldn't expect anything but professionalism out of him, but he looks like a porn star so I'm also half expecting him to break out his willy at any moment. Amy would be thrilled.

"I was home." Underneath the table, my leg bounces relentlessly. Just reliving this moment is making me feel anxious. I hope I'm not sweating through my deodorant right now. Just to be safe I keep my arms tucked into my sides.

"Did you recognize the person?" His blue eyes are watching me carefully. Is he trying to read me in some way?

"Actually, um, it was the guy I went out on a date with. One date," I stutter. "It was, uh, not a very good one though. He did give me his number. I gave it to the police but, like, maybe you could use it also."

Nick looks intrigued and picks up his phone. "Yes, I'll take the number."

I pull out my phone and scroll through my contact, presenting it to him when I find it. He looks at my phone then punches the number into his.

"Can you give me the name he gave to you?"

"That's where it starts getting weird." I shuffle in my seat.

"Yeah, this dude is a real piece of work," Amy interrupts.

I ignore her and begin scrolling through my phone to find the screenshots from his many dating profiles. "When we were out, he referred to himself as Timothy at first. Then he said to call him Christian. Then later Dylan. That and I found all these profiles he has on the app after our date. Six different names in total."

Nick picks up his phone and takes pictures of each of the screenshots on my phone. His jaw clenches as he thinks.

"What happened when he broke in while you were home?"

"I asked him repeatedly to leave but somehow he got in." I swallow. "He kept saying he wanted to talk to me. That it was important. I tried to get away from him, but he cornered me. Eventually, I was able to lock myself in the bathroom and he ended up leaving some time between then and when Amy showed up."

"You don't know what he was talking about?" Nick pondered.

I gave a nervous laugh. "Well, I wasn't really interested in what he wanted to talk about because I felt threatened when he tried to barge his way in here. But no, I don't have a clue."

"And this was the first date you two had been on?" His eyebrows raised.

"Yes."

"So, you are single then?"

I glance at Amy who is grinning like a fool. This is an odd question. He couldn't be interested in me. I'm too plain jane for someone like him. Plus, the last devilishly handsome man I tried to date turned out to be a criminal. So . . .

"Yes." This information must be important to the investigation then. Or the weird porn scene I envisioned when he first got here might be playing out.

"Okay, I think I have the gist of it. Can I give you my number so you can call me if you think of anything else that might be relevant to the case?"

"No, won't we have another appointment in a week?" Mom had given me an incredibly detailed description of just what Nick would be doing. He would be stopping by weekly until the case was solved and Timothy was taken in by the police. "I can just tell you then."

"Really," He smiled. "I must insist. If you need anything at all you can call me at any hour, and I'll pick up."

"I couldn't bother you like that."

Nick gives me a sly wink. "It's my job." He picks up my phone before I can protest again and plugs his name and number into my contact list.

"It was nice meeting you, Amy." He shakes her hand carefully as if she might devour him where he stands. "Wonderful meeting you too, Pickle." He gives the dog a playful pat on his head. Pickle wags his tail in response.

"You'll be hearing from me soon, Miss Waske." Nick stands, pocketing his phone and dips his head toward me politely.

"Call her, Jade." Amy pipes up again as he starts to head toward the door.

I'm already standing and heading to see him out. Amy causes the heated blush to work over my cheeks again. She never knows when to quit.

"I wish you well. Until next time, *Jade.*" He whispers my name as if it's a sin on his lips. With a short wave, he opens my door and closes it swiftly behind him.

6

OFF HIS ROCKER

My apartment for once feels empty. Each room so big it could swallow me whole. Amy needs to be at her own home tonight so that leaves me by myself for the first night since the incident. I've already checked the doors and the windows to make sure they are locked twice. Yet, here I am. Again, I tug on the handle to make sure the door doesn't open and then make my way to the window to check that too.

It's all locked. Pickle isn't worried, it appears by the way he is lazily draped over the couch watching me pace back and forth. He is such a good dog. How did I get so lucky?

I squeeze my sweaty palms into fists and head toward the bedroom. "Come on, Pickle," I call over my shoulder. The pitter-patter of his paws against the hardwood flooring tells me he is following.

My teeth sink into my lip just enough for me to feel discomfort. It's a bad habit, chewing on my lip, if I keep it up I'll leave my lip raw.

I set my phone down on my nightstand close enough I can grab it quickly. How fast can I dial 911? Hopefully, fast enough if I need to. My fingers run over the rough knob on my lamp, but I pull my hand back.

I'll keep the light on tonight.

Scaredy-cat.

The comfort of my pillow welcomes me as I sink down into it and adjust my grey comforter up until it's tucked under my chin. Pickle happily jumps up and stands by my head expectantly. I sigh. Knowingly, I hold up the blanket so Pickle can worm his way under the covers and curl himself against my legs.

Exhaustion weighs on my eyelids. My mind, however, runs rapidly leaving me fighting for sleep. I try to focus on the pace of Pickle's calm breathing. Then eventually I start counting in my head. I make it to four hundred before I lose myself to my unconscious being.

My mouth quirks into a smile as the children run about the yard. Their joyous laughs lifting my spirit as I pluck fresh tomatoes from the garden. Dirt lines my nails. My hands look older, more weathered than I remember.

Carefully, I place the tomatoes in my hands in the woven basket at my side and haul up my bounty with a grunt. This season has been prosperous, and we will be well set and ready for the upcoming winter.

Wait. I don't know how to garden. Yet, somehow, I do? Somehow, I know it's my children playing with sticks and climbing trees a few yards away.

Steady footsteps approach. With a quick turn, I expect to see one of the three kids to come running up to me, but it's not. It's a man.

"Here, let me help you with that." He plucks the basket from my hands with ease. A small grin plays on his lips before he leans down to place a kiss against my cheek.

This man is my home, I think to myself.

"How has your day been?" I walk alongside him, wiping the dirt from my hands on the small apron tied around my waist.

"I got the leak in the roof fixed. I think later I might plant some flowers in front of the house too. Really give us something to be proud of." He beams down at me.

"Oh, that's wonderful Tim!" I pat his back in approval. "Where are the others?"

"Garrett is off taking a nap. Javen is out back fixating on how much we have saved up already from the season. Then Dylan and the others, I think, will be on their way back home from the market shortly."

I pause.

"What's wrong?" Tim blinks, his eyebrows lifting.

Tim, short for Timothy. Javen. Dylan.

These names are so familiar. A small bit of fear creeps up my spine stifling this happy moment.

"I, uh," my brows furrow. "Who are you?"

"Mariah, I'm your husband. Are you okay?" Tim stops, setting the basket at his feet. Calloused hands trace the side of my face stopping only once to tuck a stray strand of hair behind my ear.

"Husband." I swallow heavily. "Who are the others exactly?"

He gives me a worried look. "Garret, Javen, Dylan, and the others?"

I give a slow nod.

"Also, your husbands." He squints at me suspiciously before he laughs and smiles. "Is this some sort of role play game? That could be fun."

I go to tell him no, but I'm cut off by a frightened scream. We both turn toward the kids. Two of them are barreling toward us at full speed, their eyes wide and their mouths parted as they scream again. The third lay limp in the hands of a dark creature.

The Huntress.

Tim and I race toward the children. Kye and Ruth fight to get to us through the tall weeds in the field. My heart beats wildly in my chest as I worry for Eva now in the hands of our enemy. I don't know how I know this; I don't know how my body is instinctually moving to protect the kids as I pull small daggers out of my waistband and send them flying towards the huntress.

She dodges them without blinking.

"Take the kids and run," Timothy yells, the faint squeal of a weapon pulled from its sheath whistles in the air.

"I've already got the others." The huntress smiles, her pointed teeth glistening like metal in the afternoon sun. "You're the last to go."

Cold air fills my lungs. I can still hear the gasp that woke me from my sleep. Blinking slowly, I try to catch my breath and slow the chaotic beating of my heart. The damp sheets cling to my body as I try to sit up.

A scream is caught in my throat. My body freezes, frigid with fear.

"I don't mean to startle you," he says. He leans casually against the wall without moving. The piercing gaze of his eyes seems gentler as he watches me.

My attention stays on him for a moment before it sweeps to Pickle who happily stands next to this strange man begging for love. When he doesn't move Pickle sits down at his feet expectantly.

I try to gulp down saliva to help the dryness of my throat. *What do I do? How can I protect myself?*

Stall.

"Who am I talking to?" *What name does he want me to call him this time?*

"Garrett." He inclines his head toward me.

I haven't heard Garrett yet and I don't recall a profile with that name either.

"Hmm," I sit myself up in bed pushing myself closer to my phone. "Why are you here?"

Garrett smiles but barely, his lips hardly move. "I know it's weird, but I've always enjoyed watching you sleep. You're just so peaceful."

Always. Oh, God. This man is crazy. Off his rocker crazy.

"You know I hardly know you right? We have only been on one date."

His small grin falls and his gaze drops to the ground. "You used to know me."

With his attention focused at his feet, I snatch up my phone and plug in my passcode. My fingers tremble with every movement I make.

Garrett catches my movement and looks back up at me. "Please don't call for anyone. I only want a moment. I don't take control of this mind often."

I stop and stare up at him. He seems so normal if you just look at him. No one would ever know how mentally ill he was. He might not want to hurt me, but he could accidentally.

My eyes already burn as tears well within them. This has been the week from hell, and it seems to only be getting worse. Will he kidnap me and cut me up into tiny little pieces next? Lock me up forever "for my own protection"?

"I'm scared," I whisper. "I don't know what to do."

Garrett looks startled. His hands drop to his sides as he stands up straight. "We would never hurt you."

"Please, leave me alone." I try again.

His Adam's apple bobs in his throat. Garrett takes his time before he speaks again.

"Jade, can you help us?"

"I don't want to help you." Help. He is always asking for help. Only a doctor could help him, and I am no doctor.

Neither of us moves and I fear I may have just signed my own death certificate. Garrett stares at me blinking slowly, his chest still as if he is holding his breath. I blink back unable to do anything further.

One blink, he stands, looking worried and mournful, the next blink, he is gone.

I lose my breath. My bed creaks as I stand on it looking around my room for the man who is no longer there. Was he ever there to begin with? Am I the one losing my marbles? For good measure, I pinch my arm then slap my cheeks a little bit. I'm awake. This is real life.

Leaping over my throw pillows that have scattered on the

ground I grab my taser and hold it close to me while I dial my phone with the other hand.

"Jade? Hello?" His voice is heavy with sleep on the other end.

"Nick. He was here."

7

MORE THAN MEETS THE EYE

His blonde curls are messily standing on end on one side of his head while they lay flattened on the other. Nick really came here straight from his bed. While he didn't take the time to comb his hair, he did dress in a pair of loose-fitting jeans and an off-white t-shirt.

I take note of everything he is doing while my teeth grind against my fingernails. It isn't easy to stop fidgeting and anytime I take my eyes off Nick, my mind wanders to Garrett.

Nick sighs. He has checked every window and every lock. He is thorough and observant. Skills I have yet to acquire, apparently.

"Well, there isn't any signs of forced entry and everything was locked when I got here."

I nod slowly realizing he is only getting to the point that I've gone mad. Awesome.

"Does anyone other then you have a spare key?"

"Amy does. But that's it."

Nick's hand takes its time rubbing at his eyes before he brings it to skim over the stubble on his chin. "You may need to give her a call just to make sure she still has it in her possession."

"I'm sorry," I begin. It's highly unlikely she lost the key. Amy may be a party animal, but she is also the most loyal caring person I know. "It's just, I uh, it's like he was here one second then the next he just vanished. Materialized into thin air."

Nick purses his lips and steps closer. I can smell the tangy sweet scent of his body wash that lingers on his skin.

"Okay." He slips out of the jacket he had on over his shirt. "Do you mind if I sleep on the couch?"

I'm hesitant to even answer. "No?"

"Well, Jade, you've been pushed to your limits with stress and fear this week. You're likely having some sort of PTSD episode. I don't think he was here tonight. Let me stay with you, it could calm your nerves."

"So, I am crazy?" And I sound even crazier asking that question out loud in a strained high-pitched version of my voice. The kind of voice I have had in the past when I've been on the verge of a mental break down. *Oh, God. He is too pretty to see me ugly cry this early.* I refuse to blink trying to hold any and all tears that threaten to spill over.

The light and airy laugh that escapes him eases me, and my shoulders relax. One side of his lips lifts in a simple grin. With one large step, he comes within reaching distance of me, a gap he closes quickly as he places his arms on my shoulders. His gaze is soft, sympathetic as he makes eye contact.

"You're not crazy. You just need some time and maybe a little company."

"I couldn't be a bother like that." Heat blooms across my cheeks while my teeth scrape roughly against my lip, a nervous habit I'll likely never break.

Nick drops his hands, leaving me with a small shudder down my spine as his fingertips trail down my arms on their way to his side. He means well. Yet, with the constant reminder of how close I had come to being a victim, it left my stomach churning in the worst way. I lean back away from him.

Thankfully, he takes the hint. His hands casually find his

pockets and he glances away making light of checking out the small souvenir coffee mug on my side table. It gives him the excuse to take a step away from me. Nick is smart. I'm glad he can read people well and is polite enough to respect them.

With a rough cough, he looks back at me, scanning me from head to toe. "Your parents are paying me well. It's really the least I can do."

Oh, yes. I'm a job to him, that's all. I shrug pushing my child-like crush as far down into the depths of my mind as I can before I make more of a fool out of myself.

Together we stand in silence. My elderly neighbors fast asleep around us, unaware of the frightening events that have taken place next to them. Hopefully, my late-night restlessness hasn't woken them at all. Yet, I'm sure if it does, I'll likely hear from Mrs. Hemmings. Cranky old crow too nosy for her own good, that woman. I'm in shock she didn't come waddling in with her cane the day the cops were here.

Nick eases himself onto my couch. He sits for a moment as if to examine the comfort of the furniture before he lays himself down, crossing his legs, and placing his arms behind his head.

Must be comfortable enough.

"Welp, goodnight," Nick says with his eyes closed. The image of contentment.

I find myself awkwardly hugging my arms over my chest. Apparently, it's just that easy for him. Good looks must have just made life that much better. Ug, I think to myself, suddenly remembering how I must look in my pajamas without makeup, my hair likely a frizz ball. Dang, if it was Halloween I could likely pass as a witch without even purchasing a costume.

And he saw me like this. Better take those teenage angst feelings of mine and forget about them. I've lost my chance now. *RIP Jade and her pride.*

"Jade." His voice brings me back to the reality of my living room. Nick cracks one eye open. "Go to sleep."

"Oh," I whisper. "Sorry, goodnight."

I scuttle away to my room, my heart calming. He's like a paid bodyguard. I'm safe now.

SWEET SCENTS LIFT the heavy sleep that leaves me tied up in my sheets. The palm of my hand runs over my mouth to wipe away the drool that hangs off me in a string attached to the pillow. I blink. Everything is still fuzzy in that early morning haze that I have to fight out of until I get my first cup of coffee.

Pickle's spot where he lays with me is empty and cold, an unusual way for me to wake up when his kisses are normally what greets me. I flop my arm across my bed reaching till my fingertips graze the cool metal of my phone case. One glance and my eyes are wide open.

Crap. It's nine o'clock. I'm late for my first class this morning.

"Gah!" I sputter as I throw myself out of bed and stumble out of my room with the blankets still wrapped around my feet. With as much grace as I can muster, I detangle myself just to take a fumbling step forward and jam my pinky toe into the end table by my couch.

I bite my lip to hold in a painful screech that's welling in my throat. *Get yourself together girl.*

"Ouch. Are you okay?" Nick's deep voice makes me open my eyes when I didn't realize I squeezed them shut.

"I'm alright. Yes." I straighten my posture pushing down the complaints about my now aching toe. My attention drifts over him and the plate he is holding. French Toast. With a deep breath, the familiar smell greets me again. I didn't know I even had the ingredients for french toast in my cabinets.

Giving the couch and the end table that offended me a wide berth I make my way to join him. The frizz of my hair sticks out in my peripheral, my fingers eagerly combing it down. Nick smiles. His hands are sure and unwavering as he plops down a plate of food. For dramatic effect, he sprinkles the last bit of powdered sugar above it with a small flick of his fingers.

"Hope you don't mind." He pushes the plate over the countertop to me. "My Grandma always said a night of sleep and a warm breakfast can fix any problem. So . . ."

"So . . ." I chuckle. "I'm not sure that applies to stalkers and insomnia."

Nick shrugs. Beside him, Pickle looks up expectantly and without any attempt to hide it Nick drops a piece of food at his feet. Somehow, I'm not surprised that Pickle left me to beg for food.

"Trying to buy his love?" I ask. My fork scrapes the plate creating an annoying sound that hurts my teeth. I grimace but pick up the bite and chew as I watch Nick carefully.

"Oh, it's already bought."

The smug look on his face somehow accentuates his incredibly chiseled jawline. My eyes trace the perfect line along his face. He crouches low. Pickle greets him with endless dripping kisses along Nick's cheek. A slobbery mess Nick doesn't seem to mind.

"You know, I've been thinking." Nick stands, swiping his arm across his cheek. "Maybe we could go to the History Museum."

I slow my efforts of chewing my breakfast. *Like just the two of us? Like a date? Like has he lost his mind and now all of a sudden wants to take me, a human being that also resembles a potato on my good days, out?*

"The History Museum?"

"Yeah, I'm busy most of this week, but on Friday we could go check out their new exhibit."

"The two of us? As people?" *As people? Why the hell did you just say that, Jade? What else are you going to go as? Aliens?*

Dishes clink together as Nick neatly stacks them in the sink. His head bobs from side to side as if he is considering my statement. *Perhaps he will suggest something else we could go as together. Dogs. Birds. Planes. Or freaking Transformers since it's up in the air if we go in our human forms. We're "more than meets the eye." Jesus Christ. I need a therapist.*

"Yeah, I think it would do you a lot of good to just get out and get your mind off of things."

"Right," I say. I glance at the clock on the wall. At this point, I'm so late to class I shouldn't even bother thinking about going.

But maybe it was worth it. A smile crawls across my face hidden from Nick as I turn away for a moment to collect myself and the butterflies having a rave in my stomach.

Because I've got a date. A date with Nick Johnson.

Fuck, yeah.

8

NOT A DATE, DATE

EVERYTHING IS GOING PERFECT. This is the best my hair has ever looked and my outfit is the right blend of dressy but not over the top. Nothing between us is awkward. Finally, my luck is improving!

Other people mill about taking in the extravagant works on display most of them talking in hushed tones. No one gives us a second glance. Well even if they are I'm hardly taking my eyes off my date.

Nick whistles in a low tone as he looks down his nose at a hanging art piece. "Classic."

The painting is a woman staring with a blank face while her husband frowns behind her. Nothing special in my opinion but I guess I'm not a professional so I wouldn't know. Really, I hate museums. I mean who wants to just stand around all day looking at pictures of people you don't know? I guess a lot of people, or these wouldn't exist. I, however, am not one. I'll bet Nick knows his stuff.

"It looks nice." I nod along.

Thoughtfully, he places his hand along his jaw. The small heel of my sandal clicks lightly against the ground as I follow him on to the next painting. When he stops his hair shines underneath the brilliant sun that pores in from the large windows at the entrance. He looks like an angel.

An angel come to save me.

God. That's so corny.

"You know," Nick swivels on his heels to see me as he walks backward. "I hadn't told you yet, but I think I've finally found the guy who tried to attack you."

Everything within me tightens. My stomach is a twisted knot at the thought. It's been over a week without any issues. I was starting to feel normal. Starting.

I fake a smile. "Oh, I'm glad!"

"Yeah, he looks like he might be the CEO of a large company though, so he has a lot of money to fight with. But I'll see what we can do. I've got to confirm it's the right guy still"

"How will you confirm it?"

"I'll take a picture of him and show you."

I swallow the lump in my throat. Nick smirks.

"Don't worry, I'll take care of everything. Just trust me."

And I do trust him, don't I? Yes, yes, I do. I hook my fingers into my back pockets looking at each display. The open space is filled with the sound of classical music and we let it swallow up our silence.

Inside my pocket, my phone vibrates. Decidedly I ignore it but then it buzzes again. Nick seems so interested in whatever that old-timey picture of a hay bale has going on with it he doesn't seem to pay me any mind.

It's Amy.

What are you doing?

Talk to him.

What the hell? I frown down at my phone and quickly respond back.

Amy, what are you talking about?

Then buzz buzz there she is again.

This is the most boring date ever. Talk to the poor man.

Oh my God. That little whore. I try to keep my face calm as I let my attention drift around to find my friend, but I just know my mouth is open in surprise. With her hair pulled back in a low ponytail and her eyes covered with sunglasses, Amy leans quietly against a wall just far enough away I would have never known she was there.

"Nick," I begin. He tilts his head at me but doesn't take his eyes off the painting. "I'm gonna run to the restroom. I'll be right back."

"Okay." He shrugs.

I grit my teeth thinking of all the terrible things I want to say to my friend right now. Like, why the hell is she spying on me? When she sees me coming she stiffens up like a board.

Without stopping to think I don't bother to slow down as I grab her hand on my way past her and drag her along.

"Amy, what are you doing here?"

Dramatically, she lifts her sunglasses off her face and sighs. "The last time you went on a date it was with a psychopath. I had to make sure this one turned out better."

"It's Nick. We already know he isn't a psychopath."

"You can never be too safe." Amy tries to act like she so concerned but really, she is just nosey.

"I thought this sort of thing only happened in movies." I rub my temples. This can't really be my life. This has to be another one of those utterly realistic dreams. Except it's not.

"Amy?" Nicks voice breaks over my shoulder.

Somehow this situation got worse. What did I do to deserve this type of karma or whatever bad juju has suddenly fallen on me?

"Oh, hi Nick." Amy waves with a smile.

"What are you doing here?" Nick grins back.

"You know just wanted to check out some art . . . stuff. Sculptures. Paintings. Other clay like things."

Wow, really convincing.

Nick hums. "You should join us."

Amy laughs real shrill like, the sound even bothers my ears.

I cringe and give her an annoyed look. She meets my gaze as if to ask the question of if she should. *No, you should not join us.* I try to say with telepathy.

"No, no. I can't interrupt your date." She awkwardly gives us a dismissive wave.

"Oh, we aren't on a date. You're fine. We're just trying to get Jade out of the house more to help make sure she doesn't have another PTSD episode or something."

Excuse me?

My cheeks burn as the blush works its way across my face. We aren't on a date? You had me fooled, Nick. Why am I so dumb and naive?

Amy's smile falters. I bet my own face doesn't look too much different at the moment either. Is Nick just leading me on?

"Right." I laugh nervously. "You can join us, Ames." My hand is balled up into a fist and I try to playfully punch her arm, but I know it had a little too much force behind it.

She holds her arm where I got her, and her frown deepens. "You know what? I'll just let you two finish your . . . not date."

Sadly, that's what this is. It's a *not* date.

An almost did but didn't quite make it, not date.

Silently, in the way only best friends do, we have a conversation with just our eyes. A back and forth on if she should stay or go. At this point, I wish she would stay. I don't want to just hang with Nick on a not date, date. I'm too ashamed I even thought our date was a thing.

Finally, after a slightly awkward glance from Nick, Amy shrugs. "Okay, okay. You twisted my arm."

I give her a tight smile and we move into the room Amy had been stalking us from. As a group, we pretend to be interested in the artwork, but I believe we were all actually too deep in thought replaying what just happened in our heads. At least I am.

"Jade!' Amy gasps. With a big wave of her arm, she gestures

for me to join her at a painting in the corner. "Look at this. Holy cow, you could pass as twins!"

The painting is . . . me but dressed in long robes peering longingly out of a window. This is so creepy.

"Stand next to it! I've got to get a picture of you with it. This is uncanny."

Stiffly, I stand next to the painting while she snaps the picture on her phone.

"Great," I mumble, "I've always wanted to be a meme."

"You know at all times there are at least seven people on earth who look almost exactly like you." Nick glances at Amy's picture looking mighty impressed. "It's like you just met one of them. Crazy."

Crazy. What's really crazy, Nick, is that I'm stuck on this not date with you and my best friend for who knows how much longer?

9

SINFUL

Hands graze my body stopping to give attention to the most sensitive parts. Lips meet mine in a gentle needing way that makes me want to give so much more. My body trembles with pleasure. I'm not bothered by the moans that escape me as it seems to only push my partner to do more glorious things to me.

Partner. Partners.

Slowly, I realize it's not one set of hands but many. Some staying for longer heated moments some passing by in fleeting brushstrokes.

I love it. I love them. Every single moment of it.

Please don't let this stop.

"Don't ever leave me," *I whisper.*

The rhythm of all our bodies together slows. Hips grind against mine reveling in emotion that somehow connects us all.

"We will never leave you." *Wet hot air tickles along me ear with the words, a trail of kisses presses down my neck.*

Two hands firmly hold my hips, their thumbs brushing over my hip bones again and again. "Never." *I pant as the group does their sinfully good work on me.*

"Never." *Many voices repeat in various gruff and husky tones.*

I try to smile but am lost to dangerously good sensations that leave me parting my mouth to let out my own devilish cry.

They'll never leave me.

My eyes flutter open and I can still feel their hands pressed to my skin. My lips still tingle with the warmth of a lover's caress. I don't know who they are, but I really truly don't ever want them to leave. Selfishly, I want them all to myself forever.

All. All of them. Not one but many.

What an odd feeling and an odd concept to think that I could potentially love more than one person in that way. What would my mom say? That is just unheard of in our family.

Staring up at the darkness above me I sigh. I don't need to worry about that because I can't even find one man to love me anyway.

My fingers skim along the top of my pajama pants, my thoughts still on the steamy dream. I let my fingers brush just under my waistband when I notice one edge of my bed dips down just a bit. Pulling my hand away, I reach out thinking I'm about to push Pickle off the bed.

I mean this is a private moment I'm about to have with myself.

Smooth skin meets my touch, not at all the soft fur I was expecting. I squeal grabbing my phone to use as a light. With the dim glow, I cast shadows against my wall. Timothy sitting at the edge of my bed.

"You're remembering your past lives, aren't you?" he says quietly.

"I'm sorry?" I curl up letting my arms wrap around my knees still trying to keep my phone pointed at him.

"Would you like me to turn on the light?"

"Yes, please." I'm less nervous this time, less frightened. I realized he hadn't touched me yet, hadn't ever really tried to hurt me. He just made me uneasy.

So, I'll try to text Nick and get him here while Timothy sits in my bedroom. Catch him in the act. Then, I'm moving, end of story.

With a flick of the light switch, I can see Timothy's hair isn't neatly combed anymore, his eyes hooded and sleepy with dark bags underneath them. He looks exhausted like he hasn't slept in the entire week that I hadn't seen him at all. I was just starting to think I was in the clear, that he would leave me alone. Clearly, that was a joke.

"I haven't seen you in a while." Somehow, I'm staying calm, so I turn my phone back to face me.

"You asked me to leave you alone. I tried, I really tried but I knew you would start to remember, and it would be confusing, and I didn't want you to go through it alone." He pauses eyeing me thoughtfully. "The other's think I'm selfish. I'm just greedy like that. I just want your time."

"The others? Timothy? Dylan? Christian?" This is the real question that has eaten at me every time. Why so many names? Why so many personalities? This man has something wrong with him and somehow, *I'm* the solution.

"Yes."

"How many are there?" I'm stalling. Yet, I find myself genuinely curious.

No. NO. This man is breaking and entering. Don't feel sorry for him even if he is messed up in that twisted head of his.

"Seven, including myself."

Seven, holy shit. I fight to keep my mouth from falling open. Seven people in one brain. It must be seriously noisy in there.

"Wow. And who am I speaking to now?"

"My name is Javen." He bows his head.

"Javen," I say his name slowly, tasting the familiarity on my lips. "Javen, why do you think I've been dreaming about my past life."

Causally, I try and unlock my phone without actually giving

it much of a look. I fail the first time. Then the second. But the third time, it opens up.

"Because you are. This is how it's meant to go. We meet and it triggers you to start remembering. I wanted to give you as much time as possible, but the Huntress will be coming for you soon."

"The Huntress. I remember that name."

My brain feels foggy, but the mechanics are turning, it's like something is actually beginning to click into place inside of me. The excited feeling you get while you're on a roller coaster builds inside my stomach. Excitement and fear.

Javen smiles a bit, looking hopeful. "The Huntress is a very, very bad demon and her one job is to keep us apart."

Is it the fact that I've had so many dreams this week with these names in them that they are all so familiar to me now? Was my subconscious just pulling from my reality in the most confusing way? Or is Javen right?

"Javen, what's wrong with you?" I scroll to my text messages, finding Nick's name as Javen covers his face, dragging down his features when he does.

"The only thing wrong with me, with us, is that we need you to get us out of this tiny fragile human body."

"Me?" I stutter. What the hell does he think I'm going to do? As subtle as possible I gently type out *help* and press send.

"Please put your phone down." Javen stiffens, his hands curling and uncurling in his lap.

I do as he asks, praying Nick takes the hint and comes to save me.

"Sorry. How can I help you?" The words sound pushy even as I say them.

"I want to you hold my hand and say a spell with me."

Say a spell. So, I'm a witch now, huh?

"I don't have magic. This isn't a fictional novel where you come to tell me you're about to take me off to wizarding school and fly me off on some broom."

His lips pursed. Each word is short, utterly enunciated. "It's not magic. It is the supernatural. But it's dark, evil. It's what we are made of."

He leans forward, close enough I can feel his breath hitting my skin.

"In this life, you're the hero in your story, maybe even a victim. But in the original, you're the villain."

"I thought this huntress was the villain?" I lean forward letting my face come within an inch of him.

His breath hitches in his chest, his eyes flicking from my gaze to my lips then back up again before he manages to say, "She's our villain. But we're the villains in many other people's stories."

"Tell me what you are. Tell me what I am."

"Release us." He counters.

"Tell me or I will do no such thing."

He reaches for my hand, but I pull away. I straighten and watch as he does the same. He is debating on if he is going to actually tell me or not.

Roughly he clears his throat. "We are the embodiment of everything wrong with the human world. This temporary home. We are persuasive. So much so that no human can resist us and the power we have to sway their minds. Least none we have come into contact with yet."

"If you're so powerful, how come you haven't used these *powers* on me?"

"It's in the binding. There is little we can do in this form. Somethings, like being able to enter your apartment without using a door are easy. Others . . . swaying the mind . . . not possible."

"So, you are a wizard? A bad wizard?" The arch in my eyebrows and squint of my eyes told him enough that I didn't believe a word he said.

I expect him to start again, to explain in greater detail, or even to show me some of this magic he speaks of but instead, he tilts his head to the ceiling and laughs. It's an easy laugh, genuine enough. He really found humor in what I said.

"A wizard?" He laughs again.

"Okay, judging by how your reacting, you're clearly not a wizard." I deadpan.

As his laughter dies down, he tries to regain a serious composure. His lips though still slightly curve up into a happy grin. He stands up holding his hands out at his sides.

"Jade, we are the embodiment of what you would know as the seven deadly sins."

I don't react. Part of me wants to laugh like he did at the absurdity of what he is saying. The other part of me though nods in agreement knowing it's true.

"So, say what you are telling me is correct and not some silly made up thing by a crazy man with multiple personalities. What am I to you?"

"You're the love of our lives."

The words hung between us. The love of *our* lives. My dreams with the men . . . all the men. Seven. Seven men. I see bits of it now playing like a movie in my head. Clips of all the dreams that felt fuzzy at the time but now are becoming clearer.

"What am I?" Do I want to know? Do I somehow already know? Suddenly, I'm over examining my life. Who my parents are, what my goals after college are, my friends— Amy. Is it all a lie? Is this reality just a dream that will end when I wake up to a new, very different life?

"You are literally the devil's advocate."

"Oh."

What else do I say? I don't particularly feel evil. The devil is a bad guy, common knowledge based on religion. But no one ever said the seven deadly sins were living beings or that the devil had an actual advocate.

"Will you say the words now? Will you release us? I know it's so much to take in and I promise we will answer everything. Though once we are released you will likely begin regaining more and more memories from previous lives."

"Previous lives." My lips felt numb as I repeated after him.

"Well, yes. Technically, you've died many times. Your spirit is always reborn though."

My heart feels like it's beating in a sluggish rhythm that I can feel pulse inside my head. I blink. Javen reaches out and takes my hand.

"*Septem Animarum,*" He looks at me expectantly.

My hands are trembling in his grasp. His thumb gently strokes against my skin, his hands steady.

"*Septem Animarum,*" I repeat. Heat surges between our palms.

"*Ut sinus te. Set liberum chao.*"

As I follow his lead, saying just what he says, I stare with wide eyes at our hands. They glow a vibrant green color, building until it's blinding. His hand rips away from mine and I fall back against my headboard covering my face.

He cries out a terrifying moan, but I don't move until the light that envelops us fades away. I consider keeping my eyes closed. *If I can't see him, them. They can't see me.*

"Oh, my Satan. She's done it. It's worked," a new voice says.

"I'm so happy to only hear my own voice inside my head," a deep grumble from somewhere else in the room says.

"Jade?" someone whispers next to me.

Compared to the unearthly glow of dark magic we just performed, somehow, my bedroom light is so dim. The yellow light reveals not just the one body I had seen before but many. I count them, my eyes jumping from one to the other.

They're all so different from each other. None of them even resemble the man I knew before. One, two, three, four, five, six, and seven.

I push aside the hand of the one who is leaning down to me with concern etching his features. Sliding from the bed, my shaking knees threaten to drop me to the floor, and the man behind me catches me. He stands me upright and backs away.

It's like I know them now. I recognize them.

I point my finger at each of them saying their names with a new confidence.

"Ebon, lust." The definition of tall, dark, and handsome. His black hair is slicked back, and a bad boy grin has my heart skipping a beat when I meet his coal grey eyes.

"Timothy, pride." Blonde hair hangs into his sky-blue gaze, his chin lifting as he stands taller.

"Garrett, sloth." He stands with an easy smirk, his hands tucked into his pockets. Red curls in effortless disarray atop his head.

"Christian, gluttony." He keeps his brown eyes on me as he licks his lips.

"Mark, envy."

Mark purses his lips. "It took you long enough to get to me."

Garett snorts, "But he isn't jealous or anything."

I smile at the joke continuing on as my nerves begin to calm.

"Dylan, wrath." His mousy brown hair is tossed to one side, his fists clenching so hard his knuckles have lost their color.

I twist back to the one who helped me stand, my finger bumping against his chest. "Javen, greed." He gives me a small nod. Javen's tight curls twist so close to his head you can hardly tell he even has curls, yellow eyes watching happily from under dominate eyebrows.

"You'll remember more as we go. But for now, for your very safety, we have to leave." Javen clasps both hands over my shoulders.

"What's going to happen next?" I ask carefully.

Timothy speaks up from behind me. "We don't know, we've never gotten this far."

"You what?" I begin but Javen snaps his fingers and suddenly we are no longer in my apartment.

I'm not sure if Nick ever got my text message. But if he does, if he comes to my apartment to save me from what I thought was my certain doom, what still may be my end, he won't find me.

He won't find anyone.

ALSO BY NIKKI HUNTER

Check out more great reads from Nikki Hunter!

The Royal Harem Series

The Hundred Year Curse
The Curse of the Sea
The Legend of the Cursed Princess

The Magic of the Jin Series

The Needed
The Wanted
The Taken
The Forgiven

The Rising from Ruin Saga

Dawn of Danger
Day of Ruin

NOCTURNE

NIKKI LANDIS

Copyright © 2019 Nikki Landis
All Rights Reserved.

No part of this publication may be reproduced, distributed, or transmitted in any form or by any means, including photocopying, recording, or other electronic or mechanical methods, without the prior written permission of the publisher, except in the case of brief quotations embodied in critical reviews and certain other noncommercial uses permitted by copyright law.

This is a work of fiction. Names, places, and incidents are products of the author's imagination or are used fictitiously and are not to be construed as real. Any resemblance to actual events, locales, organizations, or persons, living or dead, is entirely coincidental.

Cover Art by Erica Petit Illustrations
Edited by

❦ Created with Vellum

NOCTURNE

The feral, uncontrollable state of a vampire when consumed by bloodlust and lost in the vile pit of everlasting darkness . . .

ABOUT THIS BOOK

Dead by morning...
Skye Colt has always been a hunter. Raised to be one of the best, she faces life as it comes and lives each moment like it's her last.
Until everything changes and a single brutal attack forces her on a one-way suicide mission. Vengeance is her only thought until three handsome and irritating men intervene. Nothing prepares her for the shocking truth, or the revelations made on Dead Island.
With her soul on the line, will she trust the trio of protectors enough to help avenge her sister's murder? Or will Skye be tempted by the sensual allure of immortality?

1

SKYE

THE SHARP EDGE of the hunter's knife gleamed in the encroaching twilight as he stood on the small vessel's deck, slicing and gutting fish for the evening meal. I watched with vague interest, mostly bored with the trip and trying to hide my impatience. When I booked this boat over a month ago, I'd been told it was one of the fastest ships in the harbor and expected to reach the island long before nightfall.

Someone was a lying sack of shit.

When I returned to the mainland, I was going to give that scheduler a piece of my mind and it wouldn't be pleasant. If I managed to return home at all. I wasn't under any delusions that my ridiculous plan would be successful. Hell, I'd be happy if I was able to walk on the island and kill half the evil bastards that murdered my sister and hunted our clan down to extinction.

Three years later and my sister's death was still as haunting and painful as the day it occurred. Whenever I closed my eyes the only thing I could see was the fear in her eyes and the copious amounts of blood that never seemed to fade. Visions of frightening apparitions and fangs that dripped with venom dominated my dreams. Nightmares had plagued my nights ever since I was forced to watch her murder. Maybe I would never recover. Fatigue had settled bone-deep into my body and my soul was weary. Perhaps I decided to act on this foolish impulse now because I knew it was a one-way trip.

A suicide mission.

Maybe I should have told the hunters who owned this boat there was a possibility I wouldn't need passage back. They were a wild bunch and from what I could tell, weren't fond of passengers or women. Sort of boggled the mind when they were the ones responsible. I could have booked any vessel. Why get bent out of shape because of me? Don't put your boat up for rental if you don't want people to actually, you know, *rent* it.

"So, Skye, is it?" The oldest brother asked. He seemed to be the one in charge and the only man who bothered to speak to me since we left the docks over three hours prior. His sexy dark looks were a welcome distraction from the sun's relentless glare over the ocean's surface. Mossy green eyes held my gaze with a combination of curiosity and boredom. I didn't miss the way he perused my entire body as we spoke. His focused attention slid over every inch with unhurried assessment.

"Yes, Rhun, we established that when I stepped onto the Maiden's Virtue."

He rubbed the stubble on his chin thoughtfully as his gaze switched to his brother. "Ash, you hear her say her name earlier?"

A grunt followed as Ash continued filleting fish and then ripped the skin from the flesh. The muscles in his arms flexed and moved beneath the taut layer of tanned skin. He was as ruggedly handsome as Rhun and twice as distracting without a shirt to cover his sculpted frame.

"I think I heard her," the youngest brother announced, walking onto the deck in nothing but his birthday suit.

No lie. He was stark naked, sporting a semi-hard cock, and

damn near perfectly formed physique. What did their mama feed these boys? I'd never seen a trio of men more perfectly proportioned. Tall and devilishly sinful, they were any woman's wet dream.

My eyes widened and then averted as the two remaining brothers chuckled.

"I'm taking a swim, Rhun. Back in a minute."

"Sure thing, Kepp."

The man in question winked and then dove overboard to go swim with the sharks or whatever else seemed to make total sense on this ship. His tight and perfectly formed tanned ass didn't escape my notice. No lines where swim trunks or even a speedo were visible. Obviously, he preferred to be naked.

Sighing with mild annoyance, I turned back to Rhun and noticed that Ash was gone. He must have taken the fish inside to cook. My stomach growled at the thought as my gaze shifted to the empty cabin doorway.

"He might share if you ask."

Why I suddenly felt like that was some kind of sexual innuendo, I wasn't sure. "No, I'll be fine."

Rhun made a sound in his throat like he knew I was lying. "Not fond of fresh fish?"

My eyes narrowed. "I'm not fond of a lot of things."

He nodded, stroking his chin again which increased my irritation another notch. "Like delays?"

Smartass.

"You could say that," I admitted, deciding the conversation was over. I didn't know what the deal was with this trio of weirdos, but I was officially keeping to myself until we arrived at our destination. It wasn't like it would matter. I was probably gonna be dead in less than twenty-four hours anyway. Rhun must have sensed I was making a getaway because he stood in front of me so fast, I swear I didn't do more than blink.

"Why do you want to travel to Dead Island?"

Snorting, I still thought it was humorous that an island full of bloodsucking monsters was called Dead Island. Of course, it was in Spanish but still amusing. Didn't anyone realize dinosaurs had already cornered that market in fiction? Didn't anyone appreciate the irony?

"I paid for passage, not secrets. If you require them before coming aboard you should let your customers know ahead of time."

With that comment, I left him standing there with a strange expression on his face, something of a cross between annoyance, anger, and disbelief.

Get a clue, buddy.

Naked Kepp climbed aboard a half-hour later and I had to wonder how he managed to do so when the ship never stopped moving. He tried to smile as our eyes met but I quickly averted my gaze away and sat with my stuff. My concentration was mostly focused on the appearance of the island which was within view now. Sporadic lights proved it wasn't deserted. For the first time in three years, I felt a stirring deep within.

I swear to avenge you, Serina.

"For you sis," I whispered, reaching into my pocket and pulling out my own knife. This wasn't any normal blade. Enchanted by the Sven Witches, I paid a heavy price for the dagger's power. Etched into the steel were runes and magical carvings that would aid in my quest.

Every possession that I owned or meant anything to me was located inside the satchel slung across my shoulders. Lightweight and durable, it would provide what I needed to last the night.

Sucking in a breath, I released it slowly and stood.

As soon as we docked, I was on my way to kill vampires.

2

RHUN

"Hi, I'm Skye," the dark-haired beauty announced as I spun and found her climbing aboard my fucking ship like I gave her an invitation. "Your only passenger for the trip."

Fuck me.

"We weren't supposed to have anyone on board tonight," I grumbled, snatching the invoice from her hand with more frustration than I intended. *Shit.* There it was in black and white. She was paid for a round trip passage to Dead Island and back.

Who the fuck messed this up? I'd left specific instructions with Pete. No passengers this weekend.

"Listen, sweetheart, I'm sorry. There's some kind of misunderstanding. We aren't accepting renters for another week."

Her eyes narrowed as her arms crossed over her chest. "I'm afraid I'm going to have to insist you honor the agreement. It's paid in full. I've kept my end of the contract."

Dammit.

"I have no problem reimbursing you the full cost."

"Not acceptable. I have to be on that island tonight. There are no other vessels available."

I already knew that was true. Most of the boats this time of year were filled quickly due to the summer weather and the lure of the islands. Reluctant and aggravated, I had to accept. "Alright. Climb aboard."

Maybe I should have offered to grab her bag or reached out to help her, but I was pissed and didn't give a shit. The last thing I needed was a cute little piece of ass distracting Kepp or Ash before we dumped her off as quickly as possible. Dead Island. Yeah, sure honey. I wasn't taking her anywhere near the bloodsuckers. She could die on her own dime, not mine.

By the time she realized that we'd taken her to a resort, we'd be long gone.

Skye made herself comfortable on the deck as I mumbled curses under my breath and went below to warn the others.

Ash was in the galley making coffee as Kepp sat at the dinette and finished a sandwich. Both looked up when I entered.

"We've got company. She's booked passage to Dead Island."

"What kind of company?" Ash lifted his mug and met my frustrated gaze.

"Female, stubborn, and a severe pain in the ass."

"Sounds like my type," Kepp laughed. He jumped up and proceeded to peek at her from the stairs. Striding back to his seat, he snorted with mild amusement. "She's gorgeous, Rhun. Mind if I stake a claim?"

Don't lose your temper. Five, four, three, two, one . . .

"What the hell are you talking about, boy?" I scolded. "This isn't a pleasure cruise. Keep your dick in your pants." I couldn't name the reason why I was so irritated by my best friend's son. Landon had entrusted me with his greatest treasure, the boy he died saving. I always took that to heart and wasn't about to let the kid get into serious trouble. Right now, I'd throw him to the sharks to get that shit-eating grin off his face.

"Right," Kepp drawled, clearly enjoying my reaction, "loosen up a bit, old man."

Ash chuckled loudly as he finished his coffee. "I've got fish to clean for dinner. I'm going to observe our guest and see if I can figure out why she's on board. Seems less likely this is a coincidence and she's got a connection to our kind. Whether she is one or not remains to be seen. No one asks to go to Dead Island unless they're a hunter."

"Right," I quickly agreed, "and she's only got one bag. I don't think this girl is planning on staying around long which makes me suspicious."

"I'm on it," Ash replied as he left and made his way up on deck.

"Want me to talk to her?"

No fucken way. "I'll be the one to interact. You two gather what information you can. Perhaps you can distract her and see what's in her bag."

Kepp nodded, slapping me on the back as he rose from the chair. "Should I be worried you're gonna be tongue-tied in her presence?"

He ducked as I swung and missed him by more than a foot. "Smartass. Go on."

Kepp joined the others on deck as I inhaled a deep, calming breath. Something about Skye was familiar but I couldn't quite place where I'd seen her face before. Was she a hunter? I doubted it. She was dressed like all the rest of the vacationers with expensive jewelry, high-end clothing, and makeup— in the sweltering heat. Maybe I was making a snap decision based on her looks, but I'd be surprised if she was anything other than some spoiled rich chick who was used to having her way. Hell, I'd probably only recognized her because she was on some tabloid.

Deciding not to waste more time, I joined the crew on deck. Kepp was nowhere to be found but Ash was watching Skye with more than a passing interest. She didn't appear to be concerned around a trio of unknown men which made me wonder what her motivation was behind this trip. The more I watched her the more I noticed how carefully she regarded the world and how strangely she acted. Her eyes assessed everyone and everything with a calculating purpose. Her bag was never far from her side and she kept glancing at it like every possession she owned was inside. Sadness lingered more than once which made me want to hear her story.

Walking close, I ticked my head in her direction.

"So, Skye, is it?" I asked, intrigued enough to start up a conversation.

"Yes, Rhun, we established that when I stepped onto the Maiden's Virtue."

Fuck. The way she said my name made all the blood in my body travel south. I was sporting a hard-on so fast I may as well be fifteen again . . . and that was a good thirty years prior.

Rubbing the stubble on my chin thoughtfully, my gaze shifted across the deck as I attempted to gain control over my traitorous body. "Ash, you hear her say her name earlier?"

A grunt followed as he continued filleting fish and then ripped the skin from the flesh. He was playing his part well. I couldn't tell he was interested in her presence at all.

"I think I heard her," Kepp announced, walking onto the deck as naked as the day his mama had him.

Dammit.

Why the hell did he always try to piss me off? I asked him to distract our guest not try to show off his package. She gobbled up every square inch of his body too as I resisted the urge to roll my eyes like some preteen girl. He swaggered her way like he was modeling the goods and offering them for free. Fuck if she wasn't halfway interested in the idea. I saw her visible shiver that confirmed it.

Skye's eyes widened before she averted her gaze as Ash and I both chuckled at her blush.

"I'm taking a swim, Rhun. Back in a minute."

"Sure thing, Kepp."

I swear that boy was making me turn gray before my time. Hiding a sigh, I turned back to our passenger.

"Why do you want to travel to Dead Island?" My curiosity was too great to ignore. I needed to know why Skye was here and I didn't care if she took offense to my questions.

"I paid for passage, not secrets. If you require them before coming aboard you should let your customers know ahead of time."

I was dismissed like a naughty child and promptly ignored as she turned her back.

Pissed, annoyed, surprised, and completely turned on— I decided I would enjoy getting to know Skye on her return trip back to the mainland. That is if she didn't book another vessel after being pissed that we dropped her off at the wrong location. Maybe I'd wait around to see her reaction.

Kepp was back sooner than I thought, and he went below deck to dress. It wasn't long before we were gliding into the pier. I was distracted by the necessities of the boat and didn't notice Skye's escape.

Looking up, I realized she was gone.

"Where the fuck did that female go?" I wondered, tying off the boat with a heavy growl.

This trip was going to be more trouble than it was worth.

3

SKYE

I was on the wrong damn island.

Those sneaky bastards brought me here in the hope that I was bluffing.

Turning on my heel, I was back at the boat before they disembarked. "What the hell is going on?"

Rhun lifted his pretty pale green eyes from the water and shrugged. "You said you had your reasons. So do we."

Sarcastic bastard.

Inhaling and exhaling at least twice, I managed to calm down enough to apply reason. "Listen, if you lost the one person you loved most in this world, if they were savagely taken and murdered, would you do everything in your power to avenge their death?"

The three men stiffened and turned as one in my direction.

"Yes," Ash answered, speaking for the first time. "Get on the damn boat, Skye."

Relieved, I hopped back over and helped to untie the vessel so we could swing back out to sea. "Thank you," I finally answered, fighting back tears.

It wasn't long before we were back on open water.

Rhun took the rope I was twisting in nervousness from my

hands and guided me below deck until we stopped at the dinette. There was just enough room for the four of us. Sighing, I knew I would be expected to tell my story and I wasn't sure if I could. Too many emotions churned within and I lowered my head to my arms as they rested against the table.

"Who was it?"

I was pretty sure it was Ash that asked.

"My sister," I choked, lifting my head. "I'm going to that island and I'm going to kill every last one of those bloodsucking monsters. You can just drop me off. I don't plan on a return trip."

Silence filled the small space as I leaned back, crossing my arms.

"You're not Ginny's girl, are you?" Rhun swallowed hard. "Damn. I'm sorry, Skye. This would have been a much different trip if you'd told us who you were and why you needed passage."

I shrugged. "It doesn't matter. This is about revenge for my family. I don't know you or anything about you. Being a hunter is a lone job. You all know that. The amount of people I trust in this world I can count on one hand."

"We do," Ash admitted gruffly. "Trust is earned. No doubt about that." He shoved his hand through his thick hair and scowled. "You can't do this alone, honey. I'm not going to let you."

You don't have a choice, mister.

"That would be a costly mistake." My voice was so low and full of venom I hardly registered the sound. "Let me pass."

"No."

Stunned, I shot to my feet and shoved but the behemoth in front of me was a solid wall of muscle and caught my wrists faster than I could blink. "Stop. This is foolish. Dying won't bring her back."

He didn't know shit about my life or loss.

"Ash," I begged, "please. You have to let me do this."

"You didn't listen to my words. I said you weren't going *alone*."

My brain finally caught up to what he was suggesting, and I ceased all my struggles. His hold relaxed but he still held my body close. "You're coming?"

"We all are," Kepp intervened.

Right about the time he spoke was when I realized Rhun had asked about Ginny. His gaze locked on mine the second I turned in his direction. "She was like a mother to me and Serina."

He nodded. "Ginny loved you both. Never failed to talk about the beautiful young hunters who kicked ass and held their own. She was super proud and embellished more stories with us than you probably want to be revealed."

Dammit. Ginny always overshared, especially once she started drinking. Owning her own bar meant she had way more access than she needed.

"I don't think she had to embellish anything," Kepp declared, leaning forward until we were face to face. "You still ride that bull?"

His eyes smoldered as a wicked grin curved my lips. "Every Saturday night at Dark Horse."

"Fuck," Ash murmured, "you girls hold the title."

"What title?" Rhun asked, clearly annoyed.

Ginny's bar was aptly named the Dark Horse. Every weekend bar patrons lined up to ride her mechanical bull. The beast was massive, heavy, and mean as a hornet. He unseated everyone but me and Serina.

"Longest ride," I declared, winking at the big man as I ticked my head in his direction, "while drunk."

Kepp let out a wild howl and slapped the table as Ash broke out in laughter.

"Ginny taught us how to hold on to a bucking bull and we perfected her technique." Yeah, so my words were probably a little more sexual than I intended but the guys were riveted. "I hold the record."

"Must be the hips," Kepp declared as he licked his lips. "Damn, I can't believe we've never seen you as many times as we've been there."

"It *is* the hips and how you control them," I admitted, "but Ginny didn't like us out on the floor. I'm sure we've been there often at the same time. She usually asked us to stay in the party room. We only let our favorites in."

"Then when did you ride?"

"After hours."

The guys laughed as I pushed off the table and stood. No more wasting time. It was already dark, and the night was all we had. "I'm ready. Let's get to the island."

"Hold on, honey," Ash asked, "we don't have a plan."

"Don't need one," I assured him.

"I disagree," Rhun contradicted, "I won't allow you to be slaughtered on some wild half-cocked plan of revenge. This isn't your backyard. It's the fucken jungle, Skye."

Placing one hand on my hip, I poked a finger into his chest. "Don't get bossy. I know how to handle myself."

"That remains to be seen."

"Fuck off, Rhun."

His eyes narrowed. "Don't tempt me, *sweetheart*."

We were staring each other down almost nose to nose. He was a good six inches taller, but I lifted up on my tiptoes, so he didn't think I was intimidated. "Call me that again and you're going to regret it."

"Oh, I highly doubt that, *sugar*."

"I'm not your sweetheart or your sugar," I retorted.

"Not yet."

Blinking, I did a double-take. "What?"

Ash and Kepp were watching our showdown with interest.

"Don't make me spank your naughty little ass, Skye. I may

enjoy it far too much." With that, Rhun spun around and stomped up the stairs as I sank into his empty seat.

"What just happened?"

"Well, honey, you just had a little love spat with Rhun. He enjoyed it far too much and went off to rub one out," Ash declared, shaking his head with laughter.

Kepp placed his hand over mine. "I've never seen him get riled up over a woman. Watch out, little spitfire. He isn't messing around."

Sighing, I tossed them both an impatient look. "We should be serious. The island can't be far."

"It's not," Ash assured me, "I was only waiting on Rhun."

"Is he the one in charge?" Just my luck.

"Of course. No one takes a shit, bats an eye, or allows sexy little hunters on board without his permission."

"Wonderful," I muttered under my breath.

"Don't worry, baby. He's got nothin' on me," Kepp declared.

"Right," I laughed. "I'm going up. You two coming?"

Their heads shook in unison.

"We'll give you a minute."

"Wow, thanks, Ash." Traitor.

"You've got this, honey."

Clearly, he missed my sarcasm.

Rhun was busy digging around in a few bags that were open on the deck. Daggers, wooden stakes, spears, pistols, and about every other weapon you could imagine were contained within.

"That's quite an arsenal."

He didn't look up. "Protection is vital, especially if you want to survive."

No shit.

"I know that. I'm not stupid, Rhun."

"No one said you were but deciding to hand your life over to these hellspawns isn't going to change the fact that Serina is gone." He sighed, finally turning my way. "I speak from experience."

You're still a douche.

"I think we got off on the wrong foot . . ." I began.

"Nah, we're good." He turned back to the open duffel bags and started arming himself. Once he was done, he stood and sauntered my way with purpose. "Show me what you got."

"Now?"

"Yes."

"Forget it. I need to reserve my energy." Fighting Rhun was a bad idea. All that hard muscle combined with his attitude would surely be too much to handle. I'd rather focus on the damn bloodsuckers.

"I was talking about your weapons," he clarified, smirking as he folded his tree-trunk arms across his chest, "but if you think you can take me, sugar. Let's give it a try."

Oh, I was *soooo* tempted to knock him on his ass.

"Tell me you aren't planning to go hunting like this," he gestured, hand sweeping over my body with disapproval. "You're a walking disaster waiting to happen."

"Why? Because I dress with style?" I was teasing him, but he didn't know me well enough to figure it out. Shrugging out of the black jacket with ruched elbow sleeves, I set it aside followed by the layered silver necklaces I wore. My long top with lace details was next as I whipped out a hair tie and pulled my long dark hair up into a ponytail. The rest of my outfit was much more practical— black tank, dark jeans with a little stretch, boots that laced halfway up my calves, and armbands that secured additional throwing knives within easy reach. I strapped more blades to each thigh after I tightened the belt around my waist.

"I suppose I pass inspection now," I announced sarcastically. "Time to eradicate our enemy."

4

ASHER

WE DROPPED anchor and took a small dinghy to shore, approaching the coastline cautiously. Dead Island was named this way intentionally. It wasn't a joke.

Vampires had lived among the ruins for centuries, but they weren't the same monsters that lived in popular culture. No sparkles or compulsion that made women swoon at their feet. The bite wasn't an instant aphrodisiac and didn't make panties disintegrate with lust.

These hellspawn were vicious, feral, bloodthirsty creatures of horror.

The only desire was to feed. Once the task was completed, they moved on. Corpses piled up as necks were ripped into with malicious intent. No hint of humanity, remorse, or awareness remained. They weren't conscious of thought. No moral compass guided their choices. Vampires were created without a purpose. There was no reason they existed. Like a serial killer that kept attacking victims and raising the body count, vampires couldn't be allowed to wreak havoc and destruction. Their very existence was against nature.

Humanity didn't have a chance of survival without help.

A supernatural entity had to be created in order to eliminate the threat.

Enter the hunters.

Our one job since creation had been to fight against the paranormal creatures that threatened our world. We confronted and destroyed any beasts that harmed humans. It was our birthright. After centuries of conflict and war, our bloodlines evolved. As the creatures of night sharpened their skills, we developed our own unique skill set and abilities to counteract.

This was the way of the hunter.

A life of unrest and supreme sacrifice. All were prepared to meet their fate.

Most of us were lonely and often relationships never worked, even the ones that formed between fellow hunters. Our lives were too complicated, too unsettled. Emotions ran high. Jobs were difficult and stressful. Children born in this life often felt it was a curse. We roamed like gypsies and it wasn't an easy life.

Serina and Skye had experienced this firsthand.

Maybe I felt compassion, maybe it was the attraction. Whatever the reason, I felt compelled to protect Skye and keep her near. We were close to the same age and although she didn't remember, we had met once before. It was years ago now when her sister was still alive, and I'd entered the Dark Horse alone after a particularly nasty assignment.

"Hey there, handsome. What can I get you?"

"Something strong," I responded, slapping a few bills on the counter.

"Rough gig?"

"You could say that," I drawled, watching the way her jeans molded to her sexy ass as she turned around and reached for a glass.

She caught me as she spun around and winked, setting the bottle of rum on the bar.

"I think you could use the captain. He's great at keeping company."

Snorting, I picked up the shot and downed it, letting the warmth trickle down my throat and into the pit of my belly. "It's gonna take a lot more than that."

"Sounds like you need to unburden yourself. Usually I'm not the one to tend bar. That privilege belongs to the Duncan brothers but since Ginny is out and took them with her, I got stuck serving drinks and offering a friendly ear."

"My lucky day," I observed, taking a seat at one of the stools. "How come I haven't seen you around?"

"I don't like big crowds," she laughed, "and my sister and I are usually hunting."

"Ah," I nodded, understanding what she meant. "Where's your sister now?"

She hooked a thumb over her shoulder at the crowd throwing darts. "Winning, as usual."

The girl was a near replica of the beauty in front of me but didn't hold the same allure. "So, what's your name?"

"Skye," she answered, reaching out her hand as we shook. "Nice to meet you . . ."

"Asher," I filled in, "but my friends call me Ash."

"Well, Ash," she paused, and I nodded at the use of the nickname, "I'd say you have a lot of stories to tell. All I have is time. Care to settle in for a bit?"

Hell yes!

"Sure thing, honey. Ever corner a were during a full moon?"

Shaking her head, she glanced outside at the full moon. "That what your bad night is about?"

"Yep, got the wound to prove it, too." Lifting my shirt, I showed off the claw marks slashed across my torso. "Damn near cut into my innards."

She tsk'ed with her tongue and poured me another shot. "I'd say you need more than liquor."

"I do," I admitted, placing my hand over hers. "I'm not implying anything too serious, babe. You, me, that bottle, and a quiet corner to talk. What do you say?"

Shocked when she tossed down her towel and agreed, I led her into the corner booth where we talked, laughed, and told stories until nearly three a.m. Sad to see our time end, I leaned forward and pressed my lips to hers. I didn't know if it was the liquor or something more, but I felt that kiss deep down in my core and my head spun in response.

"Tell me, honey, if you want to take this further. I'm no mind reader."

She smiled softly and brushed her fingers over my cheek. "Ask me some other time, hero. I may just take you up on it."

I NEVER SAW her again no matter how many times I dragged Rhun and Kepp back to the bar. She seemed to have disappeared off the face of the earth. The guys were beginning to think I made the whole thing up. I missed her every night since. Fate had brought Skye back into my life and I wasn't about to squander the chance to initiate a little more this time.

"Why don't we split up?" I suggested, slipping my arm around her shoulders. "We can cover more ground and meet back here in a couple of hours."

Skye smiled, winking my way. "Sounds good to me." She checked her watch. "How about midnight?"

Rhun's lip curled as if he was fighting every instinct to agree. "Fine. Don't be late." He spun on his heel and stomped off in the opposite direction as Kepp smirked.

"Guess that means we're off."

Once we were alone, I moved my arm and gestured straight ahead. "After you, honey."

The island was mostly jungle but there were areas where

miles of grass led to the rocky cliff edge and then dropped to the sandy shore below. Lust vegetation grew everywhere and made it difficult to locate the vampire nests. Tropical and lush almost to the point of suffocation, the overgrown trees and vegetation.

We didn't get far before the first drops of moisture began to fall from the sky. Skye screeched as we rushed through the leaves and tried to find shelter. There wasn't much protection from the elements. Rainforests were typically wet year-round, and this island was no exception.

"Hey, what's that?"

Stumbling forward as the rain fell heavier, we managed to find what appeared to be the entrance to a cave.

"Careful. Let me go first," I ordered, pushing ahead as I pulled out my blade. "We don't know what we'll find."

Shivering, she nodded, brushing the extra water from her skin. "I'm right behind you."

Hardly a visible light, I ended up using the screen of my cell phone temporarily. Kepp had glow sticks and flashlights in his pack but I didn't want the light bright enough to betray our location. Who knew where the damn bloodsuckers made their dens on this godforsaken island?

Tugging on my arm, Skye pointed with a gasp, "Ash, look."

Tilting my head upward, I saw what she meant.

The entire ceiling was covered in bodies . . . and they were hanging *upside down*. Swinging lightly, they weren't moving. My heart hammered in my chest as I imagined every single one of those batshit crazy fuckers awakening all at once.

Shit.

"What's the matter with them?" Skye asked with a soft whisper, creeping closer.

My hand shot out before she could make a sound and awaken them prematurely. "Careful, they can still react to stimulus. They're in stasis."

"Sleeping?"

Nodding, I pulled her closer and lowered my head to whisper in her ear. "We don't want to push them into the next phase too quickly."

"What do you mean?"

"On the island, there's something here that keeps the vampires in this state. They don't fall into the same level of unconsciousness on the mainland. We've been keeping track and cross-referencing eye-witness accounts."

"Damn."

"We were planning on coming this weekend to find out more," I divulged. No point in keeping secrets between hunters. She needed to know all of the facts.

Skye's big brown eyes filled with sorrow and I knew she was thinking of her sister. "Their heightened awareness is longer than I remembered. When they attacked our compound, I saw a much different monster than the one who destroyed my parents and Ginny. I'm afraid they're evolving."

"They are, honey," I agreed. "It's the *nocturne*."

"I've heard that word before. Ginny talked about it a few times."

Her light fresh scent engulfed my senses as she turned, and our lips were only a few inches apart. For a split second, I nearly kissed her. "Do you know what it is?"

"Kind of. Bloodlust?"

My body became hyperaware of our close proximity as I swallowed before answering. "The feral, uncontrollable state of a vampire when consumed by bloodlust and lost in the vile pit of everlasting darkness. They are faster, stronger, more agile, and can use their power to seduce and manipulate us. As a result, they're nearly impossible to kill."

"Shit," she cursed. "That sounds like what happened to Serina."

"Why do you say that?"

"My sister didn't fight the bloodsucker who bit her so

savagely. She was drawn to him, mesmerized in a way I've never seen before. It was terrifying."

"Three years ago, right? The same time the vampire attacks increased."

"Yeah, do you know something?"

Shaking my head, I wasn't sure. "Just a suspicion. Maybe the *nocturne*, the increased attacks, and your sister's death are all related."

"Why would my sister be involved? That doesn't make sense." Her voice rose slightly, and I had to clamp my hand over her mouth as a few of the vermin wiggled above us.

"I'm only suggesting they could somehow be connected, nothing more."

Skye sagged against my chest, her head falling to my shoulder as I moved my hand away. "I dream about her every night. *Every single night*, Ash. It's pure torture."

Cupping her cheek, I brushed my thumb across her soft skin. "Grief is difficult to overcome. I know about such nightmares. I've had my fair share in the past."

"We can't let these creatures survive. We've got to kill them *all*."

I didn't tell Skye the reason why Rhun was so uptight was because he lost his own mother and sister to the same fate. His best friend Landon was murdered only a year later. Rhun took Landon's son Keppler and watched over him, training him as his father would have done. Years later, Rhun and Kepp were as close as brothers. The age difference only led to mutual respect and a high regard for one another. Rhun was determined to exact justice and seek revenge. We built up our arsenal and loaded my boat, a shared promise between the three of us.

We won't leave the island until every last one of these bloodsucking demons were destroyed.

5

SKYE

Scraping sounds on the rock from the vampire's talons could be heard as I leaned against Ash, taking comfort in his warmth and compassion. He was quieter than the other two but no less flirtatious when the mood seemed to strike. His breath was always laced with a hint of cinnamon, but I never noticed if he was hiding a stick of gum in his mouth or if he gargled that flavor intentionally. His blue eyes were like dark pits of ocean blue and sparkled often with mischief. He enjoyed teasing his fellow hunters and I felt a bit silly thinking they were all brothers in the beginning.

Thick red hair fell nearly to his shoulders and I couldn't help the thought that he reminded me quite a bit of that handsome actor who played the part of the Scottish character Jamie in Outlander. Ash was ruggedly handsome with firm muscles that bunched under the skin as he moved and a strong jawline with a light dusting of stubble. He was paler than the other two but no less attractive.

In fact, he was the most dashing of the three.

Rhun was arrogant and grumpy, full of pride. Kepp, a bit too playful and somewhat of a practical joker. I could tell much about their individual personalities already. Ash, he was the most intellectual of the bunch. He internalized what happened around him with a fiercely protective and offensive stance. I liked his firm but gentle nature. Ash made me feel safe in a way that I hadn't in a long time.

"We should rendezvous with Rhun. He'll want to know what we found."

Ash made sure I exited the cave first as he stayed close by my side and watched for any sign that the vampires in stasis were awakening.

"You know, I can't help wondering what the deal is with Rhun." I didn't think Ash was surprised that I asked.

Chuckling, his piercing gaze met mine for a few heart-stopping seconds. "He's had it rough. It's his story to tell but let's just say he understands your pain on a level that I wish to never experience."

"His family?"

"Yes," Ash confirmed sadly. "Don't hold too much against him."

"I won't," I promised. "Thanks, Ash."

We were silent a few minutes as we made our way back toward the others. Thinking back to the first time we met, I decided to approach the subject since he hadn't indicated that he remembered. That kiss we shared was far too sensual and erotic to forget. I had missed him since that night in Dark Horse.

Maybe I just wanted to find my hero. Maybe I needed something to anchor all my hate since my sister died. All I knew was that I loathed secrets, lies, and situations that made me uncomfortable.

"Are you going to pretend like we didn't meet and kiss at Dark Horse the entire time we're on this damn island?"

He faltered, his feet nearly tripping over one another. "I was under the impression you forgot."

"Nope," I contradicted, "in fact, I'm trying to remember why we only ended up kissing."

A slow wide grin lifted his lips. "Too drunk? Too sober? I'm not sure."

Chuckling, I shook my head. "I think I was too nervous."

"And now?"

My lips curved upward in an impish grin. "I'm not."

Stopping, I tugged him closer as my fingers gripped the material of his shirt and lifted up on my tiptoes. The memory of that night and his kiss was seared into my brain. I wanted to experience his passion again. I needed to feel the strength of his arms and the security of his embrace. Heat infused my core and for a moment I wanted to leave the reality behind that I may be dead by morning.

Ash didn't hesitate but lowered his head and captured my lips with the experience and desire of a man who knew what he wanted and was used to having his way. His kiss dominated my mouth as our tongues collided and I was roughly pressed up against something hard. I was too distracted to notice if it was the trunk of a tree or something else. His grip was nearly painful, but it was the way his body molded to mine that caused the moan to surface from deep in my throat.

I *wanted* Ash.

If I survived this night, I'd be sure to finish what we started.

"Skye," he murmured huskily, "if we make it off this island, you're *mine*."

I didn't care if it was only a promise of hot sex, for once I wanted to give in to my desires. I'd been closed off and numb for years, fighting against any and all emotion in order to forget the loss of my sister and Ginny and the truth that their deaths had been the single most traumatic experience of my life. Loneliness ate away at my insides until I forgot what it was like to share a moment with another soul. Ash reminded me it was okay to let a little happiness in again. As long as I didn't forget my purpose.

"You got it, handsome."

He grinned wickedly and reached for my hand, pulling us

away from the large fronds and overgrown vegetation that made it impossible to walk without great effort. I was grateful it was dark and not the middle of the day. The humid air was stifling but I could imagine it was probably sweltering with the combination of the sun. With nothing but the moon and stars to guide us, I was still sweaty thanks to the humidity. The jeans weren't helping but I refused to remove them.

Rhun was pacing as we arrived and growled when he saw our entwined hands. I couldn't pretend that sound didn't do naughty things to my insides, but I wasn't going to act like Ash and I did anything wrong. After all, I would kiss whoever I damn well pleased.

Kepp tilted his head to the side, glancing at our hands and shaking his head. "I'm jealous."

"Shut up, Kepp."

Rhun turned his back and walked away, leaving for a good ten minutes before he came back more composed. "What did you find?"

"Caves, and plenty of them. Damn bloodsuckers are in stasis."

"That's what we found, Ash." Kepp shook his head. "Damn near woke them up when the rain started."

"We didn't, though, which is good," Rhun added, "vampires like those dark caves. Best place for a nest on the whole island. They're fairly safe dangling from the ceiling."

"Not for long," I interjected. "I say we torch them all."

Ash laughed. "We need to take them out, but we also need a plan. We don't know enough about this island. It's time we explored a little more, so we aren't making decisions based on incomplete information. Rhun?"

"I think we should split off again. This island is huge and there's no way we covered every inch of it yet. We need to map out the locations and number of bloodsuckers in each hive. I don't want to miss a nest later."

Rhun was right. Feeling foolish for ever thinking I could do this alone, I swallowed hard and met his frown. "I never considered the island to be such a vast breeding ground. It's terrifying to think I could have been here alone."

Rhun opened his mouth to reply but Kepp beat him to it.

"Hey, Skye, come with me this time."

Kepp reached for my hand and I took it, stepping back into the wild unknown.

6

KEPPLER

"How many caves did you find with Ash?"

"Only one," Skye admitted, "but I have a feeling there's a lot more if you found one with Rhun."

"We found two, but I think you're right. I'm worried about how many of these fuckers are gonna get loose when they wake up. How long does stasis last? We're still not sure."

This was still in the information gathering stage. We didn't know nearly enough about the vampires and their nests, how stasis affected their hunting and feeding habits, or how they fell under the *nocturne* frenzy.

"Best idea is to assume it's a lot. I just don't want to run into them all if they're *nocturne*."

I snorted as if the idea was funny. "Can you imagine Rhun's reaction? I bet he'd lose his shit."

Laughing, Skye shrugged. "I think we'd be too busy running for our lives."

"You're right about that. Hundreds of bloodsuckers all hell bent on my destruction? I'm gone!"

The first cave we found was similar to the two I had located with Rhun. "Is this like the cave you found with Ash?"

"Yep, right down to the creepy vampires sleeping upside

down and the sickly smell of bat shit."

Attempting to hide my humor and remain quiet, I shook my head. "They sure do stink."

"Rot and death," she agreed.

The hair on the back of my neck began to prickle as I gazed around inside. "This is going to sound weird, but . . . I feel like we're being watched."

"Let's finish what we came here for and then get out."

Outside the cave, we documented our findings and continued on, trekking through the rainforest in the dead of night as if it was perfectly normal and logical to be doing so. It wasn't too much longer before we found a sloping incline and followed it down to a ravine. At the bottom of a hill was a muddy embankment full of discarded leaves and debris. We followed alongside until the ground gave way and we nearly fell into a hollow pit. I grabbed Skye's arm just in time as she clutched at my body frantically.

"I almost died!"

Smirking, I held her close. "No, but it would have been painful when you landed." Grabbing a flashlight from my pack, I turned it on low and swept the light over the ground. The pit was covered in human bones and the remnants of a recent meal. Corpses with mangled bits of hair and ripped, dirty clothing were pressed up against the sides.

"Shit," she cursed.

"That's a fucken graveyard," I gulped, gesturing to all the bodies. "Damn bloodsuckers."

"Sticking around here is a bad idea. I don't care if they're all supposed to be sleeping or not."

"You're right."

"I'm going to make a few notes while I can see with your flashlight."

"Alright." I gave her a minute and then stowed the flashlight back in my pack as we used the moon to guide our way to safety.

"This is crazy, Kepp. What the hell was I thinking? I never should have come to this damn island."

"Hey," I remarked gently, grabbing her chin and tilting her head up. "This is what we do. Hunters are born to eradicate our enemy. You're not alone and you're going to get through this. We *all* will," I assured her.

Skye leaned forward and pressed her cheek over my heart as her arms encircled my waist. "You're sweet. Thanks, Kepp."

Clearing my throat, I squeezed her tight before letting go. "I think we should head back. We've got more than enough information to share." Scratching the side of my head, I rubbed my hand over the short length of dark hair. "I'm worried. Bloodsuckers are most active at night. They're nocturnal creatures by nature. Why are they in stasis for so long?"

"It doesn't make sense," Skye agreed, "and I have a bad feeling."

"Yeah."

Sighing, I led the way to our rendezvous point but stopped to mark another cave on our makeshift map. Seven in total over the last few hours. The entire island was a maze of caves and inlets. Each one was filled with a nest and almost all were equidistant from the next. I found the spacing an interesting fact. Were they deliberately created a certain distance from the next hive? Would stretching the distance compromise their safety?

Rhun and Ash were talking low as we approached, both their expressions tense. I didn't know what they were discussing but I could guess it had something to do with the sexy little hunter next to my side. Whatever the drama, I didn't give a shit. I wasn't getting involved. Right now, any argument was unimportant.

"We need a plan. Things don't add up and we don't have a lot of time."

"Well, we could always try to take out one of the nests," Ash offered.

"That's risky," Rhun growled, "what if they all awaken at the same time? There are hundreds of the bastards, more than we originally thought."

"What I don't understand," I added, glancing at each one in turn, "is how these vampires are being made. Bloodsuckers aren't born, they're *created*."

Skye's eyes widened. "You're right. I don't know why I didn't think of that earlier. There has to be someone creating new offspring."

"Exactly," I agreed. "We need to find out what's happening before we expose ourselves. There's no other option. If we fail and the whole island is awakened . . ." I paused, shaking my head, "it could be disastrous for the mainland."

"Hundreds of vampires unleashed all at once," Ash added. "Kepp is right. We need to search harder. We're missing something."

The crunching of leaves drew our attention as we all silenced.

A deeply disturbing presence could be felt as it approached but it wasn't entirely vampire nor was it human. The skin on the back of my neck began to tingle again and I jumped in front of Skye as Ash crouched low next to my side. Rhun pulled out his double blades and stood ready.

We were prepared for battle . . . but not the shocking revelation to come.

A young woman that bore a striking resemblance to the feisty and beautiful hunter that joined our group emerged from between the trees. Something about her wasn't quite right. It was only when her lips parted, and I spotted her gleaming fangs that I understood.

A horrified scream launched from Skye's throat as her long-lost sister stood in front of us, her wicked smile proof she was no longer the hunter her sister once knew.

"Hello, Skye."

7

SKYE

"Serina," I whispered, shocked, appalled, and horrified by her transformation.

"I was beginning to wonder if you'd ever venture this far. The effort to bring you here was exhausting."

Taking a deep breath, I hoped to calm my anxiously beating heart. "What effort?"

"All those nightmares. The pain was positively . . . *delicious.*"

Startled, I began trembling with the knowledge that I had been manipulated from the moment the vampires attacked our compound. A calculating and devious plan had continued to wreak havoc on my life ever since, but I never ever would have thought that my sister would join their ranks.

"You were dead," I accused, "and it seems that fact hasn't changed."

The smile that curved her blood-red lips sent a chill down my spine. "How good of you to notice. Don't you think, honey?"

To say I felt betrayed by the man who approached and slid his arm around her waist was an understatement. Glenn Foster — the hunter who supposedly helped to bury my sister's body

— stood exactly as I remembered except for the matching fangs.

"Hello, sexy. You're as ravishing as I remember."

His words were meant to rile me up, but I wasn't rising to the bait. "I can't say the same."

Sickened by the knowledge that my sister had become a creature of the night, I was so overwhelmed with emotion that I wasn't thinking clearly. I wanted to wrap my hands around Glenn's throat and cut off his ability to speak as he whispered poisonous words in her ear.

"Charming as this reunion is, I need to borrow my sister. Won't you come along, dear?"

"I'm not going anywhere with you."

Rhun angled his body so that he would take the brunt of any surprise attack. "You'll have to kill all of us first."

Serina smiled as she sauntered forward, swinging her hips seductively as she approached Rhun. He didn't back down, but I could see the tension in his jaw. "That's the plan. Of course, it would be a lot more fun if you struggle."

"Please struggle," Glenn laughed, hissing as he bared his fangs. "I enjoy playing with my food."

Pushing through Ash and Kepp, I made the only reasonable choice. If I could spare others suffering, I would do so. The guys had a chance at freedom if I didn't cause a scene. "I'll go. The others will leave the island and never return."

Kepp protested but Ash shoved him back. "Is this what you want, Skye?"

Nodding, I kept my focus solely on the two vampires directly in front. Raw emotion threatened to surface but I wouldn't let the shock and horror take root. I tried not to think of the last three years and the painful realization that I had mourned for Serina when all along she'd been living as a monster. A bloodsucker. My greatest enemy.

Betrayal caused my heart to harden. The woman before me wasn't my sister. Any feelings that I felt were for the hunter who was now destroyed. Inhaling deeply, I focused on what mattered— stopping her any way that I could.

"Delightful. Aren't you all so accommodating?"

The sarcasm in her voice grated on each and every one of my nerves. Serina had been a sweet-tempered girl and was rarely sarcastic or rude. This foreign body was nothing like my sister. Further proof that the vampire I would destroy wasn't someone I loved. It would make this easier when the moment came.

"Lead on. I'm ready," I replied stiffly, letting the last of my sorrow fade way.

Glenn and Serina laughed as they linked arms and began to walk away from the group. I didn't acknowledge the guys because I knew they would do what was necessary. My sacrifice didn't matter. This wasn't about one single individual. Hunters knew that our lives were on borrowed time. The only thing that mattered was destroying these bastards before they had a chance to leave the island. If my death could save thousands, I would gladly bear that burden.

I never heard Rhun, Ash, or Kepp leave but I did notice when I was completely alone.

Serina and Glenn began moving so quickly I couldn't keep up, even when I ran. Their laughter echoed among the trees and hid their presence in shadows. The night wasn't my friend.

Keeping on a straight path through the trees and overgrown jungle, it wasn't long before I spotted torches set up along the ground. My feet became more cautious as I followed the amber lights deeper into the hidden wild. The sounds of night should have accompanied my lonely trek, but eerie silence was all that followed the billowing smoke and flickering flames to my left and right.

I couldn't help but feel like I was being corralled to a specific location. Every instinct in my body insisted that I flee before it was too late. Hunters could feel the presence of immortals and easily detected when a vile or evil entity was nearby. My entire body was attuned to the fact that I wasn't alone. The fine hairs on the back of my neck tickled as I kept vigilant.

Attacking now would be a brilliant strategy of the enemy.

I was alone, vulnerable, and tired from the long and endless night. My feet were beginning to throb from being in my boots so long and my body needed nourishment. Thankfully I still had water in my canteen, but I would soon finish it off.

Up ahead a shadow had emerged. As I drew closer, I could see the figure was a man. He seemed to wait patiently until I was close enough and then a dazzling smile transformed his stoic features. Sensual green eyes sparkled like emeralds and met my own before they dropped to devour my entire body, stripping my clothes from my body in a way that made my knees weaken.

"Welcome, Skye Colt. I've been waiting a long time to meet you."

8

RHUN

"You're a dick, Rhun."

Ignoring Ash, I grabbed the edge of the dinghy and started pushing it out into the water.

"Hey," Kepp yelled, standing on shore with his fists at his sides. "I'm not alright with leaving her behind."

"Me either," Ash added, glaring my way.

Sighing, I ticked my head toward the beach. "Don't be stupid. Get in the damn boat."

Neither listened. Swearing under my breath, I tried to keep my voice low. "We need a strategy. *Let's go*," I emphasized.

Ash seemed to finally understand what I meant. "Like Chebeague Island?"

Finally, he was clued in. Chebeague Island was close to Maine and another hive of bloodsuckers we'd exterminated a few years ago. We had to leave the island by ferry to gather supplies and return to eradicate those who were left behind. It wasn't the size of the nests we found here but just as dangerous.

Our eyes met and I nodded. "Yes."

Kepp relaxed and helped to push the small boat out far enough that we could haul ourselves inside. Once a little distance had been reached between us and the island, I finally spoke up.

"Look, there's no logical explanation for the way shit just went down. Why the fuck did Serina Colt show up out of nowhere? How in the hell is she a vampire? Aren't either of you suspicious?"

Kepp held up his hand. "Are we rescuing Skye or not?"

Fucking hell. Don't they understand a damn thing?

"Yes," I growled, trying not to think of how she might suffer before we returned. "That's not up for debate."

Kepp visibly relaxed. "Then I don't care what the plan is," he gulped hard, "As long as we get our little spitfire back."

Blinking, I didn't think about how she affected each one of us until this moment. "She *is* ours."

Ash chuckled, shaking his head. "Damn, Rhun. I thought you'd never admit it."

"We can talk to her about it later. Just so you both know; I'm staking a claim. All three of us. No reason to argue about it."

Ash and Kepp both sat up straighter and I took that as confirmation of my words.

"Right now," I continued, "I'm more concerned with what's happening on that island."

"Like the fact that vampires are mindless drones who kill and feed without mercy, yet Serina and Glenn seem to be some evolved version that allows their human personalities, intelligence, and cognitive awareness to remain. That's not something we've discovered before now."

Ash was right.

"Yes, that's new. I want to know why they need Skye. It doesn't make sense to keep her alive. Humans serve no purpose for vampires other than a food source. Why not kill us all?"

"Exactly. We were allowed to escape which leads me to believe that it doesn't matter if they killed us on the island or not." Kepp stroked his chin as he spoke, his brows bunching together as he frowned. "There's only one explanation that makes sense. The fucken bloodsuckers don't care if we escaped because they aren't staying on that island."

"I hate to agree but you're right. All the caves, the nests, the vampires in stasis— they're creating an army." Ash slammed his hand down on the seat in frustration. "We have to go back and destroy those hives before they unleash on the mainland. It'll be a goddamn massacre."

Our job as hunters was to prevent this exact scenario from happening. "We need to call in a few favors. Once we're back on the Maiden's Virtue, I want you to use the satellite phone and warn our fellow hunters, Kepp."

He nodded; his expression grim.

"Ash, we need a plan on how we're eliminating those nests. We're also going to need plenty of distractions. Do we still have all those firecrackers?"

"Yep, stored safely below deck. I'll gather them up."

"Good." Rubbing the back of my neck, an idea began to form. "How much explosives do we have? Enough to collapse all the cave entrances?"

Ash's grin widened. He was the demolition expert among us and kept inventory on all our supplies. "We should. Are you suggesting we bury all those bloodsuckers? I don't think it will work, not for long."

"If we leave Greek fire in the nests and set up the explosives, they should ignite all at the same time," I suggested.

"In theory. If some of the canisters don't explode then we haven't successfully destroyed the bastards, only delayed the inevitable and seriously pissed them off. If they go *nocturne*, we're in deep shit," Ash admitted, "but I think it's worth the chance to see what happens. We still don't know how these caves are connected."

"Or how the hives are connected," Kepp added. "Are they all on the same central hub? Will killing one awaken them all? It's a risk we have to take."

"Then that's the plan," I decided. "Except for Skye. We risk harming her by taking care of the nests first, but I don't see how there's another option."

"If we go after her first, then the bloodsuckers all awaken, we've doomed us all. She's strong and she's smart," Kepp acknowledged, "and she's a fierce hunter. Skye knows we have to take out the nests first. She'll be counting on that."

"I agree." Ash sighed, scrubbing his hand across his face. "Skye will be expecting us to remove all threats before we come for her. It's how she was raised. Ginny taught those girls everything she knew."

"Precisely why a part of me thinks this is a trap. Serina was a hunter, too."

The silence grew between us as we approached the Maiden's Virtue.

Kepp was the one to speak first. "There's not another option. We have to proceed with the plan. Eliminate the enemy and remove all barriers to success, one at a time. I don't see how we've got a chance if we don't exterminate those vermin first."

"That's the problem," Ash conceded, "we aren't seeing the big picture. That's the most disturbing of all. Whatever Serina has planned, it involves her sister, those nests, and a missing piece we have no idea about. We're flying blind and that shit is dangerous."

"Then we watch our backs, stay sharp, and be ready for anything. We've got a better chance of survival if we move quickly and efficiently. Let's move our vessel farther down the coast of the island. We need to gather our supplies and get back onshore as soon as possible."

Time to enact phase one.

9

SKYE

SOMETHING about the powerful man who stood before me was creepy and unnerving. While easily handsome and charming to a fault, his presence pushed in on my body and bullied it until I was close enough to reach out and touch him if I so desired. He wore an expensive tailored black suit with a crisp white button-down shirt that gaped a little at the top and revealed the attractive luster of his skin. The scent of cherry and whiskey combined with a clean scent that was nearly intoxicating and tugged on my senses. His dark hair was long and swept back in a way that seemed to focus on his mesmerizing gaze.

Nearly tongue-tied, I refused to speak.

"I'm Edmondo," he purred, his voice a seductive and deep lure that could reach out and catch almost any female he wanted. "Welcome to my island."

Tilting my head to the side, I contemplated his words before speaking. "Interesting. I thought this island belonged to all of the bloodsuckers."

His warm chuckle released into the air and surrounded my slender frame with physical fingers that stroked along my skin as they caressed every exposed inch. He was pure sin. A wet dream.

And a powerful vampire.

"You do not disappoint, love. Please," he gestured, "follow me for some refreshment."

I knew he wanted me to walk ahead but I refused and ignored his obvious disapproval as he glided further almost hovering above the ground until the path ahead opened onto a wide grassy field. The perfectly manicured lawn was a stark contrast to the rainforest that lay only a few yards away in any direction, leading all the way to the coast. The scent of salt and fresh flowers tinged the air with a fragrant bloom.

It wasn't the change in scenery that grasped my attention but the gothic castle that suddenly appeared, looming down upon us as we approached. Circular towers reached upward from the left and right sides as the stone structure beckoned like some dark apparition in the night.

Wide-eyed, I couldn't help my reaction.

How was such beauty hidden from the world? Some ancient form of magic? A glamour?

"I see you have an appreciation for luxury, as do I."

"Of course, I'm not blind."

"No, certainly not, love. I would be rather disappointed if you were."

He led the way around the vast estate until we reached a deck that overlooked the ocean and what I could only assume was a breathtaking view in the light of day. Tables had been erected beneath strands of twinkling white lights that dangled by loops far above my head. Laden with multiple dishes of cuisine, fresh fruits and vegetables, and an ice sculpture of a mermaid. Everything was bright and delectable, full of color and tempting.

I wondered why the mermaid didn't melt in the heat and humidity...

"You seek to entice me?" I asked as he turned my way. "Why, Edmondo?"

He growled lightly at my use of his name and brushed his fingers across my cheek. "Turnabout is fair play, is it not?"

"What are you saying?" His tendency to speak in riddle was annoying already.

"You're completely irresistible, pet. I find it hard to keep my distance."

Snorting with mild humor, I met his smoldering gaze and didn't turn away. "I imagine that's the case with all living, breathing humans. Blood is your lifeline."

He laughed, sweeping me into his arms as soft music began to filter into the air. A perfect gentleman and a fantastic dance partner, he was playing a dangerous game with his planned and obvious seduction.

"You're positively delicious in every way."

"I bet you say that to all the girls," I murmured, mildly amused. I couldn't help thinking he was the best actor I'd ever met. Talented and determined, he was frighteningly charismatic.

"Only to the ones I want to devour," he admitted with a wink. "You, love, are entirely above them all."

"How flattering," I replied, playing along, "but hardly convincing."

"How shall I prove it?" He swept me over to an empty seat and bowed, kissing my hand as he backed away. "Maybe a little entertainment?"

I was certain our idea of entertainment was nothing alike.

"If you must." Why provoke him by refusing? There was nothing to be gained by making him angry and everything to learn if he continued his playful game.

"Oh, I insist, Skye," he rumbled, his eyes glowing brighter. "I've yet to truly begin."

The use of my name was purposeful. "As you wish."

Maybe I was suspecting bloody bodies or ravenous

vampires to flood the area and to suddenly be attacked but I was shocked when a troop of gypsy performers began to dance, juggle, breathe fire, and enthrall me with their performance. For a moment, I forgot that this was nothing but a ruse. I relaxed against my seat only to be startled by Edmondo's voice next to my ear. He'd moved behind me so swiftly and secretly that I hadn't noticed. On his knees, he began whispering intimately.

"Aren't they enjoyable?"

The dancers chose partners of the opposite sex and were soon grinding against one another, rubbing and caressing as the scene before me changed and the air filled with lust and desire. Moans of rapture could be heard as the couples stripped. Hands and mouths sought pleasure from their partner as a literal orgy soon consumed the scene.

"I admit," he purred, "I'm incredibly aroused. What about you, love?"

I saw no purpose in what he was trying to accomplish other than stalling for time. Immediately on the defensive, I rose to my feet and spun, shoving a finger into his chest. "I think we've had enough games tonight."

"I politely disagree." One hand rose and, in the light, I caught the long black nails that were carefully filed into points. "Come, let us find our own amusement. Maybe a glass of wine is in order."

I refused. He brought a chilled goblet to my chair anyway.

"Sit, Skye. We have much to discuss."

"I'm tired of this. Get to the point, *vampire*."

He rose and sat to my left; his lips quirked up in amusement. "You have one of the strongest wills I have ever encountered," he admitted, tapping his raised fingers against one another, "I simply love the challenge."

"I can see that," I replied dryly.

"A shame you have no patience. We could have had a grand evening."

"I'm sure your definition and mine are quite different."

"You must learn to control your impulses, love. The rewards are worth the wait."

"Do you speak from experience?" I taunted, placing the untouched goblet on the table. "Or are you simply philosophical as well as delusional?"

Yeah, pissing him off was a bad idea. At this point, I didn't care.

Something had to give, and I wasn't going to be distracted from the truth or my sister any longer.

10

ASHER

"I guess it's now or never," I surmised, a grim smile on my lips. Thoughts of Skye took center stage in my head and I hoped she was alright.

Hold on, honey. We're coming.

Rhun picked up his bag and slung it over his shoulder. "Once your designated caves have been collapsed, we meet back here. If you have any trouble, contact via the walkie talkie. Emergency use only. Got it?" He passed them out and switched his on. "I'm on two."

The batteries should last long enough to take care of business. Dawn was only a few hours away now. The sunrise would bring safety as it prevented the bloodsuckers from hunting. The old tales were true in that regard. Vampires literally combust in the sunlight, right after they begin to sizzle and burn. It's morbidly fascinating.

Kepp and I agreed with Rhun and set our walkie talkies to the same frequency as the three of us separated. I had the east side of the island and the trip was difficult if not downright impossible. The moon had nearly disappeared behind the clouds and the temperature was starting to rise the closer we came to sunrise. Sweat dripped in places I didn't want to think about. I'd long since ditched a shirt but I was still hot and uncomfortable. We filled our canteens and had a quick snack on the boat so at least I wasn't starving or dehydrated.

My main concern was Skye. She never ate all evening or night and that would weaken her considerably. Maybe she had something in her bag. It was possible.

Don't give up, little spitfire.

The first cave was emptier than I remembered but I set up the Greek fire and left the canisters in place as I added the explosives and backtracked to the entrance. More explosives were added outside and in strategic spots that would ensure the whole area collapsed. Wiping sweat from my brow, I picked up my pack and headed to the next location on my map.

The following two caves were more of the same. Bloodsuckers in stasis and eerie silence. An uneasy feeling began to grow, and I couldn't place the source. Was I worried about Skye? Or was there something else causing my senses to heighten?

I couldn't shake the feeling that I was being watched and observed. What if someone was only waiting for me to walk away in order to dismantle the explosives? What if the humidity caused them to malfunction?

Once my five caves were done, I made my way back and checked each cave one more time to be sure nothing had been tampered with. Everything appeared the same, no different than when I left. I noticed the damn bloodsuckers were still sleeping peacefully and although they moved occasionally didn't appear to be aware of my presence.

Fucken vermin.

Nothing left but to return to Kepp and Rhun, I made my way to our rendezvous point. I was the first to arrive. Kepp was next, sweat dripping down the side of his face as he cursed under his breath.

"Like a goddamn sauna."

Chuckling, I had to agree.

Rhun arrived shortly after and he seemed the coolest, calmest, and collected of us all. He didn't hesitate to issue the command we waited to hear. "Let's get these bastards. On my count . . . five, four, three, two . . . now!"

Each of us dialed our cellphones at the same time and the simultaneous electrical current was enough to jolt a small detonator charge, which in turn set off the main explosives that we planted. It was a fairly simple bomb. The cellphones were excellent triggers. I'd done it before when I set off fireworks at home. If you knew technology, this didn't take more than a few extra parts and about ten minutes to modify.

A series of small booms could be heard as the ground rumbled beneath our feet.

Triple grins appeared on each of our faces as we realized our success.

"Now," Rhun announced, "time to make sure all those caves are indeed collapsed. We go together this time. I don't want anyone ambushed alone."

About ninety percent of the caves had successfully collapsed. We could hear the screeching inside more than one as the bloodsuckers were burned into a crisp. The caves would become their tombs and I didn't care about their suffering. The creatures deserved their fate.

Good riddance.

Two caves were only partially collapsed. One was nearly untouched.

The two partially collapsed tombs had vampires screeching as they tried to escape the Greek fire that had successfully lit inside. Rhun pulled more explosives from his pack and manually lit them as we scrambled away. The two caves were buried within a few seconds as the vampires were successfully trapped inside. The Greek fire would finish them off within minutes.

We crept up to the final cave and listened for any sign that the bloodsuckers had awakened. It was far too quiet.

"I think we should go in," I suggested, "there's no reason to think they're awake if the Greek fire canisters didn't explode."

"Unless they're all connected, as we thought," Kepp interjected.

"Right," I mumbled, temporarily forgetting that crucial detail.

Rhun clasped a hand on my shoulder. "No worries. Proceed cautiously. We don't know what we'll find, and I don't want any surprises."

Rhun led the way inside as we kept close to the cavern walls and tried not to give away our location. Vampires had heightened senses which meant their ability to hear was so fine they could discern a crunching leaf miles away. A large boulder partially blocked our passage and we carefully slid through the small gap. The cave was so dark I could barely see in front more than a few inches. My eyes adjusted but it wasn't enough. I didn't dare use my phone.

Noises like light fluttering could be heard above as we approached the nest.

Rhun was moving around and I knew he was gathering the Greek fire canisters that littered the ground. There was no point in leaving them. We liked to keep a sizable inventory in case of emergency. He stopped next to my side as I heard his low even breathing.

Rhun or Kepp reached out and tugged on my sleeve. I knew what they were saying. The bloodsuckers were waking up. Mild screeching echoed from above.

Shit.

They had to be connected. This was confirmation. All those dying bloodsuckers were communicating with the ones still in stasis.

I did the only thing I could think of at that moment. I shoved Rhun and Kepp back as I shouted, "run!"

Lighting a row of firecrackers, I threw them up in the air, not realizing I had also lit something else.

"Was that a stick of dynamite?"

"Fuck!" Rhun yelled as he scrambled backward, and we all tripped over one another in our haste.

"Holy shit!"

The firecrackers went off the same moment as the stick of dynamite ignited. The only thing I could think of was getting the hell out of there before we ended up in little pieces. If the Greek fire had been on the ground, we all would have been ignited and not even running to the ocean would douse those flames.

I was a fucken idiot.

Popping noises combined with the rattling and exploding sounds were almost deafening. The cave lit up as the bodies of the bloodsucking demons burst into pieces above our head. Blood, goo, and body parts rained down upon our heads as Rhun and Kepp cursed and tried to run away from the disgusting mess. Shaking my head, I stayed put and lifted my bag over my head until the last of the carnage had hit the ground.

Thinking it was safe, I removed the bag and lifted my head in time to have a splat of vampire innards land directly on my face. I might have hurled my guts out if my mouth had been open. As it was, I dry heaved and slumped against the cavern wall, cursing my luck.

"Are you fucking kidding me?" I grumbled, wiping the guck from the eyes. "A bloodsucker shower."

Kepp chuckled, shaking his head, and then began laughing louder until Rhun and I joined in. "This is priceless. Somebody take a pic with your cell. Dude, we need to have this as a memento."

Rhun snapped a couple of 12-hour emergency light sticks that glowed an eerie grin and swiped across his phone. A few seconds later we were immortalized forever covered in exploded bloodsuckers.

"Skye is going to wonder what the hell we've been doing," I noted with humor.

"We need to find her. Something tells me she's in danger and we should hurry."

Rhun's words focused our attention and we left the cave, running through the jungle as if our asses were on fire as we searched for any sign of our sexy hunter friend.

Rows of torches could be seen up ahead as my gut churned. It could be a trap and nearly always was when it came to hunting supernaturals. "This way!" I shouted as I ran ahead.

It wasn't long before we found a hidden trail that led to a vast property— complete with a foreboding gothic castle. Turrets and spires twisted upward as the entire thing seemed to growl menacingly in our direction.

"What the fuck?" Kepp wondered aloud.

I didn't slow down, too concerned about Skye.

Female cries of rage and screaming drew my attention as I rounded the corner and found a sacrificial altar with twin stone pillars on each side looming directly ahead. Chained and bloody, the Colt sisters were at the mercy of a group of bloodsuckers, one clearly the leader as he turned and snarled, fangs gleaming in the firelight where a bowl of churning blood seemed to bubble and gurgle beneath hovering flames.

11

SKYE

"Delusional?" Edmondo laughed, his gaze piercing mine almost to the point of pain. "I do believe you're becoming grumpy, Skye. Would you like some refreshment? Something to nibble on?"

Like my neck?

The wine glass was pushed back in my direction, but I declined. "No, thank you."

"You make it difficult to be a good host. Is there nothing I can do to show my sincerity?"

Not really.

"Call my sister and end this charade."

"So soon?" He clucked his tongue in disappointment. "I rather enjoy keeping you to myself."

"All good things must come to an end, right? Pleasure can't dictate every moment, or we would be lost inside ourselves endlessly," I announced with a wink, catching him off guard. My intent was to keep him guessing and uncertain and hoped I was succeeding. The guys would need time to destroy those nests and all the vampires hidden within the caves.

"You see with the eyes of a discerning soul," he murmured,

picking up my hand and caressing the top of my skin. "A woman worthy of the gift I can bestow."

Right. At least he wasn't trying to hide that part of his plan. If he thought I'd be swayed by all of this luxury and power, he was a fool.

Was my sister so easily seduced? Did she find him so irresistible that she betrayed the oath of the hunter? Did Edmondo torture or threaten Serina into submission?

"You think ill of me," he announced, his emerald gaze holding my own and refusing to break away. "I did not harm your sister, nor did I force her to choose. She made her own choices as you must also."

"It sounds simple but we both know that it's not."

"No," he agreed, "perhaps it is best I call to her now. My need for you grows and this night is passing much too quickly."

His revelation sent an icy chill deep into my bones. I was being manipulated and coerced but I didn't exactly know how he was accomplishing it. For a moment my fear was palpable, and he closed his eyes, inhaling as his fangs gleamed in the light for the first time.

"Forgive my reaction," he apologized as he saw the horror I couldn't hide on my face. "Your emotions are so vivid they are almost physical manifestations that I can see, touch, and lick with pleasure."

I shivered at the imagery his words evoked.

"Serina," he called, dropping my hand, "return to my side, beloved."

My sister was absent one moment, standing before me the next. Her movements were far quicker than the human eye could discern. Her beauty was heightened by the soft lights and the gossamer gown she wore of bright white.

"My bride, Serina," he replied as I gasped, "say hello to your sister."

Bride? What the hell?

Jumping to my feet, I shook my head, the chair crashing

over on its side. "No. Tell me this isn't true, Rina." Shocked and appalled, I reverted to using her old nickname from childhood.

Amused laughter was the only response. "The sooner you realize this is your reality, the easier it will be to join us."

Join? Why the hell would I do that?

"You're not my sister," I replied with venom, backing away. "I will destroy you, vampire," I promised, pulling the blades from my thighs quickly, "and exterminate you once and for all."

Clapping averted my attention and I was tackled to the ground. I could smell the mild decay of death and the metallic scent of blood that usually accompanied bloodsuckers as I was hauled to my feet.

"Don't move," Glenn warned, his tongue gliding along my neck. "I would love to suck you dry."

A vicious snarl transformed the elegant and handsome Edmondo into a bloodthirsty beast. He lurched forward and grabbed Glenn by the throat, lifting him off the ground as the others cowered and lowered to their knees. "You do not touch what belongs to me. Ever," he roared, tossing Glenn to the ground. "Take my brides to the altar. *Now*."

Brides? What the fuck?

"Get your hands off me!" I screamed, struggling against the hold of my captors.

"Cease your struggles, Skye," Edmondo ordered, "if there is even one scratch on your body, I will be incredibly displeased."

"Brides?" Serina screeched, turning to Edmondo. "What deception is this?"

"None, my beautiful bride," he soothed, "you must ready for the ceremony."

She relaxed, placing a kiss on his cheek. "Of course."

Panicked, I fought the entire distance as we were steered in the opposite direction than I arrived, following a path lit up by more torches that led to a raised platform. Two stone pillars were erected on either side of an altar long ago stained by the blood of its victims. Chains dangled as they swung precariously in the wind and hung down from the pillars where metal rings attached to the front, just inches from the top. I was shackled at the ankles and wrists to the pillar on the right as Serina stood and let Edmondo place her on the left.

The sick bastard leaned in and pressed his lips on hers, grinding his hips as he gripped her waist, nearly devouring Serina as moans of pleasure reached my ears. He thrust in slow circles as if he was preparing to bed her other than ruthlessly leaving her in chains and his monstrous desires. Pulling up the edge of her white gown, he stuck his hand between her legs and proceeded to bring her to orgasm. Right here, in front of everyone.

My eyes closed as I tried to block the sounds issuing from her throat. Tears threatened to leak from my eyes, but I wouldn't allow sorrow to creep in now. My time on this earth was numbered. I knew he meant to kill us both despite the act. This ruthless vampire was stealing his own pleasure before he ended us both at the same time.

As my thoughts latched onto that one detail, my eyes opened in shock. Twins. There was great power in siblings born on the same day, the closer they were in minutes, the better. We were born only five minutes apart. Edmondo must have a reason for bringing us here at the same time.

"My lord," a strange female voice greeted, "I am ready and await your instruction."

Edmondo withdrew from my sister and placed a kiss on her forehead. "You've done well. A pity I cannot keep you."

Serina's gasp was audible even from a distance. "You lying sack of shit!"

He lifted a hand and smacked her so hard she fell limp, dangling by the chains. "I've warned you about your insults for the last time. Goodbye, darling. It was fun while it lasted."

Serina whined but didn't lift her head.

Furious, I held my tongue only because I needed my wits for what was to come.

Edmondo sauntered my way and lifted his hands wide, his lip curling up on one side as he smiled deviously. "My bride deserves only the best. Tonight, I strengthen my power and hold over this world. I will possess the bloodline of the greatest hunter family in existence and consummate our union. Victorine, begin your spell."

As his words began to sink in, I became fully aware of the fact that he was sacrificing my sister at the same moment that he was planning on taking me as a bride. Struggling against the chains, I tried to slip my wrists through the metal cuffs, but they were too tight.

Magical vibrations danced across my skin as the witch Victorine began her spell. She approached Serina first and lifted a sharp blade, slicing across her stomach and allowing her blood to drip into the bowl she held below to catch the crimson fluid. When she backed away, blood continued to drip down the white gown and stained the delicate fabric. Serina whimpered as the witch walked to the altar and placed the blood in a much larger bowl, pouring it into the stone basin. Herbs were tossed in next as Victorine continued to chant, sparks flying into the air as the mixture bubbled.

"Are you ready, my lord?"

Edmondo nodded, slicing into his wrist with his teeth and approaching the bowl as he let the dark red blood flow into the mixture. The air crackled while the droplets fell into the liquid and it hissed and churned until he stepped back.

"Well done. The sacrifice has been accepted. Only your chosen remains. Shall I gather her blood?"

"No," he growled, turning in my direction. "None harm my queen. I will gather a sample."

As my eyes met the green glow of Edmondo's gaze, he placed a hand over his heart. "Beloved, you are mine. I am yours. After this night, we are one."

Shocked to find his lips against my own only seconds later,

I didn't realize that he had sliced into my wrist until I felt the blood oozing from the wound.

"Forgive me, this is the only time I shall ever harm you."

"Get away from her!"

Turning away from the deceitful vampire, I found Rhun, Ash, and Kepp fully armed and covered in what appeared to be dark blood.

"Rhun!" I screamed, terrified by my mistake when Edmondo hissed and spun around, ready to tear them all apart.

12

KEPPLER

"What have you done?"

Maybe it was a little too obvious the blood and grime on our bodies belonged to his spawn.

Lifting my middle finger, I flipped him off. "Exactly what we plan to do to you."

Rhun and Ash crouched, ready for the attack we knew was coming.

The vampire waved his hand as the bloodsuckers in the vicinity immediately attacked.

It didn't escape my notice that he turned back to Skye and grabbed her chin, forcing a kiss onto her lips. Roaring loudly, I began attacking the vampires with renewed zeal. As the vermin rushed forward, I caught a glimpse of their crimson eyes and extended fangs, sharp claws, and fast reflexes.

Fuck. They were *nocturne*.

Rhun's double blades were slicing through the ones he was able to catch but the fuckers were incredibly fast and agile. Ash preferred his single sword and swung the blade with scary efficiency. I was the odd man out. I didn't like to mess with heavy cumbersome blades. I was skilled with martial arts and

Chinese throwing stars, small throwing knives, and nunchucks.

Many said nunchucks were clumsy and not useful in attacks. They were wrong. The sticks were an outstanding weapon if you knew how to use them properly, which I did. My training kicked in and I lost count of the bodies that fell beneath my feet only to meet the deadly end of my brothers-in-arms and their blades.

Rhun broke away from the group and rushed toward the vampire with his hands on Skye.

"His name is Edmondo!" she screamed.

The vampire king?

Was Skye familiar with the lore? No wonder he had the twins chained to the pillars. This was a ritual sacrifice!

My brethren came to the same realization almost immediately as it occurred to me that I would have to destroy the witch and prevent the completion of her spell. The vampire king was going to murder one sister and take the other twin into his bed, spawning a new breed of bloodsucking demons with the enhanced senses of a hunter.

No fucking way.

I couldn't allow that to happen.

Ash beat me to the witch and sliced with his sword, decapitating her so fast it took a few seconds for the head to separate from her body and fall to the ground in a squishy plop. Her body twitched and quickly followed as Ash plunged the sword deep into her chest and pierced her heart, twisting until the organ was shredded in her chest.

The vampire king rushed forward and swiped with his claws, slicing into Ash's torso.

Rhun cried out in rage as he leaped into the air and his feet pushed off the stone pillar, lining up his trajectory perfectly as he stabbed both of his blades into the vampire king's shoulders. The blades were imbedded into his body as he spun and hissed. For a moment, he seemed to be in control and then the poison that coated the blades with Greek fire began to wreak havoc upon his immortal flesh.

The vampire started to shimmer as he tried to use his power to escape.

He was unsuccessful.

I watched with morbid fascination and glee as he shook and convulsed, burning from the inside out. The only thing hunters found in centuries that seemed to have a lasting effect and permanent death for vampires. Greek fire couldn't be extinguished. It wasn't easily affected by magic. There was no cure, no stopping its finality.

Vampires burned as if the sun was literally inside their bodies and didn't cease until they were nothing but piles of black ash.

"Edmondo!"

Serina's wail of horror was the only sound as the final vampire was defeated and he burst into greenish tinted flames. His flesh was consumed as he roared his defiance until the last second. Moments later blackened bits of ash drifted down to the perfectly manicured lawn.

"Help me out of this!" Skye pleaded as Ash broke her shackles and pulled her into his embrace, planting a kiss on her lips exactly as I wanted to do.

She hugged him back and ran to Serina as I met her there, a barrier in case her sister tried to attack. "We don't know what's happening with her yet," I cautioned.

"Hey, I know, Kepp." She pressed a kiss to my cheek and turned toward Serina.

"Sis?"

Serina blinked, her eyes glassy. "Skye-bear?"

Huh?

"Oh, Rina," she blubbered, hugging her sister close. "I thought I lost you forever!"

"I thought I *was* lost forever," she admitted. "It was a total and complete nightmare."

Inhaling, I could find no hint of her previously vampire scent. No death, no decay, nothing rotten. She was human again. Full hunter. The death of an original vampire often released his spawn from the *thrall*. In this case, Serina was exceptionally lucky.

Ash helped Skye to release her sister as the two girls seemed to hug for eternity.

Clearing my throat, I indicated the rising sun. "Looks like your transformation was just in time."

"You mean I would have . . ." she trailed off, shuddering as her gaze met each of us in turn. "You saved me. How can I ever thank you?"

Ash grinned, gripping her shoulder. "Be ready to help us out when we need the favor returned."

"Done," she agreed, looking my way. "Your names?"

Skye flushed and pointed to each of us in turn. "Kepp, Ash, and Rhun."

The introductions complete, we sighed collectively as the toll of the night began to seep into our bones.

"What are your plans now?" Ash asked, his eyes devouring Skye as she spoke with her sister.

"The same as always," Skye answered, placing a hand on her curvy hip. "Hunt."

"Maybe after a few days of rest," Serina added.

Skye lifted her head and her gaze met our fearless leader. "And you?"

Rhun tugged Skye close as his mouth crushed down on hers. "That, *sugar*, is just a promise of what's to come. We need a little vacation." His finger brushed along her cheek as his gaze held hers. "Anywhere you go, I'll follow."

13

SKYE

Loud music blared from the speakers as the waitress slammed a couple of pitchers down on the table and we all scrambled for a glass. The beer was cold and refreshing, the perfect beverage to quench our thirst. We had been back in town for only a day when we met at the bar and decided to share drinks as we recapped our perilous adventure.

I still couldn't believe Serina was alive and well. The torment of losing her had diminished but the trauma of that island would take a bit longer to recover from completely. She laughed with the guys as Rhun reached for my hand, bringing it to his lips.

"She'll be fine." Already, he understood me far better than I could ever have believed.

"I know," I conceded, "but I worry that the trauma of her ordeal has been buried too easily. What if—"

"It's a bad idea to start any sentence with those words," he whispered, placing a finger against my lips. "I'd rather cover your body in kisses and spend the time we have together in more pleasing ways."

"Oh?" I asked, leaning in closer. "Is that an invitation?"

"Open and always available. I'm too old to mess around, Skye. If you want me, I'm yours."

My lips met his in a passionate but firm kiss. "I accept that offer."

"What about us?" Kepp asked as Ash's gaze let me know he felt the same way.

Three very different men but each with a distinct and attractive personality. I had fallen for each of them. Rhun, Ash, and Kepp— all for different reasons and in different ways.

"I think we need to decide how this is going to work."

Serina's laugh interrupted our serious discussion. "I say you take all of them upstairs and show them why you're the mechanical bull champion."

The heat in the room went up several degrees as each of my guys responded to her words. Ash nodded. Kepp grinned wider. Rhun cleared his throat and squeezed my hand as he held it.

"Very funny, sis."

"I have a few friends I need to catch up with," she announced, rising to her feet as she finished her beer. "Three years is a long time to be away. A girl has needs."

My jaw dropped as she laughed and made her way to the dance floor, joining the bodies that were swaying to the beat.

Rhun stood and held out his hand. "Ready?"

I placed my hand in his palm and led them up the stairs and into the private room that I had owned for years. Ginny made sure the bar was ours and when she died it was left to me and Serina. We owned equal parts and kept our living accommodations above. The Dark Horse was home. I couldn't imagine living anywhere else.

I used the key to let us all inside and began walking toward the king-size bed located in the master suite. Both Serina and I shared the space since the entire floor had been converted into an apartment with separate master bedrooms for each of us. We could entertain at the same time and not bother the other.

Each suite had a connected bathroom and a full bar. Lounge chairs and other furniture completed the large open space where we could sit with friends away from the bed but still enjoy company if we wanted privacy.

Rhun tugged me toward the bed and I knew if I wanted to stop this I could at any moment. His lips met mine as we lowered to the mattress. I leaned into the kiss and was rewarded with a low sexy growl. His hands lifted my shirt over my head as he pressed light kisses to my exposed skin. Ash knelt on the bed and quietly undressed before his hands began to massage my feet. Kepp was close to my head as he massaged my temples and I let out a small groan.

"That feels wonderful."

"It's only the beginning," Ash answered as he tugged my jeans down my hips and off, followed by my lacey thong. "Damn, that's sexy, honey."

"I think her pretty pink pussy is even sexier," Rhun murmured as his stomach met the mattress and he spread my thighs apart. "I need a taste."

Kepp's hands moved from my temples slowly down my throat to massage my breasts as Ash lowered his head and sucked a pink nipple into his mouth. His tongue circled the flesh until I had goosebumps rise up on my skin. Soft moans left my throat as Rhun's talented tongue delved between my folds and found the perfect spot to devour.

The combined sensations sent my body into dizzying heights of pleasure. I'd never had multiple partners all at once. I didn't know what to expect but this felt natural. Everything about what we were sharing just seemed *right*.

"Skye, sweetheart, you're absolutely delicious."

My hips began to grind against Rhun's face as he licked and sucked with expertise. "You're going to make me come."

"That's the plan, sugar."

His fingers soon joined his tongue as he glided them in and

out, his lips sucking on my clit as I reached the peak and crashed over the edge.

"Oh, God!" I exclaimed, coming hard on his tongue as he held my hips in place. He lapped up my release and then lifted his head as the spasms subsided, but the waves of pleasure still crashed over every inch of my body.

"I need you, baby."

Rhun climbed upward as he lined up his hard cock and my eyes widened at the impressive size and girth. "Don't be afraid, sweetheart. I plan on making you come at least twice."

He thrust inside as I dug my nails into his back and my head tilted back, my tongue meeting Kepp's as he kissed me thoroughly. Ash was still suckling at my breasts as Rhun picked up his tempo and began moving faster. Ash's hand slid down my stomach until he found my clit and pinched, my body jolting with the pleasurable pain.

"Make her come hard, Rhun. I want her next."

He nodded with a grin and thrust harder, his ass cheeks clenching as I tried to grip them with my fingers.

"More!" I shouted as he slammed home, fucking me so hard that I nearly saw stars.

My orgasm hit with such ferocity that I bit my lips to keep from screaming, crying out his name. "Rhun!"

He thrust a few more times before his own release, collapsing for a few seconds before he placed a loving kiss on my lips.

Ash took his place as he moved and lowered his head while he kissed me, his tongue colliding with my own. His kisses were the most erotic of the three and I had a feeling he was an exceptional lover. He was inside me before I could blink and took his time, gliding in and out with a consistent rhythm that immediately began to build the pleasure inside again.

He pulled back and slammed inside before rolling over on his back and guiding my hips as I began to ride him. Kepp made a sound of pleasure as I reached over and grasped his erection, pumping up and down slowly as he moved his hips.

"Are you willing to take us both at once?" he asked huskily, moving behind me as he placed kisses all over my neck. His hot breath tickled my ear as goosebumps rose up on my flesh. "I'd love to penetrate you at the same time as Ash. The pleasure will be incredible for us all."

Nodding, I leaned forward as I felt his fingers press against the tight hole.

"Do you have any lube?"

I gestured to the nightstand as Rhun opened the drawer and all my toys were exposed. "Naughty girl, I approve." Rhun handed the tube to Kepp as he covered his length and began to stroke while his fingers massaged the area. One finger pressed inside as he rubbed the lube over the entrance.

A sound of incredible pleasure left my lips as Ash began stroking my pussy and Kepp glided his finger in and out, adding another and then one more until three fingers were in my tight hole. It was almost too much. I wasn't new to anal, but it had been a long time.

"Are you ready?" Kepp kissed the back of my neck as I felt him gently push his way inside, little by little, gradually letting my body adjust to the feeling and his fat cock.

"Yes," I moaned, "you feel amazing."

"So do you, baby."

He was soon seated within as both guys stilled and allowed me to adapt to the double penetration. Slowly, they both began to move and soon found a rhythm that worked and enabled us all to enjoy the ecstasy of our combined flesh. Ash and Kepp were groaning as I swiveled my hips and the three of us became lost in the pleasure until our bodies could take no more. We came at the same time, my walls clamping down on Ash as he thrust a final time and released. Kepp roared my name as he collapsed against my back and the three of us breathed together like one individual body but three shared souls.

Reaching out, I felt Rhun grab my hand and pull it to his lips. "We all care for you, Skye. I'm bold enough to say we feel much more."

Ash cupped my cheek. "You're it for me."

Kepp withdrew from my body and hugged me from behind. "I can say the same."

"Just as you're all it for me."

I slid down on the bed and was rewarded with my guys snuggling close as our eyes drifted closed.

A smile on my lips, I had never been happier than this moment, sharing my love with them all.

THANK YOU

Thank you for reading!

If you enjoyed the story please leave a review to help others decide on the book.

PLAYLIST

Sexy Back— Rivethead
Blood— Breaking Benjamin
E.T.— Rivethead
The Hunter— Adam Jensen
Bury a Friend— Billie Eilish

ALSO BY NIKKI LANDIS

Fight for Light Crossover Novels, Dark Paranormal Romance— Angels, Demons:

Fallen from Grace I Seduction of Darkness I Kiss of Fate

Fight for Light Prequels, Paranormal Romance:

Forgotten Oath I Forgotten Reign

Descendants of Nephilim, Dark Paranormal Romance— Shifters, Angels, Demons:

- *Fight for Light* Series -

Silver Moon (Lycan War) I Reaper's Curse

Fight for Light, Dark Paranormal Romance/Slow Burn Reverse Harem:

The Guardian I The Harbinger I The Meridian I The Imposition I The Revenant I The Awakening I The Covenant I The Reckoning

Short Story/Novellas: - *Fight for Light* Series -

Reaper's Folly I Fractured

NightWalkers, Vampire Paranormal Romance:

Dark Promise I Dark Vengeance I Dark Persuasion I Dark Deception I Dark Dominion I Dark Destiny I TBA

Transitions, Paranormal Suspense Romance:

Zodiac Killer I The Gift I The Forsaken I TBA

Freedom Fighters, Post-Apocalyptic Military Romance:

Refugee Road I Midnight Surrender I Crimson Dawn

Alien Alphas of Pilathna, Sci-Fi Romance:

Dungari Rise I Dungari Reclaim I Dungari Rage I TBA

Braxtharian Warriors, Sci-Fi Romance:
Seekers (The Last Oracle) I Scarred I TBA

Volatile Vixens, Dark Paranormal/Sci-Fi Romance:
Harleigh I Ivey I Kat I Siren I Harleigh (Part 2) I TBA

Sinners Syndicate, *Volatile Vixens* Sidekick Series, Dark Paranormal/Sci-Fi Romance:
Onyx I Blaze I Chaos I TBA

The Collective, *Volatile Vixens* Master Series, Dark Paranormal/Sci-Fi Romance:
Joker I Sinister I TBA

Dark Divide, Post-Apocalyptic Romance/Vampires:
Extinction I Dragon I Fallen Skies I Beast I Grim I TBA

Ravage Riders MC, Sci-Fi/Paranormal Romance/Crime Fiction:
Sins of the Father I Sinners & Saints I Sinner's Lament I TBA

Lords of Wrath MC, Dark Paranormal Romance/Crime Fiction— Hell Hounds:
Tarek I Bullet I Vicious I Dodge I TBA

Royal Bastards MC, Dark Paranormal Romance/Crime Fiction— Steel Horseman:
Devil's Ride I Devil's Rejects I Devil's Throne I TBA

Hellfire & Halos, Dark Paranormal Romance/Reverse Harem— Angels, Demons:
Greed I Wrath I TBA

Xavier Academy, Dark Paranormal Romance/Reverse Harem—

Witches:

Wicked Intentions I Wicked Secrets I TBA

Mystic Hallows Harem, Dark Paranormal Romance/Reverse Harem, Episodes #1 - #13:

Black Magic Voodoo I Toil & Trouble I Witching Hour I Third Eye Blind I Day of the Dead I TBA

Last of Us, Post-Apocalyptic Romance/Horror— Zombies:

Ground Zero I Lone Survivor I TBA

Cedar Creek Shifters, Paranormal Romance— Wolves:

Haunted Wolf I Obsessed Wolf I Possessive Wolf I Rebel Wolf I TBA

Timber Mountain Shifters, Paranormal Romance— Bears:

Un-*Bear*-Able Desire I TBA

Erotic Horror Short Story: A Haunted Horror of Visceral Regrets—

Pieces of Heaven

Anthologies:

Blood & Silver I Captivated I Guardian I Forest of the Fearless I Saved Between the Sheets I Ruined Between the Sheets I Obsessive Temptation I Summer Solstice I Kingdom of Salt & Sirens I Magic & Mayhem I Fire & Ice I Prophecy of Magic I Falling Into Chaos I Immortal Lust

ABOUT THE AUTHOR

Nikki Landis is an award-winning and Amazon bestselling author of paranormal, sci-fi, and reverse harem romance. An Ohio native, she resides in the Buckeye state with her husband and amazing family.

Nikki's Newsletter
Website
Facebook
Reader's Group
Twitter
Goodreads
Bookbub
Pinterest
Instagram

Made in the USA
Columbia, SC
06 March 2020